SUPERWORLD

PART THREE

BENJAMIN KEYWORTH

Podium

To Victoria,

Who married me, for some reason

Cover design by Dalia and Sam

ISBN: 978-1-0394-5673-0

Published in 2025 by Podium Publishing
www.podiumentertainment.com

SUPERWORLD

PROLOGUE
THE HANDS OF DEATH

Ten thousand miles apart, two men who had never met prepared to die.

For men of a similar age, facing similar fates, they had very little in common. The first, Tse Chi-li, was long, lean, and wiry, a native son of Jiangxi with hair like black straw and a face riddled craterous with pockmarks. He moved very little and said even less, quietly awaiting his final step to annihilation with the same fatalistic silence with which he had approached all steps leading up. He sat in his cell in Ganzhou, staring unwavering at a rough-edged, thumb-size divot in the gray cement floor, and whatever thoughts swirled dark inside his head stirred no ripples on the surface.

The second man, Cyrus Corbin, had never been so laconic. Six foot four and two hundred and forty pounds, he was a hulking cudgel of a man, his head clean-shaven and an assortment of crude tattoos etched black and gray across his body. His skin, a ruddy veneer stretched across vascular, steroid-built muscles, was white but flayed tan by a lifetime of sunburn, and the beard that dangled over his chest was a near half foot of coarse, unkempt wire.

Unlike Tse Chi-li, Cyrus had no qualms about making his displeasure known; he swore with vitriol and violence at every shadow that passed outside his Houston prison cell, lurching forward and slamming into the unyielding stone walls whenever anyone dared walk by.

Neither man knew the other existed, and if they had, neither would likely have cared.

Though they might have, had they known what would come next.

*   *   *

Tse Chi-li finished his last meal—jaa-jyang-myen and huíguōròu—in silence, then placed the chopsticks and bowls back neatly on the serving tray. He dabbed his hands, lips, and cheeks with the soft cotton hand towel, then folded it over twice and set it down at the entrance to his cell beside the empty steel tray and small porcelain baijiu cup. He rose, rapped three times against the metal bars, then retreated four steps to turn and face inward, kneeling unspeaking, his hands held behind him.

He wore plain, simple clothes: a white button-up shirt and gray loose-fitting pants, both pressed and freshly laundered—small gifts from the guards, like the rice wine; tokens of comfort and respect. The men who guarded Tse Chi-li were not his friends nor friends of his employer, but neither did they have any desire to incur either's wrath.

From behind him, Tse heard the rattle of his cell door opening. His lips twitched as footsteps scuffed across the concrete floor, but he otherwise gave no resistance as a firm grip slid his hands into long steel-mesh gloves. The guards behind him murmured words, and with neither protest nor complaint, Tse allowed his arms to be drawn through a carbon fiber straitjacket; then, encased and restrained, he opened his eyes, turned, and was led from his cell in silence.

The guards in the hallway outside nodded to him as he passed, and the calls that came through the bars from his fellow Ganzhou Prison inmates echoed well-wishes and support. His arms bound, Tse Chi-li nevertheless walked on his own motion, guards' hands light on either elbow; silent and unflinching, even in the face of death.

A ferrous nematomancer, Tse Chi-li had worked eleven years as a paid killer for the Triads, able to extend thin metal cords from his fingers that wormed and burrowed beneath his victims' skin. He had been convicted of murdering thirteen people. He was thought to have killed hundreds more.

When Cyrus Corbin's time came, it came with darkness. His last meal had been a bucket of Southern fried chicken, onion rings, biscuits, mashed potatoes, and gravy. They'd given him a family pack of gummy bears too, as well as a pitcher of beer, which of course Cyrus had chugged down in one swallow then smashed against the wall in the hope of getting a shard of glass worth shanking with. He made no effort to hide this; subtlety was not Corbin's strong suit.

His room, a ten-by-twelve tomb of featureless cement, contained nothing beyond a cot and a lidless steel toilet, a neon light in the center of the roof, and a Perspex camera in the top right. The walls were sealed with fire retardant, and at any spike in temperature, the reinforced steel door would lock, the food slot would seal, and all air would be vented from the room. It was a cell designed to hold a pyromancer, and there was a neutralizer stationed on the cellblock around the clock in case any of the safeguards failed. Cyrus knew all this, supposedly, yet nevertheless tried to burn his way to freedom at least once every six hours.

Today, though, when the venting started, it was not in reaction to any insurrection: the light in the cell just abruptly went out. Cyrus leapt to his feet—flames racing up his forearms and across his prisoner yellows—as all around him the room hissed with a familiar, ominous rush. The giant convict howled, leveling every curse he could muster, roaring of mongrels, race traitors, and impure blood, swearing he'd burn their families alive.

The hiss seethed on, indifferent, sucking out the sound of his slurs. A few seconds later, the fire spewing from Cyrus's hands wavered, followed shortly by his shouting, and then, like always, he fell to his knees, gasping, and collapsed unconscious on the floor.

The men who entered his cell a minute later wore full body armor modified from firefighting gear and were accompanied by two neutralizers. They cuffed the unconscious Corbin, strapped him to a gurney, and injected him with a paralyzing agent from the neck down before wheeling him out. All had been briefed on what to expect.

Cyrus Corbin, pyromancer and avowed white nationalist; sentenced to death for burning alive a bus full of black children. A man who had rejected all attempts at telepathic rehabilitation, who had never shown any remorse. There were prisoners in the Houston penitentiary who got second chances. Cyrus's were up.

At 8:30 a.m. Central Daylight Time, separated by half a world, Tse Chi-li and Cyrus Corbin were led through their respective jails toward the rooms where they would die.

* * *

Tse Chi-li's guards walked him down and around a winding corridor, through patches of shadow and artificial light, until finally, they came to a halt before a steel bulkhead. There was no ceremony or fanfare, no audience—only two men standing, waiting, in black business suits. The first, a stout, balding Chinese official, moved in front of Tse, waving the guards a step back.

"There is still a chance for you, Chi-li," he said in Cantonese. "Give us the names of your associates. One way or another, we'll find them. There is still time for clemency."

The prisoner did not meet his eyes, merely continued staring straight ahead. After a few seconds' silence, the squat man in the suit shook his head and motioned to the guards. One of the wardens spun the wheel of the door. With a heavy creak, it swung open, and Tse Chi-li was pushed inside.

The chamber to which Cyrus Corbin was dragged was rectangular, with rows of chairs on one side facing a long viewing window. The guards pulled the door open, dragging the unconscious man inside before unbuckling, unloading, and rebuckling him upright to a white multi-point restraint bed standing alone in the center of the room.

Outside the chamber, a crowd gathered. Led in by guards in twos or threes, some old, some younger, they filled the rows of green plastic chairs assembled outside the one-way window looking in. Some were stony faced, some murmured, some sobbed. Most were African American, and most were dressed in black church clothes. The outliers were the lieutenant governor of Texas and the state's chief prosecutor, who sat side by side and silent at the end of the front row, in their respective blazers and business skirts.

The former took some quiet, vindictive pleasure in seeing justice wrought against these lowlifes; the latter always forced herself to attend these executions to remind her of the true consequences of her success.

All of them—officials, guards, and guests—had signed aggressive, comprehensive nondisclosure agreements, and all of them had agreed, after the event, to have all details from today's events telepathically purged. There were no phones permitted in the hall, no photography. Those who attended today would leave only with the knowledge that Cyrus Corbin was dead, and a final vision of his corpse.

* * *

In his death chamber, Tse stood, unobserved. The room was stark and windowless, circular, lined with white square tiles and devoid of feature, with an open space in the center where once might have stood a one-man bed.

Tse had requested to die standing, and the lack of restraints was not unusual, given his composure and lack of resistance or escape attempts thus far. Yet, as he turned, still restrained in his straitjacket, his eyes fell upon the sole object occupying the room.

For the first time since he had awoken this morning, a soft exclamation fell from the hitman's lips.

Alone in the execution room, Cyrus Corbin began to stir. His lips curled into a snarl, his eyes struggled open, and a mumbled slurry of swear words began trickling from his tongue. He ground his jaw, his mouth dry, and blinked as the world slowly returned to focus beneath his hazy, blurry eyes.

Cyrus grunted, straining against the feeling of lead weighing his muscles, trying to swing his arms or move his legs and pour fire from his fists. But below his neck, he felt nothing. He bared his teeth, looking downward, taking in the buckled leather restraints, the bands across his paralyzed legs and torso.

He twisted his neck, starting to shout and howl, to rage toward the two-way mirror and all the jungle bloods and bootlip lovers he knew were watching. But then, a moment later, his eyes reached what lay in the room's corner, and he fell abruptly silent.

A metal bed, and the body of a Chinese teenager.

A steel table, upon which lay a black child.

Tse Chi-li stepped cautiously toward the body, his brow furrowed, his footsteps muffled, his arms still taut and bound. But for being dead, the corpse could have been living: the boy's hair was clean and cut, his lanky limbs loose in a neat if not overlarge black suit, his eyes closed, his hands crossed against his chest.

The cheeks and lips had a pallor to them, but Tse could see no sign of injury, of what had caused the teenager's passing. Yet, he knew he was dead because Tse Chi-li had killed him, had coursed metal worms beneath his skin and through his bones and veins. A nobody, a middleman, some street kid who had possessed the stupidity, the impertinence, to flee with the take after a particularly good week.

He had needed to be punished, naturally, and Tse remembered the lines of the boy's face like he remembered every kill. Remembered how he had screamed while blood poured down his forehead, how he had begged—not that it had done him any good.

It was not the state of the body that perturbed him. Bodies were often healed, he knew, prior to interment, for funerary purposes and familial comfort. A trained healer could repair any body, even a dead one, though nothing could return the spark of life once snuffed out.

Yet he could not understand what it was doing here. Why this one? It had not been his most recent kill, nor his most notorious. Perhaps the youngest . . . But at that moment, the door on the other side of the room opened, and Tse Chi-li turned to look.

Cyrus Corbin stared at the dead baby, his mouth hanging slightly open, still unable to move from the neck down. If it hadn't clearly been dead, the kid could have been alive, its skin clear, its eyes closed, with chubby cheeks and chubby thighs. Its skin was pale and ashen, and it wore nothing but a diaper, but Cyrus couldn't see what'd killed it—just that it was dead, clearly. He had no idea whose baby that was. He had never seen it before in his life.

"What is this? One last present?!" he shouted. Cyrus strained his neck against the gurney, glaring at the mirror between him and the hall. "This supposed to make me feel bad?! Some dead coon?! You think this ain't a good start?!"

There was no response. Almost without wanting to, Cyrus's gaze drew back to the baby. Why the hell was it—Wait. From the bus? Nah. It couldn't be. But as Cyrus stared and, for the first time, maybe, reflected, the door on the far side of the room opened, and the murderer's head turned.

A young man stepped into Tse Chi-li's chamber. Maybe 175 centimeters tall, with cropped black hair and an egg-shaped face, he wore a pure-white suit over a black satin shirt. His gaze was downcast as he walked into the room, and he did not raise it to meet Tse Chi-li's eyes.

* * *

A Chinese guy stepped into Cyrus Corbin's chamber. Five foot nine, maybe twenty-something, with Asian skin, Asian hair, and Asian eyes, he wore a sleek black suit, a white shirt, and no tie.

He glanced around the room, taking in Cyrus and the baby—and he lingered there, on the child, for a few seconds before he turned and looked the white man dead-on.

"Are you my executioner?" Tse queried in Cantonese. The white-suited man did not respond, continuing to avert his gaze. Tse felt a sudden flare of irritation. "Show respect when I speak to you. Be quick if you are to do this. I deserve an honorable death."

The silent young man said nothing, his eyes continuing not to leave the ground. Tse Chi-li glared and took a step toward him. The boy did not move nor flare with any display of powers.

"What is this silence? Are you a telepath, come to pry my secrets? That was not our arrangement." He took another step forward. "You will steal nothing from me, dog. My will is iron. My knowledge travels with me to the grave."

It was not clear if his words were having any effect. Yet, as he spoke, the young man's head turned—not toward Tse but to the stainless-steel mortician's trolley upon which the teenager's body lay. After a few seconds of hesitation, the white-suited man walked over and, still without a word and without looking at Tse, placed his bare hands upon the corpse's arm.

A moment passed. Then another.

And then, with a sudden gasp, the body stirred.

"Uuh," it mumbled, and as Tse stood frozen, rooted to the spot, color began to flow back through the dead man's limbs, a trickle of movement like warm water slipping beneath spring ice.

Tse Chi-li stared as the boy's fingers twitched, as his eyelids fluttered, as his lips moved.

"No . . ." the corpse murmured, shifting groggily on the table. "No . . ."

His movements were slow, his words slurred, his eyes unfocused. But there was no escaping it. There was no denying what had just occurred.

The dead boy was alive.

"Impossible . . ." Tse whispered. Without realizing it, he'd taken a step backward. "Impossible . . ."

The white-suited man released his hand from around the dead teenager's arm and turned silently away. With Tse Chi-li's victim still mumbling on its gurney, the man in white walked back across the room and pulled open the door from whence he'd come.

And it was only here, at this final moment—for the briefest, fleeting second—that he turned and met the prisoner's gaze.

"I don't understand," Tse murmured. His pale eyes, normally so cold and unwavering, stared at the young man, wide with shock. The white-suited figure gave no answer, merely turned and closed the door, leaving the killer and his living victim alone.

A second passed, and then another.

"I don't understand," Tse Chi-li whispered again. He turned back to the table and took an unconscious step toward the stirring teenager, his own body trembling, his hands still bound. "I don't—"

And without pain or warning, without another sound, Tse Chi-li dropped dead.

"Who the hell are you?" Cyrus demanded. He struggled again to break free, to unleash fire and incinerate this mongrel, but neither Cyrus's arms nor legs nor powers seemed to be working. The Chinese man said nothing, glaring at Cyrus with unconcealed contempt. The prisoner stopped struggling and sneered.

"You wanna go, you slant-eyed ape? You want a piece? You cut me loose, and I'll wipe that look off your flat face, you inbred yellow—"

The Chinese man unclipped the press studs sealing together the wrists of his long sleeves, freeing the base of his black leather gloves. Without looking down or breaking his stare, he pulled one hand free from the gloves, then the other, flexing his long, pale fingers flexed beneath the artificial light.

"Don't you touch me, you filthy gook," Cyrus Corbin swore. "Don't you dare. I'm Aryan Brotherhood; you lay a finger on me, and I'll—"

The stranger stepped over to his gurney, placing his bare hands on the prisoner's flesh.

And without another word, without warning or resistance, Cyrus Corbin simply died.

Suddenly, the chamber fell silent. The prisoner's bald head drooped, his eyes lolling open, a thin chain of saliva beginning to spindle down his chin. Beyond the two-way mirror, the gathering crowd fell into a hush. The young man stepped away from the body then reached into his suit's breast pocket and removed a pair of black latex gloves. He pulled them over his hands, then put his leather gloves back on over the top of them, then sealed both pairs beneath the sleeves of his shirt and redid the gloves' press studs.

The executioner turned and looked at the mirror, gave a single, silent nod, and walked from the room without uttering a sound.

A second passed, then another.

All was quiet.

And then, in the corner of the room, on the stainless steel table, the baby began to cry.

FAME

"Ladies and gentlemen, tonight's guests need no introduction."

In homes and bars across America—in hospitals, on phones, in booths manned by security guards—fifty million screens sat tuned to the same image. Tonight's episode had been advertised for weeks on billboards, on bus sides, and online. Internationally simulcast live, the ratings were predicted to eclipse the Super Bowl. The cost of ad time was in the millions. NBC had spared no expense.

Before a light-studded backdrop of a shining city skyline, Jay Leno, host of *The Tonight Show*, stood with his gray hair and impeccable suit, beaming at the cameras and studio audience with his hands held in front of him, practically bouncing on his heels. His tie, usually an unremarkable shade of blue or burgundy, was—for tonight only—a glorious, shimmering gold.

"Sometimes on *The Tonight Show*," he said, "we get to interview those on the frontlines of history. More rarely—though not never—we actually *make* history. Tonight, we get to do both." His wry smile beamed. "He was an ordinary kid from the suburbs who, on paper at least, had an extraordinary power. She was an empath: unpopular, unknown, until the paparazzi snapped her in the Legion's ranks. A year ago, nobody knew who they were. Today, well, they're household names."

He paused. "I won't say any more. Because nothing more needs to be said." The host's chest swelled. "You know who they are!" Off camera and arrayed before him, the studio audience cheered. "You *saw* who they are!" The cheering intensified. "And tonight, we hear their story.

"Ladies and gentlemen, the moment you've all been waiting for. Tonight only, exclusive to NBC, exclusive to *The Tonight Show*, in an hour-long, never-before-seen special, for their *first ever interview since they saved the world*"—the audience's cheering rose to a fever pitch—"without further ado, please welcome, Matthew Callaghan and Jane Walker; *Matt the Human and Lady Dawn!*"

The studio erupted, the band played, the curtains parted, and Matt and Jane stepped forth.

Matthew Callaghan, nineteen, came first, looking as he always did: average height, light skinned, and brown haired, his features still soft and unremarkable, yet now recognized across the globe. He wore a plain black suit, a reasonably decent fit, which despite all backstage prepping still hung slightly askew, like it'd been worn once to prom and then maybe again to a first-job interview.

As he stepped out onto the stage, cameras gleaming in his face and lights shining in his eyes, his mouth split into a nervous yet optimistic grin. He gave the audience a sheepish wave as they in turn erupted in thunderous applause, clamoring to their feet, the studio enveloped by clapping, whistling, and cheers.

For a moment, Matt stood alone in the spotlight—and then, from between the curtains, came Jane, following three steps behind. Suddenly, there was no one else to focus on. Taller than Matt, her head held high, her features striking, she wore a shimmering gold dress descending into an ankle-length skirt of silver sequins, the top cut asymmetrical and patterned in intricate detail, the bottom flowing like ultrafine dragon scales with a split at the thigh.

Tall and Amazonian, with piercing eyes, a Gothic-script *E* tattooed black on her right cheek, and hair a curtain of flowing bronze, Jane Walker shone with a radiance and presence that any Hollywood starlet would have killed to have—right up until her entrance finished, and she flinched ever so slightly, recoiling instinctively from the light and noise.

Yet, a second later, Jane recovered, and the crowd grew, if possible, even louder. Her grin solidified and she straightened, then punched a fist up into the air.

The studio turned deafening. With a sweep of her hair, Jane turned to where Matt was waiting, watching a few steps away with a wry smile and his hands behind his back, and reached out to take his hand. They raised their arms together.

The crowd went ballistic. And the cameras continued to roll. As all around the world, images of them flew: the ordinary man and the superhuman woman, united as one.

"Welcome, welcome! Come, sit—"

The host's laughter poked through the speakers of the tiny TV screen, caught and clarified over the audience's cheers. Set atop a peeling wooden table left half forgotten in the corner of the warehouse, the sound of the portable television buzzed low and borderline inaudible, its weak light suffusing only the nearest few feet with a dull and shifting glow.

It was a clear and cloudless night, and the almost-full moon overhead streamed bright through barred windows set high in a ceiling of corrugated iron. The concrete floor lay speckled and dusty, cluttered with thick wooden benches and steel shelving that threw out long webs of shadow beneath the moonlight. Over by the roller doors, a single lightbulb flickered, making feeble orange resistance against the sweeping midnight blue.

A group of men stood inside the warehouse, armed and tense and silent. They moved only occasionally to shift discreetly beneath the straps of their bulletproof vests or quietly reposition their assault rifles. A dozen large, experienced soldiers, they clustered loosely throughout the abandoned space, their eyes moving over every corner of the room as the figure at their center, a thin older man in a gray checkered suit, sat quietly on a metal foldout chair, waiting patiently.

The man's skin was olive and wrinkled, his hair retreated to mere sideburns and wisps of combed-over gray. His hooked, prominent nose supported round spectacles through which he continued to read a newspaper, keeping an indifferent back to the television, making no move to turn it off.

"Sit down, get comfortable—"

The pair sat on the talk-show couch, Matt taking the seat closest to the host's desk, Jane sitting by his side. He crossed his feet; Jane kept her back straight. Both wore nervous, excited grins.

"So, gosh," began Leno. "Just, so great to have you on the show. I— Are you good there? Is your dress okay? I know you're probably more used to a cape . . ."

The crowd laughed while Jane said nothing, though her lips twitched in an anxious smile.

"I had wondered, see, if you would wear the cape—"

"Didn't want to sit on it," Jane replied.

"—then, yeah, exactly! Then I got to thinking, that probably can't be comfortable, you know; you sit on it, maybe you flop it over your lap, it pulls on your shoulders . . . I think that's why we never, you know, we never see superheroes sitting."

There was another laugh. The host paused, stealing a quick smirk at the audience before looking expectantly, almost paternally, between his two guests.

"How are you? You good?"

Matt and Jane glanced at each other.

"We're good, yeah. We're good."

"Nervous?" the host asked. Matt sucked in air between his teeth.

"A little," he confessed. Again, the audience laughed. Matt flashed a brief glance over at them, his mouth twitching into a reluctant grin, and he seemed to relax a little, appearing slightly reassured. Leno leaned over, his expression open and inviting.

"Don't be nervous, don't be nervous. This is your first big interview?"

"Yep."

"Since everything went down?"

"Yep."

"Six months."

"Feels longer," said Matt, making a face. The crowd laughed.

The host pursed his lips in faux fascination. "A lot's been happening, hasn't it? I hear—I understand you've had some legal issues."

"Ah, yes," Matt replied, half chuckling. He reclined into the couch. "One or two." The audience hollered their support. Matt flicked them a quick smile.

"That's crazy," Leno said. "That's crazy to me. Who'd sue—You're a national hero; who'd sue you?"

Matt shrugged, looking like a man trying his best to appear indifferent. "The government."

"He's here."

A voice crackled over the radio. The soldier on whose vest the radio was attached—a tall, hard-faced man in his midforties—nodded and whirled his finger around in a circle to the others nearby. Weapons clattered and rose as the guards spread out into loose positions through-out the warehouse.

The old thin man raised his eyes, folded up his newspaper, and tucked it neatly beneath the breast pocket of his coat.

"So . . . I'm human," Matt admitted. The studio audience erupted with cheers, and again, Matt turned to look at them, grinning and nodding a few times. He waited for the crowd to fall silent, his expression a little bashful. "Which everybody now knows—"

"Which they didn't before," interrupted Jay.

"Which they didn't before. But now they do."

"Bit hard to walk that one back."

"Bit hard," agreed Matt. The audience laughed. "After announcing it on national TV."

"Yeah, I think I know a few people who might've been watching," the host replied. This triggered more laughter.

"Yeah, so obviously, that's out there now," explained Matt. "And, you know, scientifically, I think, it's a big deal because we don't know *why* I'm human."

"You just are."

"I just am. I didn't choose it."

"You didn't wake up one day and go, 'You know what's lame? Superpowers.'"

More laughter.

"No. And I've got no idea, right? I didn't choose to be like this; it's just . . . I am."

"Right."

"So I'm sitting in the hospital, two days after, you know, the whole Black Death thing, and I get this call from one of my doctors, and they're like: 'There's someone downstairs from the Pentagon. They say you have to go with them. They want a blood sample.'"

Disgruntled murmurs rippled across the audience. Matt turned on the couch to face them.

"I know, right? I . . . I . . ."

"What did you say?" asked Leno, turning Matt's attention back to him.

"No!" Matt replied, almost indignant. The room broke into cheering, and Matt's face split into a relieved grin. "I mean, I said, this is my body, this is my . . . choice of what to do with it, and I . . . I don't know what you want my blood for."

There was more cheering. Beside him, Jane reached over and squeezed Matt's hand. He glanced at her, seeming to take encouragement, before turning back to their host.

"So then," he continued, "things get nasty. The hospital has their lawyers, and they're going, 'This is a patients' rights issue,' and suddenly, they've got their own legal battle. But then, you know, I get better, right? And I get out, and I go home, and suddenly . . . there're warrants. There're people at my house."

"I saw this," Leno remarked. He gestured around to the crowd, to the murmurs of agreement. "I think we all saw this. Incredible, really. Larry, play the video, play the video."

The screen behind the interview desk switched from a vague city skyline to footage of a suburban street and a crowd of people divided down two distinct lines. On the left stood trucks and cop cars, police and army officers, black-clad SWAT teams, all fanned out in a loose assembly behind one harried-looking captain holding a ream of documents in his right hand.

A bald, stocky white man in combat fatigues, he wore no helmet and a pained expression as he looked over at the second, much larger group arrayed against him: a tightly packed rabble of civilians standing mutinously between the authorities and the Callaghans' house.

They were of no specific age or uniform, although many carried flags or placards, and as the groups squared off, their ranks raced with rebellious mutterings and the flicker of powers. At the forefront, recoiling slightly back into the first layer of the crowd, stood Matt in jeans and a blue sweater. And in front of him stood Jane, in the white-gold uniform of Lady Dawn.

The wind whipped around the assembled. Jane's gold cape fluttered. Helicopters, both police and media, circled overhead. The papers the officer was holding fluttered against his hand as he struggled to make himself heard.

"I am ordering you to disperse!" he shouted. "You are disrupting authorized police proceedings!" He held the papers higher. "This is a warrant for the arrest of Mister Matthew Callaghan! This is a federal court order! You are obstructing the provision of justice!"

Angry mutterings bristled throughout the crowd. The officer's expression was strained. Only Jane remained impassive, her arms folded across her chest, her face blank.

"If you do not comply with our instructions!" he shouted, battling to be heard beneath the blades of the helicopters, "We are authorized to use force!"

Standing alone at the head of the assembled civilian crowd, Jane raised an eyebrow. She turned and glanced at the mutinous mob amassed behind her, across whom a myriad of powers flickered and arced, and who outnumbered the assembled law enforcement agents five to one. She turned back, unfolded her arms, and looked the captain dead in the eye.

"Okay," she said. "Use it."

And then her eyes and the *E* tattooed on her cheek blazed with gold and a blast of wind erupted around her, buffeting the police and protestors with pulsing, billowing light. Jane stood there, fists curled and eyes ablaze, and did not so much as move as behind her a thousand powers sprang to life.

The pale-faced police officer took a step back.

Back in the studio, the audience roared.

"Wow," laughed *The Tonight Show* host, the sound of his voice intermingling with that of the crowd. "Wow-wow-wow. And I think my wife's scary when I leave the toilet seat up. Wow."

Sitting next to Matt, Jane raised her chin as laughter ran the length of the studio, looking very self-satisfied. The host turned to her.

"And did they keep trying to arrest him after that?"

"They did not," she replied, smug. The crowd cheered.

Leno gestured to Matt. "What were they trying to arrest you for?"

"For breaking empath laws, ironically," Matt answered. "Submitting fraudulent information to the DPR. For faking clairvoyancy."

"What, like lying on your driver's license?"

"Yeah."

"And they sent a SWAT team."

"Well," Matt said with a slight grimace, "to be fair, though, I don't know if the SWAT team wanted to be there. I don't think the cops were very keen."

"No, I can imagine."

"Anyway, we appealed the warrant the next day. I mean we, the ACLU."

"That's the American Civil Liberties Union, right?"

"Yeah. They've been really supportive. Everyone's been really supportive. And from there, it was in court."

"Right. And what happened last Tuesday?"

"Last Tuesday?" echoed Matt. He leaned back in his seat. "Last Tuesday, we got the Supreme Court decision."

"And?"

"We won."

The cheer that went up throughout the studio was electric. The host slapped the table, beaming and adding in his "Yeah, yeah, yeah!" Matt grinned out at the assembled audience as they once more rose in standing ovation, then raised his hand beside his head and gave a two-fingered peace sign.

They came through the south-side entrance: a large man and a thick, greasy-haired woman, both in tight black shirts and cargo pants, both wearing sunglasses. Between them, in front so they flanked him on either side, walked a short, slick-haired man in a blue pinstripe suit, his brown leather dress shoes clacking the concrete with every step.

They approached the waiting soldiers cautiously, heads turning as they took in their numbers, their positions, their guns. Traces of unease flickered across the newcomers' faces, though they nevertheless continued forward, advancing until the two groups stood ten or so feet apart.

"Thought you'd come alone," said the lead newcomer, the man in the blue pinstripe suit. He was lean and wiry, perhaps midtwenties to thirties, with too much product in hair the color of a rat's fur, and an unrefined hunch in his shoulders that no amount of expensive clothing could uncurl. He clicked his tongue at the old man sitting on the chair in front of him, rotating a well-chewed piece of gum.

The gray, vulturelike man remained sitting, and remained impassive. "Did you?" His eyes flicked once to both the man's companions. The newcomer bristled.

"Yeah, well, it's for my protection, innit? This ain't just a collector's item no more. This is serious."

"And on that note," said the old man, sounding bored, "let's see it."

The TV continued to blare in the background, undisturbed and ignored.

"Alright, let's take it back a second," the host continued. "Let's start at the beginning. You're an ordinary guy; you're living an ordinary life—except you don't have a power."

"Yep."

"When did you first find that out?"

Matt hesitated. "When I was about twelve," he answered truthfully, "I started getting worried. I . . . I went around trying to figure out what it might be. Like, I tried reading people's minds, I tried talking to our dog"—the audience laughed—"and just, nothing, you know? And, like, I remember . . . I'd just turned thirteen, and we'd had sex ed, and I was lying awake in bed that night going, 'Man . . . something's wrong with me. What if I genuinely don't have a power?'"

The audience murmured. Leno looked sympathetic.

"That must have been a scary place for a kid."

"It was scary! And it was only a couple of years after the Neutroheal thing happened. Do you remember Neutroheal?"

"That was . . . Ah, yeah! That was the girl with Down syndrome, right?"

"Right! And I'm like, 'What if I'm like that? What if people want to study me?'"

"What if the government sends SWAT teams to take my blood?" That got a laugh, though it quickly darkened into discontented murmurings. Leno shot the crowd a quick, sly smirk.

Matt grimaced. "Exactly," he said. "So . . . I don't know; I just went off. I came up with this dumb, thirteen-year-old's plan where I was going to pretend to be a clairvoyant, but just kind of a not very good one?" More laughter, more lighthearted this time. "And then, I don't know, I just . . . kept doing it. I read books about, you know, trick clairvoyancy, and I watched videos, and I just kept on faking it and faking it and—"

"And nobody caught on."

"Nobody caught on!" Matt threw up his hands. "I don't know. It's unbelievable, in retrospect. How did I . . . How did nobody catch me?

How come no one looked at this more closely? But I guess that's the way the world works a lot of the time, you know? You keep your head down, you act confident, and you just *do things*, and people just sort of . . . assume you know what you're doing. People just ignore you."

The host nodded sagely while the audience tittered with a mixture of amusement, amazement, and agreement. He gestured to Jane. "And then she shows up."

"Then she shows up," Matt said with an overdramatic sigh. The audience laughed as Jane fixed him with an expression of mock hurt. He grinned and patted the back of her hand before continuing. "So, ah, yeah, Jane shows up. She transfers to our school—"

"Senior year?"

"Senior year. And then I'm walking home from school one day, and I see her, and we get to talking, and then I'm just sort of not thinking, and I take her hand."

"Oh." The host's voice curled rich and falsely mortified, and the crowd let out a brief burst of laughter. "Oh no. You held her hand? But you weren't even married." More laughter.

"I know!" agreed Matt. "Thinking about it now, I'm like, dude, are you kidding me? I'm so stupid. But yeah, I just . . . forgot. I don't know. Brain fart. I forgot she was an empath."

"Touch-based empath, right. And then, of course, she felt you had no powers."

"She felt I had no powers."

"How did you react to that?" Leno asked, turning to Jane. Jane shrugged.

"I thought he might've been a giant baby," she replied. The studio cracked with laughter.

The host chuckled. "So, your secret's out," he pressed on. "Someone knows. And then, as if that isn't bad enough, a few months later . . ."

"The Legion of Heroes."

"The Legion of Heroes." Leno turned toward the studio audience, who erupted in a ringing cheer. The host smiled. "Yeah. Ah-ha. Yeah, the Legion, exactly." He let the cheering fade, then turned back to his guests. "God, they've had a tough run."

Matt nodded, grimacing his agreement. "I know, right? So obviously, they'd been notified by the DPR or something that there was an adult clairvoyant, because I'm eighteen now, and they come to my school, and they're like—"

"'Hey, kid, how'd you like to become a superhero?'"

"'Hey, come train your powers at the Academy,' exactly."

"What went through your head when you heard that?"

Matt's face split into a sheepish grin, and he glanced between the host and the cameras. "Ahh . . . nothing I can say on TV."

The room rang with laughter. Leno let it run its course for a few moments before raising his hands. "Okay, okay. So you say no, right?"

"No, I say yes."

"You say yes?!"

"Well, I can't just say *no*," Matt explained, "because then it might look like I was actually hiding something. I had to come up with an excuse, see, why they couldn't take me."

"Right, it had to seem legitimate."

"Right. So I say, 'Hey, this is Jane; she's a pretty incredible fighter'—because she was, actually, even back then—'so hey, I'm glad you want me, that's great, but if you want me, you have to take her, because that's fair.'"

A murmur from the crowd. Leno leaned back, his hands on the table. "That's very noble of you."

"Noble?" Matt scowled. "I thought they hated her. I thought it'd make them buzz off!"

The audience laughed, though it quickly turned into an "Aww," as Jane made a face. The host shook his head, chuckling as he turned to her.

"He's mean, isn't he?" he asked tongue in cheek, gesturing to Matt.

"He's lucky he's cute," she replied. Leno laughed.

"Alright, so, Jane," he continued, turning to the girl more fully. "You always wanted to be a superhero?"

"Yeah."

"Ever since you were a kid."

"Yeah."

"So for you, this is a dream come true."

"Pretty much."

"Was being part of the Legion everything you thought it was going to be?" the host asked. Jane hesitated a moment.

"It was tough," she said finally. "You had to work hard. But I think . . . they're good people."

"Well, that's great to hear. So, they take you in, both of you"—they nodded—"and then you're there, Jane, working hard, and you're there"—he gestured to Matt—"what?"

"Trying to get expelled," Matt finished, causing another wave of laughter to erupt from the audience.

"And how did that go?" Leno asked.

"I don't know . . ." Matt replied, mock reluctant. "Don't kids watch this show?"

There was more laughter from the crowd. Jay Leno raised an eyebrow.

"Alright, alright. Yeah, maybe we shouldn't go into that," he said, raising his hands. "That's my bad for asking." Another peal of laughter. "Ah, anyhow, but you didn't get expelled."

"No."

"You were a failure at failing." The crowd laughed.

"Yeah, exactly. It sucked; I couldn't get it right. Because I'm trying to maintain this balance, right, like I'm trying to keep going with this fake clairvoyancy so I don't get uncovered, but at the same time, I keep acting out, and I'm being such a bad student and . . ."

"They really wanted your clairvoyancy."

"They really wanted my clairvoyancy! And it's like, come on, guys, seriously, *these aren't the droids you're looking for.* What do I have to do?" There was more laughter.

The host smiled—then his tone turned serious. "And then, I guess, we come to the darker stuff."

"Yeah." Matt's mouth set into a line, and he gave a jerky, almost forced nod. "My, um . . . One of my friends, at the Academy. Guy named Ed. Genius. He, ah . . . Well, everyone thought he killed himself."

A sympathetic murmur rolled through the crowd. The host's face was a mask of impeccable sympathy. "I'm so sorry to hear that. That must have been tough."

"Yeah, it . . . it sucked."

Leno turned to the camera. "And I just want to remind everyone, for our viewers at home, that if you are having a hard time out there—you know, sometimes life is tough—hang in there, alright? There is help available. Larry, can we . . . Yep, we've just put up a number; this is the number of the American Foundation for Suicide Prevention. If you're feeling down, if you need someone to talk to, this is the number to call. Mental health matters, doesn't it? I think we can all agree."

"Absolutely," said Matt, nodding along with the encouraging noises from the crowd. "It's really important. You're never alone. There's always help."

"Absolutely. There's that number up there. So, you thought your friend committed suicide."

"Yes."

"Except he didn't."

"Turns out, no."

"It was the Black Death."

"The Black Death. He'd . . . um . . . Ed, he'd . . ." Matt paused, suddenly teary. He drew a shaky breath.

"It's okay. It's okay." Leno reached over and put a gentle hand on Matt's arm, then turned to the crowd. "I think we've all lost people. I mean, we talk about this stuff, and we're happy—I think everyone's happy—that it's all over, but the tragedy; we can never forget, this man took people's lives." Murmurs of agreement rippled through the studio. "Thousands, millions of lives. That's not something you just get over, okay? That's not something you just get over. For you. For any of us." He paused as Matt sniffed. "It's alright, take your time, take your time."

"No, it's—I'm fine," assured Matt. "I'm fine. You're right, he—he killed *so many* people. And . . . Ed was just one more, wasn't he? He . . . found him out; he figured out Heydrich was faking it, faking being Captain Dawn, and so . . . he killed him. Just like that. Just another death on the list."

"But that got you thinking," the host continued, steering the conversation gently away. "Didn't it?"

"It did," Matt agreed, "because I knew him, Ed, and it didn't make sense to me. It didn't make sense that he'd killed himself."

"So you started investigating."

"Both of us. Jane and I. We started looking into . . . into suspicious deaths. Into Captain Dawn's past."

"Yeah."

"And we found . . . It was horrific."

"Oh God, I . . . I shudder. I shudder to think."

"He'd been killing—Heydrich—he'd been killing hundreds of people, secretly. Maybe thousands."

"Jesus, it just never ends."

"No, it doesn't. He'd been killing these people, all these people who knew the original Captain Dawn at some point, like his old classmates and neighbors and teachers, and . . . it was psychotic!"

"He was a son of a bitch," said Leno. He turned to the crowd. "I don't know if I can say that; I don't know if that sort of language is okay on commercial television, but screw it, I'm going to say it: he was an absolute son of a bitch." The studio rang with clapping and cheers. "Rarely, I think, do we see someone who so clearly just embodies . . . the worst of humanity. The absolute worst. He was a monster. And if we never see the likes of him again, the world will be a better place."

The room descended into thunderous applause. Leno waved the noise down with his hands. "Let's just, I think, take a moment of silence to remember everyone who's been lost. Would you—Would you be alright . . . ?"

"Absolutely."

"Of course."

"Yeah. Let's just—Everyone, yep, okay. Just for a moment."

And for the first time, truly, since Matt and Jane first stepped out onto the stage, silence descended on the studio.

A few moments passed before eventually, Leno looked up.

"Thank you. Thank you, everyone. I think we needed to do that. Because, look, tonight—tonight might not be about the victims—"

"No, but they're such an important part," added Matt.

"Absolutely, such a pivotal, pivotal part. But I don't think anyone's ever going to forget that. I'm certainly not." There were more sounds of agreement, a couple of interspersed sobs. "But look, I think we've had that moment—and tonight isn't about everyone we've lost. We've had days for that, we've had times, but tonight? That's not what tonight's about. Because we're always going to remember them, but sometimes, in the midst of all this horribleness, you've got to focus on what's good. On the good guys. On you two."

"Or it's all too bleak."

"Or it's all too bleak. Exactly!" Leno turned to the crowd. "When tragedy strikes, look for the helpers. That's what, I think, Mr. Rogers used to say. Look for the good people, look for the good parts of mankind. And that's what tonight's about." He lifted a hand toward the ceiling. "To the good people."

"TO THE GOOD PEOPLE!"

The studio took up the words, raising them like a toast, then descended into applause. When the noise finally died down, Leno pressed forward.

"So. Sorry. Getting back to your story. So, you discovered the truth."

"We did, sort of. We knew something was wrong."

"And then Heydrich found out that you'd told people."

"Yeah."

"And at that point, well . . . the game's up."

"Yeah, the truth's out there."

"Which, I think, is where most of us"—he gestured to the cameras and the audience—"where the rest of the world becomes, you know, becomes aware of what's going on . . ."

"Yeah."

"There was that broadcast." Leno's mouth twitched, and a murmur ran through the crowd. The memory was still fresh. "Had he confronted you before then? About outing him?"

"Yes," said Matt. "He, um . . . I was hiding in the desert. And he came down and talked to me. And he wasn't really angry, you know; he was almost sort of . . . pleased? I don't know. I think, for me, what was the hardest part of keeping my secret all those years, about being human, was having no one to talk to about it."

He looked at the crowd. "And I think one of the things we forget about the Black Death, about Klaus Heydrich, is that underneath it all, underneath all the horrible things he did and all his powers . . . he was still just a man, you know? He was still . . . flawed. He wasn't a god."

The host nodded his agreement. "Is that what you were thinking, when he came after you?" He paused and turned to the crowd. "Because can I just say, personally, I was terrified. Can I say that?" He looked at the audience, who murmured their agreement. "I'm not ashamed to admit it: I was terrified; I think we all were. And I mention that because it's so easily overlooked; it's so easy to . . . to get swept up in that fact that, at the end there, yeah, there was this happy ending, but in the moment . . . it was terrifying!"

He let out a short, strained laugh and shook his head. "This demon, this monster, this . . . the worst person in history, literally threatening to conquer the planet, and I . . . What did you do? How did you feel? Not just seeing this on television but being there, on the ground, right there in front of him, going, 'Holy crap, he's coming for me'?"

Matt paused, screwing up his face as he considered his answer.

"I just . . ." he started finally. "I was just trying to focus on what came next. I knew . . . I knew I couldn't run from him. I knew there was nothing I could say or do. But I just kept looking at him, and I kept thinking, 'You're not better than me; you're just some guy.'" A cheer went up among the assembled audience, and Matt flashed them a lopsided grin. "I don't know; is that stupid? It was probably pretty stupid. But I'm just like, alright, let's do this. You think I'm a clairvoyant? Fine. And so, I told him he was going to lose."

Leno gawked at him. "You said that to his face?"

"I did, I told him." Matt nodded as murmurs rippled throughout the crowd. "I said, 'If you take my blood, you're going to die.' And then, I let him read my mind so he would think I was clairvoyant."

"How do you get around through the day?" Leno asked, with complete sincerity, before adding, "With those gigantic balls?"

Laughter erupted from the audience, and to the right of him, Jane joined in. Matt gave the crowd a sheepish grin. After a few moments, the host waved everyone back down, and he turned to Matt, still smiling.

"Seriously, though, what were you thinking? Are you mad?"

"Honestly?" replied Matt. "Mainly, I just didn't want him to kill me. I thought, he's going to be so angry if he figures out I'm lying, that he's gone to all this trouble to get me, and then it turns out there's no point. I didn't want to tick him off."

"But you could have just given up. You didn't need to say that."

Matt's eyebrows furrowed. "I guess . . . I wanted to stall him?" he replied. "I just . . . I was trying to keep him talking. I don't know, buy everyone else some time." He paused. "No, it was more than that," he admitted finally. "I . . . I wanted to mess with him. It was sort of like this . . . this feeling, this *screw you*, this . . . I couldn't do anything else, right? I couldn't stop him."

"Right."

"Right. But I had to do something, anything, anything that could help. And so, I think that maybe, *maybe*, I can scare him. Maybe if he believes I am who I say I am, if I believe I am who I say I am, I can make him think this is a bad idea. Because he's just some guy. Deep down inside, he's just some guy, some scared little kid who doesn't know what he's doing any more than any of us, making it all up as he goes along, same as me. Doesn't matter if he has all the powers or none of them.

"And it was a long shot—it was always going to be a long shot—but at the same time I'm thinking, 'Well, one way or another, he's not getting a clairvoyant, so . . . why not?'" There was more murmuring from the crowd. "Because if he thinks he's getting clairvoyant powers, and then he doesn't, and I've told him taking my blood means he's losing, then . . . he's never going to be able to get that out of his head, is he? There's always going to be this deep-seated seed of panic. Like, 'I've taken this power; I should be able to see the future, but I can't. I can't see what's coming, I don't feel any different—and I'm terrified I'm going to lose.'"

Matt leaned in toward Leno, staring intently. "And see, this is where the psychology of it comes in. Because he doesn't know what being clairvoyant feels like, does he? And I've made this prediction that he's going to lose, and he believes I'm real, so he can't forget it. So he's worrying about losing, but at the same time, feeling that feeling and going, 'Oh God, is this what predicting my own death feels like?' And maybe that would shake him; maybe that might spiral and spiral and spiral until maybe, *maybe*, it's really messing with his head. Maybe. Who knows."

"Wow," said Leno. He looked genuinely stunned. "So you're facing off against the greatest mass murderer in history, and you're playing mind games." The audience laughed. The host shook his head. "Like I said, wow. Remind me to never play you in poker."

Matt grinned as there was more laughter. "So yeah." He shrugged. "That's about it."

"So you didn't know your blood was going to affect him?" Leno asked. "That didn't cross your mind?"

"I mean, a part of me . . ." Matt started, but he stopped himself. "I mean, I wondered, I guess? Maybe a little? But I just thought it would do nothing, you know? I wasn't expecting anything special. I didn't want him to take my blood because, you know, I didn't want to bleed to death, but if he was going to take it, then maybe I wanted him to feel a little scared about it, you know? Just in case, I don't know, somewhere down the line, maybe, that fear turned into something. Maybe made him panic. Maybe made him do something stupid. Give someone stronger the upper hand."

"Which brings us, I think, to Jane," said the host. "Jane"—he turned to her—"talk to me. Tell me what happened. Tell us how you came to be, standing there, holding the power of Dawn."

"Steady on, guv," the man in the pinstriped suit replied. He fixed the thin old man with a smirk, though no humor reached his eyes. "Let's see them first."

The old man made no move to get up from his chair, instead sliding his gaze over to the nearest soldier with a soft, weary sigh. "Jackson," he said mildly, "give Mister Salt his diamonds."

The tall, hard-faced soldier scowled, appearing displeased at the order; perhaps at the thought of handing anything to Mr. Salt, who was grinning at him like a particularly overfed weasel, or perhaps just displeased in general. He swung his assault rifle to the side, walked over to one of the heavy wooden benches, and flipped it easily upside down. On the underside was bolted a rectangular lockbox. Jackson's fingers dug in around the short edge of the metal and pulled, tearing the top open with a rending screech. The soldier reached inside the strongbox and pulled out a leather briefcase.

"Strong lad, ain't cha?" remarked Mr. Salt. The muscular man said nothing, merely scowled. He flipped the table back to how he had found it, then walked toward the group of newcomers, one hand on the briefcase handle, the other on his gun.

"Go ahead, take it," said the thin man, waving dismissively toward his blue-suited counterpart. "Count them. We're in no hurry."

"Yeah?" The Englishman grinned. He reached out and snatched the briefcase from the soldier's outstretched hand, pulling it close as if to covet. "Awful trusting of ya. Not worried I'll rabbit?"

"You can run if you like, Mister Salt," the old man said mildly, "the lives of thieves don't concern me. If you want to end yours so abruptly, if you think we can't stop or find you—Well, that's your decision."

The man they called Mister Salt kept grinning, although the expression grew somewhat strained. He glanced down at the briefcase then up at the old man, the nearby soldiers, and Jackson, then back at his crew.

"Just jerking your chain." He smirked, though his greasy words now somewhat lacked their original luster. He turned the briefcase around so the clasps were facing him, still giving the soldiers the odd nervous eye, and clicked the lid open. The thief let out a long whistle.

"Whew. Jesus. Alright." He balanced the open case with one hand and lifted out one of the diamonds, holding it up to the moonlight. It was the size of a fingernail. "And these're all proper, ey? Ain't gonna de-Midas if I shake 'em too much? Not laced through with some poor sap's DNA?"

"They are not transmuted, nor bioorganically derived," the thin man assured him. "Pure diamonds, natural. Perform any test you like."

Mister Salt gestured to his companion, the large man in the black shirt who looked like his mother was a gargoyle from some second-rate church. "Mind if I . . . you know."

His counterpart gestured. "Be my guest."

Salt eyed the old man with some suspicion, but nevertheless, snapped the briefcase shut. He stepped over to his hunched, hulking accomplice and handed him a fistful of the diamonds, which the big man in turn held up to his eye. He licked one, smelled one, tapped it gingerly against his teeth—then he pulled out a small, glue-gun-like device from his back pocket and pressed it gently against the diamond's side. The device beeped, and a scattering of red-to-green lights lit up along the LED screen on the side. The giant nodded.

"It's real."

"Well, I'll be." Mr. Salt turned back to the man in the chair, who had watched the scene unfold with passive indifference. "You really just handing me half a billion in diamonds. Just like that."

"Money is no object," the man replied, "so long as you deliver what you promised."

"Oh, I always deliver. You know that. Expensive—"

"But worth your salt. Yes. The nomenclature is fascinating. Skip to the point. Do you have it or not?" Around the warehouse, the soldiers' grips on their weapons tightened.

The Englishman held up his hands.

"Alright, guv, alright. Jesus. No need to be tense. Man of my word, ainnai? Pep?" He glanced back at the thickset woman behind him. The two exchanged nods, then the woman opened her hand, and a shimmering blue oval of light materialized vertically in the air beside her.

She stuck her arm through, disappearing up to her shoulder as she rummaged around inside the portal, drawing her hand back out a few moments later clutching a black velvet jewellery box. She turned around, holding it in front of her, glancing at the soldiers nervously, before passing it to Mister Salt. All eyes bored into the box.

Slowly, slowly, like a two-bit game show host revealing the grand prize, the blue-suited thief gently pried the lid open, revealing its tiny, precious contents.

A black bed of satin.

And a single strand of hair.

"Give it to me," the thin man demanded, and though his voice held no agitation or urgency, nor was there any room for argument. "Please."

The thief held the flat jewellery box in his hand, balanced loosely between his fingers. He flicked a furtive glance toward the assembled mob.

Then he snapped the lid shut.

"See, I'm a man of my word," he mused. He twisted his heel on the concrete, making a small, scuffing squeak. His eyes flicked to meet the old man's. "But still, I've gotta wonda. Lotta effin' power I'm holdin' 'ere. Lotta effin' import. You think I dunno what this is?" He held up the box. "You think I dunno what it means? Why should I give it to you? Huh? Why should you 'av it?"

And for the first time since he'd gotten there, he pointed at the TV.

"Why should you 'av tha power ta kill tha Black Death?"

"He attacked me," Jane recounted, "and then he blew up the Academy."

"But he didn't kill you?"

"No. Not most of us. Giselle got people out."

"This is Giselle Pixus, new head of the Legion?"

"Yeah."

"Right. She pulled everyone out."

"Yeah. And then we went to Detroit, and we tried to fight, and . . ." Jane paused, her face falling. After a few moments, the host rescued her.

"I think we can all say you fought bravely."

"Yeah."

"Look, it's a terrible thing what happened," said Leno. "You know, we all saw it, and I . . . I don't want to dwell too much on this again because I know these are painful memories for a lot of people, but I still have to ask . . . So you tried to stop him. You fought bravely. But this is the Black Death."

"Yeah. He destroyed us."

"Yeah. And the whole world saw that, I think, which was in a way even scarier than his announcement, because suddenly, this is real, isn't it? This is happening, and these are the best fighters in the world—and they can't do anything."

"Yeah."

"And see, this is the part I want to know about," the host said, leaning in, "because then, he turns the camera off, and it's clear he's going to talk to you. What happened then?"

Jane paused for a moment before she spoke, her face deliberately blank. "He wanted me to join him. To be with him. As an empath. As . . . his wife."

The crowd gasped, the revulsion palpable. Leno shook his head.

"It's just layer after layer of despicable, isn't it?"

"Yeah."

"So what'd you tell him?"

"I told him to—" And Jane let loose a deluge of violent swear words that streamed out live on national television to an ecstatic, overwhelming cheer from the crowd and the mock consternation of Jay Leno.

"Okay, okay. Let's, ah, let's take it down a notch," he said, grimacing, although the expression didn't reach his eyes, and it was clear he was trying to hold back a grin. People were standing up among the crowd, shouting and punching their fists. With a triumphant smile, Jane raised her chin to them. For a moment, her eyes glowed and a rush of golden light streamed through her *E*. The crowd went crazy.

"Alright, alright, come on now," said the host, waving the crowd down until they settled. "Come on. I think, Jane, we can all agree—I don't know, maybe we need to take a vote on it, but to me that sounds like exactly the right answer." The audience erupted with further cheering. Once more, Leno had to wait for the noise to subside.

"Alright," he said finally. "So, he propositions you, and you say no. What then?"

"I try to blow his head off." More barks of laughter, followed by more cheers. Jane grinned while the host rolled his eyes in mock despair.

"You try to blow his head off. And how'd that go?"

"Not great."

"Not great, no, I can imagine. But he left you alive?"

"Yeah," replied Jane. "He didn't want to kill me. He . . ." She let out a long sigh, then sat up a little straighter and continued speaking matter-of-factly. "He beat me up pretty bloody. But then, he teleported me to Morningstar. To the Academy. Or the ruins, I guess."

"Why'd he take you there?"

Jane made a face. "He wanted to show me it was hopeless," she answered. "He wanted to try and change my mind. About being with him. He said he loved me."

The host recoiled as dark murmurs rippled across the crowd. "Jesus."

"Yeah."

"But he'd killed your mom!"

"Yeah. That was . . . yeah."

"But he didn't seem to care."

"No, he kept trying. He said we could be . . . king and queen, if we wanted. Have, I don't know, some empath dynasty. I don't know. He wanted us to be like Caitlin Reid and Captain Dawn."

"Sick. Absolutely twisted."

"Yeah. He dragged me over to the ruins of their old room, and there's the display case with her costume in it. Intact somehow." Jane paused and shook her head, her mouth taut. "And then he turns to me, and he's going on and on, and he reaches into his coat and he pulls out this locket, this like . . . love heart on a chain."

"He gave you jewelry?"

"Yeah. And he goes, 'This was hers; it could be yours. This could be us. We could rule.' Then he puts it in my hand and teleports away."

"Jesus. Leaving you lying there in the ruins."

"Yeah." Jane shifted in her seat. "And I . . . I don't know what came over me. I don't know why I did it. Maybe . . . I was looking for some kind of strength? Some kind of inspiration or, I don't know, something? But I opened the locket, and it was one of those big ones, you know, with a picture of the people on each side?"

The host nodded. "I know the type."

"Yeah. And there's this photo of them, Walter and Caitlin, Captain Dawn, and I . . . I look at them, and I touch it, and it's clear it hasn't been opened since she died."

"Right." Across the studio, it was as if the audience were leaning forward, almost holding their collective breath.

"And then, I don't know: I'm clumsy, I'm hurt, my finger slips, and I touch the photo of Caitlin, and I accidentally knock her picture, and . . ." Jane looked up at the crowd. "There was hair behind it. Brown hair."

"Wait," the host said. He leaned back, realization spreading over his face. "No. It can't be."

"Yeah," replied Jane. "It was. It was her hair, because I knew the color, and then it's like I'm dreaming because I'm thinking, 'If her hair's behind her picture . . . and there's a picture of him . . .'" Her voice trailed off as she glanced up at Leno, looking slightly guilty. "And . . . yeah."

"No way."

"Yeah."

"Because that was an old-fashioned thing, wasn't it? A lock of the hair?"

"Yeah, hair in a locket. And I touch it—his hair—and I remember my hands were shaking so hard, just *trembling*, and I touched it, and I could feel it still glowing deep inside. I could feel the power, and it was like . . . I heard his voice."

The studio was breathlessly silent. Leno leaned in.

"What did it say?" he whispered.

"It said . . ." Jane's voice caught but she steadied herself. She sat up straighter. "It was like it said, 'I'm here. I'm with you.' And I felt this warmth—this incredible, beautiful warmth—and I knew, somehow, this was why I was there. This was what I was supposed to do."

"So you took it."

"I took it. And I broke the case, and I put on Caitlin's armor because my own was all beat up, and it kind of fit?" The audience laughed. "And then I just . . . yeah. I knew what I had to do."

"Wow," said the host. "Just wow. Absolutely incredible. And of course, we all know what happened next—we all saw it. I have to say, I have never been more invested in anything I have seen on TV *in my life*." Chuckles went up among the crowd. "And I work in television!" More laughter. Leno turned back to Jane. "And then you beat him."

"We beat him. Matt helped. So did a lot of people."

"I remember. Our marketing director at the time—Sally—I remember her bursting into the break room and going, 'We have to get there, now!' because she was psychic, see, and I'm going, 'What in the hell are you talking about?' but she was grabbing everyone's hands and being like, 'Come on, we're going to project.'"

"It was crazy."

"Oh, I completely agree. Absolute lunacy. I remember saying, I said to Sally, 'What the hell do you think this is going to accomplish? Aren't we just going to tick him off?' But no, I didn't realize, it was the distraction."

"It was the distraction."

"You were already engaged, mentally, in the fight, and then these tens of thousands of voices—You know, it was just an annoyance, but—"

"But it was enough to distract him. It gave me time. And we destroyed him."

Once more, the studio erupted with noise as every person in the audience rose to their feet in a deafening, cacophonous roar. Leno clapped too, shaking his head.

"All thanks to a lock of hair."

Inside the warehouse, nobody moved. Nobody so much as breathed. Spread out between the shelves and tables, the soldiers tensed, hands gripping their weapons. The big man behind Salt trembled, his meaty hand clutched tight around the diamond, the woman next to him breathing quickly, her fingers slowly fanning out, eyes darting between the barrels of every glinting gun.

Only Salt and the old man appeared unmoved by the sudden tension, but of the two of them, Salt's free hand tremored, and small drips of sweat beaded atop his forehead. The buyer, on the other hand, seemed completely unperturbed.

"See, I know wha dis is," Salt repeated. "I know wha it can do. I know wha it's used for." He pointed again at the TV. "And now s'as everyone, see? Not just our little secret. They all know what it's for."

"Mr. Glasscock—"

"Salt! It's effin' Salt, I—You—"

"Mr. Salt," the spectacled man said plainly, without a hint of emotion or malice. "Or whatever you choose to call yourself." He smiled a thin, bland smile that washed over his wizened features like a wave of gray dishwater and flaking paint. "I'm not in the habit of wasting time nor reneging on an agreement. You get the diamonds. We get the hair. It's as simple as that."

"No, not 'at simple," the thief replied. He took a step back, shaking his head, causing a scattering of clatter as every gun in the room rose half an inch. Salt froze to the spot, then his head continued shaking. "This 'ere? This is national security." He held up the velvet box, letting it glimmer in the moonlight. "This is a game changer. This 'ere's priceless."

"Then name your price," the buyer interjected, "and we will pay it."

The Englishman froze. His mouth hung open. He glanced quickly back at the other members of his crew, then at the armed men around him.

"It's not just money," he said, almost pleading. "Look, I ain't no monster. Imma crook, sure, but I still got family. Folks I gotta do right by. This . . ." His eyes lingered on the box. "I gotta know where this's going. In good conscience, I can't jus' let it go."

"Mr. Salt," sighed the old man, sounding thoroughly bored. "You came here voluntarily. You stole the hair, and you brought it to us. Nobody made you. Nobody forced you. Which means either you had no idea what you were stealing—which I highly doubt—or you came here possessing a willingness, however tepid, to part with what you stole. Your moral concerns are noted, but let's not kid ourselves; even if I assured you I was on the side of angels, you would have no way of knowing it was true."

The greasy-haired thief's mouth twitched, and he looked distinctly uncomfortable, though he made no move to run. The spectacled man let out a deep sigh.

"Very well. Let us play this game. I am a collector. A scientist. A philanthropist. I have no ability to take the power of Captain Dawn for myself, nor the desire to use it to rule the world. I am curious." He paused. "And I am wealthy. So, it becomes then, Mr. Salt—and I think we've known this all along—less a matter of whether what I've said has assuaged your conscience and more of three simple words: *Name. Your. Price.*"

For a moment, Salt said nothing, simply twisted uncomfortably in place. Behind and to either side of him, both his thick-built associates whispered, trying to catch his attention, but he paid neither any heed.

Finally, Salt met the buyer's eyes.

"Double," he muttered.

"Excuse me?"

"You 'eard me. Double. A billion dollas. And nunna this sequenced bills or wire funds. I wan' diamonds, pure diamonds, like—"

"Done," the man answered curtly, cutting him off. The thief halted midsentence and stood there, mouth agape. Still sitting on his folding chair, his counterpart ignored him, instead nodding to the soldier to his left. "Jackson. Take the case from him, then give him the extra briefcases. Both of them."

Salt's mouth hung slightly open, and his jaw started to work, but try as he might, he couldn't seem to summon either words or resistance. Still scowling, as he had been the entire time, the lead soldier Jackson strode over and yanked the jewelry box from the Englishman's hands, then returned and placed it in the old man's lap.

One after the other, Jackson then grabbed, overturned, and eviscerated two more heavy wooden worktables, tearing open the metal boxes bolted onto their respective undersides and pulling out identical leather briefcases. With one in each hand, he stalked back over to Salt, where he flung both cases unceremoniously into the Englishman's arms, who staggered beneath the sudden weight.

"But dis is . . . But dis is . . ." he mumbled. He stumbled, seemingly delirious, gawking at the two cases in his hand and the other resting at his feet. "I gotta authenticate . . . gotta check . . ."

"You do what you have to do," the buyer told him. He had already beckoned another of the soldiers over, who, without speaking, had opened a silver carry case and was setting up a specialized-looking microscope. "Just do it quietly. Confirm the DNA."

The microscope soldier nodded and, reverently, as though carrying something infinitely delicate, took the box from the old man's hands. He pinched the hair inside between forefinger and thumb and, gently, placed it on the microscope's glass slide, twisting various knobs and dials. Breathless seconds passed as he stared through the eyepiece.

"It's his," the examining soldier said finally.

"Are you certain?"

"SNPs match heritage records."

"Then our business here is concluded," said the buyer. He turned back to Mr. Salt. "You have your payment—three times what was agreed. One-point-five billion dollars, real and uncontaminated. You can leave now. You'll no doubt want to confirm your haul." He pulled the last word into the barest hint of a sneer.

The British thief stood speechless, the two briefcases still in his arms. Suddenly, Salt snapped out of his trance and gestured hurriedly for his companions, who trundled quickly into place, the hulking man grabbing onto the first briefcase with one hand as he and the woman held Salt on either side. Salt closed his eyes, knuckles white around the two other cases, his lips murmuring.

"Oh, and Mr. Glasscock?"

The thief's eyes opened to find the old man fixing him with that same, implacable smile. A shiver ran down his spine.

"What?"

"Before you go, a word of caution. I want you to consider, for a moment, what has taken place here." The buyer gestured broadly around him—to the warehouse, to the darkness, to the armed, glowering guards. "We chose this place. We outnumbered you. We could have prepared, I think you'll realize, any number of traps or methods to prevent your escape.

"You are slippery, I don't doubt it, but at a certain point, sheer numbers"—he gestured again at the awaiting soldiers—"can create a stranglehold on odds. We didn't do that. We did not rob you or cheat you or make any attempt to take our payment back. Think on that. We let you walk in here, extort us for a billion dollars, and walk out. Do you know why we did that? Do you know what that means?"

He paused. Salt shook his head.

"I'll tell you," said the old man. "We did it because we are those for whom a billion dollars is irrelevant. For whom the diamonds you carry are irrelevant. Think on that. Think of how much power we must hold if that kind of money does not matter. Think of how feeble you are, how little you mean in comparison. We gave a billion dollars to a man we were indifferent to."

His smile broadened. "Imagine what resources we would expend if you suddenly became important to us. If, for example, you ever spoke of our deal or what you'd seen here tonight. If you told anyone what you'd done."

The old, thin man leaned forward, and Salt and his companions flinched. "Imagine how thoroughly we could tear you and everyone you love apart if we learned, in any way, that you'd betrayed us."

The Englishman gulped.

Suddenly, the man in the glasses leaned back, reclining in his thin metal chair. "Go on now. Get going. Teleport away. Enjoy your newfound luxury, once you pass the sleepless nights you'll undoubtedly spend ensuring every one of those diamonds isn't booby-trapped. They're not, for your information. Like I said, we only care about your silence. Not your wealth."

Then he waved them away, and with patches of sweat staining beneath his armpits, the thief clung tight to his companions and vanished in a rush of sulfurous smoke.

"So what's been happening since then?" Leno asked. "How're you settling into this new life where everyone knows who you are? Because you're famous; you're celebrities now, aren't you?"

"It's weird," agreed Matt. "I can't go anywhere. People recognize me on the street."

"I like it when it's kids," said Jane. "Kids always wave at me."

"I get fan mail," added Matt. "I mean, she gets more"—he jerked his thumb at Jane—"but I still get fan mail, and it's like, hey, that's really nice of you, but . . . you know I can't actually *do anything*, right?"

"Oh, come on now, that's not fair; don't beat yourself up," the host replied as the audience laughed.

"The weirdest thing is girls," Matt continued. "I get fan mail from *girls*."

"What?" Jane growled. Her eyes narrowed and suddenly flared with golden energy. The audience laughed, though perhaps a bit warily, as she continued to glare at Matt, who grinned and, completely unafraid, leaned over to kiss her on the forehead. A moment later, the light seeping from Jane's eyes dissipated, and she also broke into a grin. The crowd relaxed into laughter.

"No, but it hasn't been all sunny," Matt continued, turning back to their host. "The legal stuff, obviously; that's been challenging, but the ACLU have been fantastic, and it's been really great hearing from everyone out there, you know? Hearing we've got so much support."

The room rang with more cheers while Matt raised an appreciative hand.

"Um, what else," he wondered. He crossed and uncrossed his legs, relaxing into the lounge. "Oh, there are a bunch of people who're trying to kill me. Yep, that's a whole new thing."

Gasps around the studio. Leno's brows furrowed, incredulous. "Kill you?"

"Yep, put a bullet in me. That's pretty great."

"You specifically? Not Jane? Are they Heydrich supporters, or—?"

"No, they're mostly American, I think. And I think . . ." He paused, scrunching up his face. "If I'm remembering correctly, Jane is like Frankenstein? Or possibly a man?"

Jane nodded, nonchalant, as if she'd heard all this before, while Matt mimed having muscular arms. Matt shook his head and cleared his throat. "So it's like a conspiracy theory, see? Like a second amendment thing," he explained with mild exasperation.

"Apparently, I've already given the government my blood, and they're using it to make an anti-powers vaccine for, I don't know, the Illuminati or something. And then Jane is a secret government supersoldier who's going to force everyone to get vaccinated so they can take over the world. Something like that."

The host stared at him, blinking. "Oh. So then why were you going to court?"

"Oh, that's all misdirection, obviously," Matt answered, completely nonchalant. "Yeah, I'm just pretending like I don't want to give people my blood so all the sheeple don't figure out I've betrayed them. By the time anyone realizes, it's going to be too late."

"Wow," replied Leno. "So the Supreme Court's in on this too?"

"Oh, for sure," said Matt. "The Supreme Court, the police, the government, hospitals, you. You're in on it too, Jay. We had a meeting about this last week."

"Oh God, I completely forgot. I got distracted watching the Mets game."

"Well, don't worry; it's all in the newsletter."

"Phew." The host wiped his brow in mock relief while the audience laughed. "Still, I gotta say, you're remarkably laid back about this. People trying to kill you?"

"Yeah. Look, Jay, I'm not going to lie: at first, it was a bit frustrating; you sort of just want to grab these people and shake them by the neck and say, 'What the hell do you think I'm doing?!' But hey, I'm used to it now. I've adjusted. I got a second lock on my door. I've got one of those little duress alarms. And my girlfriend can vaporize city blocks, so, you know, we'll see how we go." There was a sudden surge of laughter, and Matt flashed the audience a wry grin.

"So you guys are dating, then?" asked Leno. A large *Oooh* went up from the crowd. Matt and Jane glanced at each other.

"Nah," Matt replied, grinning back at the crowd. "Friends with benefits." Jane rolled her eyes as the room laughed. Matt took her hand.

"No, we're together," he corrected, smiling and more serious. "Just taking it one day at a time. Going through all this craziness, you know. She's got my back."

"Yeah," Jane echoed, and she smiled at him. The audience let out an *Aww* as Jane poked Matt on the arm. "Tell them about the cult people."

"Oh yeah! The cult people."

"What cult people?" Leno asked, looking from one to the other. "There's a cult?"

"There is," confirmed Matt. "It's sort of like the conspiracy guys I was telling you about, but, like, the other end of the spectrum?" He paused, and when the host didn't interrupt, Matt took a deep breath. "So, there's this Christian group, see? The Eastborough Baptist Church. In Sedgwick, Kansas. You might have heard of them? They're very vocal."

"Wait," said Leno. "That name sounds familiar. Do they—Are they the ones that picket funerals?"

"Exactly. That's them."

"Right, yeah . . . Larry, see if we've got any—yep, photos of the—There we go." The screen behind the host changed, replaced by a picture of a group of protestors holding very rude multicolored signs. "That's them?"

"That's the one."

"And wait, they're protesting you?"

"No, no, the opposite," Matt explained. "They're, like, huge fans of me. They think I'm the messiah."

The audience exploded with incredulous laughter. Leno reeled back. "What?!"

"Yeah, I'm serious. I'm one hundred percent serious. They're—Look, I'll try to get this straight." He leaned forward, furrowing his brow. "So they believe that powers are evil, right? Because they're temptations from the Devil, the apple of Eden, or whatever. They believe—again, I think I'm remembering this right—they think only God should be able to do the supernatural, so by using superpowers, we are . . . going against God."

"Wow, that's . . . bizarre."

"Yeah, but that's why they protest at funerals of soldiers and firefighters and stuff, because those are professions that use powers quite regularly *and* are part of the government, and they think . . ." Matt struggled to find the words, gesturing over with his hands. "They think because the government hasn't outlawed powers, the government is pro-powers, so the government is evil, and so anyone who works for the government is evil and, I don't know, pushing Satan's agenda. Or something."

"Right," said Leno, nodding in mock-sage agreement. "I get you. I mean, I feel like they maybe skipped a few steps. They've got powers, right?"

"Oh yeah," replied Matt. "Absolutely, yes. To the best of my knowledge, every one of them has a superpower. I guess maybe they try not to use them? Which, I mean, to me, who's over here powerless, it's sort of like, 'Guys, come on . . . you're killing me.'"

The audience laughed.

"But that's their whole thing," Matt continued. "They think powers are the Devil, which means me, who has no powers, must be untainted by the Devil, which makes me the chosen one."

Matt grinned at Leno and shrugged, causing the talk show host to laugh while the studio roared.

"But you're not the messiah," Leno said finally.

"No," replied Matt. "I'm just a very naughty boy."

The audience was in stitches. Jane's gaze remained on Matt, halfway between pained and amused.

"So *they* want you to be their messiah," Leno concluded, "the conspiracy theorists want you dead. What do *you* want, Matt? What's next for you?"

"I don't know, man," sighed Matt, a little overdramatic. "I just want to go to college."

"Have you had any offers?" The host looked over at the crowd. "Because if you haven't, after today, I think you might."

The old man watched the three thieves go with one and a half billion dollars' worth of diamonds and made no move to stop them. A few seconds passed in silence as the sulfuric teleportation vapors dissipated. Then he glanced back.

"Back in the case," he commanded the guard with the microscope, who had already gingerly returned the hair of Captain Dawn to its velvet jewelry box and was packing his equipment away.

"Sir," scowled Jackson, the lead soldier, his voice gruff and angry. It was the first time he had spoken since the sellers had arrived.

"What?"

"That's it? You're just going to let them go?"

"Did you not hear anything I just said?" replied the spectacled man. His mouth hardened into a taut line. "Let them go. It's impossible to know what kind of fail-safes these people have, should they not come home alive." He shook his head, the wisps of thin gray hair shifting. "We've bought a sword of Damocles. Fear is a far better guarantee of silence."

"But—"

"You're paid for your firepower, Jackson, not your counsel. Take a team, secure the perimeter. Make sure our friends are wise and have departed."

The soldier's square face puckered into a scowl, but regardless, after a few seconds, he pointed sharply at several of the nearby men and motioned them to approach. The old man pulled out his newspaper, appearing not to listen as the unit commander snapped quiet orders, and the selected guards began dutifully spreading out toward the exits. It took approximately fifteen minutes and most of the Arts and Culture section before all of them returned.

"All clear, sir," Jackson reported through partially gritted teeth.

"Excellent. Phase two, then. Send your teleporter. Bring our friend up."

"And Jane," Leno continued. "What about you? Obviously, there's been the stuff with Matt, your front-yard heroics"—the crowd laughed—"but what about moving forward? Is being Lady Dawn something you're going to keep doing?"

"Absolutely," Jane said. "This is me. This is what I want to do. I'm here to help. I'm working with the Legion, and we . . ." She hesitated before she straightened up, choosing her words. "The original Captain Dawn, I think he didn't want to misuse his powers. And I think he got to the point, even before Africa, where he was so worried about doing something wrong that he was scared of trying to do something right, you know?"

She looked at the assembled audience. "But I want to be different. I . . . It is a miracle that I have this power. That any part of Captain Dawn survived. And I believe—I *know* that I'm supposed to be helping people. So that's what I've been doing. That's what I'm going to keep doing."

"That's amazing," Leno said. "Really, it truly is. You know, I've seen footage of you in action. Actually, Larry, if you've got it ready, if we can roll that tape—This was from the news a few weeks back."

The screen behind him flashed to show footage of a skyscraper on fire across several stories.

Jane nodded. "Singapore. A chemical fire. The firefighters were having trouble—"

"Yeah. And then see, here you come."

Suddenly on-screen, a figure dove from the clouds: a golden missile, a needle of light, which flew straight through the fire-torn window with such force that the flames around it momentarily went out. A second later, Jane reappeared, arms laden with a half dozen people, whom she carried down to safety.

"Just incredible. Incredible."

"The firefighters did most of the work," Jane replied, though she still sat straighter and with a slight blush. "It was just the smoke; it was getting pretty toxic, and the power of Dawn can sort of push it away, I guess, if you hold it around yourself, if you concentrate . . ."

"The costume, then, I've got to ask," said Leno. "Why doesn't it get destroyed while you're fighting? It must be made out of some incredible stuff."

"It's a polycarbonate weave," Jane answered, matter-of-factly. "But I think it's mostly the power. Look here, I'll show you . . ."

There was a bit of shuffling and rearrangement as Jane moved herself up to the closest camera and held her arm out, close enough to see the goose bumps and little hairs.

The host leaned in.

"See that glow?"

"Yeah, I do. I see it."

"It's all along—"

"Yeah, it goes all along your body."

"Try and touch it."

"Sorry?"

"Touch it. Try and touch it. Try and poke through."

The audience laughed. Leno looked bashful.

"If you say so," he said, triggering more laughter. He moved his hand around Jane's wrist and tried to squeeze down, but about a quarter of an inch from her skin, his fingers met an invisible force, and try as he might, he couldn't push any farther.

"Oh wow! Wow, it's like a—Sort of like a force field, almost. It's—Gosh, it's warm!"

"Yeah," said Jane. She withdrew her arm, and as the studio audience clapped, they both returned to their seats. "It's the energy; it's sort of coming out all the time, and it goes through, or maybe over clothes, I don't know, but—but most of the time, they stay intact."

"Well, good, great. I mean, I suppose the alternative is you end up fighting naked."

"I'd watch it," said Matt, raising his hand, which got a laugh.

"Please. God. No. Please."

In the darkness of the warehouse, the teleporting soldier reappeared—but not alone. Now, he dragged with him a shaking shadow of a man, a trembling, mangled figure clad in nought but rags, his hands shackled in thick iron manacles bound tight behind his back.

All around the moonlit room, the looming soldiers drew closer, almost on instinct, like sharks sensing blood. For there was blood. Their captive's skin was scarred and mottled, both feet pummeled into a pulp. And his eyes. Where once had sat his eyeballs, now he bore only ragged, gaping holes.

The teleporting soldier, sent to drag him from captivity, hauled the man across the concrete floor like a sack of broken meat. He threw him, shivering and sobbing, at the old man's feet.

"That's sufficient," the buyer murmured. "Thank you, gentlemen. You may go."

"But, sir, I—"

"You may go now, Jackson. All of you. Our friend here and I are going to have a little talk."

He turned and smiled at the squad commander, holding out his palm. For a moment, the soldier looked conflicted—then he handed the old man the box.

"Move out!" he commanded, and as one, the guards clustered together, pulling reluctantly away from their broken, trembling prey. With practiced familiarity, the soldiers moved into an open space and placed their hands upon their squadron's teleporter, who scrunched up his eyes. For a few moments, the night air hung with the soft sounds of shuffling and concentration. Then, there was a pop, a waft of sulfur, and the armed guards disappeared.

Leaving only the old man and the blinded prisoner in the warehouse, alone.

Pale and skinny, with jaw-length black hair hanging lank and blood-ied against hollow cheeks and a trembling underbite, the prisoner shook at the sudden sound and subsequent silence, beginning to frantically rock and sob.

"Arthur, no, Arthur, shh," cooed the man in the glasses. He did not rise from his chair nor reach out to offer any comfort, merely continued to sit, to stare at the body shaking at his feet. "Arthur. I'm not here to hurt you. There's no need to be afraid. It will all be over soon. I promise."

"Oh God," the man named Arthur wailed. The old man shook his head.

"Not like that. I'm not going to kill you, Arthur. Unless you try to escape. But I need something from you. Something very simple. Do you understand what I'm trying to say?"

"No," the prisoner whimpered. "No. No."

"Shh, Arthur. Shh. Just a simple task—one simple thing—and you'll be taken for healing. We'll get you back your eyes."

The captive suddenly froze. He hunched into himself, peering blindly up toward the sound of the old man's voice.

"You . . . You . . . I'm not going to die?"

"That's entirely up to you, Arthur," the man said mildly. "Just know that I've got a gun to your head, and if I see you being uncooperative, I will shoot you without hesitation."

"Oh God," Arthur whispered.

"Shh, shh, shh. All will be fine. Now, just stay there, wait there a moment, while I make a quick call."

For the first time since he'd arrived, the buyer stood. Keeping careful distance from the blind man sprawled piteously across the concrete, the old man shuffled a few feet across the warehouse, wherein he reached into his pocket and pulled out a cell phone. Its screen glowed, flickering with a steady uptick of numbers—an ongoing videocall. The feed of the receiver was blank. Delicately, the thin, gray-suited man perched the phone atop one of the wooden tables, propping it up against an empty paint tin with the camera facing back toward the prisoner and the chair.

"Can you see?" he asked.

"Yes," a voice replied. The old man nodded before shuffling back to the chair so he was within the camera's view. He sat down gingerly, then reached into his breast pocket and withdrew the black velvet jewelry case.

"Arthur," he said calmly, in a voice that betrayed no hint of the horrors the prisoner had endured. "I'm going to hand you a box. It's a gift box, like one that might hold a necklace. Like you'd buy from a jewelry store. Hold out your hands, okay?"

The blind man whimpered, blood and mucus dripping from the sockets of his empty eyes, but he held out his arms. His hands shook violently.

"Arthur. I need you to be steady. I'm going to give you the box. You're going to open it. You're going to feel very gently what's inside it. You're going to take what is inside it. You're going to hold it. You're going to be very careful. If you drop it, I'll have to kill you."

"Oh God," Arthur sobbed, his hands shaking even harder.

"No, no, none of that. Do this one thing, and I'll take you to the hospital. You'll be healed. You'll get your sight back. You want that, don't you?"

"Yes." A whisper.

"Then hold on to what I'm about to give you. Hold it very tight."

The buyer reached out toward the trembling man and slowly, slowly, lowered the case into his hands. Arthur flinched the moment the box made contact, but only for an instant; the next second, he caught himself so violently that the tension in his muscles threatened to snap the case in half. But he kept hold of himself.

Steadily, steadily, the captive's fingers fumbled around the box's edges, feeling the shape, the gap, the hinges. He turned the case around, his broken fingernails prying slowly around the edge. The box creaked open. The hair lay inside, soft and gold.

"Gently now," the old man reminded, almost caring, almost kind. Arthur's arms continued to shake, but his hands remained steady, brought still by sheer terror and force of will. His fingers slid softly over the velvet lining, searching for aberrations, more tender in fear than the barest lover's touch.

"I . . . I feel something," mumbled Arthur. "I think . . . it feels like hair."

"Good," the thin man replied, leaning forward with a smile that Arthur could not see. "Good. You've got it firmly?"

"Yes."

"Excellent. What do you feel?"

"I . . . I feel . . . nothing."

"Nothing from the hair?"

"No, I . . . What is this? What do you want?"

"Arthur," the man said patiently. "I want you to do something for me."

"W-What?"

"I want you to absorb the power from that hair."

"I . ." The blind man stammered, and suddenly, the fear on his face was palpable, stuttering and sick. "I-I can't. I can't feel anything. It's not . . . Please, I can't do it; there's not—"

"Arthur," chided the man, and there was disappointment now in his patient teacher's tone. "I need you to make a real effort. If you can't do this, I'll have to kill you. I don't want to kill you, Arthur. But I need you to absorb that hair's power."

"Oh God. Oh God, please, I can't. That's not how my powers work. They have to be a person; they have to be living—"

"They are living, Arthur. That's a real person's hair. Absorb it, Arthur. Absorb it, or I'm going to kill you."

"Oh God. Oh God, please." The blind man scrunched up his face, his entire body shaking, his teeth chattering uncontrollably, as all that was left of him clenched around this single, solitary hair. Desperate. Clutching.

"Please-please-please-please-please—"

"Five, Arthur. Four."

"Please. PLEASE! No, I'm trying; I swear I'm trying. I'm trying. There's nothing there—!"

"Three."

"NO! No, I promise—I swear to you—there's nothing there. THERE'S NOTHING THERE!"

"Two."

"No-no-no-no-no-no-no, oh God, please, please, hnnnnngh, hnnnnngh, hnnnnngh—"

"One."

"I'M SORRY!"

Silence.

The endless dark. The sound of a chair being pushed back, scraping. The sound of shuffling. Then the old man's distant voice.

"Satisfactory?"

"Yes."

"Any further need for him?"

"No."

"As you wish." There was further shuffling, and suddenly, Arthur heard the thin man speak once more, close by.

"I'm very proud of you, Arthur. You've done very well. Now, put the hair back into the box. Yes, gently; that's right. There you are. Hand me the box. Yes. Excellent. Now, stay there. A healer will come soon."

"Please," the blind man whimpered.

"Shh. Shh. You've done well. It will all be over. Soon, this will all be a bad dream."

With the case tucked safely in his pocket, the thin, gray-haired man shuffled back toward the table. He retrieved his phone, reoriented the camera toward himself, and started off toward the front door of the warehouse.

"The healer will arrive in an hour. As will a telepath."

"I'll be long gone."

"Good."

A pause.

"He made a genuine effort."

"I know."

"Do you need another?"

"No. I've seen enough."

The speaker ended the call, leaving the old man in silence—save for the whimpers of the broken empath, huddling in blood and sweat behind him, and the sound of the small television, blaring oblivious into the dark.

"Look, we're almost out of time. Matt and Jane, I want to say thank you so much for coming on *The Tonight Show*, and thank you so much for everything you've done. It's really—It has been an absolute pleasure, an absolute privilege. Thank you."

"Thank you, Jay.

"Thank you."

Claps and cheers.

"Is there anything you want to say?" the host asked. "Anybody watching at home, anyone you want to say hi to?" He looked between Jane and Matt, the latter of whom shrugged.

"Shout-out to my family, I guess," said Matt. "Thanks for supporting me, and I'm sorry—I'm sorry I had to lie. Um . . ." He paused, thinking. "Shout-out to Jonas and Sarah. Shout-out to everyone back at Morningstar; Giselle, Wally, Will. You're all as much heroes as I am; much more, probably. And I guess . . . shout-out to everyone, generally. Everyone who lost someone throughout all this horrible crap. I'm thinking of you. We're all thinking of you. And . . . here's hoping this is the end of it. Here's hoping it gets better from—from here on out."

The studio erupted in thunderous applause and Matt nodded, chewing his cheek and glancing for approval back at the host. Out of the corner of his eye, he shot a brief glance at Jane, who for a second—and for the first time since they'd come on the show—looked genuinely uncomfortable.

"I . . . ah . . . I'd like to . . . Yeah. What Matt said," said Jane. Then she hesitated, shuffling slightly in her seat. "And, um, to my dad, too. Hi. Dad. Hope . . . Hope you enjoyed the show."

"I'm sure he loved it," Leno replied. He fixed them both with a truly magnanimous smile. "Matt Callaghan. Jane Walker. From all of us here in the studio at NBC and at home, let me just say thank you, once more."

He turned to the crowd. "Ladies and gentlemen, live across America and around the world, exclusive to *The Tonight Show*, I give you: Matt the Human and Lady Dawn!"

Matt and Jane rose, waving, and the world followed in standing ovation.

*   *   *

"Well, that went pretty well."

The pair of them, Matt Callaghan and Jane Walker, stood backstage as *Today Show* aides rushed around packing up their stuff. Everything they'd brought with them was going in Matt's backpack—Jane liked to keep her hands free in case of attack.

"Hmph," Jane grunted. She continued to glare at the NBC employees rushing around. One of them, a long black-haired Latina girl who couldn't have been much older than she was, hurried over.

"Ms. Walker, what did your coat—?"

"I didn't have a coat," Jane growled, narrowing her eyes. The aide flinched and hurried off in the opposite direction.

"Be nice," Matt chided.

"Hngh," Jane grunted again.

"*Hngh*? What's 'Hngh'? Use your words."

Jane ignored him. "We need to get out of here."

"We *are* getting out of here," Matt replied. "Just cool it a sec. I told Dad I'd get Leno's autograph. And Taylor wanted Kevin Eubanks's? Come on." He sidled over and put his hand reassuringly around her hip. "We're not in a rush."

"The longer we stay—"

"Yeah, yeah. Threats of imminent murder. I know. Just relax."

"I don't know how you can say that," Jane grumbled. She looked around the long hallway full of scattered props. "You're the one they keep trying to shoot."

"Yes, well, I have complete confidence in my bodyguard."

"Don't joke. This is serious."

"I know, Jane. I'm taking it seriously." He glanced up and down the hall. "Ooh, I think that's Andre with my sandwiches."

The portly, black-suited page with thinning hair and a bowl cut waddled over and handed Matt a brown paper bag.

"Here you go, Mr. Callaghan. Straight from the craft table."

"A gentleman and a scholar, Andre, thank you." Matt opened his backpack and began shifting space for the bag of sandwiches, wedging them delicately between his Converses and civilian clothes. Behind him, Jane rolled her eyes hard enough to pull a muscle.

"I wasn't sure which ones you wanted," Andre stammered, "so I got you two of each; if that's not enough—"

"Andre, my man, that is plenty. Thank you. I'd give you a tip, but—"

"No, please," said the page, giddy. "Don't mention it; it's nothing. It's just my job."

"And you do it splendidly. Autographs?"

"Got them." He handed Matt some signed photos. "Mr. Leno and Mr. Eubanks say they're sorry you can't stay."

"As am I. But well done. We good to go?" He shot a look over at the nearby burly NBC security guard, who nodded and pushed open the door to the fire stairs.

"Birds are on the move," he called into his earpiece; then, "Good luck, Mr. Callaghan. Lady Dawn."

"Thanks," Matt thanked him, but Jane was already moving, pulling Matt out the fire escape and down into the concrete stairwell. The door slammed shut behind them as they began to circle down.

"Okay, so security plan says we're getting off at—"

"B1. But we're actually taking the back exit from—"

"B4. Got it." They marched onward in silence, Jane leading the way, checking impatiently around every rail and bend.

A few moments of concentrated walking passed as they descended floor by floor.

"Sandwiches. Seriously."

"Hey, I've been starving myself all week to look skinny. Or, well"—he rehefted the backpack—"you know. Less fat."

"You're not fat."

"That's very kind of you."

They continued walking.

"Do you think they bought it?" Jane asked eventually, her eyes still fixed resolutely forward. Behind her, Matt shrugged.

"Why wouldn't they? It makes sense. It's reasonable."

"What, that the Black Death was carrying around a locket with . . ." Her voice trailed off as they passed the door to level twenty-three.

"Better than the alternative," Matt said darkly. "Better than . . . you know . . . Pokémon."

Pokémon was the pair's code word for *time travel*. They'd started using the phrase between them in case anybody accidentally overheard what they were saying in public.

"Goddamn Pokémon."

"Speaking of," said Matt, "any more signs of . . . you know . . . ?"

"The Pokémon trainer?"

"Yeah, him."

"Apart from one time when I was thinking about playing Pokémon and he showed up to tell me not to because I'd get very, very sick?"

"Yeah, apart from that."

"No." Jane's mouth twitched in a line. Matt frowned.

"I wonder if he's done now. Like this is mission complete."

"Maybe." Jane allowed herself a moment to hope. "I mean, the Black Death's done. What could possibly be worse?"

"See, now you've done it," Matt complained. They continued to trudge down the stairs. "Now everything's definitely going to hell."

They lapsed into silence, continuing down the concrete spiral.

"What you said back there, about other girls," Jane said, "Did you mean that?"

"Jane," Matt replied, sounding exasperated. "It was a joke."

"Yeah, I know. I just . . . Do girls really send you letters?"

"What?" he complained. "Is that so hard to believe?" Ahead of him, Jane narrowed her eyes.

"No."

Matt struggled not to roll his eyes. "I bet you have more groupies than I do."

"That's . . . That's not fair."

"What isn't?"

"I . . ." Jane shook her head. "Never mind."

"Jane," Matt drawled, lacing the girl's name with equal parts affection and scorn, "I am not going to leave you for a groupie. I love you. Stop being dumb."

Jane grumbled something under her breath but nevertheless looked mildly placated. Matt leaned forward and squeezed her hand. They continued to descend.

Finally, they reached the bottom of the stairwell.

"B4," Matt confirmed, nodding at the number beside the doorway. "See? Easy-peasy. You've got to go to B4 *before* you leave the building."

"Genius. Come on." Jane shouldered open the door and moved through, Matt following closely behind. He didn't know a hundred percent where they were going—Jane had been the one who had gone over the maps, and it seemed safer to leave these sorts of things to someone who knew tactically what they were doing. Academy training and all that.

"Is that a Maserati . . . ?" Matt wondered as she pulled him past a very low, very fast-looking car.

"No distractions. Come on." She rounded a cement pillar and locked eyes on the south-side door. "There's our exit."

"Well done."

"Shut up." She turned to him. "Remember: no hesitation. Hang on once we see sky."

"I know how to get carried," Matt grumbled. Then he added, "If we were just going to fly out of here, why didn't we take the roof?"

"Too predictable. Gotta keep the bad guys guessing."

"Ah. Knew there was a reason." He leaned up and kissed her on the cheek. "And they say you can't have looks and brains."

"They say you don't have either." She smirked.

"Hey, that's mean. I have fangirls, you know."

"Yeah, yeah. Come on." She pushed open the fire escape door, and the pair stepped outside.

Into a sudden wave of noise and light.

"MATT!"

"MATT!"

"JANE!"

"LADY DAWN!"

The two recoiled. Somehow, the alleyway they'd come out into wasn't empty but heaving—milling with a throng of fans and photographers, paparazzi, people holding up placards.

Jane took a step back, trying to keep her face from breaking into despair and shock.

"How?" she hissed. "What—?!"

"Stay calm."

"MATT!"

"LADY DAWN!"

"GIVE US A KISS!"

"GIVE ME YOUR AUTOGRAPH!"

The door had opened up into a laneway and two small concrete stairs. The pair now stood at the top of those stairs, facing the heaving, flashing crowd standing between them and a clean escape. Matt leaned in close.

"Ah, well," he muttered. "Nothing for it. Through the adoring throng."

"Matt—"

"Come on. Happy face."

He straightened up, smiling toward the crowd with a wave, which caused another surge of shrieking and a blinding flash of camera bulbs. Jane forced herself not to grimace. They were not enemies, she tried to tell herself. These people were on their side.

She tried to move her lips into something resembling a smile and raised her hand up into what felt like a stunted, mechanical wave. The crowd shrieked regardless.

She descended the two small steps as members of NBC's security team came pushing through from the alleyway exits, shouting at the crowd in a vain attempt to maintain order, trying to clear a path. Jane gripped Matt's hand just tight enough not to break it, and then began moving shoulder first through the scrum.

"JANE! JANE!"

"LADY DAWN!"

"MATT!"

"WE LOVE YOU!"

"SHOW US THE LIGHT!"

I'll show you the light in a second, Jane glowered. She resisted the urge to blast out and flatten the entire freaking lot of them. Ahead of her, the security guards were making almost no progress against the legion of fans who were pressing in trying to get a closer look. Necks craned; people flew. A few of them had spider-climbed up the walls, and another teetered over the crowd on elasticized legs.

"Excuse me." Matt smiled, following behind her. "Excuse me. Sorry. Coming through."

Jane glanced back to see that with the free hand she wasn't holding, Matt had scooped up a felt-tipped marker and was messily signing a scrap of paper. She gritted her teeth so hard they hurt.

"Excuse me," she repeated, shouldering her way forward. "Excuse me. Yes. Thank you. Move."

Shouts and screams. The discordant flash of lights. A sea of faces. Movement and sound.

The world sucked in around them, and Jane felt her chest growing tight, her breathing nervous. She forced herself to breathe, took a moment to close her eyes, then continued pushing slowly through the crowd. Her heart was beginning to pound.

"Come on," she told Matt, though she didn't know if he could hear her, didn't know if she could hear herself. There was so much noise, people pressing in all around them . . . She turned, glancing across the crowd, looking for flashes of powers.

She turned back to see Matt following, her hand still in his, his body almost submerged by the excited throng. He smiled.

"It's okay," he assured her. Despite his size and how close they loomed, he seemed unflustered by the people, by their yelling and calling and pawing, grasping hands. He paused and stopped squeezing after her, turning around to answer someone in the crowd. "It's okay."

And at that moment, behind him, an invisible space flickered, and there appeared a man holding a gun. And before Jane could do anything—before anybody could flinch or scream or run—the man drew the weapon, pointed it at Matt's head, and fired.

"*NO!*"

INTERLUDE

I awaken at 6:48 a.m., for that is my custom.

I rest no more than twelve minutes—one unit; a fifth of an hour—so that I am about my day by the seventh chime. Over-rest is as debilitating as under-rest and renders soft one's body and mind. I cannot afford to be soft.

Vigilance is the soil of greatness.

When I awake, I check the cameras to ensure my house is empty. Bedroom, bathroom, hallway, staircase, entrance hall, living room, kitchen, dining room, study, garage. Only when I am certain I am alone do I rise.

Vigilance is the price of responsibility.

I make my bed as soon as I leave it, for cleanliness is next to godliness, and an ordered house brings an ordered mind. I run on the treadmill for thirty minutes to maintain fitness and cardiovascular health. I set the speakers to play Franz Schubert's Four Impromptus, D 935, for classical music stimulates mental acuity.

I cease. I wash myself. I see to my appearance. How a man presents himself is how he is known to the world. I brush my teeth for the count of one hundred and twenty, rinse and swirl mouthwash, apply cleanser, hydrating serum, then moisturiser with an active SPF component.

Vigilance is the safeguard of prosperity.

I dress. My shirts are ready, pressed and starched by my own hand, for I must be self-reliant. I select a pastel blue, for yesterday I selected a pastel purple, and the progressing gradient serves to effectively mark the days. I put on a white undershirt, I put on trousers, I put on socks.

I put on a pair of medical-grade, powder-free, disposable, nonsterile, food-safe black latex gloves, size medium. I put on a pair of tan leather overgloves from my collection, a decision I permit myself to make at random to allow for spontaneity.

I put on the selected shirt. I check that my gloves are sealed beneath the sleeves and that the sleeves are correctly buttoned, once, twice, three times.

Vigilance is the foundation of safety.

I recheck the cameras. I descend. In the kitchen, I prepare a breakfast of bircher muesli with Greek yogurt and seasonal fruits. In the dining room, I consume my meal, along with five hundred millilitres of chilled, filtered tap water, which I mentally convert to sixteen fluid ounces to assist my American cultural acclimation. I sit in silence and stare along a twelve-seat dining table which has only ever sat one person.

It is 8:12 a.m. I have not yet killed anyone I did not mean to. It is the only measure of success.

MATT CALLAGHAN, DECEASED

CASES ADJUDGED

IN THE

SUPREME COURT OF THE UNITED STATES

AT

OCTOBER TERM, 2000

UNITED STATES *v.* CALLAGHAN

CERTIORARI TO THE UNITED STATES COURT OF APPEALS FOR
THE FEDERAL CIRCUIT

Argued August 3, 2001 – Decided August 6, 2001

(Selected Extracts)

REHNQUIST C. J., delivered the opinion of the Court, in which STEVENS, O'CONNOR, SCALIA, KENNEDY, SOUTHER, THOMAS, GINSBURG, and BREYER, JJ., joined.

. . . rarely has a case come before this Court representing so blatant a contempt for Constitutional rights. The shameless manner in which the Department of Justice has acted in this matter should not simply be a cause for condemnation but alarm, being utterly unfounded in either statute or the common law. It is rare that the Justices of this Court find themselves so united in their determination, but the Court draws no pleasure in this unity, given its catalyst in such flagrant governmental overreach . . .

. . . the United States' arguments are universally without merit. The ramshackle way in which the Appellant's myriad grounds have arisen, fallen away, and been replaced throughout these proceedings speaks to a troubling indifference on behalf of those prosecuting this matter to their fundamental duties, to the judicious exercise of litigator discretion, and to the principles of unbiased governance. It is clear to the members of this Court that the United States has pursued with unfettered obsession the attainment of a specific outcome, namely the acquisition of Mr. Callaghan's genetic material, irrespective of how or whether this outcome is supported by facts or law. This Court condemns, in the strongest possible terms, such nakedly unprincipled executive action, which is anathema to the principles of justice and the rule of law upon which this country is based. Were it not for the high public profile of Mr. Callaghan and the clear public interest in denouncing the Appellant's conduct, this application for certiorari would have been dismissed without hearing . . .

. . . The Appellant claims, in the first instance, that Mr. Callaghan has an obligation, by the mere fact of any accusation of criminal wrongdoing or, implicitly, his mere presence on United States soil, to surrender personal genetic material as a matter of course and identification. This is patently incorrect and a clear violation of the Fourth Amendment's right of the people to be secure in their persons . . .

. . . Pivoting from that contention, the Appellant next submitted in the alternative a litany of alleged criminal conduct by Mr. Callaghan that they claimed supported the issue of a warrant. Chief among these, initially, were allegations of obstruction of justice, despite clear and well settled case law that such ancillary charges are not valid if the underlying charges against the accused are not properly obtained. There then followed the dual—and a reasonable observer would think contradictory—accusations that Mr. Callaghan had breached regulations relating to the registration of powers by being unregistered or, in the alternative, that he had committed fraud by allowing the Department of Powers Registration to improperly register him as clairvoyant.

The former of these accusations is plainly nonsensical, as Mr. Callaghan was at all applicable times registered with the Department of Powers Regulation for the purposes of the relevant Acts. The latter of these accusations similarly cannot support any finding of wrongdoing, first, because Mr. Callaghan's obligations to the Department did not extend to correcting unforced errors in the Department's systems, and second, because Mr. Callaghan was a child at the time of the alleged offence.

Mr. Callaghan did not supply false information to the Department, and had the Department become aware that their conclusion regarding Mr. Callaghan being clairvoyant was wrong at a time adjacent to Mr. Callaghan's assessment, Mr. Callaghan would not have faced criminal charges. It is absurd to suggest that an act that would not have founded a warrant for arrest at the time it occurred should somehow found a warrant for arrest now. This is to say nothing of the presumption of doli incapax, which the Appellant in their leveling of accusations against Mr. Callaghan seems to have preemptively concluded did not require addressing.

The presumption is not rebutted. Matthew Callaghan was thirteen years of age at the time these alleged offences occurred, squarely within the range to which the presumption against criminal capacity applies. The Department of Powers Regulation, for its part, seems to be attempting to escape being tarred as incompetent by seeking to foster criminal responsibility onto a thirteen-year-old child. Such efforts are ineffective and, quite frankly, supremely unbecoming . . .

. . . . The Appellant also sought to rely on section 11 of the Empathic Individuals Regulation Act 1990. Section 11 states:

Empathic Testing to be Mandatory

> (1) Any law enforcement or otherwise designated official must, upon notice, issue an empathy testing order against:
>   a. Any adult whose powers are unregistered;
>   b. Any registered adult suspected to possess empathic abilities;
>   c. Any minor demonstrating empathic abilities;
>   d. Any minor who has obtained the age of 14 without demonstrating a registrable ability; or
>   e. Any person otherwise suspected to possess empathic abilities;
>   f. unless an empathy testing order has already been properly issued against and completed by that person.
> (2) Any person issued with an empathy testing order must report within 3 days to a registered testing facility and complete the federally designated empathic ability test.
> (3) Failure to comply with an empathic testing order within the given period creates a presumption of empathic abilities within the person against whom the order is issued, and is to be treated as a violation of Section 16 of this Act…

While the legitimacy of this legislation and its Constitutional viability remain untested, in circumstances where Mr. Callaghan was never issued an empathy testing order, such statutory consideration is unnecessary. The legislation clearly places upon

law enforcement or otherwise designated officials the
ability and impetus to issue empathy testing orders to
individuals falling within certain categories. Whether
Mr. Callaghan did, at any point, fall into any one of
those categories is irrelevant, as he carried no positive obligation at any point to seek out an empathic
test. As above, any failure by United States officials
to recognize Mr. Callaghan's condition does not impugn
nor criminalize Mr. Callaghan's actions . . .

. . . however, even if Mr. Callaghan was guilty of
an arrestable offense, there is no requirement either
at law or in the practice of law enforcement that an
arrested individual surrender to arresting agencies
their personal genetic material. The thrust of the
Appellant's submissions on this front, that the collection of Mr. Callaghan's blood would be no different
to the routine taking of his fingerprints and therefore should be permitted or even ordered, is risible.
Even were this Court convinced that the two are equat-
able, which we are not, the very existence of this suit
and the clear fervor with which the State has pursued
it would raise per se concerns that said procedure was
being undertaken for an improper purpose . . .

. . . We reject the State's de facto claim to Mr.
Callaghan's genetic material. We reject the Appellant's
contention that search and seizure requires no need to
show probable cause or criminal conduct. We reject the
allegation that Mr. Callaghan has engaged in criminal
conduct or that any probable cause exists upon which
a warrant for his arrest could be based. We reject
any assertion that he has engaged in obstruction of
justice in the absence of founding charges. We reject
the implicit contention that he is not entitled to the
presumption of doli incapax. We reject that he has
breached the Empathic Individuals Regulation Act and
decline to confirm that Act's constitutional validity.
We reject the assertion that the existence of criminal

charges carries with it a de facto requirement to submit to blood-drawing procedures, that such procedures are a standard part of law enforcement process, or that such procedures are not in this case being pursued unreasonably and for improper purpose . . .

. . . We award the Defendant indemnity costs.

"NO!"

Time froze. The world around Jane fell silent, swallowed by the sound of her final gasping breath. The scene crystallized, the colors shining—a painting of perfect detail, suspended forever in gloss.

The brightly lit alley, moths floating, wings shining midbeat beneath yellowed lights. The chipped brick walls, breathing softly with dust and moisture, wisping hints of steam rising from the bitumen, the distant cars, and lancing headlights. The press of people, their rippled clothes, their frozen faces caught midturn and midfall from elation to horror. Recoil, spreading like a wave from the gunshot, the slow flash of cameras, the slow drop of signs. Eyes widening in terror. Mouths opening in screams. The hands reaching out, too late, to pull Matt back.

Her own face, too, was screaming, her own body as much a part of this scene as anyone's. She saw herself in the center of it, the gold-clad widow in some medieval painting, her own hand reaching back for him, her own lips locked in a hoarse and mangled shout. Always too far away; always too late.

The shooter—his body flickering as his invisibility wavered, disrupted by the gun's sudden kick—seemed to appear from nothing; a man surfacing beneath a quicksilver veil. In that moment, in that space, every line of his face glistened in perfect detail. Pale and middle aged, with sagging bulldog cheeks and a thin, receding hairline, a bulbous nose and dumpling chin. He looked almost surprised at the life he had taken, shocked by his own accomplishment, to see his hand holding the black-barreled pistol, to see that he actually killed.

Like water sliding through ice, Jane's awareness turned glacially toward the bullet, to the spinning, slow-rolling metal burrowing free from Matt's temple, to the tip of a relentless trail of brain and viscera that—now free—moved outward, ever forward. Pieces of him, suspended in midair—debris from the flesh-stained tunnel. Droplets of blood; pieces of bone. A fine mist of gore caught for a moment before it would spray across the crowd and carry with it Matt's life and soul.

And Jane, stuck there—always—alone across a six-foot void that may as well have been eternity, always crying out, always reaching back. Always too late.

A frozen, perfect picture seared into her mind from which she could never escape.

No.

No.

NO!

Jane screamed.

A piercing shriek, raw instinct, a single urge: *undo*. Without thinking, without knowing, like bones tearing free from flesh, Jane clenched her fists and ripped herself apart from time, rearing up beneath the surface of eternity. The Earth fell away—time fell away—and in an instant, she was a blur-edged shadow, raked in every direction by a howling, freezing wind.

Infinity pulled at her—the endless plummeting darkness, the seething kaleidoscope of everything that ever was and is and could be. Yet, in that moment—in that breath—her mind held no room for pain. She did not think, and the delirium of the timeless world that would have torn apart a conscious mind was not comprehended by an instinctual one.

She had not meant to go; she just *went*, and in that briefest space of being, she had but one perfect, unyielding want.

Undo.

Jane screamed into oblivion and threw herself mere seconds, hurtling up and over and plunging back beneath the river in a single, rushing arc.

Suddenly, reality hurtled back into focus. The alleyway shone and heaved, buzzing with movement and noise. She was her. She was back. She was there between the buildings, between the people, the screaming and the cameras and the waving signs. Matt was behind her, looking across at her, glancing back. He was smiling.

"It's okay," he said.

And then, an invisible space behind him moved, and a man holding a gun appeared and pointed it at Matt's head. Jane's eyes widened, and her lips twisted in a snarl.

BANG.

The gun fired, and the shot flew harmlessly off into the air, slamming into the brickwork above the crowd with an abrupt, impotent crack. Suddenly, the unseen assassin was visible, his eyes bulging, staring up at Jane, who was now mere inches away, her hand wrapped around his wrist in a vise-grip, aiming the pistol up at the wall.

Behind them, Matt spun at the sound of the shot, his face rapidly draining of color. Jane did not look back at him; instead, her teeth bared and her eyes blazed, boring down into the shooter as she held him quailing before her. Her right hand clenched the front of his shirt, her left holding the hand with the gun as she stared at him with such unrestrained malice that the killer wilted beneath its strength.

Then Jane snarled and her eyes burned gold, and with a crack, she broke his wrist.

The man shrieked. The crowd screamed, recoiling at the sound of gunfire, and suddenly, the stillness broke into pandemonium, people scrambling backward as others pressed forward, a sudden sea of confusion swirling around three rocks.

The gun fell from the man's grasp, clattering harmlessly to the ground, and the pale, dough-faced man went limp beneath Jane's unblinking, murderous gaze.

Her teeth bared; his lips trembled.

Then Jane snapped her head forward and headbutted the assassin straight on. The man collapsed without a second thought.

All around her, the crowd fell abruptly silent. A sort of stunned hush descended as the assembled masses stared at the two of them: Jane, standing tall and burning in her sparkling dress, and the slumped, broken-nosed assassin hanging limply from one hand.

"Holy crap," said someone.

Then all at once, the alley erupted in cheers.

"Stuart Louch."

The police officer stood with one hand on her belt, the other clutching a palm-size notepad. Around her, the alleyway still buzzed with people, though much more serious and official now, the police having pushed back and cordoned off the general public.

At either entrance to the area, a crowd of onlookers still thronged, peering up and around the police tape and the interviewing officer's burlier, more scowly comrades. Some onlookers flew above the crowd, flashes snapping from their phones and cameras; a few hung from the walls, and one had giraffed up an elasticized neck for a better look. Matt tried his best to ignore them.

It had taken the police mere minutes to arrive on the scene, in force, and with no hesitation about clearing away the rowdy, excitable crowd, most of whom were clearly ecstatic to have been witness to some comic-book-style excitement firsthand.

It would have been an impressive response time, really, had it not underlined the likely reality of Matt and Jane being under some kind of surveillance, or at the very least, the police having taken the opportunity of knowing their whereabouts to stay very, very close.

That, and the fact that the NYPD had actually been second to arrive, after the Legion of Heroes. Or, well, Will and Wally, to be accurate, who had teleported in and raced over mere seconds after the attempt on Matt's life. A perk, Matt supposed dryly, of the whole thing having been broadcast live across international television.

The moment they'd arrived, the telepath and teleporter had begun shouting commands and flashing their Legion eagles to clear some space among the crowd surrounding them, and within a few minutes, had managed to secure Matt a little cordoned-off area next to a dumpster, which they continued to guard with imperious stares.

It was beside this dumpster that Matt still sat, perched glumly atop a milk crate, with the two Legionnaires flanking either side of him, their arms crossed and their expressions glowering at the policewoman like the two feudal bodyguards of some back-alley trash lord.

"That's all you got from him?" Wally demanded, interjecting unprompted in Matt's defense while the subject of said defense sat tired and resigned beside his feet. "Just a name?"

Wally Cykes, telepath, was the Legion of Heroes' second-best psychic, a redhead, and one of the least intimidating people Matt had ever known. The idea of him verbally berating a police officer was about as incongruous to Matt as Matt competing in the Olympics.

The ridiculousness was only mitigated marginally by the fact that Wally had tonight elected to wear a black knitted sweater and blue boot-cut jeans rather than one of his trademark Hawaiian shirts. Nevertheless, he was giving the policewoman no quarter.

"A name and an address," the officer said, struggling not to roll her eyes and directing her answer back to Matt. "He didn't tell us. He had his wallet in his pocket."

"Just his wallet?" Will asked. "Nothing else?"

Will Herd, teleporter, was Black, well-groomed, and could have stepped out of a group photo on page four of any Gap catalogue. He wore an open navy felt trench coat and a gray shirt, and like Wally, he was leaning slightly over Matt while staring narrow eyed at the police officer with his arms protectively crossed.

"I'm not at liberty to discuss ongoing investigations," the officer replied. "And I'm not here to trade evidence. I'm just trying to get a statement." She paused and looked at Matt. "From the victim of this attack."

"I'm fine," Matt said.

The policewoman frowned. Matt resisted the urge to roll his eyes at her subpar faux concern.

"Still," she told him, trying to sound like his well-being genuinely mattered to her, "we should have the EMTs look you over."

Matt leveled her a flat stare. "Poor attempt," he said. "Poor execution."

The officer appeared unfazed. "I'm not trying to trick you, Mr. Callaghan. We want to make sure you're alright."

"I'm not shot. Thank you. I don't need any swabs."

"It's standard procedure."

"Well, I'm a very abnormal boy."

To his left, Will let out a snort, which he quickly suppressed. The policewoman's eyes flicked up to him, then fell back down to Matt with a deadpan gaze.

"I appreciate your special status. It's why we're being so accommodating."

Accommodating was one interpretation, Matt thought darkly. Behind the interviewing officer, there was a large gap of empty space between the four of them and where the NYPD were holding back the onlookers behind the police tape. In the center of that space was the furious, rigid figure of Jane Walker, still wearing her gold-and-silver ball gown but now standing with her fists clenched and her eyes blazing golden, breathing heavily and furiously glaring at absolutely everything nearby, as if the brickwork might suddenly rear to life and attack.

Jane paced slowly, step by step, across the empty space in the alleyway with the hunched shoulders of an agitated wolf, energy lashing off her in whipcords, never moving more than about ten feet away from Matt's person. Her mild high heels, which she'd worn at Giselle Pixus's insistence, had been thrown without a second thought against some trash can, leaving Jane standing barefoot on the bitumen.

The reduction in height did nothing to make her less intimidating, and it was clear—to Matt, at least—that the police were *accommodating* Jane's presence in the same way a troop of Boy Scouts might accommodate an enraged grizzly bear.

The policewoman interviewing Matt—O'Neill, by the name on the badge above her breast pocket—briefly followed Matt's gaze over her shoulder to the stalking, glaring empath, then turned back to meet his eyes.

"Come on. We're on the same team here."

She was not an unattractive woman, Matt concluded—a pleasant face, fit, midthirties, dark hair tied up in a bun—and she used a slight sympathetic smile when she looked at him that made Matt suspect she'd been deliberately chosen to interview him over her uglier, manlier colleagues in the hope of playing on his predilections as an impressionable teenage boy.

The problem with that plan, of course, was first that you never play a player, and second that Matt could literally see his blisteringly twitchy, murderously tense girlfriend about ten feet away, seething with energy that warped the air itself and still perfectly capable of tearing his testicles off.

"My lawyer told me not to talk to cops."

"Have you spoken to your lawyer?"

"Yes."

"What did they say?"

"Not to talk to the cops."

"Right."

The policewoman paused, one side of her lip twitching in disapproval as she stared down at him, obviously trying to calculate her next approach. After a few moments, Matt relented and sighed.

"We're going to speak in the morning. We'll get something drafted. You'll have my statement by tomorrow."

"You sure that's what you want?" the officer asked, raising a slight, chiding eyebrow. It reminded Matt of the way his mother used to speak to him when he was six and started writing an incorrect answer on his math homework. "Your memory is a lot fresher right afterward. You might miss some crucial detail."

"I'll risk it, thanks," Matt replied flatly, seeping enough acid into his voice to make it clear their conversation was over.

O'Neill held up her hands in a shrug and retreated a few steps back to join her colleagues, giving a wide berth to the gold-smoking Jane and her aura of wisping light. Jane was spreading the energy out above them—Matt could tell by watching the air's eddies and currents—shaping it into a pulsing dome so as to repulse any bullets that might be shot from on high. It was a new skill. Impressive, really. She'd been practicing.

Wally watched the policewoman go with an uncharacteristic scowl.

"I could get more out of him," the psychic grumbled.

"No, you couldn't," Will replied, almost instant reproach in his voice.

"Fourth Amendment," agreed Matt.

"No one would know," Wally replied darkly, though his words didn't carry much conviction.

Matt sighed.

"Can we go now, please?" he asked. He craned his neck over at Jane. "Jane? I'm tired. I'd like to get out of this suit."

At the sound of her name, the bronze-haired empath's head snapped back toward them. After a moment or two more of glaring at suspicious bricks, Jane scowled and stomped over, golden light still rippling off her skin, though thankfully, she was considerate enough to lower the output somewhat as she approached, and by the time she'd reached the other three, the golden fire in her eyes had dimmed to the point where Matt could at least see her irises.

"Where is he?" she demanded. Jane turned her head and glared over at the police van, inside which the assassin lay handcuffed. "I want to talk to him."

The way her fingernails were digging into her palms made it very clear what *talk* meant.

"No one's dismembering anyone," Matt reprimanded her. "It's fine. I'm fine. The police have him. Let them handle this like they normally do."

"He shot you." Jane scowled.

"He shot *at* me," Matt corrected her. "You stopped him. No harm, no foul."

For some reason, this statement did not make Jane any happier. Matt fixed her with a small, sad smile.

"Look," he said, glancing between Jane, Will, and Wally and seeing their obvious reluctance. "Why are we bothering with this? We all know what he's going to say. He's going to be some sad, unaffiliated little man with very distinct views on chemtrails who spends way too much time on the Internet. Just like the rest of them. Why hang around to find out?"

The three Legion members exchanged glances with one another.

"This area's not particularly secure," Will conceded, inclining his head toward Jane.

"Not my point, but sure," said Matt, overshadowed by all three of them, as he was still sitting on a milk crate. The others didn't acknowledge he'd said anything.

"We're very public. Very visible."

"See, that sounds like you're agreeing with me, but you're actually talking about something completely different."

"I've got it," Jane growled. "Nobody's going to touch him. I want answers."

"Now you're talking about me like I'm not here. Hello."

"I'm keeping a broad sweep of the crowd," Wally informed them, glancing beyond the police lines at the hordes of curious onlookers. "Not picking up any nervousness or hostility."

"Hello. Guys. Home."

"That's only conscious thought," Jane snapped back. "What if they're disciplined? What about Psy-Block?"

"Sweetie, when you're a world-class psychic, you can tell me how to watch for gaps."

"I am a human-badger hybrid. I am dying of prostate cancer. There is a T-Rex about to eat us all."

"Azleena said the Morningstar forensics team won't be ready for another half an hour," said Will.

"Where the hell are they?" demanded Jane.

"Probably in bed." Wally shrugged.

"Bed, that sounds nice," Matt chimed in, continuing to be completely ignored.

Wally put his hands on his hips and turned to Jane, his lips pursed.

"If we leave now, it'll be hard for the Legion to claim jurisdiction over the investigation."

"I thought we trumped local authorities?"

"Yeah, but practically, there'll be issues with chain of custody." Wally looked at her. "Plus, he's not technically a member."

"Oh, bullcrap!"

"Guys, I'm really okay with the police doing it," Matt tried again, lamely. "Just let them handle it. I'm sure they'll let us know."

"I want answers," Jane said bitterly. From his place atop his milk crate, Matt looked up at her, seeing her set jaw and the way she was blinking angrily at everything nearby.

"Jane." He reached out and took her hand, gazing up at her. Jane's face pinched in anger, and she turned away, refusing to meet his eyes. Matt sighed and stood up, placing his other hand gently below Jane's shoulder blades and pressing slowly at the tension in her back.

Jane sniffed, still staring up at the alleyway rooftops, refusing to look at him. Slowly, though, the energy whirling off her began to fade.

"I'm okay," he said. "It's okay. Everything's fine."

"I know," she snapped, though a moment later, she seemed to regret her harshness. Matt didn't let it faze him. He continued to rub gently beneath her shoulders.

"Everything's going to be okay," he told her. "I'm alive."

"Yeah, but—"

"I want to go home. Let's go home."

Finally, Jane's shoulders slumped. The light that had been swirling around her faded.

"Okay," she murmured. "Okay." She glanced at Will, who nodded.

"Should we tell the cops?" he asked.

"Screw the cops." Jane scowled.

"They're just doing their job," said Matt, trying to be fair. Again, nobody seemed to listen. He sighed, and the four joined hands.

"Basement?"

"Basement."

"Hold on."

Will scrunched up his eyes. Around them, there was a surge of noise, of flashes and shouting, as the onlooking crowd suddenly realized what was about to happen. A moment later, the cold light of the alleyway was subsumed beneath pressure and darkness, and Matt felt himself hurtling through a tunnel of crushing, smothering black.

About a half second later, the sensation passed, and Matt opened his eyes to the familiar smell of sulfur and the sight of bare concrete walls.

"Ah," he said, smiling around at the ten-by-ten oppressive bunker. "Hole sweet hole."

They had teleported into a room at the bottom of 32-40 Wilsmore Crescent, a large and modern building that covered half a block and twenty-three floors. Twenty-two of those were standard residential apartments, accessible the normal way apartments were accessible: through the front door and lifts, and a lobby on the ground floor.

But unbeknownst to the other residents of Park River Arms, as it was called, a topmost level existed, not present on any strata registration or publicly available floor plan. This floor existed separately to the rest of the building, connected only to a private elevator shaft that ran straight up and down to an underground concrete bunker with no outward doors.

Three stories below the street and surrounded by solid rock, it was an inconspicuous cube of hollow concrete sitting just outside the building's anti-phasing, anti-teleportation Disruptance fields that no one would have ever suspected was present, let alone led to a secret apartment.

A secret penthouse, actually. The White Queen—Elsa Arrendel, former Norwegian aristocrat and deceased Legion second-in-command—had had the whole place purposely built in the 1980s as a private, paparazzi-proof refuge, cleverly angled to be invisible from the outside. When she'd been killed, ownership had transferred to the Legion, who'd spent the better part of a decade discreetly renting it out to philandering celebrities and the like for exorbitant profit.

Now, it belonged to Matt and Jane.

"We should put up a poster," Wally suggested, looking around at the bare concrete walls. "A bit of color or something. Such a depressing first sight to come home to."

"It's not that bad," chided Matt, waving his hand in front of his face to disperse the sulfur. "Although I do like the poster idea."

"Maybe some tropical scenery."

"That dangling cat picture that says, 'Hang in there.'"

"Will one of you idiots please call the lift," growled Jane. She pinched the bridge of her nose.

"Someone's grumpy."

"I'm just not in the mood."

"Alright, alright," relented Wally. He turned to Will. "Let's leave the lovebirds to their nest."

The teleporter raised his arm, and the telepath took it.

"Thanks for coming, guys," said Matt. He reached past them to the silver elevator doors and pressed the *up* button. "Really appreciate it."

"Just glad you weren't shot," replied Will. Behind him, Jane sniffed.

"Aren't we all?" Matt replied.

"Let us know what the police say," added Wally.

"Let us know what Legion forensics come back with," said Jane. She gave a curt nod to Will and submitted begrudgingly to Wally's one-armed hug.

"I thought you did really well," the redheaded psychic told her. He looked at Matt. "Both of you."

"Thanks, man."

"We'll debrief more later. Get some sleep."

Wally turned back to Will, and with a nod, the pair disappeared in a sulfurous *pop*. The bunker suddenly seemed less crowded and claustrophobic. Matt released a sigh, letting his shoulders droop. Jane continued to stare straight ahead.

The elevator dinged, the doors opened, and they stepped inside.

The cold concrete silence faded away into a light press of gravity and slow, distant whirring as the pair steadily rose.

"Well," Matt joked lamely, glancing across at Jane. The lift had caramel-colored wood panelling and a foot-wide mirror strip running around the middle, in which the sequins on his girlfriend's dress continued to sparkle. "What a night."

Jane gave no response other than to clench her jaw and continue to stare at the doors to the elevator.

"Come on," Matt assured her. "I'm fine."

The rising feeling ceased. Jane shook her head. The elevator pinged.

"We never should have done it," she said.

They stepped out. Matt followed Jane to their front door and watched as she pressed her finger into the scanner pad above the handle. Neither of them had a key.

"What? The interview? Of course we should have."

The lock clicked and the door swung open, allowing Jane to spin round and fix him with an incredulous gaze.

"You were shot!"

"I was *almost* shot," Matt replied, stepping past her with a dismissive wave. He strode into the apartment, shrugging out of his suit jacket and throwing it haphazardly across one of the lounge chairs before flopping down onto the couch. After a moment of glorious melting into the leather, he sat forward and began to untie his shoes.

"That doesn't make it okay!" cried Jane, striding in his wake.

Around them, the apartment stood as they had left it. The ceiling was relatively low, maybe eight or nine feet high initially, although the floor dropped down by an additional two steps a few feet in from the entrance. For a penthouse, it had relatively few windows—for privacy and security reasons—with the northern side stepping out into an indented balcony that provided Jane with a fly-out point and them both with some semblance of a view.

It was a large space, mostly open plan. There was a long wooden dining table (Arrendel's) near the balcony doors; brown leather couches, matching armchairs, and a thick glass table marking a living area in the center (Arrendel's); and a further yellow couch facing a TV and Xbox to the south (Matt's).

Floorboards ran the length of the main room, save for in the kitchen, which was marked by white tiles and a long marble island parallel to the west wall, while a doorway on the south side led off to a spare bedroom, bathroom, laundry, and gym, the last of which was foam padded to muffle any noise when weights were dropped.

Their bed—the master bedroom—was in a room in the northeast corner and had white carpet with mechanically heated underlay. The whole place was soundproofed up the wazoo and still littered with art and decorations from its original owner—although the odd beer bottle or pizza box, phone chargers, crumpled hoodies, photographs of Matt's family, and the textbooks scattered across the dining table marked the last few months of Matt and Jane's habitation, and the slow process of them making it their own.

Reclining into the brown leather couch, Matt undid his top button and pulled off his tie as Jane loomed over him with a pained expression, her arms crossed, making no move to decant herself from her sparkly dress. Matt glanced up at her and then down again, noting her bare toes splayed atop the carpet.

"Did you leave your shoes in the alleyway?" he asked. "Giselle's going to be furious."

"Stop changing the subject."

"You know some weirdo's going to find those and sniff your feet."

"Matt! Be serious!"

"I am being serious!" Matt exclaimed. He threw up his hands. "What do you want me to say? We knew it was a risk. Going outside generally *is* a risk! That's just how it is until all this blows over. Sometimes may be good; sometimes . . . crazy people!"

"They shouldn't have known we were there," Jane spat bitterly. Matt just shrugged.

"Jane, yes, I agree with you. The deception should've worked. But what do you want me to say? Sometimes, the best laid plans go tits up."

"We didn't tell anyone," Jane complained.

"That we were sneaking out the basement?"

"Yes."

"Azleena knew. Maybe she accidentally tripped something when she pulled up the building plans."

"Unlikely."

"But anyway," Matt pushed forward, "it was just bad luck. And it was fine, wasn't it? In the end? I mean, you were there; you protected me . . ." Abruptly, Matt's voice trailed off, because the look that had come over Jane's face was not relieved but pained, twisted, and wracked with guilt. She'd had the same look back in the alleyway.

"You . . . did protect me, didn't you?" he asked. Jane opened her mouth to answer, but for a few seconds, nothing but wordless protests stumbled out. The penny finally dropped. Matt's face drained of blood.

"Jane!"

"What?" she demanded, although her guilty, shifting expression put an end to any attempt at ignorance. "What?!"

"What did you do?!"

"I saved your life!" Jane shouted, voice rising in self-defense.

"You played—You time traveled?"

"Only for a few seconds!" she argued, but Matt was already on his feet, his hands thrown up in the air, his face a mask of horror. He stepped back, turning in place a few feet away, gaping at her.

"We . . . We talked about this! Jane, we"—he swore, clutching his hair—"talked about this. You promised you wouldn't!"

"I'm sorry!"

"You can't mess with this stuff!" he cried. "You can't . . . It's time travel! You screw with time, time screws back!"

"He shot you!" Jane cried, and she lunged toward him with a single vicious step. "He shot you, and I saw it. I saw your blood and your brains and the bullet and—" She choked off into a sudden sob. Her hands, clenched into fists, hung rigid in front of her.

Matt's chest deflated as his face turned, if possible, even paler. "I . . . I died?" he whispered.

"Yes," Jane snapped, her throat choking around the words. "You died, right there in front of me, and I couldn't—I couldn't just watch. I had to . . . I just . . ."

She took another angry step forward before wavering, and a moment later, collapsed down onto the couch. Her eyes closed, and she took a deep, shuddering breath before opening them again and fixing Matt with a burning look.

"I'm not just going to let you die," she spat, the sheer venom and rage belying the underlying sentiment. Matt stared at her, frozen, conflicting emotions warring across his face.

"Jane," he said finally. "It's not that I want to die. And it's not that I'm not grateful; it's just . . ." He waved his hands about, trying to find the words. "Time travel! You know! This is dangerous. You told me it's dangerous, didn't you?!"

Jane didn't answer. When she'd first traveled through time—during the Black Death's onslaught, on the outskirts of Detroit, when she hadn't known what she was doing and when she'd used the power she'd just absorbed without thinking, the Time Child having provided her with precise, pinpoint instructions—it'd been disturbing, but not deadly. Coming back, too, to 2001 from 1988 hadn't really been something she'd had to think about; she'd known instinctively where she was supposed to be and when, like she'd retained an anchor somehow to her original time.

In the six months since that day, however, every time Jane had consciously reached for the time-traveling power, it was like the very universe around her became unstuck; she caught a glimpse, a brief flash of a reality so overwhelming it threatened to shatter her mentally, and then inevitably she immediately pulled back, terrified by the sudden brush with infinity and obliteration.

In retrospect, the first time around, the Child's guidance, her own ignorance, her injuries, and the adrenaline surging through her veins had somehow inoculated Jane from the sheer magnitude of being able to move outside a single, stable timeline. That was no longer the case. Jane understood what she could do now, the enormity of it, and the moment she reached consciously to rearrange things, that awareness threatened to consume her mind.

"Was the Child there?"

"No."

"Jane!"

"Dead! You were dead!"

"And—And I appreciate that, but you—" Again, his voice faltered as he struggled to find the words. "You can't just . . . change things!"

"Why?" Jane snapped, folding her arms and glaring at him. "Why can't I change things? What's the point of having these powers if I can't"—she swore—"change things?"

"That's not what I'm saying," Matt sighed. "You know that's not what I'm talking about."

"It *is* what you're talking about! It's what you're always talking about! You're always on me, always trying to make me feel bad, like, *Urgh you can't do this; you can't do that*—"

"That's not what I'm trying to—"

"It is! You are trying to do it! You're—You're trying to—You want me to—Why should I stand by?! Why should I let bad things happen when I can stop them, when I can make it right?"

"Jane, we're not talking about being a superhero; we're talking about time travel!"

"So?!" Jane cried. "What's the difference? Why the hell can't I? I-I could do it, if I practiced, if you'd let me even try to—"

"Oh, so now it's my fault?"

"I'm not saying that!"

"Jane, it's *time*. You don't. Mess. With time travel!"

"I'm not . . . The Child! The Child messes with time travel!"

"Oh, right, so we're just doing what the Child does now? The mysterious magical death child whom we know nothing about? Yeah, sure, sounds great!"

"Why are you always against me?!"

"Against you?! Jane, I'm trying to protect you! I'm on your side!"

"I'm not the one who needs protecting!"

"I know that!" Matt exclaimed, throwing up his hands. He shook his head in despair. "I know that. You're the strong one; you can do whatever you want; there's nothing I can do to stop you. I know!"

"That's not—"

"But where does it end, Jane? Huh? Okay, you save me, great. Do you save other people? Friends? Strangers? From all bad things or only murder? Huh? Do you stop someone from being robbed? Except, why is the robber robbing people? Are they a drug addict? Broke? Did they have a bad childhood? Do you fix all that too? Do you go back in time and stop them losing their job? Do you stop them drinking? Do you go back and give them better parents?"

"You're being absurd."

It was an old, well-trodden argument. Jane did not seem to see the problem with interfering, with these unearthly powers. Matt? Well, Matt saw problems clear as day. A great big billboard sign, neon white with fresh black lettering that read "Trouble Brewing." One didn't need to be clairvoyant to see where this recklessness could be headed. Didn't need to be a genius to see the danger at hand.

"I'm being *logical*. If you change one thing, then you can change everything, and where does it stop? Does no one die? Is no one hurt? Is no one unhappy?"

"You'd rather let people die than save them?"

"We're not supposed to play God!" Matt started to swear, but caught himself, forcing the exclamation back down. De-escalate. Common ground. Resolutions. He took a deep breath, then held up what he wanted to be placating hands. "Jane, I know you. I know you! You don't like it when things are wrong; you don't want to let things go; you'll want to fix them. If you let yourself loose, then you'll—You'll just want to keep fixing. It'll never be enough!"

"He killed you!" Jane cried. "Some worthless piece of crap nobody! He killed you!"

"Well, maybe I was supposed to—"

"No," Jane cut him off, vehemently shaking her head while staring at him, her face hard as stone. "No. If that's how you're going to be, if you're going to—No, I'm not going to talk about this. I'm not—I won't—" She took a step back, head still shaking. Matt reached out and caught her wrist even as she pulled away, her arms crossed, trying to force her to look at him.

"Jane."

"No."

"Jane."

"No!"

"I am eventually going to die," he told her, holding on even as she continued to shake her head. "Me, our friends, your dad. I mean, I'm not thrilled, but it's part of life; you have to accept that."

"No. No, I don't. Why are you talking like this?"

"Because I don't want—" Matt fell silent for a moment, struggling to find the right words. "I don't want you to do something wrong. I don't want you to lose sight of yourself. You are *so, so* powerful." He squeezed her arm. "Nobody is meant to be able to do what you can do. Nobody is supposed to be that strong!"

"Oh, don't give me this—"

"With great power—"

"If you say one more word of that Spider-Man crap, I swear to God—"

"But it's true!" cried Matt. "We have to be so, so careful! Not just with the time thing but with Captain Dawn, with the superhero—"

"Oh, so now you don't like me being Lady Dawn?"

"Jesus Christ, I'm not—" Matt sighed, pulling himself short. He rubbed his temples, trying to redirect the conversation. "It's just . . . there's so much at stake."

"You think I don't know?!"

"Don't you think maybe there was a reason Captain Dawn didn't use his powers?" he asked. "Don't you think maybe he might've been scared that even with the best intentions, he'd screw up? About crushing people underfoot?"

"Please." Jane scowled, rolling her eyes. "You didn't meet him. He wasn't being a role model—he was a sad, broken man, scared because Mommy wasn't around to tell him what to do anymore." She vehemently shook her head. "I will not be like that. I can't be like that. Matt, why won't you listen?!"

"I *am* listening!"

"You're not! You always do this; you're always against me. It's like you hate me; you always—"

"Jane." Matt's deadpan voice cut her off. "Stop being ridiculous. I don't hate you."

"You do. You want to be dead; you want to be with your fangirls; you—"

"*JANE.* Come on." He continued to hold his gaze, firm and unrelenting. "We're a team. Listen. Listen! We're a team. We are trying to work this out. This is not normal. Any of it. I'm just trying to be safe."

Jane scowled, still not meeting his eyes, instead staring resolutely at the ceiling. Matt pressed on, still holding on to her arm.

"You can change the world," he told her, "really, easily change it. And there's almost nothing anyone could do to stop you. That's crazy. Isn't that crazy? You know how few people can say that? You know how few people there are who can just *make* everyone else do what they want?" He shook his head. "The Dawn stuff. The time stuff. Especially the time stuff. If you start looking at it like the key to every problem, pretty soon the whole world's going to start looking like a lock."

"You talk about me like I'm evil." Jane sniffed. Matt sighed, and his expression softened. He pulled her into a stiff, resistant hug.

"You're not evil," he reassured her. "You'll never be evil. But it's not evil the road to Hell's paved with. I'm just . . . I'm just worried about you. I'm trying to make sure you don't get lost."

Jane dropped her gaze to the floor.

"You think I'm lost?"

"I think you're trying. I know you're trying. I'm just trying to help."

They lapsed into silence, the tall, stiff girl in the gorgeous shining dress, and the rumpled, soft boy with his arms around her.

"I'm not sorry," Jane said eventually. She pulled back and finally met his gaze, though with what was very much still a glower.

"I know you're not."

"Why should it be any different?" she asked bitterly. "Why should this be different to any power?"

"Because it's *time*," Matt replied. He moved to sit on the couch, pulling Jane gently down to sit beside him. "You can't mess with time."

"He *killed* you," Jane pleaded, and her expression melted into longing, her voice infused through not with anger but a desperate need for him to understand. "He *killed* you. I can't . . . I can't just let that happen."

She pulled free from his embrace. The couple lapsed into silence, each sitting facing slightly away from the other on opposite sides of the couch. Matt shook his head and sighed.

"We should've been more careful," he said finally. Jane's face scrunched up.

"I should've been more careful," she echoed. She dropped her head into her hands. "I should've just grabbed you and blasted out the minute there were crowds."

"You didn't know."

"I panicked."

"You hadn't had time to shift," he told her, soothing, shaking his head. "You'd just been in interview mode; you were still thinking like that. Neither of us had taken our 'public relations' hats off."

"I shouldn't have let it happen."

"Jane, you went back in time to save me." Matt reached across the couch and took her hand. He held it, feeling the warmth, waiting until finally she relented and met his eyes. Her face was wracked with pain. "I will never say you don't do enough."

Her hand clenched his tight around his fingers. Matt smiled.

"Someday, I'm going to die."

"Stop saying that."

"Someday, I'm going to die. No, listen. Talking about it doesn't make it any more likely. And if it's gotta happen, it's gotta happen. We can't . . ." He shook his head. "We can't rewrite the universe so I continue living."

Jane's grip loosened, and she pulled away. Slowly, dress still jingling when she moved, she pulled her legs up onto the couch, hugging them close to her chest.

"Jane."

"Leave me alone."

"Jane."

"Go away if you want to die."

"I don't . . ." Matt sighed, exasperated. "I don't *want* to die, I just . . . When you gotta go, you gotta go. My time is my time. Like ideally, my time is, like, eighty years from now, but I just . . . I just don't want you royally screwing the world up trying to save me."

Jane continued staring straight ahead, her eyes narrowed and her arms wrapped around her knees. It was a cool night, but Matt knew she wasn't doing it for warmth. The power of Dawn meant the girl never got cold anymore.

"I'm going to protect you," she muttered, still refusing to look at him. Matt shuffled over beside her and laid his head against her shoulder.

"No," she complained, making a weak attempt to shrug him off.

"It's okay."

"Go away."

"I'm not going anywhere."

"You don't know that."

"I do. You'll see. It'll work out."

He reached an arm around her shoulders and slowly, through her half-hearted resistance, turned Jane's head to face his own.

"Everything's going to be alright."

The girl's hard expression became a mixture of longing and pain. She drew in a deep, shuddering breath then blinked rapidly, forcing her gaze up. Suddenly, without any warning, she leaned in toward Matt and kissed him, full on the lips. The boy gave into the movement, letting her push him back, wrapping his arms around the back of her dress. Slowly, they sunk down into the cool, waiting softness of the leather couch. Matt relinquished the embrace, clapped his hands, and the automatic lights faded, dousing the room in midnight.

And then slowly, from among the soft, gentle sounds that began murmuring up from the embrace of the sofa, there flowered within the darkness a soft, golden light.

INTERLUDE

You step from the car, and you are already drunk.

You pull the money clip from your breast pocket and throw notes at the limo driver, laughing as you insult his family, calling him ugly, a dog. His profuse thanks follow you and your friends as you pile out, though you are indifferent to his words. The money you leave behind is far more than he would've charged you.

One of the girls stumbles on the gutter, almost breaking a stiletto. There are shrieks of laughter as she is pulled to her feet. The bouncer sees everything and ushers you inside irrespective of her intoxication, your money clip a staff parting all seas. You ascend the staircase.

Noise. Darkness. Pulsating light. You take the highest view with the widest spaces, a king surveying the mass of strobe-lit bodies writhing two stories below. The DJ's stage, streaks of color. You fall into a lounge and let the others argue over who gets to sit next to you. The hostess brings you drinks in crystal bottles. You shout, laugh, decry, proclaim, smash a glass against the wall. Everybody loves it. Hao telekinetically spins the pieces together over the table, Xue leans in close with her tongue between her teeth and fingertips of flame, bright blue, sculpting something melting, formless, pure. You watch her work, mesmerized, as Sky drapes one long, smooth leg over yours and whispers enticements in your ear, her satin dress gliding in the violet strobe light.

More drinks. The sculpture is done. You push up, stumble, spill champagne over the railing. There is an argument, pushing. The sculpture is destroyed. The quarrel fades as quick as it came. The hostess returns; the hostess sits. You squeeze a hand around her thigh. More drinks, more laughter, then conspiratorial whispers and grinning nods. You peer deliberately away as Sky takes a shard of glass and slices the flesh beneath her left breast tissue while others stand keeping watch, blocking the line of sight of any bouncers. You turn to see her wiping blood from the plastic packet, the incision still exposed but already healing. She winks at you while everyone's backs are turned, in that brief window while the wound closes. She thinks it stirs something in you, that you like pain, you like watching. You don't. Unbidden, thoughts stir in your head of men restrained in bright rooms with open mouths and empty eyes.

A white powder arranged in lines on the table. You lean in, lean out, feel a frothing sting like baking soda bubble up your nose and burn your nasal passages. A bitter slick on the roof of your mouth. More drinks, more shrieks, more envy. Then you descend from your kingdom through a thudding, light-flecked maelstrom into the heaving mass below.

You are dancing—no, swaying—no, jumping. Your head has lolled back, you cannot move. Words are swallowed by the pulsating sky, each boat detached in this sea of people. Some no one jostles you, and your friends turn on them for you. Your eyes barely see, drifting indifferently toward the stage as your reputation almost descends to punches.

Then you see her. *Her.*

Long blonde hair, a waterfall of platinum; immaculate. Tall, chest heaving in the bass, skin like cream and honey. Her dress is white, same color as your jacket. You lock eyes. She smiles at you. And somehow, you know. Somehow, you just know.

Melody. She says her name is Melody.

THE CALLING

A Practitioner's Guide to Telepathy in the Law
The Law Society of New South Wales, 2nd edition
Selected Extracts

. . .

Scope of Ability

1.4 Telepathic abilities are broken down into six overlapping functions or effects. These are:
1. Telepathic perception of the presence of another person.
2. Telepathic perception of the thoughts of another person.
3. Telepathic communication with the mind of another person.
4. Telepathic influence or control over the actions of another person.
5. Telepathic influence or control over the autonomic nervous system of another person.
6. Telepathic modification of the thoughts, memories, or personality of another person.

. . .

1.6 Although the scope of telepathy contemplated by section 344G is vast, in reality, few telepaths have the capacity to effectively utilize their abilities to such an extent. The majority of telepaths can exercise first-, second-, and third-degree functions without difficulty and fourth-degree functions with some difficulty and to a limited extent. Adult telepaths capable of competently exercising fifth- or sixth-degree influence are rare and will usually not be encountered in a legal setting.

1.7 Expertise in telepathy does not necessarily equate with being competent at exercising higher-degree functions, nor does an inability or ineptitude with higher-degree functions indicate a lack of professionalism or incompetence. The majority of work done by professional telepaths involves first-, second-, and third-degree telepathy, and the depth of experience required to be proficient in these areas, third-degree telepathy in particular, is extensive. As such, many telepaths forego developing their aptitude for fourth-, fifth-, or sixth-degree telepathy in favor of mastering more practical skills.

. . .

Common Myths and Misconceptions about Telepathy

1.18 As a widespread, potentially intrusive and easily comprehendible power, there are a number of misconceptions about telepathy and telepaths both broadly and among specific cultures and communities. These misconceptions are exacerbated by the depiction of telepathy or similar abilities in pre-Aurora media and folklore, which can depict telepaths or creatures with telepathy as capable of a broad range of unrealistic behavior. Practitioners need to be aware of these inaccurate beliefs, both for their own knowledge and education and so that they can recognize and correct them when they are expressed by clients, witnesses, legal officers, or laypeople.

Myth: A telepathic reading damages your mind or steals your soul.
1.18 False. There is no evidence of any harm, effect, or change in personality, either short-term or long-term, resulting from properly conducted telepathic contact.

Myth: There is no way to tell if a telepath has read your mind.
1.18 False. Damage or modifications to a person's mind caused by the improper, deliberate, or malicious use of telepathy is clearly identifiable by magnetic resonance imaging (MRI) of a telepath-recipient's brain. Additionally, the thoughts of a person who has undergone telepathic alteration are typically highly perceptible to other telepaths, even in passing.

Myth: Repeated use of or contact with telepathy causes brain damage.
1.18 False. As above, there is no evidence that telepathic examination or communication, used properly, has any negative long-term effects.

<table>
<tr><td align="center">TIP</td></tr>
<tr><td>A helpful analogy to assist clients or witnesses in understanding the long-term effects of telepathy is to compare it to normal speech. In the same way that permanent hearing damage is not caused by being repeatedly spoken to at a regular volume, permanent brain damage is not caused by repeated responsible use of telepathy.</td></tr>
</table>

Myth: A telepath who makes contact with your mind instantly knows all about you.

1.18 False. As above, there are degrees of telepathy and telepathic contact, not all of which involve thought perception. A telepath engaged in routine security or noninvasive monitoring will only get a general sense of a person's current location, mood, and thoughts.

Furthermore, even in direct third-degree mental examination, a telepath neither accesses nor retains the entirety of a telepath-recipient's thoughts or memories. The total amount of information being put out or processed by an individual's brain at any given moment is often greater than a telepath can accurately interpret, given that it includes conscious, instinctual, and inarticulable thought as well as subconscious processes, sensory perception, and synaptic communication.

<table>
<tr><td align="center">TIP</td></tr>
<tr><td>Use analogies and practical explanations to help your client or witness understand the limits of telepathy. Possible examples include:

- A telepath reading your mind is like you reading a book: you cannot simply open it for a second and know everything inside.
- Your brain is an incredibly complex biological computer. When you use a computer, do you instantly know everything that's on it? Like when you look for a file on your computer, the telepath will search in your brain in certain ways to try and find what they are looking for, but they cannot perceive everything.
- Remember, the telepath is still only human, and is seeing your thoughts through their own human mind. They are not going to be able to memorize your every thought and memory in the same way that you would not be able to memorize every word you read if you were going through a large folder of documents.</td></tr>
</table>

Myth: Simply being nearby allows a telepath to know what a person is thinking.

1.25 Partially false. A telepath not seeking to make telepathic contact can nevertheless perceive powerful and uninhibited thoughts and emotions in nearby individuals in the same way that nontelepathic people can overhear conversations or perceive facial expressions . . .

. . . As addressed above, the simple fact of telepathic perception or contact does not mean that a telepath will be privy to a person's entire memories or thoughts, and it is likely that the majority of Australians pass telepaths every day without any negative repercussions.

Matt Callaghan snored.

Curled up on his side, mouth slightly open, his limbs wrapped in a tangle of sheets and blankets, Matt slept soundly in the calm and quiet night. For a while, Jane just lay there, listening to his breathing, watching the slivers of the city's starlight flit across the ceiling, the patterns stealing around the black curtain covering the bedroom window. Little light, little sound, little dark. It was so peaceful, and for a moment, all Jane wanted was to lay back and hold it tenderly in her grasp.

Matt's snoring was steady and constant, little more than a rasp or whisper. That was okay. Once upon a time, Jane might've found it annoying, or it might've kept her awake, but now, she found the sound oddly soothing. Not that it mattered either way. She wasn't tired.

The girl indulged in a few more moments' peace then rolled from their bed as quietly as she could before padding barefoot across the shaggy carpet to the other side of the room. She pulled on a hoodie, more out of habit than anything, then tiptoed from the bedroom, gently closing the door behind her—leaving Matt to his rest, and her to their sprawling apartment and the looming, vacant night.

Clank-clank. Clank-clank. Clank-clank.

The individual weights of the dumbbells rattled with each punch, unused to being jerked around with such ferocity.

Clank-clank-clank. Clank-clank. Clank.

Jane moved through the boxing routine with a sort of indifferent familiarity, weaving an uninspired combination of jabs, straights, and hooks. She wore no gloves and hit nothing save empty gym air, but she wasn't practicing striking as such. More just . . . going through the motions. Punching for punching's sake.

The dumbbells she held in each hand clanked and shuddered with every movement. A hundred pounds, one twenty—she wasn't sure what she was up to anymore. All she knew was that the bar ends were full and the spinlocks holding the weights in place looked like they were straining. Probably weren't designed to be thrown around so much.

Jane stretched out her arms, let herself fall into a plank, and began doing springing push-ups.

Clank. Thud, clank. Thud, clank. Thud, clank.

She wondered how good the apartment's soundproofing was. Muting voices through walls was one thing, but this constant pounding of dumbbells hitting the hard foam floor—it was difficult to believe no one heard that. Though so far, there'd been no complaints. Maybe the units below them thought their roof was haunted.

Jane pushed back onto her feet, balancing the right dumbbell unthinkingly against her left wrist so she could use her free hand to wipe her brow. Halfway through she realized how stupid the motion was, since she wasn't actually sweating. The corner of Jane's mouth twitched into a frown, then she grabbed the right dumbbell again, sat down on the bench, and began to unscrew the spinlocks. Weights. She needed more weights. Denser weights. Add it to the shopping list.

Jane reracked the equipment and turned the lights off before leaving, returning the gym to darkness. The iron glimmered in the light of the distant hall. How much had the White Queen lifted, Jane wondered. If she had even worked out to begin with. Probably hadn't. Probably too busy being royalty.

"Princess. Little baby princess. Go cry about it."

The crappy speaker in Jane's headset crackled with insults from some guy she'd never met. He was dead; she'd killed him, and he sounded very emotionally involved.

"What're you, twelve? Yeah, right. No, you're not. Thirteen max. Go hit puberty. You sound like a girl."

Curled up alone on the couch with her legs tucked beneath her, Jane's eyes remained focused on the TV as the soldier she was controlling clambered up and took cover behind a ledge. The living room was dark save for the flash-flashing of the TV, and quiet save for the click-clicking of the Xbox controller.

"Yeah, no, duh, idiot, I am a girl. Yeah. Yeah, I am. Nineteen. Yeah. Goddamn right I'm good."

She was alright, she guessed. Before she'd dated Matt, Jane had never really been around video games. It took a while to pick up, the way you wriggled your fingers here and your guy moved on the screen over there. But you got it after a bit of practice. After that, well, her eyes were sharp and her reflexes sharper.

"Yeah. Nah, I don't have a boyfriend. I don't know, a bit. This is my alt account. Haha yeah. I mean, if you want. It's a new phone, though, so I gotta check my number. Cool. Hold on, let's get out of the way for a second. Yeah. Yellow house, top floor. Yeah. I'll meet you there."

The sound of footsteps echoed through her headset as somebody nearby hurried up a digital flight of stairs. Jane's character crouched facing the stairwell, shotgun locked and loaded. A few seconds later, an enemy soldier came charging with reckless abandon into her line of sight. Jane blew his brains out.

"Haha. Idiot. Freaking idiot, what did you think was going to happen? No, no, jokes, sorry. I was just messing with you. I was joking. For real—no, for real this time. Yeah. No, I promise. I'm out of ammo, anyway. Yeah, I'll wait."

A few seconds' pause. Then more approaching footsteps, followed by another shotgun blast.

"Ha. Die, trash."

"Lèsè tǒng zài nǎlǐ?"

"Lachee tong zed nali?"

"Where is a trash can? *Lèsè tǒng zài nǎlǐ?*"

"Lachae tong zae nali? Where is a trash can?"

Jane squinted intently at the colored workbook on the desk in front of her, her hands pressing both off-white headphones slightly more firmly onto her ears. They had better-quality speakers than the crappy Xbox Live headset, but she still found it hard to concentrate on the individual sounds the man in the recordings was making.

She looked down at her workbook, illuminated by an adjustable desk lamp. So many different tones. So many little pictures to memorize. And so many of them looked so similar.

"*Yóuxiāng zài nǎlǐ?* Where is a post box? *Yóuxiāng zài nǎlǐ?*"

"Yoshung zai nali? Yosheyoung zai nali?"

She was getting to the back half of the workbook now, reaching the point where it felt like she was forgetting some of the words she'd learned up front. Jane gnawed her lip, concentrating on the tip of her pen as she tried to make sure the spikes of the Chinese characters she was writing were all pointing the right way.

"*Gōnggòng qìchē zhàn zài nǎlǐ?* Where is a bus stop? *Gōnggòng qìchē zhàn zài nǎlǐ?*"

"Gung-gung teacher chen zai nali? Gung-gung . . . Crap." Deep breath. "Gung-gung chi-zur-zen zai nali?"

Why couldn't the world's most spoken language be Spanish? Spanish was easy. She could make sense of Spanish. Matt had taught Spanish to his dog.

Deer Lady Dawn,

My name is Cassie. I am 6 years old. My dog has run away. Her name is Ori. She is a whyt dog with whyt hare . . .

Sitting alone at the long wooden dining table, Jane squinted at the laptop screen, the glare spreading out around her into the violet dark. Her fingers on her lips, she continued scrolling through the email, dreading the inevitable point.

Mom says that Ori is gorn and that she went to look for her but she cood not find her. It is cold and I miss Ori. She is a good dog but she can not opin dog food with out my help.

Please please please find her I love her so much evin moor then doodl bear. My hows is number 7 . . .

For what felt like an eternity, Jane read and reread the email, feeling, as with so many she received, a building sense of panic at how to respond. She knew, logically, there was nothing she could do, but how could she tell the little girl that? What did she say? Did she say anything? Did she just delete it and move on? The dog was probably dead. Oh God, the dog was probably dead.

Indecision weighed on her like a lead blanket. Jane's fingers hung paralyzed above the keyboard, her anxiety mounting as she wasted precious seconds on vacillating that could've been spent answering other requests.

Finally, she managed to tap out a reply.

Dear Cassie,

Good start, idiot.

Thank you for writing to me. I'm sorry to hear about Ori. I'm sad to say that she has probably been hit by a car or something and—

No. Jesus Christ, Jane. Come on.

It is a sad fact of life that everything dies, and sometimes, the things we love the most disappear, and there is nothing we can do about it. When I was nine, my mother—

Backspace, aggressive backspace. This is not about you.

Jane stared at the screen for a few minutes more, and then finally settled for being practical.

Dear Cassie,
Thank you for your letter. I'm sorry to hear about Ori. I can't come by and look for her right now, but I think you should tell your mom that she should call the local police station and let them know. You should also call the nearest animal pound because it's possible Ori might have been taken there by accident. She is probably microchipped, so talk to your vet.

If your mom has any friends who can turn into dogs, maybe see if they can have a look around your yard to see if they can see anything that might have spooked Ori. And if your mom knows any psychics, maybe they can also help.

Wait, could telepaths hear animals? Crap, she didn't actually know. She'd have to ask Wally.

Jane powered on.

There are also people who can talk to animals called anipaths. Ask the police if they know any. They might be able to help.

Jane leaned back from the keyboard, feeling satisfied. Then she read again the girl's desperate pleas for her to help, personally. Jane hesitated, scrunched up her face, trying to resist the overwhelming sense of guilt—then finally she sighed and leaned back in.

If I am in the area, I will fly over and see if I can see her.

There, Jane thought. Surely that was the most anyone could expect of her. She'd done good. She was doing good. Good job.

Jane clicked through to the next email, a request to help get back clothes and family heirlooms from an abusive ex-husband. She squinted at the laptop screen, trying to concentrate on the details, but soon found herself reading and rereading the same three lines. Jane closed her eyes, rubbed her temples, took a deep breath, and sighed. Then she scrolled back up.

Dear Cassie,
Following on from my last email, you should also suggest to the police, if they have someone with supersenses, that they get some of Ori's fur—

"Mmm, smells like burning dog."

Jane looked up from beside the sink, her hair tied loosely in a bun, her expression frazzled. The sun was up, dawn light streaming through the windows. On the other side of the long kitchen counter, Matt strode out from the bedroom, his face a friendly smile. He was still wearing a T-shirt and boxer shorts.

"I thought you'd be out for"—Jane glanced at the oven clock—"another hour."

"Well, there was a lot of swearing. And some . . . scents." Matt raised an eyebrow and pointed with his chin toward the benchtop. Jane grimaced, sweeping her eyes over the various plates of food she'd laid out. In theory, it was supposed to be a hearty, expansive breakfast. In reality, most of it was black.

"Sorry. Thought there was more time. I was just . . ." She sighed, turning away from the stove and putting down the spatula she'd been holding. "These were going to be test runs."

"Extensive testing," Matt commented. His nose wrinkled. "So, smoke I get, but I still can't place the burnt dog smell."

"I cooked spam."

"That's what that is."

"I meant to cook bacon. I mean, I did cook bacon. But then it burned."

"It's okay; I like bacon extra crispy."

"This is . . . ash."

Matt peered at her, bemused. "Why'd you cook it to ash?"

"It was going too slowly, so I added fire. Then I got distracted. Then there was too much fire." She pinched the bridge of her nose. "Sorry."

He shook his head and beckoned Jane over, leaning across the counter to kiss her on the cheek. "I appreciate the effort."

"This isn't my forte."

"I know. Does take some practice."

She turned back to switch off the stove, abandoning her latest omelette abomination to the same fate as its predecessors. "Try the toast," she suggested, starting to move dishes into the sink. Matt was better at stacking the dishwasher. "I think if you scrape the top off, it'll be alright."

"Restaurant quality," her boyfriend assured her, and though he smirked when he said it, his voice contained no hint of malice.

It tended to be most mornings that Jane attempted to make breakfast. Her goal, as it had been for some time now, was for Matt to wake up and find the dining room table already laden with food. It wasn't a strong goal, and it wasn't some stupid gender roles thing; she just wanted to be able to do it. And she had time to do it. And she wanted to be a good partner. And she wanted Matt to think she was nice.

Unfortunately, despite her litany of other skills, Jane Walker was perhaps persistently the worst chef in the history of mankind. Beset by a strange, almost bewildering combination of impatience, inexperience, aggravation, and just plain bad luck, she had devastated, carbonated, evaporated, and exsanguinated an entire deli's worth of foodstuffs, which might have been an issue if money had been tight. As it stood, however, Matt simply continued to find her efforts funny, and Jane continued to feed her repeated failures down the whirly death vortex garbage disposal thingy in the sink.

Matt sat down at the kitchen counter and started scraping char off some toast.

"Turned on my phone," he told her. Jane restrained a smirk.

"And?"

"Fourteen missed calls from Mom. One from Dad. Two from Rana. A few from Kate."

Rana was their lawyer at the ACLU. Kate was their agent.

"Emails?"

"I shudder to think."

"Damn." She shrugged. "Well. Sounds like you've got a fun morning."

"Yeah, yeah." Matt paused as Jane passed him the butter. "I should call Mom."

"Yeah."

"You should call your dad."

Jane felt herself stiffen. "He'll be fine."

"I know he'll be fine; he'll want to know you're fine."

"He knows I'm fine. How could I not be?"

"Alright, well, then maybe he'll want to know I'm fine."

"He watches TV."

"Lord preserve us," Matt lamented, rolling his eyes at the ceiling. He bit down, his next words garbled through a mouthful of toast. "Ish badsh enough you donk cheth your phone." He swallowed. "At least call some-one occasionally after I almost get killed."

Jane had a phone now. She didn't like it. With the exception of Matt, she found the idea of being generally contactable all the time by anyone irritating.

"I don't know where it is."

"It's in my bag. Underneath the—" He abruptly ground to a halt, then swore. Jane smirked.

"I put your sandwiches in the fridge."

"Wait, really? Goddamn, I love you."

Jane's cheeks flushed with pleasure at the offhand remark. She attempted to respond in kind, but by the time she'd opened her mouth and struggled close to forming the same sentence, Matt had already charged headfirst into another topic.

"Are you happy for me to give Rana your statement?"

Jane swallowed and forced herself to move on. "Absolutely. Lie away."

"Mildly lie."

"Little baby lies."

"A little lie-flavored garnish." He paused. "So, call Mom," Matt counted on his fingers, taking another bite of toast, chewing, and swal-lowing. "Call lawyer. Call Kate. Spend an hour and a half shooting down her latest terrible merchandising concepts. Respond to emails. Delete emails. Study with Giselle—"

"Put on pants, probably, before that happens," Jane added, trying to keep her tone light. Matt indicated to her with his finger.

"Put on pants, check. Maybe even shower. Study, lunch, study, gym—"

"Cardio," Jane interrupted.

"Cardio," agreed Matt, though he sighed as he said it. Jane had no idea why Matt seemed so resistant to her insistence that he spend half an hour every day running on the treadmill. It was a complete no-brainer. Matt had literally one job in the event anything went wrong, as she oft and repeatedly reminded him: run, run as fast as you can, and keep running until I save you. A consistent cardio routine was literally the bare minimum for that.

Plus, it improved his butt.

"Giselle leaves," Matt continued, oblivious to Jane's butt thoughts. "Dinner, maybe; you home, probably. Try not to lose my mind."

"I'll be back before then," she reassured him.

"I'm not criticizing," said Matt. He sighed, sinking to rest his head on his arms on the kitchen counter. Jane felt a rush of pity and wracked her brain for something she could do.

"What about you?" Matt asked before she could reach any brilliant revelations. "What's on your agenda?"

"I . . . You know. Superhero stuff." She paused, mouth twitching into a grimace. "I should message Will."

"Already done."

"Oh. Thank you." She leaned over and kissed him clumsily on the cheek, which Matt somehow managed to receive without any reciprocal awkwardness. "Did he say when—?"

"No, but can't imagine long."

"Right. Well, I . . ." She glanced back around at the mess-strewn kitchen. Matt rolled his eyes.

"It's fine. I'll do it."

"No, sorry, you shouldn't have to. I—"

"Just go. Jesus. What else do I have to do?" To her relief, he didn't sound too annoyed when he said it, and his eyes twinkled as he smirked.

"I really thought I'd get it done."

"And yet, your organizational powers continue to be matched only by your cooking. Go. Leave the dishes. Save the world."

He rounded the bench and hugged her, and Jane nestled her head against his neck. Then she went to get changed.

The fingerprint scanner pinged, and the door to their apartment opened. Matt, by this point, had put on pants.

"Morning, all."

"Morning, man." Will grinned as he stepped through.

"Oh my God," gushed Giselle Pixus, following close behind. "Is that Matt Callaghan? Oh my God. From TV? *Maaatttt.* Can I have your autograph?" Matt rolled his eyes good-naturedly as they walked toward each other and Giselle descended into cackling laughter.

Tall, thin, and stunning, Giselle Pixus, speedster, was the same olive-skinned Eurasian goddess she'd always been and in characteristically irrepressible spirits. Gone was her brief, bleak window of misery, extinguished the moment the real Klaus Heydrich reappeared and proved her innate kindness hadn't caused her friend's depression and death.

Gone too was any sign of the horrific burns that half a year ago had covered nine-tenths of her body, restored by superhuman healers to its original flawless self. The only slight change, if you knew to look for it, was the subtle lack of branding on any of the activewear she sported. The leggings, white top, and black jacket were all custom Legion fabrications, Matt knew, and specifically designed to be fireproof.

"Another brush with death," Giselle said in faux lamentation, holding the back of her hand to her forehead as if a Victorian lady about to faint. "Yet once more, our hero triumphs."

"Yeah, yeah. Another day, another dodge." The two met in a hug. After a moment or two, they pulled back, Giselle's arms still wrapped around his stomach. She beamed at him.

"What do we say to death?"

"None for me, thanks?"

"Close enough. *Jaaaane,*" Giselle called, detaching from Matt and leaning into the main of their apartment. "How's your loooove neeeeeest?"

Jane stuck her head out from around the door to their bedroom, face pinched into a darkened scowl. She trudged out toward the newcomers, already dressed in the uniform of Dawn—white bodice, gold sigil of breaking day, gold boots, cape, and gloves. Giselle, completely unintimidated by both Jane's large, gleaming presence or her sour expression, pranced forward and engulfed the younger woman in a hug.

"You did so good last night," she cooed when, after a moment, they pulled apart. "I saw the whole thing. I know I'm fast, but you? You were *on it*"—she snapped her finger—"like that. Eagle eyes. So good. We were so impressed."

"Thanks," Jane said awkwardly, breaking contact. She shuffled slightly in place, tugging fitfully at one of the cape's shoulders. Matt moved in quickly to change the subject.

"Shall we let these two get going?"

Giselle clapped her hands. "My, yes. So many disasters, so little time. Go, fly, shoot light at people. And you"—she rounded on Will—"go take her places and make eggy fart smells. Make the Legion proud."

"Our charismatic leader," the teleporter grieved, though he grinned as he said it. He nodded at Jane, who returned the gesture before turning back to Matt.

"Call me the second you need anything," she told him. Matt struggled not to roll his eyes, instead forcing a smile.

"I'll be fine."

"Hmm." Jane frowned. She glanced over Matt's shoulder at Giselle, who was watching the two of them with unrestrained glee and moving her fingers super fast to make two blurry love hearts. Jane's eyes narrowed.

"Go," Matt insisted. Jane returned her attention to him, still hesitant.

"It doesn't feel right."

"Come on. Life goes on. Besides, who's going to get past her?" He jerked a thumb back at Giselle, who threw up devil horns.

"No excursions," Jane warned, poking him in the chest. Matt raised his hands defensively.

"No excursions. I'll be good."

"You better be. If you die, I snap and kill everybody."

"A little dark," Matt commented, going for constructive feedback to encourage rather than dissuade his girlfriend's embryonic attempt at a joke. He gave her a quick kiss, squeezed her gloved hands, then patted her beneath the cape.

"Aww," said Giselle.

"Shut up," Jane ordered, pointing. She jerked her head at Will. "Come on."

They exited into the hallway with Jane only giving one last fleeting look behind her. The lift pinged, and the sound of stilted conversation drifted in from the elevator. The minute the doors closed, Matt's shoulders slumped, and he sighed.

"That good, huh?" Giselle commented, moving beside him, arms crossed, some of the levity dissipated. Matt shook his head.

"Big night."

"No kidding. You guys sure know how to make television."

"She worries about me," he said with a sigh.

"Dude," replied Giselle, making a face, "I worry about you. You're like the world's most murderable baby."

"If I could go one day," Matt lamented, staring up at the ceiling of the penthouse, "just *one* day without being horribly emasculated, I would die a happy man."

"Please," Giselle snorted. "Emasculated. You're better than that."

Matt considered for a moment. "It's true," he eventually conceded. "I am. Too much self-confidence. Damn loving, supportive parents."

"You're a feminist icon."

"A diamond in the rough."

Five thousand feet below the surface of the ocean, the crew of the *V.K. Konovalov* huddled in smothering silence as they listened to the walls around them creak. The air hung cold and thick with condensation. Clustered around the weak glow of electric lanterns or a pyromancer's cupped flame, their breaths fogged before their faces as they hunched beneath rough-spun blankets and pulled layers of spare clothing tight.

Two weeks ago, the *Konovalov* had left port abuzz with the kind of confidence reserved for young, fit sailors with superpowers and purpose. Eleven days later, a torpedo misfire had taken the life of their teleporter, four crew, and the submarine's generator. Suddenly, they were no longer silent hunters stalking the depths. Suddenly, they were helpless men trapped in a titanium tube, a coffin slowly sinking toward the yearning void.

The submarine sat silent now, motionless on the ocean floor, an insignificant bubble of metal waiting to be popped by the crushing, freezing dark. Its crew huddled close as the air grew thick, their powers suddenly useless, feeling the weight of death's fingers pressing in all around. They whispered soft stories, scared promises—and flinched to a man, every one of them, at the hull's every groan and whimper, every movement, every creak.

Suddenly, without warning, the submarine shifted, and the world around them lurched. Hands grabbed doors and railings; men shouted while others cried. Some stayed silent, waiting for the crack that heralded their inevitable death.

But a moment later, their fear froze in wonder as the *Konovalov* sailors felt themselves slowly, gradually, beginning to rise.

Though none of them could see it, outside, a sudden rush of light illuminated the seafloor's darkness. From beneath the submarine, a figure rose, pushing between the metal and sand, the hull suddenly lifting atop a wave of flowing gold. The stranger rose to kneeling—Atlas bearing Earth—and slowly, slowly, the golden light spread, pushing outward, pushing up.

With a heave, the figure kicked off from the bottom of the ocean. Slowly, slowly, from the water's endless depths, the dark metal of the *Konovalov* rose, buoyed by a single, solitary light at its base and center burning in a relentless ascent.

Inside, the submariners held on to the walls and each other, listening in terror to the creaks and rumbling, the floor shaking beneath their feet. Then suddenly, after what felt like an eternity, the rising stopped, and to their disbelief, they felt the walls of the vessel begin to rock, to pitch in gentle rhythm against the lap and bob of waves. Men scrambled, lanterns dropped, blankets discarded. Hands rushed to check dials, radios, and periscopes.

Their instruments spoke true. They had surfaced. They were alive.

Between the ensuing tears and shouting, relentless swearing and passionate embraces, one man, Dimitry, stumbled awestruck to push open the exit hatch, peeking his skinny head nervously out into the blue, sunlit sky. He blinked over and again, his head ringing as his ears popped, blinded by the sudden sunlight, barely able to believe what he was seeing.

He looked around, spotting no other ships, no source of rescue—only the sea for a hundred miles around him, lapping ceaseless and calm.

Then the water to the left of the submarine broke, and a figure shot from the ocean in a comet of gold, rising twenty feet above the *Konovalov* to hang suspended in the air. A woman. A shining vision of a woman, who shook loose her bronze ponytail in a fan of spray and turned to look upon him like a Valkyrie come to Earth. In that moment, with the salt wind rippling through her hair and the sun's light shining behind her, Dimitry could have sworn he stared upon a god.

The shining woman's eyes found him, a lone white head bobbing atop a submarine among the endless sea. Stunned, overawed, as if in a dream, it was all Dimitry could do to shuffle his right hand up and give an awkward, lopping wave.

In that moment, the spell broke. The girl's shoulders relaxed, an uncertain smile passed over her face, and she seemed, suddenly, far closer to being human than she had mere moments before. She raised her own hand and returned the gesture—a small, stunted wave strangely shy and all her own.

There came noise from down below, pushing and grunts—calls to let others up. Dimitry simply ignored them, ignored all of them, instead continuing to stare, mesmerized, as the girl or goddess turned, looked off into the heavens, and, without a word, flew up.

He watched her go in wistful reverie, not quite believing what he'd just witnessed, unsure if he wanted to sigh or smile or sob.

It was 11:00 a.m. and Matt was bored.

Cooped up, low-key stressed, and bored. He didn't think any of those sentiments were unreasonable. He'd been studying for the last three hours, everyone in the world knew his identity, a large number of people were trying to kill him, and he wasn't allowed outside.

It was bizarre for Matt to find himself looking back with fondness at his days at the Academy, at vast swathes of time spent indulging in pointless nonsense interspersed with the occasional rush of adrenaline at someone almost uncovering his half-baked clairvoyant falsehood. At least back then, most people hadn't cared about his existence. At least then, he could touch grass.

Matt sighed and tried to force his eyes back down to the textbook. Across the dining room table, Giselle flicked him a small, concerned look.

They were studying law. Matt officially, Giselle unofficially; him as a special-consideration distance student for prelaw at Columbia, her just as someone who listened to the same lectures as him and happened to share his textbooks. Not that you'd know that was the way of it—Giselle seemed to lap Matt as effortlessly in academics as she did at actual running. Goddamn polymaths. Nobody in his life was normal anymore.

The idea had been inspired, originally, by their ACLU lawyer, Rana, and Matt's frustration at not being able to clearly understand about fifty percent of what was going on. Well, alright, maybe closer to twenty percent; Rana had very good interpersonal skills and the ability to compress complex legal concepts into words for normal humans. But it was still overwhelming for Matt to review documents that he was expected to sign off on so riddled with legal jargon they may as well have been written in French.

Matt hated feeling stupid. He didn't have the urge to be intimidatingly smart—that would've been unrealistic—but he hated feeling dumb or like major life decisions were being effectively made for him, especially when documents he was expected to sign were just being shoved in his face. Hence, prelaw. Hence, his admission to Columbia, which he was quite certain would absolutely never have happened if it weren't for Rana's good word and his not-insignificant celebrity.

So, Matt had enrolled in college in a fit of intellectual defiance and in what had seemed like a good idea at the time, to both whittle down the hours in this newly precautionary phase of his existence, and maybe come out the other end with a good qualification once everything had settled down.

Except then the defiant urge to do something bold and bettering had faded, and Matt found himself stuck with the reality of studying law, which was reading a metric ton of incredibly long, dry judgments written by old dead men and coming to the slow, dawning realization that you knew nothing about anything and were in fact profoundly stupid.

"Want to take a break?" Giselle asked.

To do what? Matt wanted to bitterly reply. They weren't allowed to go anywhere. Well, *he* wasn't allowed to go anywhere—Giselle could leave, but she typically wouldn't go far without him. It seemed consensus among his friends and the Legion of Heroes—who were now pretty much one and the same—that he was not safe to be left alone.

Someone always needed to be babysitting, in case today was the day the stupid, murderous Second Amendment pricks somehow figured out which apartment he was in, remotely traced his IP address, spider-climbed the walls, set the building on fire, or dropped an anvil on his head from space. None of which had actually happened yet, but all of which remained technically possible.

There had been four attempts to murder Matt in the past six months, not including Klaus Heydrich or the man who'd shot/shot at him last night. The first had been in the second week after he'd come home from the hospital; he'd been in his room, in bed, asleep, as had all his family, when a speedster had raced past their home and lit up the place with a semiautomatic pistol.

Fortunately for the Callaghans, this attempt had been plagued by poor planning and worse execution, with the majority of the bullets leveled at the ground floor while the family's bedrooms were upstairs, and the shooter, going several hundred miles an hour, having the stability and aim control of a Jell-o-cube-riding rodeo.

Between the recoil, the superspeed, the low caliber of the handheld weapon, and—Matt suspected—the would-be assassin's probable last-minute guilt about shooting up a suburban family, the majority of bullets had lodged themselves in the brickwork, the carpet, the garage, or the front lawn.

Nobody had been hurt, but it had been enough to alert the police and the Legion that something was afoot, and that Matt might legitimately be in danger. The shooter had been picked up by police after the bullets were traced back to the store he'd purchased the gun from, and the attacker had been identified as a thirty-five-year-old assistant manager at a Missouri Ford dealership with no affiliation with any terrorist groups, a once-a-month visitation arrangement with his twin daughters, and a history of unmanaged depression.

The second attempt had come two weeks later, about a month after Matt's return home. This one, scarily, had been much more sophisticated: a twenty-eight-year-old dishonourably discharged ex-marine sniper teleporting into a tree across the road from the Callaghans' house and setting up aim at Matt's window with a high-powered rifle.

This, too, had been foiled, but not by the shooter's incompetence; rather, it was the Legion bodyguards, specifically Wally Cykes, who had telepathically sensed the arrival of a new hostile entity and quickly alerted the rest of the Legion to its presence. This time, it was Jane who'd caught the culprit, descending from the sky like a furious golden meteor and pulverizing the tree and the assailant before the latter had time to escape.

Jane had snapped the gun in half and beaten the man near lifeless; Matt had reimbursed the neighbors for the tree the next day. Again, the attacker had no affiliations, having purchased the gun illegally and spent the three days beforehand alone in a threadbare apartment strung out on a diet of energy drinks, onion rings, and dextroamphetamines.

This attack, then, being more sinister and frightening than the first one, had been enough to convince the Callaghans they had to move. They'd relocated to an anonymized safe house—with the Legion and the State Department working together to set them up with new identities and a new home—only for that, too, to somehow get found out and shot at after barely a month.

This time, the attacker had sat in a car out of sight of the Callaghans' new residence and fired bullets around the corner, attempting to use his electromagnetic powers to bend the projectiles in precise and unnatural arcs, which was a dangerous idea, in theory.

Unfortunately—or fortunately, depending on which side of the gun you were on—it turned out that bullets moved very fast, and that human reactions moved (comparatively) very slowly, meaning that the majority of shots fired by the amateur assassin had not so much curved with deadly precision as wobbled a little bit and flew across the street into an old lady's prized gardenias.

When Giselle Pixus had found him, alerted by the sound of gunshots, the twenty-two-year-old Walmart pallet loader had been swearing furiously, so distracted trying to recalculate and reload his twin pistols that he'd failed to notice the Legion speedster approaching until his tires were slashed and he was cable-tied to a nearby telephone pole.

From there, there had been no more new identities. It was clear—to Jane and the Legion, at least—that whatever official relocation services were being provided were not secure; that there were holes in the government's security, unwitting or intentional, through which confidential information could leak out.

To find the hole, let alone plug it, would have required a level of effort and coordination that the police and the State Department were, quite frankly, unwilling to supply, being reluctant to admit they had a problem in the first place, and then equally resistant to the idea of any third party, even the Legion of Heroes, trawling for it in their data banks.

So, this time, the Legion didn't bother; beds were made, space was cleared, and the Callaghans were simply relocated to Morningstar Academy, the Legion's freshly rebuilt base of operations, where they were set up in a little side-wing cottage home once made for founding member Ironbound and his kids and wife.

There, now, the attacks on Matt's family stopped. It was one thing, it seemed, for a lone shooter to talk themselves into driving a few states over and taking potshots at regular people in the heart of Middle America, but another thing entirely to attempt a one-man assault on the home and training ground of the very-negatively-toward-unwanted-guests-inclined Legion of Heroes and their dazzling array of superpowers and death.

Even with Morningstar in a state of rebuilding, and the Academy being slowly repopulated with fresh faces, the prospect of launching an attack was obviously too daunting. Matt's family, it seemed—at least for the time being—were safe.

But it soon became clear that Matt wasn't. The fourth attack, at around ten thirty in the morning on a mild, windy Tuesday, had taken place outside the ACLU offices as Matt and one of Rana's paralegals had stepped out to visit a nearby coffee cart for midmorning coffee and bear claws.

The assassin—a tall, wispy-bearded twenty-four-year-old—had strode across the street, phased intangible through an underpass, drawn a combat shotgun from his black leather trench coat, and leveled it ten feet from Matt Callaghan's chest.

Luckily, this attacker's decision to dress exactly as one would imagine a would-be shooter to dress themselves, i.e., in black cargo pants, black combat boots, and wraparound black sunglasses, made his approach stand out somewhat, and Matt's accompanying paralegal, Daisy, had, with bulging eyes, hypervoiced the assassin so thoroughly that the shotgun had flown out of his hands and smacked him barrel first in the eye socket.

A crowd of angry onlookers had then descended on the man, who within seconds had found himself dazed, deafened, disarmed, and bound with someone's purple cat-patterned necktie to the wheels of the coffee cart, his head shoved in the underbelly so that its basic-range Disruptance would prevent him from phasing out. Matt had made sure to generously tip the cart owner.

This attacker, it had turned out, lived with his parents and had dropped out of filmmaking class at the local community college five months ago after the abrupt and messy end to a long-term relationship. There was something about the way he'd sobbed while being arrested, and how banal he'd looked once his sunglasses were removed, that Matt found particularly unsettling. He was just some guy. They were all just some guy.

Regardless, the verdict had been unanimous: Matt was not allowed outside anymore. Not alone, not under any circumstances, and if a venture out became absolutely necessary, then only ever accompanied by a trusted, fully inducted member of the Legion of Heroes.

Jane's preference was, of course, for his guardian to be her and her alone, but sometimes, that wasn't possible—Lady Dawn had places to be and people to rescue. At their home, too, it was decided (over Matt's frustrated but impotent protests) that Matt needed a bodyguard. Acolytes were okay for this, so long as they'd proven trustworthy, but again, Jane's preference was for it to be a full Legion member or her. Preferably her.

When it came to Matt, Jane Walker viewed anyone who wasn't her with suspicion, if not of their intentions, then at the very least their ability to competently keep her boyfriend from being shot. This paranoia was in part why the pair had moved into the Park River apartment rather than with Matt's family at the Academy, as on balance, the possibility of one of the new Acolytes being some sort of deep-cover infiltrator seemed to the relentlessly paranoid Jane greater than the benefit of more eyes and powers.

And so, only a few months after they'd first started dating, Matt and Jane had moved in together. It had been a quick progression, as far as romance went, but then again, so was the whole of their relationship. It was somewhat understandable. Ever since they first kissed outside the hospital, Matt and Jane had been largely inseparable, with the latter determined to keep the former ever under her protective, possessive eye, and the former fast becoming the latter's emotional anchor and support.

These long hours of togetherness, coupled with their existing friendship and—let's be honest—probably teenage hormones, meant that, to Matt and Jane, it felt like they had been together for years. Moving in, therefore, had been simply a natural progression.

And it had been going well; the two melded around each other with natural ease, were supportive in their cohabitation, and it was only the threat of the outside world—really, the need to keep Matt safe—which seemed to sow discord in their otherwise happy relationship.

Matt, for his part, found the constant need for protection equal parts ridiculous, understandable, and exhausting. When he was outside, yeah, sure, the precautions made sense. But Jane's insistence on having someone babysit him at all hours here, in this secret unmarked penthouse nobody knew about, with fingerprint scanners, bulletproof glass, and blast proofing just seemed like overkill. Unnecessary, soul-destroying overkill.

It'd been three months now, give or take, since the last attack. Matt had been preparing, mentally, to make the case to Jane that maybe the madness had passed, that perhaps they could relax a little, start transitioning toward eventual freedom, maybe just at home, so he could at least poop in privacy without someone listening to him grunt.

And then came last night's knob jockey, planned and poised to strike with laser precision in their one visible opening. They'd put so much work into security checks: the crew, the studio audience. The effing sandwich guy. And then, somehow, word of where they'd be leaving had gotten out, and some invisible butt monkey had been there ready to put a bullet into Matt's brain. Or not put a bullet in his brain. Matt tried not to think about the whole time travel mechanics too hard, lest he go cross-eyed and kill himself.

The decision by all his would-be assassins to use guns spoke to a pathology that Matt found interesting, if not disturbing. Although not exactly rare, guns weren't overly easy to get nowadays, especially not new or high-functioning ones. Despite past attitudes, as he understood them, and the whole Second Amendment thing, Matt had never known this to cause a huge amount of consternation; after all, if you could shoot laser beams out of your eyes or throw trucks at people, not having a little pew-pew pea pistol for personal protection wasn't really that big a deal.

But the decision to specifically use firearms—the one deadly method explicitly preserved in the Constitution that was so heavily linked to this notion of personal sovereignty and rights—spoke to a certain mindset or belief system among his attackers that was disturbingly unified, even if their actual affiliations weren't.

It would almost have been better, Matt pondered ruefully, if they had all been part of some shadowy organization committed to killing him. An organization, at least, could be found, combated, broken. But a bunch of random strangers individually arriving at the same murderous conclusion? Christ. That was like trying to prevent cancer.

This latest attacker was exactly the same, or at least—Giselle reported—as far as Legion forensics could tell. A vacuum repairman in his midforties, no partner, eight-years divorced. He owned a single-stroke fishing boat moored at a local marina, a Kelpie cross named Cyclone, and a criminal history of nothing worse than the occasional drive through a red light and low-range blood alcohol.

And he had, seemingly completely independently and of his own accord, come to the unshakable conclusion that Matt Callaghan's existence posed an intolerable threat to mankind. He was an ordinary person, who through simply reading on the Internet, had become convinced beyond convincing that he needed to take someone's life.

The idea scared Matt more than he cared to admit.

The cavemouth was dark as Jane descended slowly.

Around her, the rocks glistened with damp and moss, promising cold to the touch and an easy slip if her steps weren't careful. The way was lit, barely, by mottled sunlight filtered through the jungle canopy. Beneath the overhanging stone, the light faded gradually as Jane made her way cautiously through. She had mixed feelings about caves.

On the one hand, they were quiet, cool, shadowed places awash in natural tranquility. On the other, it was easy to lace them with explosives or hide a neutralizer somewhere, waiting to dampen her powers before she could realize and escape. To protect against this, Jane kept a small stream of energy burning between her toes, invisible beneath her boots but ready to alert her should her powers start to waver.

She continued cautiously down into the cave, letting a tiny amount of light glow around her fingers so she could see where she was going.

The walls glistened, slick and wet. Her gloved hand trailed along the rock.

Jane heard and saw the rebels around the same time they saw her.

There came ahead the sound of muttering, of scrambling feet and hurried movement. Slowly, Jane rounded a large, impeding boulder, glancing up as the cave's low roof opened into an expansive cavern a hundred feet high and at least that again across, tapering in the uneven distance into a slow and gradual downward slope.

Pinpricks of light—glowworms or moss—speckled the stalactite ceiling. Beneath it, Jane's gaze took in a horde of disheveled people: men, women, children, makeshift accommodations, wooden shacks dotted with white gas lamps and battery lanterns, piles of rucksacks, food, and clothes.

From the depths of the cavern, faces emerged, spurned out of hiding by the sound of movement—or sensing, perhaps, the sudden escalation of tension and panic brought on by the white-gold newcomer's arrival. Before long, a crowd had gathered. Murmurs rippled, frightened and awed.

Jane stopped in place at the top of the rough-cut steps to the cavern's entrance, not wanting to approach any further so as to maintain a clear path out and her position on the high ground, but also so as not to look like she was advancing. She didn't put her hands up—she wasn't surrendering to these people—but neither did she take a stance or power up.

"*Look twice, act once,*" Matt repeatedly told her. "*You're not a gold-colored hammer.*"

From the massing crowd of scared, hungry Bolivians—their faces drawn and their clothes rough—a man in a patched white shirt and no shoes stepped forward.

"*Dama Alba,*" he murmured, holding his hands half up in trepidation, as if scared she was going to blast him where he stood. His lips trembled, and he broke into a stream of what sounded like reverent pleading or explanation but which, unfortunately, Jane could barely understand a word of. Spanish. Goddamn Spanish. Why had she decided to learn Chinese?

"No . . . *habla* . . . *hablo* . . . Spani—*español,*" she managed, screwing up her face, trying to remember. "No . . . um . . . need . . . *por favor* . . . English. *Inglés?*"

The leader of the crowd looked at her, then called something out to the people around him. There was a flurry of murmurs around the cave until eventually a young girl, maybe ten or twelve with her dark hair in a long braid, was ushered forward to stand beside the spokesman. Clutching a thin green smock, she glanced up at Jane with evident anxiety.

The man spoke again, and this time, the girl translated his words into nervous English.

"Lady Dawn," she said, "please, don't hurt us. We are not be meaning to harm you." The man in the white shirt continued to speak low beside her, and after a moment, the girl continued. "We are not be meaning to harm anyone. Please. We are . . . desperado. Desperate. They come and to take us away."

"I'm not here to hurt anyone," Jane reassured them. She paused for a moment and glanced at the girl. "Translate that." There was a brief pause before, mentally, Jane heard Matt's chastisement. "Please," she added. She forced an attempt at a smile.

The girl continued to look nervous, but nevertheless, translated Jane's words. Jane took that as encouragement to press on. "There's been reports of fighting," she said. "The men out there, they say you are fugitives. That you are stealing, attacking their town."

"It is our town," the leader replied, all of a sudden angry, his voice rising above his nervousness after what Jane said was translated by the girl. "They are invaders. They are trying to be taking—to take what is our properties, saying we owe them under *la regla*—the rules? The law."

"What law?" Jane asked, her brow furrowed. "You all owe them money? How is that?"

"The water," someone in the crowd piped up in English, and there were agitated mutters of agreement as their spokesman turned, backed by vigorous nods.

"*Sí, el agua*," he echoed, then through the girl continued. "They say the water no longer belongs to us. They say it all belongs to them. That we must pay to use it. Even the rainwater. Even the—" The girl abruptly stopped translating and looked fearfully up at Jane, clearly terrified she'd be angry at the gap in her vocabulary. "The . . . person who is water? Who become water? *Lo siento*, I do not—"

"Aquamorph," Jane growled. She narrowed her eyes and turned back toward the cavern entrance, where outside, armed soldiers were waiting for her *intervention*. She was not angry at the girl. "That was not what I was told."

"Please," the leader begged. "We do not want to be here. We are not thieves. But there are too many, and they come in force . . . the governor's men . . . We cannot afford . . ."

"I understand," said Jane. She turned her back to the cavern, cape swishing golden in the lantern light. "You and you"—she pointed at the man and girl—"come with me. We're going to resolve this."

There was a murmuring in the crowd. The leader glanced back at his townsfolk, seemingly afraid. He clutched the little girl's hand.

"What are you going to do?" he asked through her.

Jane's lips curled, and suddenly, the dark of the cave shone with waves of thick, billowing light. The people amassed before her fell silent to reverence and awe.

"Good," she answered as her eyes burned.

"These sandwiches are actually not bad," commented Giselle, reappearing with what appeared to be a pesto chicken avocado from behind the fridge door. Matt glanced over from across the room, brain foggy with contract law.

"Help yourself. I forgot to eat them last night. Not soggy?"

"Nah, they're pretty good." Giselle's mouth and hands momentarily blurred, and the pesto chicken sandwich she'd been holding vanished, replaced for fresh consideration by a tuna salad. Matt nodded at the bag.

"Just leave a chicken schnitzel. If I'm going to have one, it'll be—"

His phone rang. Matt glanced down at it buzzing on the table. He frowned at the unknown number.

"Don't answer it," Giselle told him, though it was less a warning and more an exasperated sigh.

"I can always just hang up."

"Someone could trace you."

"Azleena put on that scrambler VPN thingy."

"I just don't understand. I mean, fine. On your head." She rolled her eyes.

Matt answered the phone.

"Hello?"

"Chosen prophet. Holy one."

Matt sighed and put the call on speakerphone. "Hello, Pastor Fredericks."

On the other side of the room, Giselle shook her beautiful head in despair. *How does he keep getting your number*, she mouthed.

"I witnessed Satan's attack on you last night. Praise God for He protects you. He shields his chosen son from harm."

"Phil," replied Matt, "please, we've been over this. I'm just a person."

"Humility, even in the face of undeniable evidence. The Lord was humble when he first walked among men. They tried to strike him down too, the nonbelievers. The Romans and the Pharisees." Fredericks's voice over the phone was husky, laced rich with fervor and devotion. "But nothing can stop the will of God. It is a sign, Matthew Callaghan. Even in your name, a prophecy. Matthew, the great witness, the disciple. Callaghan, of war and of strife. The battle is coming for the soul of this nation. You will lead us."

The pastor's voice ascended into sermon. "Then I saw Heaven standing open, and there before me was a white horse. And its rider is called Faithful and True. With righteousness He judges and wages war. He has eyes like blazing fire, and many royal crowns on His head. He has a name written on Him that only He Himself knows. He is dressed in a robe dipped in blood, and His name is the Word of God."

By this point, Matt had his head on the table.

"Phil, I don't own any crowns," he told him. "And I can't even ride a horse."

Beside him, Giselle had tiptoed over and placed a plate bearing the chicken schnitzel sandwich down in front of him. She pointed at the cell phone with silent, incredulous movements, gesturing for Matt to hang up. Matt just leaned back and rolled his eyes.

"The vessel does not matter. All that matters is the calling. Lead us, oh divine one. Tell us your will. Take up your destined mantle. Show us the way."

"Stop picketing funerals," Matt demanded, perhaps a bit more grumpy than usual, it having been less than twenty-four hours since he'd been shot. "Leave the poor families alone. And stop hating gay people. No one cares anymore."

"You would condemn the sinners to the lake of fire. Yes. They have had their chance to repent. No more ministrations. The Lord's table is full."

"No," said Matt, throwing up his hands at the phone even though he knew the pastor couldn't see him. "No, that's not even slightly . . . Just don't be a dick. That's my one commandment. Don't be a dick to anyone."

The phone fell momentarily silent.

"The words you speak," Pastor Fredericks said finally, "are of your old life. The innocence of the sacred child. Truly, God has blessed you to retain it, for only within His heart flows endless love for His children. But God is fire and iron too. So, too, He smites those who ignore his commandments."

He launched into another Bible verse. "But God said: 'You shall not eat of the fruit of the tree that is in the middle of the garden, nor shall you touch it, or you shall die.' But the serpent said to the woman, 'You will not die, for God knows that when you eat of it, your eyes will be opened, and you will be like God.'" He paused. "We have all eaten of the apple, Matthew Callaghan. We are all cursed by its taint. Only you have been born free of it. Only you have spat it out."

"I've spat out taint," said Matt, dryly. "Gross."

"Praise God and all his mercy."

"Pastor, please stop calling. I'm serious. I'm begging you—this really has to stop. I'm not trying to be mean, and I appreciate you being . . ." he struggled for the word ". . . fond of me, but I promise. I swear to you. I'm not some divine vessel."

"Every day you say you're not, Matthew Callaghan, witness of war, prophet of strife. Every day you denounce your calling. And every day you remain all that is pure in this world, clean against this sick corruption, and ever more we know that we must place our hands upon you nonetheless."

"I'm going to hang up now," Matt sighed.

"Go in peace to love and serve the Lord."

"In the name of Christ, go away."

Matt hung up. "That man is going to be the death of me," he complained after a moment.

Giselle, who had sat back down in her original study position at the dining room table, shrugged, indifferent. "Better him than the other shooters?"

"Ha-ha."

"For real, though—I don't know why you keep engaging," said Giselle. Matt rubbed his eyes.

"He's mostly harmless."

"Mostly?"

"And I don't know, I figure if I keep telling them to be better people, maybe one day they'll actually listen?"

"You're very patient," Giselle told him, sucking her fingers free of chicken grease. "You could just get a restraining order."

"I think I like having at least one group dedicated to keeping me alive," Matt mused.

"Hey," the speedster replied, sounding insulted.

"Sorry. Two groups."

"We can let them protect you if you like."

"Please no," said Matt, putting his face in his hands. "They'd make me read their leaflets."

Leaves rustled in the distance. Jane pulled back the branch in front of her, peering down into the valley below. She looked at her two scientist companions, the young, stubble-bound Iranian man and the lean, dark-haired French woman, who were both looking decidedly uncomfortable standing beside Will in their khaki hiking gear.

"Let me get this straight," Jane said. "You put stem cells—human stem cells, and human organs, inside a bunch of monkeys."

"Chimpanzees, technically," the guy, Pejhman, corrected. "And bonobos." Jane stared at him with an expression of incredulous disbelief, causing him to blush and shut up.

"Chimpanzees and bonobos," she repeated, her words back-of-the-freezer frosty. "Dozens of chimpanzees and bonobos, which you crammed full of human DNA. And gave brain transplants."

"There was some unintended growth in the cerebral cortex," the female scientist, Vanessa, protested, "but we didn't actually *transplant* any brains—"

"Grew a bunch of supermonkey brains in a bunch of human-DNA-coded monkeys, who have since gone rogue and"—she stared at them, incredulous—"developed superpowers."

The two scientists hung their heads in what Jane sincerely hoped was shame.

"Yes."

"Yes."

"Superpowered monkeys."

"I'm afraid so."

In the middle of the Madagascan rainforest, overlooking a distant research facility from which there came the far-off sounds of hooting and the occasional screech or explosion, Jane Walker leaned back, put her gloved hands on her hips, and let out a long, exasperated chain of profanity.

"That's not necessary," Vanessa grumbled.

"Shut it," snapped Jane, jabbing a finger at her. "Shut your stupid, supermonkey-making hole." She turned to Will, who was struggling not to laugh.

"I told you we had a big day." He shrugged.

"Unbelievable. Absolutely goddamn un-"—more swear words—"believable." She rounded on the scientists. "So what do you want me to do? Are they actually intelligent? Do I . . ." She pinched the bridge of her nose and sucked in a ragged breath. "I can't believe I'm actually saying this: do I have to go down there and negotiate with a society of intelligent supermonkeys?"

"The brain growth isn't stable," Vanessa insisted, nodding with an enthusiasm that was both unnerving and completely inappropriate. "The cells are degenerating. All throughout their bodies. A month from now, they'll all be dead from cancer, but in the meantime, we don't know . . . um . . ."

"Right, if they'll go Planet of the Apes, Simon West, or just hurl poop at each other." Jane squeezed her eyes shut, feeling the beginning of a one hundred percent nonphysical headache. "Good, well, you're under arrest—you're both under arrest—after all this is over. For reckless experimentation or cruelty to animals or . . . something."

"They were lab-grown primates!" Pejhman protested as Vanessa stammered in with, "But under Madagascan law—"

"I literally do not care," Jane interrupted. She pointed an accusing finger at the scientists. "This is, quite possibly, the stupidest thing I've ever had to do. You go all science-happy gene splicing, and now I've got to go down into the jungle and murder a bunch of supermonkeys. Somebody—somebody!—is going to get punished for this, so help me

God. I like monkeys!" Jane threw up her hands. "I actually like monkeys! They're fluffy and clever, and my mom was a wildlife photographer—"

Unfortunately, the rest of Jane's recollections about her mother were forever lost, for at that exact moment, the canopy shook, and before any of the humans could react, a gigantic chimpanzee came hurtling down from the trees. With patches missing from its fur and its long, fanglike teeth bared, the creature careened screeching toward them, a picture of primate derangement that only moments later grew even more concerning as bright red lasers erupted from its eyes.

"Son of a—!" Jane exclaimed, stumbling as a blast of red energy slammed into her, staggered but less hurt than stunned. The chimpanzee, obviously used to whatever it looked at being instantly vaporized, kept hurtling toward her, its amber eyes widening and the tone of its hoots changing rapidly as its momentum continued carrying it forward.

Jane, her poise quickly recovered, snarled and snapped her arm up, catching the attacking primate on the chin and coat hanger-ing it with a thud into the dirt. The shrieking stopped abruptly.

Jane stared down at the prone body of the chimpanzee, lying gurgling among the leaf litter and the mud.

"Monkeys," she muttered, incredulous. "Murderous mother"—she swore again—"monkeys." She patted angrily at the tendrils of smoke wafting up from her uniform. "Fine. Just . . . Fine!"

Jane rounded on the scientists, her hands balled into fists. "Don't. Move," she snarled; then, without waiting another moment, she grabbed the stunned laser ape by one leg and hurled it like a furry cannonball toward the compound, rocketing off in its wake a moment later in a streak of blazing gold. There was a thud, a crash, some distant screeching—and then a cacophony of hoots began to echo up from the valley floor.

Matt lay back on the lounge with his head facing the ceiling and tried not to think about all the things he wanted to do.

He wanted to go to a party. A real party, with people he didn't know and people who didn't know him from television.

He wanted to go to a pizza parlor. He wanted to go to the movies.

He wanted to ride his bike somewhere. Go hiking. Go Rollerblading, as if that was something he had ever done. Go skiing, even, though he'd only previously been to Aspen twice.

Play basketball, despite never being any good. Go ice-skating, though he was bad at that too. Go to the beach, get sunburnt from being too pale, ick out at waves full of seaweed, and recall in person how much he hated sand. Get drunk in someone's garage. Try to fake ID his way into a bar. Play laser tag. Go dancing. Get high on a hill. Gaze up at the stars.

He wanted to go to college, to learn from a professor whom he could see and who could look knowingly back at him and make him feel accountable, instead of hiding anonymous and distracted behind a computer screen.

He wanted to sit in a classroom and learn in real life, to complain, compare, and commiserate with classmates, not feel the edge of his mind and vision blur from hours spent trying to concentrate on a laptop.

He wanted his world to be larger than this small, stifling corner, which somewhere between the beginning of his isolation and now had turned from a sanctuary into a trap.

Somehow, going out last night had made things worse. Maybe it had been seeing people, all the buildup, the excitement, but whatever it was, to return now to the same confined existence felt . . . suffocating. He understood why he needed to stay inside for the time being; he understood it was for his own good, and that it was the right thing to do. He didn't dispute Jane's oft-stated and quite rational concerns, nor did he disagree with any particular point. He just wished he could go out. That was it. That was the sum of it.

But it would all be over soon. Maybe not tomorrow, maybe not this week, but eventually . . . surely. The court case had finished, the interview was done, the truth was out there. Surely his fifteen minutes of fame were close to expiring; surely everyone would lose interest soon. And then, once the excitement died down, Matt could just fade away like any washed-up celebrity, destined for nothing more thrilling than being question eight in a round of bar trivia. A little more delay, a little more patience—and then normality. Back to all the things he wished he could be doing. Back to what he was always meant for. A normal life.

Matt Callaghan lay with his head back on the couch and allowed himself to feel these feelings of despair and injustice, impatience and longing, because even though they weren't helpful right now, they were legitimate, and simply because he was the master of his mind didn't mean he shouldn't show his emotions some respect.

Giselle's voice echoed out over the couch, and with a weary sigh, Matt dutifully poked his melancholy head up.

"What was that?" he asked, eyes opening.

"They're on their way back," the speedster repeated, still over at the dining table. She had been on her laptop doing conference calls with various Academy contacts, organizing . . . who knows, whatever there was to organize for the Legion, talking into a wireless headset, her words quickly slipping past his attention into a pleasant background hum.

Matt righted himself and sat back up on the couch, wiping crumbs off his shirt. Gross. Had he showered today? Yes, he thought so, this morning after Jane's dumb cardio. Or was that yesterday? Definitely within the last day or two.

A few minutes passed, then the scanner lock beeped, the door swung open, and Jane strode into the apartment covered in blood.

"Not on the carpet!" Matt immediately objected, launching to his feet and pointing at his gore-splattered girlfriend. Jane slid to a stop and glared at him, but Matt unflinchingly held his ground.

"Fly," he commanded. "Slowly. Straight to the bathroom. Straight to the shower." He paused. "I'm assuming none of that is yours."

"No," Jane glowered.

"Good. Levitation, shower, laundry. You look like Carrie gone to prom."

"Who?" Jane grumbled, but she nevertheless bit back any further complaining and floated ignobly past him into their bedroom, mud-slicked golden boots trailing a few inches from the ground. Matt watched her go with an expression of incredulity.

"What'd she do, massacre an entire village?" he asked Will, who'd closed the door after following in behind her. The teleporter, Matt noted, was wearing a hundred percent less blood.

"Renegade supermonkeys," replied Will. He gave Giselle a friendly wave, which the speedster returned.

"Supermonkeys, of course," replied Matt, not even bothering to ask.

The three of them descended onto the couch, Giselle and Will chatting happily about the day's events while they waited for Jane to shower in preparation for their upcoming Legion meeting. Matt idly checked his phone, half listening, and noticed he had a missed video call from Taylor. He called him back.

"Hey," his old Northridge friend answered after a few rings. From his background, he looked to be in a Starbucks somewhere. "Yo. How are you?"

"Hanging in there, baby," Matt replied. "You know. Got you Kevin Eubanks."

"My man." The copper transmuter paused, though Matt noticed his smile was slightly strained. "Congrats on, you know, living."

"You know me. Born lucky."

"Born ugly, more like. Can't believe they let you on TV."

"Screw you, I looked good."

"Nah, nah, I'm just messing with you." On the cramped box of the phone screen, Matt saw Taylor pause. "Really, though, man, how you doing? You alright?"

"I'm okay." Matt sighed. "I mean no, I'm not okay; I was freaking terrified, but I'm fine now. I'm home, and Jane's here, the apartment's safe, and—"

"What the hell are you doing?"

Matt twisted around in the couch to find Jane looming over him. She had emerged from the bedroom, her hair damp and free from chunks of monkey viscera, having reverted to her usual jeans and a gray hoodie. Her wide eyes bored into him like she'd just caught him taking a dump on the carpet, and her mouth hung half open in an incredulous scowl.

"What?" asked Matt, stupefied by her furious expression. "I'm talking to Taylor."

"Hey, Ja—!"

Jane didn't say a word. Instead, with a single ferocious movement, she leaned down, snatched the phone from Matt's hand, and hit *End Call*. Matt sprang to his feet.

"Hey!" he cried, incredulous. "What the hell?"

"Don't you *what the hell* me!" Jane snapped back at him, her expression thunderous. "What the hell is wrong with you?!"

"Nothing's wrong with me, I was just talking!"

"Just talking? On a video call? To some outsider, from our secure apartment, who—"

"Who what? I've been friends with for seven years? What, do you think Taylor's going to betray me now?"

"We don't know!" Jane exclaimed, throwing up her hands, her rough fingers still gripping tight to Matt's phone. Across from the couple, Giselle and Will had ceased their conversation and turned with blank expressions toward the pair. "You didn't ask me! All calls, unless they're securely made—"

"Oh, so now I'm not even allowed to talk to people without—"

"Maybe, if you keep showing off our house to your random—"

"He's not some—"

"Hey!" Giselle's sharp whistle rang out over the top of their argument. Both Matt and Jane fell abruptly silent. They turned to face the speedster, who fixed them both with a hard gaze. "Enough!"

"He shouldn't be—" Jane began to argue, but the words spluttered and faded as Giselle's eyebrows raised, if possible, even higher. Jane retreated into scowling silence.

"Thank you," said the head of the Legion. She looked between the two of them, though her gaze lingered on Jane. "You finished? We good? You want to domestic a little more, or can we get to this meeting on time?"

Matt kept his arms crossed and said nothing. Jane rolled her eyes.

"I'm fine," she said. "We're fine. It's nothing. Let's just go."

Her expression unwavering, Giselle gestured over to the dining room table where she'd set up hers and two other laptops, the webcams facing toward four empty chairs. Will rose from his armchair, maintaining a pointed silence, and the four of them began heading over. As they crossed the room, Matt eyed Jane's jumper.

"There's a toothpaste stain," he told her.

"So?" his girlfriend scowled.

"So, shouldn't you dress more formal?"

"Why?" Jane replied, staring at him with a mixture of irritation and genuine stupidity. Outside the apartment, the sun was just beginning to set.

"I don't know, professionalism? Gravitas? Position of—"

"Jane, honey, you look great," Giselle interrupted, cutting Matt off with a glare. "Let's go. People are waiting, chop-chop." The couple fell silent. Matt rolled his eyes before sinking down into one of two chairs positioned in front of one of the laptops. A moment later, Jane sat down next to him, her arms crossed, simmering.

A few seconds of silence passed before Matt sighed and begrudgingly leaned over to log onto Jane's computer for her. His girlfriend muttered something that lesser men might have mistaken for thanks, remaining as allergic to remembering passwords as she was to boundaries or personal hygiene.

"Hello, Giselle, can you—can you hear me?"

"I can hear you," the speedster answered as Wally's voice echoed out of the computers' speakers. Matt leaned over again and muted Jane's microphone to stop the reverb. "I can hear you. Can you see me?"

The preliminary back-and-forth continued as more participants from the Academy and members of the Legion joined the call from across the globe. Apart from occasionally prodding Jane to sit up straighter and stop scowling, the response to which was sullen and muted at best, Matt soon found himself zoning out.

"First and foremost, of course, I'd like to acknowledge our heroic dead . . ."

There were probably a great number of people around the world who would have killed to sit in on a Legion of Heroes internal conference. If Matt had had to guess, pre-Academy, what a meeting of the world's foremost superheroes would look like, he would have imagined a lot of dramatic speeches, fiery denouncements, and fists banging on tables.

But it turned out, having now sat in on a few of them, that meetings between people with the power to change the world were pretty much the same as meetings between anyone. The Legion might've been a super organization, but it was still a human one. And now that there was officially an active membership, and with so many of the Ashes—trainees from the original Legion—gone, and the institution no longer beholden to the fake Captain Dawn, Giselle and the others *were* the organization. There were rules to enliven. Strategy to discuss. Minutes to take.

"I think, personally, if we're going to provide an official response . . ."

Engaged, generously, in about five percent of what was going on, Matt took the opportunity to send Taylor a quick apology text and then to check his email. It wasn't that his opinion wasn't listened to at these meetings; it was just that he was sort of . . . unqualified. Superheroing had never been his speciality, nor his interest. He had no particular powers, everybody knew now, nor any real insights worth adding.

He was part of the Legion, sure, and beloved in his own special way, but sometimes, Matt felt more like a mascot, the team's earnest little puppy who everyone was constantly concerned might wander in front of a truck. Then there was his unofficial yet no less widely known status as Jane's romantic partner (marital bickering aside), which carried with it its own license to speak.

Everyone shut up and stayed silent when he said something because if they didn't, the power of Dawn glared gold daggers at them. But that didn't mean Matt really received anything more than polite attention. A boyfriend or a dog. It was good to have a choice.

"It's not as one-sided as that—"

"I'm not trying to be disingenuous—"

There were unread messages in his mailbox. Quite a few of them, which was hardly unusual these days. Matt the Human had fanboys, fangirls, extensive legal battles, and merchandising contracts. Most got filtered through their agent. His inbox still needed clearing several times a day.

". . . been a very effective program . . ."

An email from Azleena, Morningstar's new resident genius, caught his eye, a forward from the police to Legion forensics. Standard information exchange, a simple file-sharing link. Though he'd already heard the key points, Matt opened it anyway, scanning over the attachments with an impassive eye.

"Maybe if we put together a memorandum . . ."

Arrest report. Fingerprints. The perpetrator had, once he got an attorney present, consented to controlled psychic interrogation. The transcripts of those were always a bit trippy, being chain-of-thought auto-generated by a computer. There was a verbal record, too, which was much more procedural.

Did you talk to anyone before you did it?
No. I just knew it was right.
Where did you get the firearm?
Liberty Arms gun store. Near the Applebee's.
And the bullets?
Same place.
How much did you pay?
$8,999.90.

Nine thousand dollars for a freaking gun, Matt mentally whistled. Around him, the Legion's conversation had turned to a chemical spill in

Mongolia. Despite her initial slouching beside him, Jane was now riled up and actively involved, arguing loudly for Legion intervention. Others on the call pushed back. Matt read on.

How did you know where to find them?
Who?
Mr. Callaghan. Ms. Walker.
I don't . . . I plead the Fifth.
You're not on trial here, Mr. Louch. You're not in the witness stand. Are you saying your answer would incriminate you?
I believe my client seeks to exercise his Miranda Right.
He's welcome to. Except I was under the impression Mr. Louch was cooperating. That's the only way you're getting any time off this sentence.
You don't have to answer that, Stuart.
[PAUSE ON TAPE]
I had a hunch.
You had a hunch?
Yeah. I was reading some people on Bluin, and they were saying—
Bluin?
It's a message board. A news-sharing site. You can join groups according to what you're interested in. For like fishing, or TV shows, or political . . .
Noted. Continue.

Matt's ears pricked up as his family was mentioned, but it turned out they were just talking about getting age-appropriate tutors for his sister Sarah's schooling. They'd covered this ground before; it was down to considering CVs. He turned back to the transcript.

Someone on the NeverSurrender BluBoard was posting speculation about where they were going to be. Because we knew they were going to have to come in for filming. Someone said their aunt was in the crowd. The studio audience. So we knew it was the usual building in New York.
And someone knew the security arrangements?
No. Just speculation. People talking about what they thought. What they'd do. Making plans. Theories. Someone wrote that they'd try to sneak out the back. I don't know. I thought it made sense.
You flew five hundred miles on a hunch?
Wouldn't you? If you knew your liberty was in danger? Patriots act.

What my client means to say is that this was his mindset at the time.
Yeah. Of course.
What happened when you arrived?
I waited. There was a crowd. I kept myself cloaked, and then, I don't know. I took a shot, but she stopped me.
Jane Walker?
Yeah.
Who, I'd like to point out, violently assaulted my client.
You're welcome to make sympathy your defense.

Coincidence. It all came down to goddamn coincidence. A million idiots typing on a million keyboards until eventually one of them struck the truth. Matt rubbed his eyes with the back of his hand and tried to zone back into what the Legion were saying. They'd moved onto admissions grading. He zoned back out.

As he continued to sit there, though, Matt realized something was bothering him. Not the gunman's words or his explanations. Not his demeanor, which even through the emotionless pages of a typescript, Matt thought seemed to contain a little bit of remorse. He didn't know for sure, but Matt had read a few of these things by now, and felt like he could decently interpret.

No, it was . . . something different. Something about the whole thing. Something just felt . . . incongruous. He scrolled back to the top of the document.

State your name for the record.
Stuart Milton Louch.
Occupation?
Vacuum repairman, Great Lakes Vacuum and Electrical.

A vacuum repairman. A divorced vacuum repairman, with a home loan and two teenage kids. Matt felt himself frown. Vacuum repairman, and he'd gone out and paid nine thousand dollars for a gun, plus airfares? Was vacuum repair that much of a lucrative profession that between a mortgage, child support, living expenses, and alimony, a repairman would have nearly ten thousand dollars just lying around?

He flicked through to the police's subpoenaed financial records. One bank account, no credit cards. No new loan applications either. *He's a fanatic*, Matt reminded himself. *He traveled halfway across the country to kill you.* Surely it made sense that if someone believed enough to commit murder, they believed enough to empty their savings account.

Yet, it wasn't the belief that niggled at him. No, it was the . . . organization. The way this guy had looked last night, and now the police photos of him . . . he just didn't strike Matt as the sort of man who was good with money. If Matt had been walking down the street and seen Stuart Louch pass him, he would have pegged him as a man who lived paycheck to paycheck; not from any empirical evidence, but just . . . he had that look. Call it years of people watching. Call it gut instinct.

". . . to better identify our needs moving forward . . ."

Matt flicked over to the telepathic autoscript. There was an art to reading these, he'd found. You had to sort of unfocus your eyes and read not so much the words on the page but the vague direction they were heading. It was important not to get bogged down in any particular rambling phrase or detail; one rode the waves of echoing internalization and drifted where they seemed to go.

Gunmetal bullet. The man walks into the shop, and he's nervous, though he tells himself there is no reason to be afraid, there's no way they can know. Pen on the line, inked blue, dark intentions. I will wait fourteen days.

Did you wait?

Yes. I saw it on a billboard. How could I not know. My heart raced; herein lies my opportunity. A when, a where, and I am refraction, pure and glass. Let never my conscience find me. He is but a boy barely older than my son. Put it away, drown it.

Regretting, then, the purchase.

No, not to water blood to liberty. Of tyrants, heroes, even innocent to the slaughter. It cannot wait; it must be done. Unfortunate. Thoughts as I cannot think them, he is a good boy. Bluin board, PreserveHumanity, "What if he had a disease?" "One for the many." One day, my children will thank me. They would. Will they?

A long stretch of thought then—a long and winding diatribe about his children, a sense of purpose, a sense of loss. These things went on for dozens of pages, at times quite in depth. Matt continued to hold his mind loose and kept scanning.

And then, there, at the bottom of the page, he saw it.

Providence, then. The lottery ticket.

Matt's heart skipped a beat.

He clicked back into the gunman's bank records. There; three months ago. He had cashed a lottery ticket—twenty thousand, four hundred and thirty-two dollars—a week after it had been bought. Nobody in the police had thought anything of it. It was a coincidence. He'd just so happened to have the cash.

Except—

Except—

Matt's heart raced.

Suddenly alert, suddenly awake, he pulled up the man's bank statements, racing line by line through transactions, fingers trembling, feeling like his eyes were going to burn into the screen. Around him, the sound of the meeting blurred completely into white noise, distant words, irrelevant. All irrelevant, until he knew—until he found—

No. There was nothing there. Matt searched again, scrolling up through weeks, months, years. Nothing. Nothing again, and nothing. No odd deposits. No withdrawals at casinos or transactions with the special code given by banks for gambling purchases.

In the last two years, Stuart Louch had only bought and cashed one lottery ticket. One ticket, and he had won twenty thousand dollars. Enough to buy a gun and a plane ticket. Enough to get in place to kill.

Matt's heart felt like it was about to beat right out of his chest.

Coincidence. Coincidence. It had to be a coincidence. Except . . .

Who did they know that used the lottery?

INTERLUDE

I kill approximately one person per week. Sometimes more. Sometimes fewer. A message comes to my cell phone twenty-four hours before I am needed, along with details of the convicted's crimes. That is part of my contract with the United States Department of Justice. I want to know who I am killing. I want to know the reason I am taking their life.

Exactly a day later, a car comes. An unadorned car, black, white, or silver in color, always a different make and model, neither expensive nor cheap. It pulls up outside the house and makes no noise. I know it is them because the timing is impeccable. I know it is them because the driver gets out and opens the door.

I walk out, I walk in, I sit down, I close the door. It takes approximately eight seconds. The risk of outside contact during this period is low, though not negligible. But the man in the car will not open the door until he can see there is no one present on the footpath. The contract ordains this also.

I am driven to an airport, a private jet. The car pulls up to the mobile passenger stairs, and I get out, walk up, close the hatch, sit down. The cockpit door is locked, and there is no one save the pilot aboard. We take off in silence and land in silence, and I stay seated the entire time. Were there to be an emergency, I know where to find the exits, life vest, and parachute.

The plane lands. I stand up, open the hatch, walk down the stairs, and into another waiting car. Again, I am driven. The car twists and turns and pulls up at that day's prison. There is an empty hallway, a waiting door. My door is opened, the driver stands clear, I step outside. I see no one, speak to no one, my path clear from beginning to end.

Save for the dead man.

Usually, they are men. Rarely women, though not never, and when they are, their crimes are the worst imaginable. I read all of them through. I think about all of them, about their victims, imagine how it must have felt, how they suffered. I force myself to envision every image, every detail. He who imparts justice must understand crime. I am not a mindless tool.

When I step into the final room, I meet responses of many varieties. Confusion. Realization. Anger, fear, hatred, acceptance. Contempt. Some of them plead, some threaten, some bargain. Some say nothing, like if they do not consent to my presence, then I cannot end their lives. None of it matters. I do not say a word. I look at them, and I picture their atrocities, and when they draw their final breath beneath my fingertips, it feels just.

I read when I am not killing people.

I read books. Every Tuesday, when Emily comes, I receive new books. A book is a window to another world, another life.

I no longer read newspapers. Once, when a newspaper was being delivered, it was thrown through my front window, and the telekinetic American teenager who had been delivering it came to my door to apologize. Had coincidence pulled but a few more strings, I could have accidentally touched and killed him. I canceled my subscription immediately.

I do not read catalogues, pamphlets, or flyers. At one time, I experimented with having no mailbox in an attempt to avoid receiving anything of that nature, but those distributing promotional material soon began slipping it beneath my door. I now have a mailbox. It is a condition of my contract that whoever transports me on the way back from an execution empties it of unsolicited material. If they did not, the box would get full, and people might start bringing flyers to my door again. That risk is unacceptable.

I read the Internet. It is an endless, teeming ocean of new ideas and information. Sometimes, I even write on the Internet too, communicate with other people, though never openly and never using the name Qiang or my surname, or anything else that could identify me.

On the Internet, everyone is equal. People speak freely or, well, freely enough. I read about things that interest me. I read about other places in the world, about life and death. I read discussions between real people in real time. I feel like I am there, like I am one of them, like they care about me, like I am learning. Like they will notice when I am gone.

I find myself reading the Internet more and more.

It is Tuesday, and I wake up at 5:00 a.m.

I do not rest further, nor do I wait for my alarm to sound. I check the cameras, confirm the house is free from intruders, and get up. I run on the treadmill; I listen to Schubert's Fantasie in F Minor. I shower, I brush my teeth, I apply skincare products, I dress, I button, I pull on my gloves. Today is my best shirt, the pink one. Salmon. I have read on the Internet that women are attracted to modern, educated men who are well groomed and confident enough to wear nontraditional but not garish colors.

Over the shirt I don a suit jacket, black to match my gloves. It makes me sick to think that perhaps they look unusual, but there is nothing I can do about it. The black jacket hides them best, makes them seem coordinated rather than frightening.

Let her think I am cold. Please, let her just think I am cold.

I check my buttons no less than fifteen times, because today is the day of highest risk, and I must not—I cannot—fail at this juncture. Vigilance has its heart in repetition.

I recheck the cameras. I descend. I have breakfast. I clean my plate, and then I sit in silence in the living room, staring at the crack around the edge of the curtains, watching the empty footpath, the front lawn. I wring my hands together in my lap, tap my feet without meaning to. I cannot summon the concentration to read. I know it is irresponsible—that I should be using this time to better myself—but I cannot resist. I have to wait.

"Morning," I whisper to no one. "Morning. Morning. Morning."

Finally, at 10:17, her van pulls up on the street outside. I clutch both arms of the chair, throat suddenly tight. I hear her footsteps on the path, on the one-two concrete steps. I hear her shuffle some boxes down. I hear the doorbell.

I close my eyes and count to twelve, then I rise from my seat and go to her.

I open the door.

"Morning," she says, and she smiles at me, and in that moment, just that moment, all is well.

"Morning," I reply.

Emily. Perfect Emily. She is half an inch shorter than me, fair skinned, with dimpled cheeks and a splash of freckles beneath her radiant eyes. Her hair is thick and wavy, red and brown, the color of potter's clay, flowing free beneath her cap and down her back in a waterfall of autumn. A neat white smile spreads up through her doll-like features, and her emerald eyes sparkle with life.

She hums as she walks; I've heard her. She is well rounded and strong, carrying every box she brings without complaint. I imagine she was raised on a farm, running through wheat fields and dust clouds. I do not know her power, but sometimes, in my dreams, I imagine her shaking off her drab olive uniform and unfurling blue gossamer wings in the morning sunlight. Her arms, like always, are bare. Her voice, as always, is warm.

"Got a few coming in today, don'tcha?" she says. I don't know whether this is a question or a statement, so I just try to smile and nod. It does not seem to perturb her.

"Do you want to start on those ones, and I'll head back to the truck?" She peers up at me expectantly, not two feet away.

"Of course," I manage to respond. She turns, and for a moment, all I can do is watch her. Then I catch myself staring and panic and, feeling sweat building inside my gloves, bend to pick up the boxes she has deposited. Fruit and vegetables. Supplies, sundries. Books. Emily is my sole link to the outside world, beyond my journeys to the prisons. She is the only thing keeping me alive.

I carry the first two boxes into the house and to the kitchen. Emily brings the next two; I take those, then the next. When it is done, I come back to the door to stand opposite her, heart churning. Now comes the riskiest part.

I reach into my suit and pull out a long white envelope. I hold it out, directly at her, my gloved right hand grasping only the barest tip. She smiles at me, reaches up, and takes it. She opens the envelope, counts the money, then looks at me with a small, wounded smile, with disbelief.

"You've gone over again."

"For your trouble."

"Come on, you're too generous, Mister Q—"

"Quinten, please." An Anglicized name; easier, more palatable.

"Quinten. I don't need this. It's too much." She smiles, looking a little amused, a little embarrassed.

"There were a lot of boxes."

"Not that many. It's my job." She puts a hand on her hip and shakes her head. "What am I going to do with you?" she asks, bemused. She slaps the envelope businesslike on her wrist, then slides it into her back pocket. "Trading must be going well, then."

I have told her I am a trader. She has not asked what I trade. She can never know the truth.

"About the same."

"Yeah? Did you see the Callaghan thing on TV the other night?"

I hesitate. "I, uh . . . I don't have a television." I resolve immediately to purchase one.

"Really? What do you do for fun?"

"I, um . . . I read."

Emily laughs. "You don't say." She points with her chin to the space on the porch where the boxes had been. "I had a look at this week's. I saw *The Amber Spyglass*? That was the only one I know."

"You know it?"

"Yeah. Have you read the first two?"

"They should all be in there."

"Aww." She makes a face and holds a gentle hand over her heart. "It's so sad. I won't spoil it. But it made me cry."

I don't know what to say. Emily pauses, then she grins up at me, mischievous.

"Your English is getting better."

"I . . . Thank you." My heart skips a beat. "Emily."

"Please; Em."

"Em." She fixes me with a warm smile.

"Same time next week?"

"And every week," I answer, breathless. Emily laughs.

"At least until I get a better job. See you." She turns and flicks a wave behind her as she strolls back down the pathway, toward the brown delivery van waiting on the road. I watch her go. The engine starts, and just like that, I am left standing alone in my silent doorway.

Just like that, Emily is gone.

It is 6:42 p.m. My eyes blur, and my head hurts. I have been staring at the computer screen for hours, reading all that I can. "10 Tips for Approaching Girls." "5 Conversation Secrets I Wish I Knew."

At first, my free hand made notes, but now, the paper lies cast aside. I despair. The more I read, the sicker I feel—more disgusted, more ashamed. No normal man must read this. No normal, complete person ever struggles with these basic fundamentals of human interaction, elusive only to failures and freaks. The more I learn, the more the depths of my inadequacy—the breadth of the chasm in my being—becomes obvious. It is unbridgeable. I have missed my chance. I am broken. I cannot be fixed.

Ding-ding. Ding-ding. My phone rings. I glance at the screen, suck a deep breath, gather my feelings, and answer.

"Hello, Liang." For the first time this week, my mouth speaks its native tongue.

"Brother."

"How are you?"

"Fine."

"Hmm." I am his junior by three minutes, yet often, I feel the older. "What news?"

"Nothing. It is simply my usual call." Silence. Even in Cantonese, the conversation is stilted.

"How is Hong Kong?"

"Raining. You can't step outside without getting drenched." Pause. "How is America?"

"It is . . ." I hesitate, looking around me. At the bookshelves laden high, the plush carpet, the expensive furniture. At emptiness, the cold and aching night. "It is the same as anywhere."

"Yes. Understandable." More silence. "And you . . . Are you well? Generally?" I hear him sound resentful even to ask.

"I am fine," I respond, the words cool. "I see you are in Hao's photos again."

"Yeah. We had a few drinks. It was his birthday."

"There seem to be many birthdays."

"It's just an HK thing. It is hard to explain. They are all low-key."

"Of course." I feel my fingers kneading together. "And you don't . . . ? They don't . . . ?"

"Of course not, Qiang," he snaps. "How would I? Why would I? I am perfectly safe."

"Of course."

The phone falls silent. Eventually, Liang's voice retreats from its defensive position.

"I am sorry for the length of time between calls. Work has been busy."

"Yes, no, of course. It is like that for me too."

"I have been meaning to come and visit you."

"Of course. Truth be told, my schedule has little space anyway. And I am reading so much that time often gets away from me. There are barely enough hours in the day."

"Truly?"

"Truly."

"Well, that is good." Pauses drip, drip, drip into the conversation. "Oh, I suppose you should know. I am seeing a girl."

My heart stops for a moment. "That's . . . How wonderful."

"It is. I think I have fallen for her."

"What is her name? Where did you meet?"

"Melody—Well, she goes by M. We met . . . ah, at a social engagement. The Chamber of Commerce. Very dull."

"That is nice for you. She has a nice name."

A momentary lull. "She wants to be a singer."

"Does she have a good voice?"

"Lovely."

"Hopefully she will succeed, then."

Another pause. Liang does not ask if I am seeing anyone. He at least has that much sensitivity.

"Well . . . keep well."

"You too. Be safe."

"Of course." A click, and the call ends. I put the phone down and stare blankly at the wall. I do not know how long I sit there. I do not know what time the tears start trickling from my eyes.

THE WATCHER'S WARNING, THE WORLD BETWEEN THE WALLS

Twisted: The Science of Peculiar Powers
by Sylvia Funkstone
Available now from Barnes & Noble, RRP $19.95
Recommended for readers ten to fourteen

Mysteries and Divines

So far in this book, we have talked about peculiar powers that come from many places; from people who are born able to use a "standard" power in a special way, to people whose powers are shaped by their own special genetics, to people whose powers have changed because of an accident, a chemical reaction, or a change in their body or mind. But there is another type of peculiar powers other than the ones you've already read about—a type that is at the same time the rarest, the most famous, and the most difficult to study. These are, of course, powers that from the moment they first materialize are absolutely, utterly unique.

There are not many people—possibly only enough to count on one hand—in recorded history whose powers fall into this category. Among scientists who research superpowers, these people are called "Divines." This is not a very helpful name, as it can wrongly give the impression that the people with these extraordinary powers are some extra level of supernatural, maybe even gods. This is not correct; underneath their gifts, they are still ordinary humans, with the same feelings and fears and flaws as you or I. But the powers they possess are extraordinary, and often so powerful that they place those who have them in a category all their own.

The first and most obvious person who comes to mind when discussing unique powers is Walter Reid, aka Captain Dawn. In all the years since the Aurora Nirvanas, no other person has possessed Captain Dawn's power of unlimited energy, which not only gives him enhanced strength, speed, and the ability to fly, but which is constantly released from his body, shrouding him in an almost impenetrable shield.

This golden energy is so potent that, when released, it can destroy almost anything, and has led to his moniker, "The Power of a Hundred Suns," which while unlikely to be technically true (nobody is really suggesting that Captain Dawn actually has energy equivalent to a hundred stars stored within his body) certainly gives an idea of the amount of power we are dealing with.

The second and third unique abilities in this category will also be familiar to fans of superheroes. "The Brothers Darkness"—twin brothers Charles and Edward Lewis—were supervillains fought by the Legion of Heroes in 1981, and are collectively the only other people to definitively be classified as "Divines." Charles's power, which is still not understood properly to this day, was to create darkness; Edward's power was to control it.

The powers of the Brothers Darkness is a mystery that has troubled scientists since the moment it was discovered. This is because, scientifically speaking, there is actually no such thing as darkness—there are only places which are not, at that moment, reflecting light. But to the shock of all observers, what Charles Lewis was able to create was darkness—a pitch black, crushingly heavy darkness that seemed to consume light from everything nearby.

This singular phenomenon, although extensively recorded, has never been properly explained, and perplexes scientists even now. The ability was so shockingly powerful, and such a fundamental violation of our understanding of the laws of physics, that it left researchers no choice but to make it the second power to ever earn the title "Divine."

From there, the list of "Divines" that have ever been identified becomes less clear-cut. There are some who argue that people who possess powers others also have, but whose strength with those powers is so beyond what anybody else can do, should be included in the "Divine" category.

Elsa Arrendel, famously, when asked about the definition, responded that the Legion of Heroes had three Divines: Captain Dawn, herself, and another person whom she failed to specify. It is not clear whom she meant by this, or if it was even accurate. But certainly, it is arguable that there are people out there whose powers are unique in how strong they are, and who overshadow others with the same ability in a way beyond any skill or training.

Then, there are people who seem to have unique abilities but whose powers do not seem to have the same strength or impact. As a foremost example of this, take Liverpool resident Charlotte Bell. Charlotte is, to the best of current knowledge, the world's only historiographer—a person with the ability to touch an item and know what has occurred nearby and where that item has been.

The implications of Charlotte's power—which have been thoroughly tested and confirmed to be real by both Scotland Yard and the FBI—are staggering. Prior to discovering Charlotte, there had never been any confirmed record of a person whose powers involved time; neither the ability to travel through time itself nor the ability to see what was going to happen in the future.

But Charlotte's ability, which supernaturally allows her to see the past in a way that defies all logic, opens the door for the question: Are other time powers possible? Are there other Divines out there, waiting to be discovered, or waiting to be born? If it is possible for someone to have power over something as fundamental as energy or darkness or time, what else is possible? Matter? Reality itself? Death?

* * *

It was a testament to Matt's years of mental discipline that he did not immediately jump up screaming. Instead, it was as if his mind and breathing had shut down—the apartment, the others, the sound of conversation, all of it spun in a blur, circling and pressing in against his forehead.

Heat spread across his face; his hands clenched into fists, balled up so hard it felt like his fingernails digging into his palms were going to draw blood. Suddenly, despite the night air, Matt felt himself sweating. It was all he could do not to shake.

He needed . . . needed somewhere to . . .

Sitting beside him, still engrossed in the discussion, Jane remained oblivious to Matt's sudden distress. Slowly, forcing himself to breathe, Matt moved his fingers over to her keyboard and typed with trembling hands into the chat box, letting her read what he wrote before deleting it.

Bathroom.

Jane spared him a brief glance and nodded. A second later, somebody on the conference call said something she disagreed with, and in an instant, she was back to arguing. Matt slowly pushed himself to his feet, his legs feeling like they were about to give way.

He stumbled away from the dining table, through his and Jane's bedroom, and into the bathroom beyond. Trembling, his hands closed the door, and the sound of discussion in the living room fell muted. Suddenly, there was silence. Suddenly, he was alone.

Matt sat—lid closed—on the toilet and sucked in deep, shuddering breaths, trying to gather his thoughts.

Almost a year ago, a reclusive Greek psychic named Cassandra Atropos had lured him and Jane to an abandoned Albanian farmstead as part of a Legion of Heroes expedition by pretending to be clairvoyant. Rather than trying to hurt them, Cassandra's goal seemed to have been to distract Klaus Heydrich, who had been hunting clairvoyant powers, long enough to give Matt *just* enough information to maneuver him where he needed to be.

Chief among this information were numbers for the following month's lottery. The point, though, was never for Matt to play them—the numbers were a red herring, readied evidence that Matt could use at the proper time to distract his Legion assessor and keep his true humanity under wraps.

Except, the numbers, the information, and the misdirection—none of it had actually come from Cassandra. Cassandra had been merely the vessel, a telepathic conduit given a glimpse into a fourth-dimensional reality overwhelming enough to make you want to gouge your eyes out. The true architect behind the whole scheme had been the Time Child, a strange and inexplicable being who flittered in and out of existence with neither name nor explanation, manipulating things for its own hidden agenda. In this instance, the lottery had been the Time Child's tool—a way of keeping Matt safe.

And now, the lottery was trying to kill him.

Which meant the Time Child was trying to kill him.

The Time Child *had* killed him.

Ho-lee shi—

Matt felt like he was going to hurl. All these attacks. All these coincidences. They'd spent ages discussing the kid, post Detroit, post everything. Hours of huddled conversation, theorizing safe from prying ears and eyes. Who they were, what they wanted, how the hell they'd just shown up. But the sudden discovery of the lottery ticket, the hand of fate swung suddenly not to save Matt's life but to end it, turned all that on its head.

Because inherent in their thinking, Matt realized now, was an assumption neither of them had realized they'd been making: that the Child was benevolent. They had assumed the boy—if it even was a boy, if it wasn't just something that looked like a boy, if it was even real, if it was even human—had their best interests at heart, because it had seemed to be working to keep them alive, or at least move them away from imminent slaughter.

Then, on top of that, there'd been Cassandra's rantings, her proclamations that they were watched over and loved, which had dovetailed nicely into the presumption that the Child genuinely cared for their safety, that it was on their side.

But that didn't need to be true. Because Cassandra could've been a liar or been lied to, set up or shown exactly what the Time Child wanted, like Matt had done when the Black Death psychically scoured his mind.

What if the Child had deliberately set out to create an impression that it was harmless? What if it had wanted them to think it was the good guy? Or, wait, what if it was actually trying to be the good guy but had such a wildly twisted understanding of right and wrong—

Or simply a broader view. Matt felt his face pale. What if the Time Child's goal hadn't simply been to save the world from the Black Death, but to save the world in general? To protect against both that enormous, lingering threat, and all threats yet to come? Threats not just to one person, but to all of superhumanity? And after destroying a tyrannical blood-based empath, what if the next biggest threat looming ahead on the timeline was something completely different, something like the ability to take away people's powers and—

Oh no. Oh God. It all made sense. One of Matt's biggest questions, something he'd never quite understood, was: if the Child had simply wanted to stop the Black Death, why hadn't he just made a vaccine from Matt's blood? Jane had thought, and he'd accepted, that it was because the process would have been too slow, that even if they'd stabbed the Black Death with some sort of anti-powers serum, Heydrich would still have had too much time to run loose.

But what if that wasn't it at all? What if the reason was actually simpler? What if the Child never wanted there to be any way to take away people's powers?

Oh God. It all made sense now. What did they actually know about the Time Child? That it played the big picture? That it was more than happy to sacrifice lives to save them? And what would be the next greatest crisis looming on the horizon, after Heydrich was eliminated?

Easy: the death of the superhuman. Matt's blood, the banality inside him, extracted and extrapolated, used to put Earth's population back under authoritarian control. To make powers a privilege, something governments didn't have to freely tolerate, something that could be gifted or taken away.

The Second Amendment people weren't crazy.

He was the next great threat to mankind.

Without even realizing it, Matt had gotten to his feet and now frantically paced back and forth around the confined space of the bathroom.

Of course. Of course! It all made sense now. The Child had needed him to defeat Heydrich, but the minute that was done, Matt was no longer an asset but a terrible, unwitting threat. The longer he lived, the longer he publicly existed, the higher the chance of his genetic makeup getting out. They'd been vigilant so far, but in a year? Ten years? Fifty? Every move he made, every goddamn flake of dandruff, all carried with it the potential to subjugate humanity . . . so the Child wanted him dead. The Child *needed* him dead. Not out of maliciousness, but for the future of Earth.

The room spun before Matt's eyes.

What did he do? What the hell did he do?! He wasn't equipped for this. This wasn't something he could prevent, something he could escape from; because on the one hand, there was the Child, a literal time traveler, an elusive, almost godlike being seemingly capable of being anywhere and doing anything, but on the other hand, there was what happened if the Child failed. The looming dystopic future it was murdering him to prevent.

Oh God. Matt's legs gave way, and he staggered back onto the toilet. If he died, the world lived. If he lived, the world lost.

Breathe. Oh God, breathe, he tried to tell himself. A dozen mental calming exercises bounced fruitlessly off his brain, clattering like colored play blocks. He didn't know—There was no—But so many things made sense now. How the killers kept finding him. How them leaving the *Today Show* had gotten out. For months now, he'd had this niggling feeling that something weird was happening. Now he understood why.

There was a conspiracy to kill him—just not in the way he'd thought.

Breathe. Oh my God. Breathe.

Well, that does it, Matt thought, his head lolling deliriously upward to look at his reflection in the bathroom mirror, ghost white. *I'm screwed.*

There was no way out of this one. Like, he'd had some wins, you know; he was reasonably resourceful, but holy crap, this was simply above his paygrade. A time traveler. A freaking *time traveler*. How was he supposed to win against a *time traveler*? He might as well have chopped off both hands and attempted to swim the Pacific.

Except—*Wait. Hold on. Wait.* Suddenly, Matt's back shot up, the top of his spine banging painfully against the tank of the toilet. His heart surged with a sudden, elated rush. He was alive. Impossibly, illogically, he—he was still alive!

Abruptly, Matt's brow furrowed. Wait, why was he still alive? That didn't make sense. The Child could easily have killed him. It could have . . . Well, heck, any number of things. A terrifying cornucopia of options, actually, Matt realized, his mind suddenly awash with Wile E. Coyote–style visions of death. Traffic accident. Air bubble in his hospital line. Ball bearing dropped out of an aircraft, cyanide in his milkshake, carbon monoxide leak, a precisely placed bot fly. God, any one of the many, many bullets that had been shot at him.

But no. The Child hadn't done any of those things.

Why *hadn't* it?

It took Matt a few seconds of staring intently, brow furrowed, at the floor tiles before the answer suddenly came to him. Jane. Jane had the Child's powers. Admittedly, she was still an amateur when it came to using them, but nevertheless, she had done it. She had successfully skimmed the surface of madness and traveled through time to save his life. Jane, the complicating factor.

Suddenly, Matt found himself leaning forward on the toilet like he was fighting a very serious poo. What if, he reasoned, what if getting Jane to copy Captain Dawn had been the only way to bring down Heydrich? And what if, logically, the only way to achieve that had been for her to take the Child's powers? What if, to the Child, that entire play had been calculated? What if they had gambled on Jane getting what they needed, going where they showed her, and then not using the ability further? Or even better, eventually giving it up?

Because—and Matt's face suddenly paled—she'd been under pressure to give it up. *He* had been pressuring her. And all the Child had to do was wait for her to listen, wait for Jane's resistance to buckle against Matt's badgering, wait for her to question herself, to believe her boyfriend's insistent argument that it was "noble."

And then, the moment she did, well, there'd be no recourse. The Child could kill Matt immediately, without mercy, bullet through the back of the head. But so long as Jane was still standing there, so long as she held the Child's power, any sudden and mysterious death Matt might suffer might send her not only reaching for the ability, but growing suspicious. Might make her practice. Might make her improve.

Holy crap. Okay. Matt's head was reeling. That was why there'd been so many unsuccessful assassins. That was why each one had come close, but he'd never truly gotten hurt. Oh my God. It all made sense now. They hadn't been meant to succeed; they'd been meant to make this last one seem organic, to draw suspicion away from the fact it was all a setup, that it was anything other than inevitable, some random lunatic acting of their own accord.

And then, what had been the hope after? That Jane would be too scared to attempt time travel? That she would, but be unable to go deep enough? That she'd try and be swept away?

A dark cloud fell over Matt's face. Because that, too, struck him as a plan most convenient. Jane destroys herself trying to save him; two rats with one rock. In one fell swoop, the Time Child would have eliminated him, the greatest threat to superhumans, and simultaneously destroyed the most powerful being on the planet, the only other person who could time travel. Who, for all Matt knew, might be number three on the Child's hit list, below him and the Black Death.

Jesus Christ. It felt like someone had replaced his bones with electricity. *Count to ten*, Matt tried to tell himself. *One, two, three . . .* He closed his eyes and ran his hands through his hair, his fingers trembling, focusing on the words—only to abruptly stop at six and for his eyes to fly open, his mind racing with another unbidden thought.

He'd made another potentially erroneous assumption, Matt realized. He'd assumed—because he supposed he hadn't seen any evidence to the contrary, and he guessed the magnitude of the Child's ability had just seemed to imply it—but he'd assumed the Child's power was unique. That it was (excluding Jane) one of those one-of-a-kind powers, sort of like Captain Dawn's, that through sheer luck or coincidence only manifested in one person.

But what if it wasn't? What if there were other people, other "Children" out there in the time web, with different ideas and agendas, various competing goals? What if it wasn't the Child—*their* Child—trying to kill him? What if it was another one? What if the reason all the assassination attempts had failed wasn't because the Child had set them up, but because they had prevented them?

Holy crap. Matt leaned forward, staring intently at the white wooden cupboards beneath the sink. Okay, God, this was—Well, this was somehow even more distressing. One mysterious time gremlin was concerning enough, but two? More? How many? What if there were hundreds of these little critters out there, shooting back and forth across the cosmos from thousands of years in the superhuman future, each infinitely screwing and unscrewing and rescrewing time? What if whether he lived or died wasn't a contingency; what if his very existence was a war?

I . . . Screw me sideways, Matt thought. His brain was so hot it was practically cooking, and he wouldn't have been surprised if any second now, he started smelling burnt toast. He went to sit down again, only to realize he already was.

Jesus. What did he do? Because this theory, though perhaps more complicated, was no less feasible, and definitely carried with it no less existential threat. A dozen time travelers didn't make things better. It made them worse. Much worse. So far, he'd only seen "their"—*their* in quotation marks—Child, the pale blue-eyed bastard, but that didn't necessarily mean anything. Maybe the others were more inconspicuous. Maybe there were rules, politics, even alliances. God help us.

How in the mother-loving heck was he supposed to navigate competing omniscient time factions? What the hell was he supposed to do?

Breathe, Matt reminded himself, *just breathe.* Although a panicked, snarky bit of his subconscious quickly added, "Because that's about all you can do." Think logically. Sort out the pieces. Which was, of course, freaking impossible once dumb time travel and multiple time travelers started *zip-zap-zooping* all over the place with their pale skin and stupid galaxy eyes. This wasn't even multiverse theory; this was . . . He didn't even know what this was. Chaos! Still. Breathe. Practical steps. What did he need to do, personally? Forget the road, focus on where to put your feet. What was the best thing he could do, right now, to maximize his chances of survival?

But do I want to survive, came the thought, blunt and unbidden. The notion took Matt slightly by surprise, as he had never considered himself even vaguely suicidal. Nevertheless, in the interest of fairness, he turned the question around and mulled it over for a few minutes, gazing with a sort of put-off expression at the drain in the tiled floor. Finally, he shooed away the notion.

Yes, he did want to live, actually. He quite enjoyed being alive, despite its many frustrations. Yes, he acknowledged the lingering "blood-stolen, tyrannical anti-powers vaccine" potential was a problem, and probably legitimately a threat. But the precursor to that was getting his blood stolen, and the thus far unspoken corollary that followed was no one being able to retrieve it.

Because it wouldn't be sufficient, he now realized and reasoned, for him and Jane to simply drop the ball—the other side, the quote, unquote, "bad guys" had to take the ball and run the field with it. They had to get his genes and hold them long enough to make their vaccine, and in the intervening period, there was Jane—all hundred suns of her and very few places in the world she could not and would not blow up. A snipped-off lock of hair or a vial of blood wasn't much use to anyone if it was incinerated by golden hellfire before it could be studied.

So, all right then. Matt wanted to keep living. It was also morally justifiable, somewhat. Not quite a revelation, but good to resolve, nonetheless. It was not necessary for Matt to be killed, and he rather enjoyed being alive, so that was settled. And if that was the way it was going to be, hypothetically, then was it possible to thread the needle, so to speak, timewise and fatewise, between having his blood stolen and ending up prematurely dead?

It might be hard, Matt acknowledged, but hadn't that sort of been what they'd already been doing? Maybe not consciously—or not conscious of the looming extratemporal element—but they'd been managing. Maybe he just needed to be more cautious on his slink back to normality. Maybe he needed to see Jane's precautions as protecting him not just from overzealous gun nuts but also against the very thing those zealots were trying to prevent. Plus homicidal Time Children.

Matt pinched his nose. Jesus Christ. What had happened to his life?

Okay. Matt took a few deep breaths. So. He should continue playing safe. But did that matter? As he'd already acknowledged, if a competent time traveler wanted to kill him, well, there wasn't much Matt could do about it.

But no, Matt suddenly realized, that was the wrong way to look at it. Whether or not time travelers were going to kill him was entirely outside his control. It was like being struck by a meteorite or dying of an aneurysm or having the Earth suddenly collide with an unseen micro black hole. There was nothing he could do about it, so worrying was pointless.

Time travelers shooting him or poisoning him or, who the hell knows, replacing his soap with a bar of anthrax, were dangers so far above his paygrade that trying to prevent them was ludicrous. They would either get him or they wouldn't. Life was just full of those inherent risks.

Suddenly, it hit Matt that maybe nothing he did mattered anyway. These were time travelers. They could literally change the future. They could see and hear him right now, knew exactly what he was going to do and why he was going to do it.

Except—and again, Matt forced himself to take a step back—that wasn't necessarily true.

It was tempting, he realized as he reviewed his own chain of thought, to equate time travel with omnipotence. But just like with the power of Dawn, when you really got down to it, time travel was just a power. It didn't make you special; it didn't make you God. The Black Death had still been able to get some hits on Jane, and she'd still been defenseless against telepathy (which she now rectified by taking Psy-Block).

She could still be tricked, could still be caught, could still be neutralized. Remember the story she'd told him about the original Captain Dawn and that neutralizer priest in Ireland? Powers be damned, that had stumped the whole Legion. And the Time Child—or Time Children, whatever there was—had to be the same. It was just a power. A big, daunting, very scary power, but still. There was no reason they wouldn't be vulnerable to telepathy or neutralization or any other kind of attack.

What had Cassandra said, all those months ago? Something about an airgap? It seemed like the Child had been reluctant to get too near Heydrich, maybe for this exact reason: because it was all well and good to be alive to possibilities, but another thing entirely to gamble on your reactions being faster than superspeed or telepathic thought.

So assuming the Time Child was playing by the same rules—and honestly, at this point, that was a pretty big assumption—but assuming it wasn't entirely divorced from the rest of the universe, that meant it had weaknesses. That meant, like all superpowered people, it only had the one ability.

Except if it was an empath, Matt corrected himself. Except no, he then corrected himself back. Jane had absorbed a power from it, and an empath couldn't absorb powers from another empath. That didn't work for some reason, he'd learned. They could only absorb from an original holder. So the Child must have been an innate time traveler, which meant it wouldn't have any other powers. Which meant—and Matt's heart suddenly raced, and he felt himself becoming disproportionately excited—that it couldn't be psychic.

It can't know what I'm thinking, Matt realized, and he almost punched the air. He had *something*. Now, even if it was just inside his head—and screw you, he was Matt Callaghan, there was no *just* about it—even if it was just internal, he had somewhere he was safe. Even if the Time Child was working against him, and even if it could supernaturally predict what he was going to do, it still couldn't see his thoughts. It could intuit, sure, and listen in, but so long as Matt kept his mouth shut, there was no way the Child could know.

Matt rose quietly, eyes unfocused, and once more began to pace with slow, deliberate steps, gently rolling one shoulder at a time. Okay, he had to be careful. Extremely careful. He couldn't—and he felt his excitement fade somewhat—he couldn't discuss any of this with Jane. Literally not a word. The instant Matt articulated his suspicions, the Time Child could hear, so he couldn't tell anyone.

He had to . . . He had to somehow figure out a way to confirm that a time traveler was trying to kill him, and then figure out a way to stop said time traveler without ever letting on what he was trying to do. With nothing but bare hands and thoughts. Also, there were potentially multiple time travelers.

Jesus. Nothing like achievable goals.

But there was no alternative. If Matt said something to Jane, the Child might notice.

And then maybe it'd have no choice but to wipe them out.

The man they called Jackson stood in the dark, driving rain as he stared down through infrared binoculars at the concrete storage units below.

Jackson was not his name. *Jackson* had been the first thing that popped into his head a lifetime ago when he'd first been asked for a moniker, an old song about a dream for bitter people, and now it was a mask he put on every time he made the world a little worse.

The others, some of the younger kids in his unit, didn't quite grasp that. They wanted code names and calling cards and kill counts, to be talked about, to be known. But you could not survive in this life, the man who called himself Jackson knew, if the murderer inside you was admirable. If it had traits you were proud of. That only made the mask cling tighter. Made it bite deeper into the flesh.

We got married in a fever, hotter than a pepper sprout. His Da's voice, singing softly out of tune, alone in the kitchen. He was fourteen again. The discordant melody. He hated that song.

"What're we waiting for?" one of the men behind him murmured. Lone Star, cryomancer, twenty-four. One of seven crouched behind him on the hilltop in black rain jackets, helmets, masks. Young. So very young.

We've been talkin' 'bout Jackson, ever since the fire went out.

"The leash will snap." Jackson made no move to look up from his binoculars, from the sight of three distant men on guard—two at the gate, one on patrol. The patroller had a German Shepherd.

"How do we know that?" the young soldier whispered. Jackson almost scoffed. How did they know? Ignorance was a thick rind on this one. You never asked those sorts of questions. You were given a fact, and you took it. Only dead men peered behind the curtain.

Well go on down to Jackson, go ahead and wreck your health. Metal egg flip scraping on a cast iron pan. Sizzling, spitting. White fried egg with black metal shavings scattered through.

As if on cue, four hundred yards away, the dog leash snapped. The German Shepherd took off, barking furiously in the downpour as it chased after some imagined shadow. Even in the darkness, Jackson could see the handler swearing, see him sprinting to give chase.

"Move."

The soldiers broke cover, flowing down the hill in a low run. Jackson's joints popped under the weight of his gear and his weapons, but the discomfort was distant, belonging to another. Mindless life; mindless movement.

When I breeze into that city, people gonna stoop and bow.

They reached the fence, ten feet tall and topped with barbed wire. Eli stuck his bare fingers through the chain links, barely flinching as he diverted the electricity away. Calder held up his hands and filled the air with a shimmering dissipation, shielding both he and the electromancer from view. The others were already at work with bolt cutters. Within seconds, they were through.

"Quickly." The man named Jackson led the remaining five, crouched low, rifles raised, following not the lying light and distending shadows but the unfailing pace length of his boots. Fifteen forward. Twenty left. Fourteen right. Thirty. He knew the maps. Had them memorized.

I'm goin' to Jackson, to turn-a loose-a my coat.

"Ain't for me," says Da, "it's for your Ma." Smiling through rotting teeth.

Three minutes until the guard.

Jackson slid to a stop, eyes rising. The lockup stood before them, a wide roller door of horizontal beige slats. An unremarkable unit in an unremarkable storage facility in some boonie town, so dull your eyes slid right off it. Anonymity, Jackson knew, was the best protection. So many terrible things were kept locked up in storage centers like these, half commercial, half empty, trusting to rain and rust and cobwebs to provide the protection no amount of titanium could match.

Except, the security always gave it away. Always too much security. Three guys, on a storm-swept night? Management could never truly let go. Therein lay their downfall.

But they'll laugh at you in Jackson.

He checked left and right the adjoining unit numbers and confirmed they were in the right spot. There'd been no doubt, but it paid to be methodical. Jackson knelt down and took hold of the steel padlock. Thick but simple metal. He squeezed, feeling it splinter in his hand.

Inside, he motioned. He wrenched up the roller door, stepping into darkness as his men followed. Goggles flashed, no lights, no torches. Every man moving to where he was needed, preordained. Packing. Disassembling.

Big goddamn thing, Jackson pondered, staring at the unit's contents. Looked worth the risk. This was the thing about these extractions— sometimes, you were stealing something innocuous. At least this was big effing machinery, lots of metal, spikes, and silicone, with a bulbous center bigger than a person. Felt like something substantial. Like the sort of gear you'd need to emulate a power.

Emulate a power. The man named Jackson, if he'd allowed himself the freedom, might have smirked at that notion. People were always going on about how difficult it was to emulate powers; ain't never no way, ain't never been done, blah, blah, blah. Yet man had been making fire with stones and axes far longer than they'd been streaming it from their fingertips. Electricity predated 1963. Was it really such a big deal, so unthinkable, that there would be other advances? It was more just the way things lined up. Sure, blocking out electromagnetic signals was a power, one the marine core ran almost every operation. But powers hadn't invented that. This machine just evened things. That didn't strike him as implausible.

I'm goin' to Jackson, and that's a fact. Dead night. Ma home. Ma sneering. He could've asked them to stop, either of them. But a boy ain't got words for that.

Jackson looked at his wrist. Thirty seconds. He gave a short, low whistle and motioned for his troops to hold. The men fell silent, packing down or having already stowed their pieces of the machinery. Jackson reached forward and pulled down the roller, cutting them off from the storm. Nobody moved; nobody spoke. Six breaths fogged quietly in utter dark. Outside, the rain continued pouring, hammering on the sheet metal. And underneath its pranging came another steady sound. *Tap, tap, tap.*

Jackson had pulled the unit's door down most of the way, but without the lock, it rested slightly out of position. Maybe two inches up, when you drew close enough. Subtle but distinct.

The guard spoke like predestiny.

"Hey. What's—?"

They moved, two halves of a pair, in one fluid motion. The guard, reaching the outer handle on the door and flinging it up. Jackson, in the same moment, his hands extending, reaching out from the waiting darkness to grab the man's face on either side. No scream. No shouting. Simply a wet, bloody crack, and chunks of a face slipping between his fingers. Like he was seventeen and breaking a watermelon.

Yeah, we're goin' to Jackson. Ain't never comin' back.

There was no talk, no "get him inside." Jackson simply turned, and in one easy motion, slid the body against the ground, motioned for his men to go around him, and watched as the soldiers made quick pace out into the rain. Jackson stepped around where the body had come to rest, wrapped his arms round the machine's center console, and lifted it carefully about a quarter inch from ceiling and floor. He carried the half ton easily, feeling nothing but a slight tingle in his hands. No pain; no burn.

He stepped outside, and in an instant, the rain came crashing back down. Cold and damp, that unmistakable drowning earthen smell. The second he was out, his deputy lowered the door and affixed a new lock, identical. The first remained with the deceased, the dust, and plundered darkness.

Move out, he wanted to tell them, wanted to give vicious snarling orders that breathed to life the sucking tightness in his chest. But he didn't. Words weren't needed. His men stalked out the way they'd come, sealed the fence, and withdrew with what they had gained beneath the veil of the howling storm.

Matt lay awake listening to the rain, staring into the darkness, and thinking about what to do. It was late, the meeting was over, and everyone but Jane was gone. Matt had retreated to bed and kept his eyes closed, pretending to be asleep, until about eleven o'clock, when he felt the covers rise and Jane get up and slip out for her usual nighttime wanderings.

Matt gave some thought to joining her—maybe letting her spot him in the gym or playing some Xbox together—but decided against it. Better not to appear restless, lest the restlessness caused some omniscient watcher some concern. So instead, he just lay there, curled up on his side under the blankets, thinking hard beneath the sound of thunder and the space of an empty wall.

I don't want to die. I just want my life to be simple. I need some way . . .

He needed some way to trap a time traveler. Except, by definition, that seemed impossible, because even if he constructed some trap under the guise of a legitimate endeavor, any perceptive time traveler would simply see themselves being trapped in the future before the trap was even laid. So it either needed to be a perfect trap—one that could ensnare a time traveler faster than that time traveler could think—or there was no point in traps at all.

Matt churned ideas over and over. Neutralizers were too slow. Disruptance fields didn't seem to affect the Time Child. His best bet, it seemed, was telepathy, because at the end of the day, whatever its abilities, the Child was still mentally human. But the telepath would have to be very, *very* good and disinclined enough, upon seeing eternity, to not go crazy and gouge their eyes out.

Could Wally do it? If he could get the psychic to read his mind, maybe; then maybe Matt could explain the situation mentally, and they could work together to do . . . something.

Ugh. Matt's brow furrowed in the darkness. How the hell was anyone supposed to lure a time traveler anywhere, let alone prevent them from seeing they were headed into a trap?

Option Two, then, because Option One had more holes in it than Jane's gym socks. Fight fire with fire. To try and get the one time traveler he *knew* was aligned with him—or well, pretty reasonably hoped was aligned with him, given they were dating—trained to the point of being able to take on the Time Child on its own turf.

Once he got past the initial sense this plan made, however, Matt found he liked it even less than Option One. It was one thing to wager his or Wally's safety on building a discreet trap nobody might fall for. It was another thing entirely to encourage his—let's face it—occasionally emotionally unstable girlfriend, whom he did genuinely love and care about, to go hurtling through the blinding madness of possibility. That was a lot to ask, not least because putting everything else aside, he was still very, very reluctant to mess with time. He'd meant every word he'd said to Jane in their arguments. Time travel just generally seemed very, very dangerous. Almost too dangerous to be a last resort.

And the problem, at the end of the day—Matt had to keep reminding himself—was that he didn't actually know anything. He was pretty sure, like maybe sixty to sixty-five percent sure, that he'd stumbled onto an extratemporal conspiracy—but he wasn't actually certain.

All he knew, definitively, was that one of his gunmen had, at some point, won some money from a lottery ticket. He had no way to confirm that was the Time Child's doing, just a hunch. Who knew, maybe Louch had just gotten lucky. Sometimes, people did win things. And it wasn't like Matt could go looking to see if the other would-be assassins had suffered similar strokes of good fortune, since the mere act now of going back and searching might make the Time Child suspicious. Or Time Children. If it was their doing. Which it might not.

Jesus Christ. Matt's thoughts spun so hard he was getting vertigo. He had no proof because by definition, a time-manipulation conspiracy would be proofless. But if there couldn't be any proof, then there being a time traveler out to kill him looked exactly the same as there not being one. And he kept coming back to Occam's razor.

What was more likely? That an unseen cabal of Time Children were secretly warring over his existence, or that some ignorant prick in a small town had won the value of a secondhand Range Rover? Jesus. How was this his life now? Why couldn't he just be like every other nineteen-year-old, anonymously blacked out on a dorm room floor?

Eventually, when it became clear that sleep would not be forthcoming, Matt gave up and reached down to where his laptop lay charging on the floor beside his bedside table. Discreetly, turning the brightness low, he opened the screen and shuffled up into a sitting position, quietly clicking around for a mental reprieve, going to places he knew he shouldn't go.

www.bluin.com

->NeverSurrender
For those determined to seek the truth. You can find uncensored information here, and anything else related. You have FREEDOM of SPEECH. This is a safe place for everyone to talk about the future and what's really happening in world events.

->PreserveHumanity
For the true humans unwilling to give up their humanity or to let it be redefined. For those proud of their powers and their way of life. Voids will not replace us.

For the past few months, ever since he first learned they existed, Matt had been quietly lurking in online groups of people who hated him. Sometimes during the day, when he needed a break from studying; sometimes at night, when he couldn't sleep, never with any particular goal in mind and never telling anyone, as he doubted anyone would approve. What was the point, he could imagine people asking him. Why immerse yourself in this nonsense?

And in many ways, they'd be right. The stuff Matt read on these subgroups was alternatively frustrating, scary, and wearily depressing, plus almost universally phenomenally stupid. Yet for some reason, he kept returning. There was just something about these obscure pockets of online loathing that called to him, that he found fascinating, and so he just kept on coming back.

*Posted by **vir-mosorus** 4 hrs. ago*
The Interview was so clearly staged it's embarrassing. 2:17, 4:32, 8:11, 16:13, 18:55, the list continues . . . Amazed the mainstream media believes anyone swallows this crap.

DDwaterbug *<> 4 hrs. ago*
9:09 when they cut to "studio audience" you can see the shadows aren't matching. And the sound quality suddenly changes, 9:11, 9:14, with different echo effect. Geez, I wonder why that might be, it's almost as if the two clips were shot in different studios /s. This is a game to them, they're laughing at us, they're not even trying anymore.
146 points <> Reply <> Share <> Report <> Save <> Follow

GoldandBlack *<> 4 hrs. ago*
Can somebody compile a supercut of all the CGI blunders? I want to show my dad.
214 points <> Reply <> Share <> Report <> Save <> Follow

For the first couple of weeks, Matt had worried that the forums' attraction lay in masochism or some deep-seated self-obsession. Day after day, as he'd felt repeatedly compelled to return to Bluin and its sister spin-offs, Matt had wondered if he had accidentally hit upon some new hereto untapped fetish, or if he was secretly filled with depression or self-loathing and was actively seeking out content designed to make him feel worse.

Yet, as the weeks passed and his mood remained stable and he continued to reflect, Matt came to realize this wasn't what was happening; he didn't hate himself, and he took no real pleasure—sometimes quite the opposite—in reading strangers' virulent contempt. The appeal, it finally dawned on him, was that all these people were discussing events he was personally involved in; things that, from lived experience, he objectively knew.

For once, and it was a bit of a revelation to realize how incredibly rare this was, he could actually read what people were writing on the Internet and say without a moment's hesitation: "No, you are unquestionably wrong." And that was in many ways a unique feeling; to be able to read people's sometimes articulate, sometimes well-sourced, sometimes rambling nonsense and say with total certainty that what they were talking about was utter crap.

amen-to-me *<> 3 hrs. ago*
Twenty+ mentions of blood and not once did they utter the word vaccine. Did they think a billion people would be watching and wouldn't notice?

Glaring omission. Guess the screenwriters were on the clock. It didn't even make sense from a totalitarian point of view. Unless . . . the dictator's grasp isn't as strong as they wanted everyone to believe. They can't lose face by admitting what actually happened. It's Dawn this and Dawn that. If they let the truth rip through the cities, there'd be mass uprisings. They're just hoping by the time everyone wakes it'll be too late.
52 points <> Reply <> Share <> Report <> Save <> Follow

TheTranscendent *<> 3 hrs. ago*
+amen-to-me *Crazy to me how nobody acts.*
7 points <> Reply <> Share <> Report <> Save <> Follow

A better-reasoned excuse might have been simply "know thy enemy," and if anyone ever confronted him, that was probably what Matt would go with. Lots of people on these forums professed to wanting him to die or suffer harm, not that they necessarily wanted to cause that harm themselves; most were circumspect enough not to be that open. Bans fell thick and fast in these places, moderators acted with impunity, and half of the subgroups he frequented were locked to private as soon as they started getting attention from mainstream Bluin users.

But there'd been multiple occasions now when Matt had hitched a ride into those private forums, included in the group of original members who retained access, like some silent loner let into a night-club early who wasn't evicted once midnight struck and it turned VIP. So long as he didn't engage, so long as he continued lurking, Matt remained unnoticed. A fly in the forum, forgotten, free to lurk unno-ticed and read.

Yeti1986 *<> 3 hrs. ago*
It's cute how main character reduces all criticism to "fringe" "crazy" people. Stuff, stuff, stuff that man with straw.
60 points <> Reply <> Share <> Report <> Save <> Follow

MovingForward2Beg *<> 2 hrs. ago*
+Yeti1986 *And light an arrow.*
16 points <> Reply <> Share <> Report <> Save <> Follow

Nerrgal <> 2 hrs. ago
*+Yeti1986 The enemy is simultaneously strong and weak. We can dismiss
them as a joke, yet look out, here on live TV, here's one to show how dangerous. Good thing the cameras were rolling and a street full of pedestri-
ans. DW verified and yet somehow we're supposed to believe a bona fide
GF just rolls through no checking? FF @ 15? Nah friend it's nonexistent.
21 points <> Reply <> Share <> Report <> Save <> Follow*

At first, a lot of what was written in these forums read like gibber-
ish, but after you hung around for a while, you sort of naturally picked
the lingo up. *Main character* was shorthand for "Matt Callaghan," since
they had the same initials and it was sort of derisive. *DW* meant "Dawn-
Watch," a website some enterprising programmer had set up a few
months back through which people could report and verify sightings of
Lady Dawn.

GF meant "green fingers," which was code for someone who took
active steps to kill him, a combination of having a "green thumb," as in a
gardener who pulled weeds, and "trigger finger." And *FF @ 15* was some
gaming reference about surrendering, which Matt didn't entirely get the
etymology of, since in this context it meant "False Flag."

References to DawnWatch always got Matt curious, so he tabbed
out of the Bluin boards and, back propped up against some pillows,
clicked over to the orange-and-gold website to determine Jane's current
whereabouts. Presently, she was "LOCATION UNKNOWN," not seen
for several hours. Last sighted in Madagascar, though that was graded
"UNCONFIRMED." Matt resisted the urge he routinely felt to sign in
and update the website to "SITTING ON MY COUCH."

For what felt like hours, Matt bounced back and forth, wading
through diatribes and conspiracy theories like a sewerage inspector torn
between interest and detachment at today's batch of toxic sludge. Would
there be corn in it? Some kernel of assassination? Maybe a watery whiff
of time travel, which Matt was always on the lookout for, but which basi-
cally never showed. And now . . .

The uncertainty came back, an increased churning in his stomach,
and a quickness to his pulse. Matt half considered getting up and asking Jane if she could get some weed—but no, it was already too late,
and the act might make the watcher suspicious. *Why are you anxious,*

he imagined the Time Child thinking. Scrawny little blond-haired bastard.

Matt closed the laptop, unusually angry at the forum morons and their lack of answers and insight. *Stupid Time Child, stop trying to save the world by killing me. Or . . . stop failing to protect me properly. Or get involved. Who the hell knows.* God, his headache was getting worse.

It was close to 2:00 a.m. now, and biology was finally beginning to assert itself. Matt wasn't Jane; he needed sleep, and his blurry eyes and the weird heat in his forehead brooked no delusions. Reluctantly, though his mind swirled with uncertain problems, before long Matt felt his eyelids growing heavy and his thoughts beginning to loop.

I don't want to die here, he thought. *I just want things to go back to the way they were. I have to beat a time traveler. I don't want to die . . . I want to go back . . . I have to beat . . .*

In the darkened bedroom, Matt closed his eyes, feeling his brain slipping toward fitful, restless slumber. His dreams, when they came, were of rows of blue-eyed children, of angry, faceless lizards, and of a clock slowly ticking out.

"Mr. Callaghan, Ms. Walker. Thank you for coming to see us."

"Ahem," Rana coughed. The FBI agent sitting across the table from them, the one who had spoken, turned her head to look at the pair's lawyer, who was sitting smugly between them with her arms folded across her lap.

"And for bringing your attorney. Ms. O'Reilly. Lovely to see you."

"Which one are you again?" their lawyer asked.

A week or so had passed. With the Today Show interview now over, Matt and Jane's lives had settled back into their regular routine—or their irregular routine, however you wanted to look at it—of Jane going off to deal with crises, and Matt staying home under rotating supervision.

Surprisingly, Matt had actually seemed less resistant to his protection lately, although he'd been oddly quiet since the shooting, which filled Jane with concern. She was starting to worry he'd taken this latest attempt on his life hard, or maybe was growing depressed from the constant confinement. Maybe the reality of it all had suddenly hit home. Or maybe Jane had done something; maybe after their last fight, he was still mad at her. He wasn't acting like it, but Jane still worried.

Today was different, though. Today, they had an appointment with the FBI at the FBI's central offices in Washington, a big light-brown building maybe six stories tall that looked like an office block slid awkwardly underneath a giant table. They were there to go over the Bureau's findings about the latest attempted murder and, Jane knew, be pressured into taking a side.

Naturally, because they weren't idiots, Matt and Jane had brought their lawyer along. Midforties, broad shouldered, and tall, with hair in thin bottle-blonde ringlets and a casual ease in the way she wore pantsuits, Rana O'Reilly of the ACLU was no-nonsense, sharp-tongued, and reminded Jane inescapably of Matt's mother. Certainly, from the way she talked, you might have assumed Matt and Jane were her children. Anyone who ever tried to get one over on them soon found Rana's displeasure plainly known.

"You're not under arrest, guys," the male FBI agent, some new man whose name she couldn't remember, said in a way that made him sound like the leader of a troop of Boy Scouts. He was tall, thick, composed, light skin rough with ancient acne scars. "We don't need to have lawyers involved. We only want to talk."

"Of course they're not under arrest," Rana replied before either Matt or Jane could open their mouths. "We have a Supreme Court judgment setting that out in black and white. Do you want me to read it for you?"

They were sitting, the five of them, in a nondescript gray-carpeted room on the third floor of the central FBI building, at either end of a long table running parallel to a window overlooking Pennsylvania Avenue. Will had teleported them in before going off to buy pancakes for some reason, leaving Matt and Jane to meet Rana inside and go through the Bureau's metal detector, which was the funniest thing Jane had done all week.

Now alone in the conference room, Matt and Jane sat in neat civilian clothes on one end of the table with Rana in between them, facing the two FBI officers on the other end—a plain-faced woman with a brown ponytail, and the sprawling salt-and-pepper-haired man in a dark gray suit who'd maintained the same dumb, unconvincing smile since they'd first sat down. He had the power to change his skin to rock, and she could click her tongue to use echolocation. Neither of them were any threat.

"I've read the judgment," the man—he might have introduced himself as Richardson—replied, unrelenting with his plastic fawning.

"That's a first," Rana remarked.

There was a pained silence. Jane struggled not to smirk.

"There's really no need for you to be here, Ms. O'Reilly," said the woman, sounding pained.

"My clients aren't legally old enough to drink," their attorney replied, "and you've been actively gunning to get a needle in one of them for six months. If you don't like me being present, we are more than happy to walk."

It always went this way. A supposedly "informal" interview. Surprise and annoyance at them bringing someone from the ACLU along. Polite suggestions that maybe they'd be better off talking alone, as though they were all here for a friendly game of bowling, and having a lawyer meant they'd have to cough up for a second lane.

Same tricks every time: offering to show them around privately, or plying them with food and drink. So sinister, yet so pathetic. Matt had much more tolerant views, but Jane disliked cops at the best of times. These slimy, pretend-to-be-your-friend cops, she hated more than most.

"Can we offer you a bear claw?" asked the FBI woman, Fiona or whatever her name was. She forced a smile at Jane and raised a pastry box. "Maybe something to drink? Tea, coffee, sparkling water?"

"Get to the point," demanded Rana, who prior to this meeting, as with all meetings, had instructed her young clients to keep their arms folded and their mouths shut.

It took a few more minutes of clumsy platitudes, but eventually, the agents relented, allowing the table to finally turn to grown-up evidence talk. Jane listened tight-lipped as the FBI wheeled out document after document on Matt's would-be assassin, including the evidence they wanted the pair to give, and the charges the killer would face.

None of it was new to her, and a lot of what they were receiving now were half facts—the Legion's own forensic investigation had already supplied and covered much more thorough details, and both Jane and Matt were well across the relevant points. This meeting wasn't about the gunman, though. It never was.

"And I suppose, in conclusion, we have concerns," the woman stated, terminating a presentation she'd been making about the attacker's background and goals. "Real concerns, really, for the both of you."

"You have concerns for the safety of the woman who killed Klaus Heydrich?" Rana asked, expertly incredulous. The FBI lady ignored her.

"Your safety," she said, leaning forward and putting her hands on the table, "is our top priority. It always has been. And we're worried—we're particularly worried—that without proper protection, you're going to remain vulnerable to these kinds of attacks."

"We know we've offered it before," Richardson added, his pock-marked brow furrowed with concern he'd likely practiced in the mirror the night before, "but we really want to offer it again. Come into protective custody. Let us set you up somewhere anonymous. There's a military base, up in Alaska, near Port Lions. The protection there is second to none. Together, cooperating, we can work to make sure this kind of tragedy can't happen anymore."

"Putting aside your heavy-handed attempt to place my clients under your authority," Rana replied, "what *is* the FBI doing to prevent these attacks? You're getting millions of our tax dollars; surely even you must be getting somewhat closer to determining the root of these threats."

Jane could see the male FBI agent struggling not to scowl. "As I think Matt and Jane both know," he responded, and the way he said their names, as though they were his favorite schoolchildren, made Jane want to blast him through the wall, "these aren't organized attacks. Nobody's coordinating them; not as far as we can see. And we have psychically verified. The only common ground between the attackers is the kind of websites they're visiting. Bluin, I think you know, and others. All quite radical, all quite libertarian; communities of anonymous individuals, mostly men, sharing conspiracy theories about what they perceive to be threats."

"And why can't you get rid of those?" Jane asked suddenly. To her left, Rana flashed her a look, and the lawyer's arm went beneath the table to Jane's wrist, flooding Jane with the looking-through-the-eyes-of-a-swarm-of-red-bees sensation of being able to see infrared and ultraviolet light. Jane ignored her.

"The websites," she demanded. "Why aren't you getting rid of them? Shut them down, stop people going. If these psychopaths are on there talking about how to kill Matt, why are they still allowed to exist?"

"They've got freedom of speech," Matt sighed from opposite her, before either FBI agent could answer. He seemed equally indifferent as he too fell under their attorney's glare. "You can't stop them talking."

"Even when it's about trying to kill you?"

Matt didn't reply, and Richardson seized on the opportunity to jump in. "There are site-wide policies; bans and some such," he said, leaning forward, clearly keen to be communicating directly. "Though those are often difficult to maintain, and irregularly enforced. More specifically, though, if you close down one forum, the participants just regroup somewhere else."

"So arrest them," Jane spat. "If you know who they are, if you're listening, arrest them. Find them, lock them up."

Matt turned in his seat to look at her. "Arrest everyone who doesn't like me?"

"If that's what it takes, then yes!"

"That's not a feasible approach," Richardson said mildly.

"Yeah, it's also immoral," Matt replied.

"Perhaps we can have this conversation another time," Rana suggested through gritted teeth. Jane ignored her.

"It's not immoral if someone hates you. It's you or them."

"They're scared. They're misinformed. They don't like me," said Matt. "None of that's a crime."

"No, the crime is attempted murder!"

"They're generally circumspect," the female agent added with a small sympathetic frown. She fell silent beneath Jane's furious gaze, which the empath spread around the entire table.

"Then do what you need to do," Jane scowled. "Do something. Show them there are consequences. Or tell me who they are, and I'll show them."

"Alright, I think that's quite enough," Rana interjected. She leveled withering glares at the both of them, grabbed one hand apiece, and pulled both Matt and Jane to standing. "Obviously, this is a topic that inspires passion and hyperbole from my clients, neither of whom are actually suggesting they would ever act outside the law. This interview is over. We will leave preventative measures and the monitoring of cyber threats to you. *Come on,*" she snapped. She began dragging the pair from the room, causing Jane to angrily shake off her hand while Matt allowed himself to be meekly led. On the other end of the table, the FBI agents both rose to their feet.

"We would be honored to share our information with you, Lady Dawn," Richardson spouted with predatory enthusiasm, trying to catch and hold Jane's eye.

"Bait," came Matt's voice, echoing from the hallway. "Obvious bait."

Jane glowered, sparing a glance back at the faces of the two eager agents; then, with her teeth clenched, she reluctantly stalked from the room, following her boyfriend and their attorney as all three of them walked free.

"I think they absolutely should have released it."

"You promise?"

"And so there I am, absolutely losing my mind because I'm thinking, 'How did it get there?!'"

It was a warm autumn night; the same kind of night they'd had a year ago, when Matt had first gathered Acolytes outside the Academy and invited them to drink, smoke, and be merry. Now, though the air floated with the same gentle cold, the world seemed irrevocably changed. So many empty spaces, shadows where people had stood only twelve months earlier. So many missing from that warm, sacred night.

Morningstar manor, headquarters and home to the Legion of Heroes, had loomed as bright as it ever did when Matt, Will, and Jane had teleported onto the edge of the adjacent forest. Expertly rebuilt—and three cheers for superhuman builders—it was in every way a replica of the great mansion it had replaced; a sprawling, multistory sandstone palace interlaced with iron windows and intricate latticework. And yet, though it had been restored in its entirety, to Matt's eyes, some detail was still missing. Some luster lost; some scars still present. Ruined no longer in body perhaps, but maybe wounded in soul.

"I mean, hindsight is twenty-twenty."

"What, you want to sniff my shirt?"

"Because I *knew* it was the middle one. I *knew*. But I'm staring there at the three pots, and there it is, on the left."

They had made their way up in relative anonymity, through back doors and passages, into a closed-off room in a far wing that had previously been some kind of Ashes' "teachers' lounge" before Klaus Heydrich's explosion had claimed both lounge and teachers. Now, or for tonight at least, it had been repurposed into a makeshift private dining space, with three long wooden tables arranged into a C-shape, the usual couches pushed to one side, odd Persian carpets over the floorboards, and mismatched chairs on which to sit. This was not a formal gathering;

not publicized, nor for any special occasion. Yet it remained, in its triviality, fundamentally important.

It was a gathering of those who'd survived.

About twenty people sat around the tables in no particular order, sixteen or so Acolytes and Ashes, plus the four members of Matt's family. Around the center sat Matt and Jane, him in a shirt and jeans, her having gone with civilian clothes over her usual white-gold uniform. They'd ended up sitting together, typically, and somehow in the middle of everything, unwittingly thrust into center stage by a spotlight and celebrity that even here they couldn't completely dodge. But though the attention seemed to drift toward them, it was, to their relief, never referred to. It was simply where they happened to fall.

"But it's so clear when you look back at it. He was not a well man. And I think there was still a lot of stigma around it . . ." "Oh absolutely . . ." "Especially for someone of his generation . . . Absolutely . . ."

"Hmm. I still don't quite believe my son's capable of doing laundry . . ."

"And I'm like: 'Did someone break in? Did someone move it?' And I'm freaking out because the door was locked, but maybe still, somehow. So I'm rummaging like crazy through my stuff . . ."

Giselle was there, too, and Will and Wally. It was hardly unusual to see them, but at least here, they smiled slightly brighter, flushed with the opportunity to host. Along with them were other remnant Ashes and Acolytes, those who had either been away from the Academy on other business when the fight in Detroit went down or incapacitated by the explosion.

There was Chris Gao, replicator, who had been up in the Carpathian Mountains with a team of researchers testing how far his copies could extend from one another. A gravity-controlling Ashes woman Matt had never spoken to but who'd been rushed to the hospital after she'd gone into early labor following the attack on Morningstar.

Neil Lomachenko, a stern Senior Acolyte with thick eyebrows, a jutting jaw, and the power to emit and absorb radiation, who hadn't even known there'd been a disaster until he emerged from the bowels of a Russian nuclear reactor he'd been patching cracks in about four hours too late.

Carla Black, regenerator, who'd been under anaesthetic in the Mayo Clinic undergoing routine ablation for her Logan's Disorder.

Becky Sandstrom, flier, who'd been hospitalized after being struck midair by a chunk of Morningstar's north wall. And the healers, hefty, voracious Delores and shrewd, mousy-haired Editha, who'd stayed behind at the Academy to search for survivors and tend to the wounded.

Then, scattered among them, were a few nervous newcomers, young Acolytes who had breached or were receiving their first glimpse of the inner circle: the new Bangladeshi genius girl, Azleena, whom Matt personally thought looked all of fifteen; Cameron, Kane, and Leticia, steel transmutation, electromagnetism, and superstrength respectively, whom Matt barely knew; and a new offsider of Giselle's, Helen, a quiet, short-haired, muscular technopath who didn't speak much and seemed to have replaced most of her body with cybernetics.

And then, of course, there were the survivors. For though the Legion had met Death in Detroit, Death had not quite managed to eradicate the Legion.

First and foremost was Natalia Baroque, telepath, who although immediately antipathically incapacitated the moment the fight started, turned out not to actually have been killed. Having gone down so early, it seemed the Black Death had simply forgotten to finish Natalia off, leaving her to struggle back to consciousness among the corpses of her comrades just as magma-spewing fissures began tearing their way through the earth.

Shaken but undeterred, she now sat a few places down from Wally Cykes, wearing a black Chanel dress and gold, needle-thin tennis brace-let, listening with characteristic dourness to her Legion co-psychic talk.

The second survivor, somewhat unexpectedly, was one of the Ashes, the pyromancer Charles Farrington. Matt had never had much to do with the slight, softly spoken middle-aged man during his brief stint at the Academy, and had honestly never spared him much thought. His "death," too, in the battle for Detroit's streets, had not been contextually remarkable—the Black Death had spat acid through his flames, which vaporized and began disintegrating his airway. A horrible way to die, for sure, but one you would've thought fairly definitive—melted lungs were usually pretty final.

Except they weren't. For when Will Herd hurriedly teleported into Detroit from the hospital, desperately trying to gather what few sur-vivors he could before the city plunged into the Earth's molten maw, he had found Charles Farrington still moving, twitching, his gray eyes locked in a kind of demented fury that the teleporter later admitted privately to Matt had scared him to the bone.

Unbeknownst to any of them, and to Matt least of all, it seemed there was something inside the unassuming Ashes man that had caused him to cling to life far longer than any sane person should have—a fervor, a determination bordering on fanaticism that had kept him pushing through unimaginable pain and clutching furiously to the last wisps of his dying breath.

It was only this persistence, this sheer bloody-minded fortitude, that had kept the pyromancer alive long enough for Will to find and get him to a hospital. He had recovered and was now one of a select few. Klaus Heydrich had tried to kill him, and Charles Farrington had refused to die.

The third survivor, impossibly, was Celeste.

Celeste Pettit, horse girl, faunamorph, last survivor of the second Legion, had turned into a dragon during the battle of Detroit and had the Black Death unceremoniously snap her neck. Normally, again, that would've been pretty conclusive. But in Celeste's case, it wasn't.

The science behind how faunamorphs worked was uncertain. Did their cells all physically split or rearrange into the subject animal, or was their human form stored somewhere inside them or in some pocket dimension, waiting to be retrieved? Were they truly becoming an animal controlled by a human mind, or merely an animal-shaped imitation, a sort of 'I-Can't-Believe-It's-Not-Cow'?

When Celeste had become a dragon, those questions had not been at the forefront of her mind, but after her neck was snapped, they suddenly saved her life. Dragon biology, clearly, was not human biology, and although breaking whatever bones or nerves the Black Death had severed would have killed a regular creature, somewhere between the dragon's gigantic form and Celeste's own human one, something had deflected the killing blow.

Maybe part of her original brain had persisted and instinctively triggered a partial reversion, preventing some of the damage. Maybe the complexity of a dragon's entirely fabricated central nervous system and internal organs meant that life persevered even with a detached spine.

Regardless of the how, by the time Will landed, was rounding up survivors, and preparing to teleport, there had been enough life remaining in Celeste for an incredibly groggy Natalia to point to the motionless dragon and deliriously insist that the faunamorph was alive.

What followed were thirty-six hours of the most intensive, complicated surgery the attending team of healers, orthopedic surgeons, and veterinarians had ever attempted. To Matt's knowledge, footage of the event was now doing the rounds at all major medical schools and had already been the subject of papers in *The Lancet, the British Journal of Veterinary Science, Gore Galore,* and *Horse & Hound.* And at the end of it all, Celeste was alive. Bloodied, shaken, bedridden for the better part of two months—but alive.

And so here, half a year later, gathered the survivors of the Legion; not to celebrate, not to commiserate, but to simply be. Because there was defiance, now, in just being.

"Oh, absolutely. I mean, when I look at my sons, and the attitudes they have, the openness with which they can talk about—" "Exactly . . ." "It's, even in one generation. Such a positive change . . ." "Right, exactly . . ."

"What'd you always say? Self-sufficient to run a household by eighteen or you've failed as a parent?"

"And I'm looking, and I'm looking, and I can't find anything else that's missing, and I'm going 'Why would someone break in here just to move a pot plant?!' And I'm legitimately losing it."

As ever happened with gatherings of this size, several conversations were happening at once. Matt's father, Michael Callaghan, and the Ashes Charles Farrington were deep in discussion about the true demise of the late Captain Dawn, the latter lamenting the mental burdens Walter Reid had carried following his wife's passing, while the former nodded sagely along and returned always to the importance of mental health. Jane, seated next to Mr. Callaghan, had inched her chair closer toward them and was listening intently, though she'd refrained from contributing anything just yet.

To her right, Matt was acting faux weary and being faux henpecked by Kathryn Callaghan, his mother, as both couched real sadness, concern, and love in the ebb and sway of gentle, familiar barbs. Matt's younger brother, Jonas, seated next to his mother, listened in with a mixture of admiration and envy as they discussed Matt's independence—missing, for the most part, subtext he would not recognize for years to come.

Then, across the other end of the tables, a large group of Legion members sat spread out around a corner, one by one trading stories of classmates who had fallen. The current speaker was Wally, and the room rang with laughter as he recounted a tale of being unknowingly tormented by Chino, the Colombian floramancer.

"And I just . . . I feel guilty. I really do." "Oh, no, don't do that to yourself . . ." "No, I mean, I do. I—" "It's not your fault. You never know what's going on behind closed doors; no one ever does." "No, but I suspected. I wondered. So many people, I think, worshipped the ground on which he walked . . ."

"Yes, well, I suppose with all your grown-up money, you probably just hire a maid." "Jane won't let me hire a maid." "Won't she? She's a good girl. Well, I'd still better come round. I shudder to think what state the house is in." "See, Jonas? Pay attention. That's what's called a Trojan Horse."

"And I spend, I kid you not, two weeks thinking something's wrong with me. I'm going . . . is it too hot? Is the sunlight somehow spreading it through the air? Am I inhaling it in my sleep? Am I losing my . . . ? Because every time I get back, the pot's in a different place, like shuffled one two three, and I swear to God I have never touched it, I swear, this plant is messing with me more than any weed I've ever smoked . . ."

The door to the room creaked open, and Matt glanced up to see Jane's father enter. The man was dressed in a blue plaid shirt and oil-stained jeans, and his face was rough with stubble, but his eyes were clear. Father and daughter caught each other's gaze from across the room and neither looked away, at least not immediately; instead, after a few moments' hesitation, there was a small, stiff exchange of nods. Jane turned back to Mr. Callaghan and Mr. Farrington's discussion as her father wound his way gradually around the edge of the tables.

"It sounds like it's been a real revelation for you." "There's been a lot of soul-searching. We don't help people by treating them like that." "No. *The same reason that makes us wrangle with a neighbour causes a war betwixt princes.*" "Montaigne. Exactly."

"What's Trojan? Like the condoms?" "Absolutely not. All those Greek myths I read you when you were little—" "Do they make condoms for horses?" "Ask Celeste." "Matt, don't encourage him. Although speaking of . . ." "One word about that and you'll never see your grandchildren." "Oh, so I am expecting grandchildren?"

"And then finally, *finally*, after legitimately a fortnight, I have this revelation; because see, the pots were pretty similar, right? You know, that red ceramic brown, but one had this little chip in it, and I suddenly realize it's not the pots that are moving, it's the *plant* . . ."

Jane's father had reached the back of the table where his daughter and Matt were seated. He glanced down at Jane, who first met then uncomfortably averted her eyes.

"Hi," he said. The word stumbled a bit coming out, and he fell silent. Then: "Sorry I'm late."

"It's fine," Jane replied, still avoiding his gaze.

"I just got caught up . . . There was a leak . . . The hot water . . ."

"It's okay," Jane mumbled. "Really."

Beside her, Matt's hand slid under the table and squeezed gently above Jane's knee. Jane didn't turn to him, but instead, after a moment, forced herself to look back up at her father. She pulled her face into something resembling a smile, which after a moment, Peter Walker returned.

Jane pushed her chair back and rose awkwardly, and for a few moments, the two of them just sort of stood there, making small indecisive motions. Finally, after a series of jerky, aborted movements, they embraced in a brief, stiff hug. Jane quickly patted her father on the back, then detached without looking at him, immediately sat back down, and returned to averting her gaze.

Peter glanced around the room with uncertainty, but a few seats along, Matt's mother smiled and indicated to a chair between Jonas and a sleeping Sarah. Relieved, Jane's father shuffled over and sat inconspicuously down.

They were both trying, Matt knew. During the fight with the Black Death, while a horde of distant minds had telepathically distracted Klaus Heydrich long enough to give Matt some mental breathing room, Jane's father had reached out and connected with Jane, filling a void of need and understanding that had been growing in his daughter since she was just a little girl. In that moment, it had been a perfect surge of self-affirmation and love.

But that was the thing about moments of soul-baring catharsis; they were just moments. Eventually, the emotions faded, and you were forced to return to the awkward reality that you were still two people carrying a lifetime of pain and baggage. Jane's relationship with her father could not heal instantly because the hurt that had grown between them had not grown instantly, and the heart needed the same time to repair as any muscle.

Which was why every second Thursday, from two to four in the afternoon, Jane and Peter Walker attended therapy with the most discreet counselor Matt's extensive research had been able to find them. What went on in those sessions, Jane didn't really discuss, and Matt didn't really push. From what she did say, it was slow, uncomfortable progress. But progress all the same.

Jane's dad, too, was technically under the Legion's protection. Unlike Matt's family, though, this seemed more courtesy than caution—few people possessed enough of a death wish to threaten the life of Lady Dawn's sole remaining and only recently reconnected parent.

"The goddamn plant is moving, and so I go next door and find Chino, and he is just laughing his ass off because he's been, you know, tapping our bedroom wall whenever he hears me leaving, being like, 'Come on, little weed plant, shuffle over a pot or two.'"

At the other end of the tables, oblivious to Peter Walker's discreet entrance, the loose confederation of Legion members broke into peals of laughter as Wally's story reached its crux. The redheaded psychic, dressed tonight in a purple Hawaiian shirt highlighted with white flowers, hiccupped into weak chuckles as he wiped away a tear.

"He was such a prick," he sniffed. The words came with a smile, but by the time they were spoken, redness blotched around Wally's eyes. Will touched him gently on his back, and the psychic turned to him, smiled, and shook his head.

"To Chino," Wally said, raising his glass.

"To Chino," those around him echoed, and around the room, the call was taken up. The other conversations nearby lapsed into temporary silence, drawn in by the Legion's toast. Wally wiped his eyes with the back of his hand and sniffed.

"He didn't like me," Giselle stated.

"No way," laughed Will.

"No," the speedster replied. "He really didn't. The first time I met him, I asked where he was from, and he said 'Colombia,' and I started talking about how much I loved their campus when I was in New York." A bark of laughter ran around the room. "I genuinely didn't know," lamented Giselle. She held the side of her head. "Genuinely, I didn't. His English was so good, I thought he must've grown up there, or . . . I don't know. He thought I was so dumb."

"James used to get tripped up on the same thing," said Wally. "I remember he'd complain about it—Chino—every time there were drills and they were dividing by country or whatever. He'd always spell Colombia with a *U*. Columbia. And Chino kept telling him, bro, that's not how you spell my country, but he just . . . every time, James would forget. Every time." Laughter washed across the tables, though the sound faded after a few moments, and the room fell silent save for distant scratching as Jonas scraped across his plate with a fork.

"He was such a knucklehead," murmured Giselle. She started back up with a smile. "James."

"Yeah."

"But he always meant well."

"Yeah."

"I remember—I remember—" She laughed. "I remember this one time, maybe . . . three months after I'd joined the Academy. Like, green as. They had us out doing these, I don't know, press tours? Like promotional sort of things, Q and A, to like show off their young people . . . I don't know!" She raised her hands to patches of laugher, smiling her usual bright grin.

"Anyway, it was him, me, and Nat, I think?"—she gestured to the psychic—"and maybe Winters. Anyway, I'm so nervous; I am—This is my first public tour, I have no idea what they're going to be asking, and I just—I just know I'm going to mess it up."

The speedster sighed. "Anyway, there I am," she said, "nineteen, scared out of my mind, and we're up onstage, and there was this guest there, I can't remember, some politician . . . some guy . . . Anyway, he's being a total creep; he's leaning over, keeps touching me, touching my hair, and saying things like . . . God, what was it . . . ? Oh, like, 'Don't be nervous, just imagine we're all naked. Can you imagine that, gorgeous? Can you imagine us naked?'"

Giselle made a face as the listeners murmured. "And then he was laughing and smiling at me, and I'm just—Ugghh!" She shuddered. "So gross. But I'm terrified, you know, because I'm nineteen, and I've just started, and he's some big important man, and I don't want to embarrass the Legion . . . which is crazy, freaking crazy, right? In retrospect, I should've just told him to get bent . . ."

She shook her head. "But I didn't, right, because I'm nineteen. I just kept sitting there, and James was sitting beside me, and I remember the whole time this guy's hitting on me, his eyes—James's—just keep getting narrower and narrower, but he's not saying anything, right? He's just sort of silently glaring this dude out.

"And so finally, the thing starts," she continued, "and Winters gets up and says something, and this guy gets up and says something, and I'm just sitting there panicking, panicking, because I am *so* nervous, so nervous. And then it's James's turn, and I'm watching him, just petrified, and as I watch, this politician guy sits down, and he slowly gets up— James. You know how he was, this enormous, gigantic dude.

"And he starts slowly walking super weird, walking super stiff, right past everyone, because they'd gotten him right down the end. And he walks past me, and he walks past Winters, and I'm going, 'What the hell is wrong with him,' because it's like he's got this rod up his back, and I'd never seen him move like this before."

She leaned in as if concerned. "And it's super weird, and I remember I thought I had this revelation, like 'Oh my God, he must be just as nervous as I am. Even though he's so big and intimidating, we're actually in the same boat.' And in the moment, it was reassuring, you know?

"But then James keeps walking, taking these slow, little, ponderous steps, until he's right in front of this politician, and just as he goes past, he gives this tiny little turn—James—this tiny little like"—she mimicked in her seat—"shuffle of the hips, you know, just so his butt was angled toward him for a moment, and there's this low, almost inaudible *pop*." Giselle paused, glancing around the faces, letting the silent anticipation grow. "And this dude, *blegh*"—she made a face—"he recoils back like he's been slapped, almost falling off his chair as he's hit full in the face by this absolutely pulverizing fart."

The room exploded with laughter, Natalia cackling like she'd stepped back from stirring a cauldron, Wally laughing so hard he was having trouble breathing. Even Jane cracked a grin. The laughter carried on for a few seconds as Giselle wiped away tears.

"I know. I know! And it was just . . . perfect, you know? Because what could this guy do? He couldn't do anything, not without making a scene, because to everyone, it just looked like he'd leaned back a little too far, you know, like he'd wobbled on his chair and had to throw his arms up so he didn't fall . . .

"But I know, and James knows, and this dude knows, because you could just see this like ripple, this *impact* hit his cheeks, like a dent, and it was all this guy could do to sit there and take it, and just glare *daggers* at James while he's giving his speech. And James just does not care. He doesn't look at him; not a single backward glance. He just says his piece about inspiration or what have you and trundles right back along, shoulders straight, never so much as glancing behind him, cool as you freaking please.

"And this dude's just got to sit there and pretend to smile, with his hair all ruffled and his suit all crumpled—and the smell!" Giselle threw back her head, almost choking on tears. "Oh God, the smell. It was so *bad*! Like something had crawled up inside his butthole and died. I just . . . It was the protein. Oh God, it must've been the protein; it . . . it was the worst thing I've ever smelled in my entire goddamn life." The room howled with laughter.

"And he just . . ." Giselle's voice cracked, and she lifted her gaze to the ceiling, shaking her head, the tears in her eyes no longer merriment but twinned through now with grief. "It was the absolute perfect thing he could've done. Right then. And he was just like that sometimes, you know? Always an ass, always getting things wrong, until sometimes, out of nowhere, he'd just do something completely right."

There was a general murmuring of agreement. "This was one of those. It was . . . spectacular. A work of art." She sniffed and wiped her eyes on her sleeve, then forced her lips into a watery smile. "A work of fart."

Everyone in the room groaned, and there was a general clattering as at least half of those present took a swig of their drinks as an almost instinctual reaction to the terrible pun. Tears still trickling down her cheeks yet smiling, defiant, Giselle raised her glass.

"To James," she said.

"To James." And once more, they took up the call.

* * *

"Matt."

In the moonlit corridor of Morningstar, Matt turned around. He was about three steps out of the bathroom, a little way from the dinner, away from everybody else. The speaker, Azleena, the Academy's new genius, stood alone in the dim light a few feet away from him, cutting a diminutive figure, her gangly, childlike limbs seeming almost out of place among Morningstar's adult-size hallways.

Seeing her there, barely five-two and maybe a hundred pounds, wearing a dark, unremarkable flower-pattern sheath dress and a pair of flat slip-ons, Matt felt his stomach churn with a sudden surge of disdain.

He didn't like Azleena, though she'd done nothing to deserve it. The genius was hardworking, loyal, helpful, and sharp. It was just that her being there was a constant reminder that Edward Rakowski wasn't, and for that, it was hard to ever truly forgive her. Matt knew the feeling wasn't rational. It didn't stop him feeling it every time she spoke.

"What?"

"You've got visitors."

Matt turned to look at her square on. The girl's face was nothing but serious. He'd never known her to joke.

"Who?"

"Eastborough Baptists."

Matt blinked, taken aback. "What? Where? How?"

Seeming to take that as a cue, Azleena stepped forward, turning her slim frame to show Matt the tablet she was holding. The screen was lit up with a blue-and-white high-definition night-vision display from a security camera pointing from atop Morningstar down the hill and across the grounds, where at the edge of the forest a group of worshippers gathered.

There were about a dozen or so, a mixture of women and men, all white and all wearing the same brown traveler's cloaks over plain shirts and suspenders for the men, or powder-blue ankle-length dresses for the women. Some carried old-fashioned wrought-iron lanterns; some held hands. All appeared to be singing. None were making any attempt to hide.

Matt recognized the one at the front, the tall man. He struggled not to groan. "I don't understand."

"They're technically trespassing," Azleena pointed out.

"How the hell do they keep doing this?" Matt murmured, not really responding to the genius's comment, just shaking his head.

"How do you want to handle it?" asked Azleena.

Matt pinched the bridge of his nose. "I don't know. Any suggestions?"

"I have a belt-fed 50-caliber antipersonnel cannon mounted on the southwest tower."

"Jesus Christ, Azleena; they look like Christmas carolers."

The dark-skinned girl shrugged. "It's September. Besides, this is private property; we don't know their intentions. Or their powers. In the present climate—"

"We don't need any more dead people. Get it through your head." Matt rubbed his temples, his teeth gritted. Azleena stood in silence, her face blank. A moment later, Matt sighed.

"Sorry."

"It's fine. It's your call."

"No, I shouldn't have snapped. It's just . . ." He shook his head. "I'm just a bit emotional. It's not you. Could you please let Giselle know? Discreetly? We can go talk to them together, just the two of us. It's technically her house."

"Copy," Azleena stated. She turned back toward the dining room before she paused, fixing him with an inscrutable expression. Matt rolled his eyes.

"Fine. You can also warm up the antipersonnel cannon. Just in case. But no firing unless I say."

The small girl's mouth split into a white-toothed and surprisingly gremlin-esque grin. "Copy, boss."

Matt wandered down to the entrance hall and was met a few minutes later by Giselle. Wordlessly, the Legion's leader took his arm like they were heading to a picnic, and the two stepped out into the waiting night, the cool autumn air whispering in the glow of the mansion.

"What'd you tell Jane?" Matt asked as they walked. Giselle flicked him a small, semisad smile.

"That I was helping you stretch your legs," she answered. "Giving you a tour of the new facilities."

"Thanks. I know she wants what's best, but . . ."

"I get it. These are your people. Weird as that is."

"Yeah."

They lapsed into silence as their footsteps padded atop the damp grass, a steady descent down to meet the procession of faithful coming up. The worshippers' lanterns bobbed in the night like will-o-wisps drifting from the forest, and the two groups met against a line of shadow where the light of Morningstar embraced the dark. They stood some ten feet apart, the cloaked faithful staring up at Matt in awe and reverence. The tall figure in front knelt to the ground.

"Chosen one," he murmured. Matt recognized his voice.

"Just Matt," he responded, forcing a smile. *Fight stupidity with kindness*, he told himself. Fight ignorance with patience. "How did you know I was here?"

"We keep a lookout," replied the man who knelt at the head of the worshippers. He looked up from beneath his hood, and Matt didn't need to see the familiar tapering face, proud nose, or gently lined skin to know him.

Pastor Phillip Fredericks. The cult leader stood slowly and removed his hood, revealing neat, dark-brown hair streaked through with gray, and soft, drab eyes behind thin frameless glasses. He was a very tall man, close to six-five, neither lean nor stocky, and possessed of a quiet, dignified presence in the way he rose, his shoulders gently unfurling and his hands clasping behind his back. Matt could imagine him being intimidating, with his unblinking stare and impressive height, but right now, there was no trace of that.

Fredericks stood downhill from Matt, keeping the young man physically above him, gazing up as though breathtakingly close to some wonder of the soul. "To watch out for you. To keep you safe."

"This is technically private property," advised Giselle, although her tone carried neither impatience nor hostility. "I know you want what's best for Matt, but I'm going to have to ask you to leave when he says so."

The pastor held out his hands. "We'll go in peace. Nobody here wants violence."

"Thank you," Giselle replied. Her eyes flicked to Matt, who drew a deep breath. He stepped forward.

"What can I do?" he asked those who believed in him. His eyes ran past Fredericks over to the assembled crowd, those who stood in his shadow, those to whom he had never spoken. A ripple of murmurs spread. One man—a short-haired, soft-looking man with a face full of dark beard—exchanged glances with his companions and took a step back so as to be flush with the rest of the group.

Pastor Fredericks turned to them, his face shifting into a slow, gentle smile.

"Be not afraid," he told them. "Let him speak to you. He is your savior as well."

There was another exchange of glances. Finally, a mousy-haired woman on the left edged forward.

"Please, chosen one," she said to Matt, "we seek only to protect you. We seek your guidance. Show us the path. Be our light."

"Yes," echoed Fredericks, turning back. "Show us the way."

This brought murmurs of agreement. Matt shook his head.

"I am thankful for your protection," he told them, weaving his gaze first to Fredericks then in turn to each of the others. "I'm thankful that you care enough about me that you want to risk your lives. But I'm not who you think I am. Truly. I am not a prophet. I'm not the son of God."

"It is as you said," murmured one woman at the back, middle-aged and with lines of worry deep across her forehead. She glanced with distress at the pastor. "He doesn't believe."

"It's true," said Matt. "I don't."

The pastor shook his head, not in the least bit swayed. "We will believe," he told them, "even if he cannot."

"I know," Matt replied—and strangely, there was no sigh when he said it.

They lapsed into silence. A gentle breeze blew across the fields, carrying with it the green-fresh smell of forest pines.

"May we pray over you, oh holy one?" the mousy-haired woman asked. Matt glanced over at the pastor, but Fredericks's face showed nothing but calm.

"You can," Matt said finally. "If it will make you happy." He turned back to the crowd, pushing the pastor from his gaze. "But in return, you have to listen. Really listen to what I have to say."

There was a soft rustling of consent. Pastor Fredericks stepped back, becoming but one of the faithful crowd as Matt moved slowly into their center, letting them encircle and lay hands upon him, their prayers soft, their heads bowed.

A few feet apart, Giselle stood watching, her arms folded, poised but not trepidatious. It was clear to both of them that whatever else these people were, they were not dangerous. This was not a night of violence, where men held evil in their hearts.

"I want you to know," Matt said as he stood in the center of the circle, "that I don't care what you believe in. Whether it's me, whether it's God, whether it's something else. Because it doesn't matter." He paused. "What matters is what you do. Be kind. Do good. Help people. Because none of us are here long. And none of us know how long we've got left."

His eyes swept over the believers encircling him in silent prayer. "Leave this world better than you found it. That's all I ask. If that's going to be my only legacy, let it be that."

Jane sat in the darkness, watching the shape of Matt's chest rise and fall.

They'd stayed over at Morningstar, in one of the guest rooms normally reserved for visiting dignitaries: a wood-panelled chamber on the highest floor with a four-poster bed, a walnut writing desk, and a pale-yellow, high-backed armchair in which Jane now sat.

Matt slept soundly; once he'd gotten back from his walk with Giselle, the Acolytes had continued toasting, getting carried away to the point where Matt had been quite drunk. He'd cried a bit, too, which always made her heart ache, as had a lot of them: Will and Wally and Giselle, Celeste, Editha, and the others. Even Matt's dad had gotten a bit emotional, though he hadn't really known anyone they were reminiscing about.

There'd been lots of toasts, lots of stories, lots of laughter. Matt had told a great one about Ed, the old Academy genius, lying to Morningstar nurses over some dumb nettle tea. Everyone had been in stitches, and then everyone had been crying. There hadn't seemed to be much wall between the two.

It all tinged Jane with sadness, but it didn't pull her down like it did the rest of them. Maybe because she hadn't known the dead as well, so they still kind of felt like strangers. Maybe indulging in grief felt fake because a lot of them hadn't really been her friends. But it also just . . . didn't feel like they were dead.

It was strange. She could still picture them, if she imagined. See the way they moved, their faces, as if they had just stepped out and down the road, as if they had gone away somewhere. Standing quiet on a misty street, waiting to return, indifferent. It felt strange. She knew they were dead. But death didn't seem so . . . permanent.

Jane reclined into the armchair, staring at the high-arched ceiling and feeling her thoughts drift along the waves of never sleep. Inside her veins, the power of Dawn hummed its warm, ceaseless tune. But beneath it, she felt now, caressing at the barest fringes . . . a second song. Wisps of azure starlight, whispering, wondering. She knew now how to hear it. Heard it coalesce in the spaces between the world.

I am all. I will be. See and know.

Jane opened her eyes, not realizing she had closed them, and for the briefest instant, she saw the bones of the Academy hung through with sapphire spider silk. Then slowly, surely, like a haze around the edges of her mind, she felt it. And she knew instinctually what was coming, watched as the cobwebs faded a moment before it occurred, as a pressure planted itself inside the back of her head.

Jane's eyes flicked up. Her pulse quickened. She sat straight against the fabric of the hard-backed chair and turned toward the shadowed corridor to see what she knew was coming. To watch as from the depths of the darkness, barely peering around the corner, came first two cobalt eyes, and then all that remained of the Time Child.

The night hung still. Jane waited, staring at him, refusing to blink. After a few moments, the blue-eyed boy motioned softly with his hand. Jane glanced over at Matt in bed, sleeping soundly, and without another word, she rose from the armchair and slipped across the room, out into the awaiting dark.

The child she faced as she rounded the corner, stepping out onto the bare wooden floors of the corridor, was exactly how she remembered him. Small and ghostly pale, with hair like fine white gold and clothes your eyes naturally slid over. He held his hands in front of him as he looked at her, this frail, demure little thing, and for a moment, Jane almost found herself feeling sympathy.

But then, once again, she saw his eyes. Oh, those eyes. Those swirling sapphire galaxies, which opened once you stared at them, drawing you in, sucking you down beneath the eldritch current. Everything he was lived within those vortexes, the rest of him malnourished, for those eyes consumed all.

For a few moments, Jane said nothing. Seeing the Child there, in the cold, calm dark of midnight seemed surreal, almost dreamlike. But this was no dream. The power of Dawn saw to that.

"What do you want?" she asked, her voice level, quiet. The boy did not reply immediately. For the longest time, he simply stared at her until, eventually, Jane began to wonder if he'd returned to being mute.

That he'd appeared here, in the middle of this supposedly secure fortress surrounded by some of the world's most dangerous superheroes and the best protection money could purchase, did not surprise Jane in the slightest. The Child had shown itself unaffected by Disruptances and nearly every other conventional limit. It moved through the back paths, she knew. Through dark places, behind the thread of things.

Once, a few months prior, she'd toyed with the idea of going back in time and attempting to stop the Black Death earlier, attempting to save the second Legion or stop the destruction of Detroit. Hell, why stop there—why not save the first Legion? Why not save Africa? Why not go even further and strangle the Black Death in his crib?

At that moment, though, the Child had appeared and warned her not to, given her a taste of the howling possibility that waited outside the sheath of a stable timeline, and the relentless danger it posed. It had been a harrowing experience, but an educational one. Now, the Child was back, when once more she was ruminating on lives that had been lost, on finality.

Could it sense her thoughts?

"*Come,*" the boy finally murmured, turning slowly on his heel. Jane hesitated to follow, and the Child glanced back at her.

"Where?"

"*Away,*" came the only reply. Jane looked over her shoulder, into the bedroom and Matt's sleeping form. He was unmoved, still tucked safely beneath the covers. As though peering through the wall, the Child followed her gaze.

"*No harm will come to him,*" he said.

"No, it won't," Jane replied, the words cold. The boy tilted his head.

"*Yes,*" he confirmed. He held out his hand. Jane hesitated only a moment before taking it, feeling the song of cavernous time echoing from beneath the Child's skin. Entwined with her own, her mind suddenly swam beneath the weight of twin oceans submerging each other, lapping, consuming, drowned.

The sensation became a cold and sinking throb. The boy stepped into the shadows, and Jane allowed herself to be led.

Nothing. Step after step, deeper into the dark they walked, onward and onward, until darkness was all that remained. A jet-black emptiness, unblemished, absolute. Jane glanced around, seeing only herself and the boy, no indication of where they were or breathed or stood.

"Where is this?" she asked. They were clearly no longer in Morningstar. She glanced around, gazing into the blackness. Somehow, though it was everywhere, the darkness was not oppressive, merely . . . blank. It didn't scare her like it once might have. What could, when inside her burned the light?

"*Outside,*" the boy replied. He released her hand, allowing her to sink a fraction and himself rise. "*A quiet moment.*"

Jane nodded, feeling the meaning of his words, if not quite understanding them.

"How long can we stay here?"

"*As long as we like.*"

Jane reached out, curious but not wary, sensing not so much resistance around her as simply . . . lack. She took a few steps, moving without difficulty around the empty void. There was no ground, no gravity, the darkness neither firm nor soft. She simply walked and desired to remain upright, and there was no impulse present to resist.

She turned back to face the Child, peering at him with quiet, curious intent.

"This isn't like last time. Why doesn't this hurt?"

The Child said nothing, instead seating itself upon a step of shadow, which shaped without resistance into a kind of formless throne. "*It is nothing. It took me a long time to find it. Far away from the life lines. Where existence is yet to tread.*"

"It took you a long time?" asked Jane. "How does that make sense? Can't you time travel? Don't you have unlimited time?"

"*Yes,*" the boy answered. "*And no. My existence is no longer linear, but there is still experience. Still failure. Still growth.*"

Jane shook her head. "No longer linear? As in, it once was?" She paused, sweeping her gaze around, then slowly scowled. "Every time I see you, or Matt sees you, you talk in riddles. Why can't you just speak clearly? Who are you? What are you? What do you want from us?"

For a few moments, the Child said nothing, merely staring at the shadows underneath them, small fingers idly twisting a small trail of darkness rising from his throne. Just as Jane thought he wasn't going to answer, the boy's blue eyes flicked up.

"*It is not my goal to deceive,*" he said. "*If I have, it's because that's what you needed in the moment.*"

"Like what the psychic said to Matt in Albania?"

"*Yes. She spoke my words. I showed her a glimpse of my mind, showed her*"—he gestured to the endless dark—"*eternity. True eternity, not this.*" He paused. "*But her purpose was not to communicate. Her purpose was to stall. I needed to buy the human time without giving away the game.*"

"Distract Heydrich."

"*Yes. Until the right moment. The right sequence of events.*"

The Child fell silent before continuing.

"*You ask who I am,*" he said. "*It is the wrong question. I had a name once, but it is just words. You ask what I am. I think you know. I am like you. I am like any of you. And fatally, I am not.*"

Slowly, the boy closed his swirling eyes, then reopened them. "*A long time ago, in a world that's yet to be, I was born. I grew. I had a mother, a father, two siblings. I went to school; I played. I lived an ordinary life surrounded by ordinary children. Then, one day, on the twelfth of September, at 9:16 a.m., my powers manifested. I did not understand them. I simply knew, as I sat inside a classroom gazing out at sunlit branches, that if I wanted to, I could leave. It was but an errant thought, yet I indulged it. And in that moment, I unwittingly untethered myself from time and hurtled screaming into eternity.*"

"*You understand, of course,*" the Child murmured. "*You've felt it—the enormity. Infinite information, possibility, where you not only see all that is and ever could be, but all that you could do. Your actions, your reactions, choices, fractals ever breaking, and from every one of them flows infinite change, infinite consequence. An endless, burning vortex. The*" *human mind cannot comprehend eternity, everything everywhere and always. I was no exception. I was ten.*

"*For a million years, I fell,*" he continued, "*detached from time and space, unable to age or sleep or scream. I went mad, of course—but after an infinite number of lifetimes, I grew bored of that and went sane again. My mind evolved. I learned how to let time flow through me; learned how to move, how to drift. How to think. To interfere.*"

"You interfered with the Black Death."

"*Yes,*" the child replied. "*Once restored to something approaching sanity, I surveyed the tapestry of superhuman existence and found it fraying, infested, and rotten. A plague named Klaus Heydrich stained all futures, horrific, intolerable. I could not abide.*"

"*Unfortunately,*" the boy continued, "*as you will soon discover, there are rules. Immutably fixed points, nails in the weave that would collapse the whole tapestry if removed. Where I walked, before my manifestation— my life before I could move through time—none of that could be varied. It cannot change. To do so would create a paradox, which would swallow creation whole.*"

"Yeah, right, so, avoid that," muttered Jane. She glanced around at the dark, then back to the Child, still seated on naught but void mist. "So, the Black Death came before you were born."

"*Yes. Africa was already broken, the Legion dead. I could rewatch their deaths, experience it, but I could not interfere. So much was fixed in my birthright.*"

"So many died."

"*The least of infinite evils,*" the Child replied, and though his voice retained its same ethereal presence, it tinged perhaps with loss. "*My hands are bound. We are reduced to terrible choices to forestall horrific fates.*" The boy paused, tilting his head slightly, staring at her. "*I killed my own grandmother. Did you know that?*"

Jane felt a slight tinge of revulsion. "No." Hesitation. "Why did you do it? How?"

"*Indirectly. I did not kill her with my own hands, merely put her in a position to die. But there is no distinction. Not for those such as us.*" He paused. "*It had to be. Without her death, the path would have frayed at a critical juncture.*"

"Do you regret it?" Jane asked.

For a moment, the Child was silent. "*It was the worst thing I have ever done,*" he told her, the answer soft.

He turned his head as Jane looked at him, staring out into the endless dark.

"*I am a slave to duty. Do you see it?*" The boy pointed out into the nothing. "*In the distance, very far. Even now, though we seek nothing, it pulls at us. While we sit here, its weight draws us back in.*" Jane followed his finger, and as she squinted, she realized he was right, that he was actually pointing to something—a miniscule pinprick of light.

"*The life threads,*" the Child told her, "*humanity, all who were and are and ever will be. We can shape them. We can guide them. They must be preserved.*"

As Jane stared, the pinprick grew larger. Brighter, like it was coming toward them. Or maybe they were hurtling toward it. Captivated, yet feeling a sudden thudding terror, Jane half turned back to the Child, but found herself unable to look away.

There was a pressure, a pain building inside her skull.

"So, what . . . ?"

"*Yes,*" the boy murmured, and though the panic in Jane's chest mounted, his voice remained small and calm. "*What now? What do I want from you? Why am I doing this? What is my goal?*"

The light was growing blinding now, the size of a TV screen against the dark walls, growing, growing ever bigger but faster, faster, never stopping, getting wider and wider until it consumed the pitch dark. And still it came.

Jane opened her mouth to scream, but found her voice had fled her. The Child stepped calmly off his formless throne, and quietly took her hand.

"*I will show you,*" he whispered, and in that moment, they were engulfed by life.

Light. Endless pulsating threads of color splitting and crossing and weaving and intertwining, stretching out into infinity from every moment, every choice. Instinctively, her eyes tried to follow one, to trace an end, a beginning, but there were no sane paths to follow, no extractable line or life.

The intensity of it was blinding, every color imaginable, everywhere, never static, for the threads were not threads but chains of moments, infinite—trillions upon trillions, a kaleidoscope of windows into the world. And then, with a surge of absolute terror, Jane remembered she was there. She existed. She could touch things, she could know things, she could change—she could interfere.

And suddenly, a howling fire ignited inside her consciousness, and she was seeing shattering fragments not only of her actions but her thoughts, her reactions to her thoughts, change upon choice upon thinking, a million, billion possibilities erupting in an impossible causal fractal, cutting into the depths of her very soul.

Yet, either through practice, terror, or the Child's presence, some piece of self-preservation prevailed. Jane stopped moving, stopped breathing, forcing herself desperately not to think, curling into a ball. The Child's tiny hand clutched hers firmly, and she allowed herself to be moved, small and useless, unable to shut out the hurricane of knowledge, staring quaking through transparent, lidless eyes.

If the Child had, at that moment, let her go, Jane had no doubt her mind would have disintegrated. She would have fallen, endlessly, with no way out and no way home, her sense of self torn apart until she was nothing but breath and gibbering.

At the edges of her vision, beyond the weave, she saw something move, and Jane wondered, in a rush of terror, whether there were others who had shared this fate before her—beings whose minds had touched eternity, stripped defenseless into broken, howling monsters destined to writhe forever in the dark. What terror could they wreak, could she bring, if she descended like this.

She gripped the boy's hand as tight as she dared, almost scared that she might break it. But the Child never wavered, and it never loosened its grip.

Through clenched, crystalline eyes, she watched them drift through the twisting universe, through singing threads engorged on moments too dense for comprehension, light and color surrounding them. The Child floated, a leaf on the wind, flowing through the gaps, the dark spaces between stormfronts, somehow knowing, somehow seeing where to go.

Again, Jane struggled to make herself invisible, to touch nothing, to be unobtrusive; to shut out the burning, the blinding, the roaring she worried now was not just sound and memories pouring through the interwoven threads but something hungry, something worse.

Eventually, somehow, it felt like they were rising, the cacophony growing dimmer—and finally, through the life threads still pulling at her, Jane felt a tiny cloud of sanity condensate, a fingernail of mental space. She opened her eyes—or allowed herself to see, having never really closed them. They hovered beneath the tapestry, above it, around it somehow, in the middle. A small, dark pocket. A gasp of stillness in this terrible, wondrous place.

"We don't have long," the Child warned. *"I must return you."* Jane made no words in reply, just gurgled a whimpering groan. *"But I will show you my purpose. I need to. Time is running out."*

"What . . . ?" Jane gasped. It was as if all moisture had been sapped from her body, blood swirling on her tongue. "Where . . . ?"

"Follow my eyes," the Child commanded, and he pointed with a finger that neither is nor was. *"Step back. Look at the greater pattern. There is a flow, irreversible."* Jane tried to do what he said, to follow. *"Beginning, middle, end. The lines flow always in one direction, from birth to death. Try not to see them but follow their path. All of them. Step back. All of it."*

Heart thundering in her chest, Jane tried to. She blurred her eyes, or what she thought were her eyes, like staring at a patterned painting, trying to see the true picture behind. Through painful gasps, she felt the stars refocus.

"I see it."

"Good. See how it moves, the great twisting cord. See how it starts, how the light flows, swift and sure in one direction. Cause and effect. Cause and effect."

"Yes," she breathed.

"Good. Now follow the flow. The entirety of human life."

Again, Jane pulled back, drawing away from the detail of each individual lifeline, letting her mind collapse until she only saw patterns, until the web of fate was only light. He was right. The threads all moved in one direction, twisting, intertwining; an infinitely complex rope. A pathway, a river, flowing onward, flowing right. Flowing toward—

Darkness.

Yearning, gaping darkness. Not the absence of light, not the calm nothing in which they had just loitered. This was . . . destruction. Malevolent, empty. A blackened pit, larger than all the stars in the universe, gaping and churning at the end of the pathway, swallowing everything whole.

More and more, unaware, the lifelines flowed into it. Irreversibly consumed, leaving nothing behind but dark. No song. No joy. No life.

It was a yearning void that screamed at her more terribly than any cacophony of thought.

"What is that?" she whispered.

And beside her, in the world between the walls, the Child looked at her, and his blue eyes spiraled into infinity.

"*That is a choice,*" he told her. "*A choice you make. Someday, soon, you will have to make it. Someday soon, you will have to choose between Matt Callaghan and eternity.*"

No.

"*I cannot guide you,*" the Child said. "*I cannot stop it. Just know that if you choose wrong, Jane Walker, heir to all creation, you will doom not only us—*"

His words became a whisper.

"*But the entire world.*"

INTERLUDE

You dance with your beloved, and the whole world spins in light.

Over and over, around and around, the music so loud it hurts, the darkness pulsing with life. The people around you wear masks, or maybe it is just their faces, drenched in ecstasy and sweat. There is a ringing at the peak of your consciousness, a brightness of delirious clouds. Your feet move, your chest throbs, your neck sways.

And in front of you Melody. *Melody.*

She wears white again, star-kissed sequins sparkling in the strobe light. Your hands are on her hips, and she's leaning into you, breathing into you, pushing back with yearning, cooing warmth. She turns and stares into your eyes, your arms resting on her sparrow-bone shoulders, heavy, intertwined. You draw her closer, swaying in time.

Her eyes are black holes, and her breath tastes like strawberries.

Back upstairs, and you fall into each other. No prudence, no privacy. Why hide? What's the point? In a darkened corner of a throbbing bar, you enmesh and interweave, and she whispers, "Baby . . . baby . . ." moaning where no one else can hear, and sending sunlit shivers down your spine.

Another bump? Another?

Anything to keep this going. Anything to swim another moment deep.

She throws up in a stall. You hold her hair. She washes her mouth with water, vodka soda, then goes right back to kissing, laughing. Nothing tastes any different. Nothing feels any worse. Downstairs again, dancing, drowning, caressing her neck with your teeth and tongue. Shimmering, ghostly goddess. She calls your name, and you come.

Someone has put you in a taxi. Friends. Who needs them? You pay the man what he needs to get you where you're going. The night is still young, its fruit ripe, her lips quivering. Stay with me, she begs as she slips white light beneath your tongue. Stay with me.

You wake up in your bedroom among scattered silk sheets, watching the sun rise over the bay. Melody is there, sprawled pale and naked as morning snow. You are a king. A conqueror. Whatever pain rattles in your head, whatever assails you, you can surmount it. Melody murmurs in her sleep, sleeping soft against your chest.

You pay a healer a working man's weekly wages to come to the penthouse and purge your hangover so you can trade today's lives with impunity and be ready to go the next night.

"No. Please. No."

The night is dark. The nail moon blinks, a distant streetlight. Behind a building, in an alleyway, in a district you don't know the name of, the love of your life lies dying.

"No. No!"

You push her chest, clumsy, hands slick with vomit, kneading the thin white pleats of her dress. Behind you, the taxi driver has stepped from his vehicle, his face a mask of concern.

"Hey, man, should I—I think you need to call an ambulance—"

But it's too late. You know it's too late. Your mind is thick and clouded, and you'd fallen asleep only momentarily, just closed your eyes for a second to rest your overloaded senses, and you thought she'd done the same. Thought that was why she wasn't moving. You never heard her vomit, didn't hear her choke.

And now you are in the alley. Now crying, screaming, your muddled brain trying to figure out how to save her, always two steps behind, always two minutes too slow. Your shaking hands scrabble to scoop chunks from her airway, but only succeed in pushing the bile sick farther down.

Your mouth closes around hers, trying to block out the putrid, acid sting, but her lips are too slick, and you cannot make a seal. Finally, against a bed of garbage, in the pouring rain, you pound on her chest, trying to keep her heart beating, trying to fill her blood with life.

A line is crossed. A stillness comes, her flesh already ceased twitching, her eyes rolled back—yet you know. Somehow, when the moment comes, you know.

Instinctively you recoil, heart hammering in your chest. Her arms slip from your hands, track marks glistening atop the veins.

"Hey, man." The taxi driver. "Dude, what the hell? We need to call someone; you can't . . . Holy crap, what the hell are we supposed to—"

Slowly, slowly, kneeling in the mud in your Gucci shoes and ten-thousand-dollar suit, rain cascading down your face, thoughts drip from your mind like clockwork. Cold, slow. Gurgling. Ceaseless.

Drip, drip, drip.

Your eyes turn back to the taxi driver. You climb unsteadily to your feet, staggering a few steps before righting yourself. Your guts clench hard. You shrug off your white jacket, revealing the black silk underneath.

"Get her turned over," you command. Somehow, you know to do this now; somehow, with death has come clarity. That old remorseless friend. "On her side. Quickly."

"Sir, I don't know. I don't know if that—"

"Quickly," you reiterate. Your eyes never leave her. "Quickly. She's just unconscious. Here"—you hold out your jacket—"use this. Warm her. Turn her over."

"She's just . . . ?" The driver looks at Melody, and perhaps he is uncertain—but the way you say it, and the money you've paid him, and the sheer desperation means his doubts are quickly discarded. He kneels beside her, ignoring the wet newspaper and rotten vegetables, and he cradles and rotates her gently over, as you should be doing—as you should have done.

"Pat her back," you tell him, your limbs cold, your voice hollow. The driver does not hear the desolation, just glances at you briefly before turning back to Melody, obediently obliging with measured slaps like a father trying to burp their suckling babe. Nothing happens. "Firmly. No." You lean down, splay your hand to show him. "Like this."

And with a single, fluid movement, your right hand strikes the back of your beloved as your left hand touches her cheek.

"Hngh!" A sudden intake of breath, followed by a rapid shuddering, coughing. Melody's body jerks to life, doubling over, spasms surging through her thin frame. She rolls over, crawling unsteadily onto her knees, hacking up chunks of vomit. The noises she makes are like a weak, wounded animal, but the sudden rush clears her airway. She is breathing. She is alive.

"Holy mother of God," the driver gasps. Palpable relief. He leans back onto his hands in the alleyway, giving the girl some distance, letting her cough and splutter it out. "Okay. Jesus. Scared the hell out of me." He shakes his head at you, relieved, as you bend down and gently wrap Melody in your embrace, holding her steady on all fours. "Get it all out, kid. Seriously, get it all out. And then I can take you to the hospital, both of you, no charge, seriously, I'm just relieved you're not—"

The man's voice stops without any warning, and in the silent street, he drops dead.

Melody moans. The cab lies abandoned. Distant streetlights flicker.

"Come on," you whisper. You clench your arm around her, feeling panic race down your spine as you try to pull her to standing. She sways, groggy, but succeeds. "We have to—We have to—"

"Baby, I don't . . ." she whispers. Her feet falter as you drag her away. Her words slur, her eyelids flutter. But she's alive. Alive. "Baby . . . baby . . ."

You limp into the dark-drenched night, a wretched, soaking little man clutching your desperate prize. The rain falls, stinging, blurring your vision, washing your hands clean of vomit. Your heart pounds with a gnawing fear like none you've ever known. There is a hollow in your chest. A trembling in your eyes.

And a taxi driver lying dead, not ten meters from his cab, silent and unmoving in the dark.

DEATH WISH

Extract, Transcript – **"God from the Fringes: The Great Debate"**
University of Notre Dame, April 1995, televised, 2 hours 52 minutes

<Topic – "The superhuman implies the existence of the divine">

<In the affirmative – Pastor Phillip Fredericks)>

<In the negative – Mr. Christopher Hitchens>

Fredericks: ". . . absurd, just absurd—"

Hitchens: "[Laughing] My opponent seems shaken by the assertion. [Pause for crowd laughter]."

Fredericks: "It is the most ridiculous thing I have ever—And if you think I'm going to stand here and—"

Hitchens: "Well, you can stand wherever you want, dear pastor, but that will not change the simple fact of the matter, which is that you are trying to stack absurdities on their head. Layer after layer after layer. Oh, well, we have something we do not yet understand; therefore, it must have been a supernatural being, surely, and it must be my supernatural being, specifically; a God who cares about us, even knows we exist, who takes part in our little tribal wars, cares who we sleep with, in what position, cares what we eat and on what day of the week. It is an absurdity.

"We are confronted with something the theists say is impossible, which I dispute, but regardless, which they say is impossible, and so their solution, therefore, is to layer more impossibilities on top. Impossibility solved by more impossibilities. Stacking turtles. And eventually, if we just throw in enough nonsense, eventually—they hope—we'll forget to question this underlying assumption and let them sneak this prehistoric god of theirs in through the back door."

Fredericks: "You cannot stand there while men are able to fly and—"

Hitchens: "Men could fly before the Aurora Nirvanas, my friend. [Pause for crowd noise]. Oh yes, they could. They flew in airplanes; they flew in helicopters. Quite a few of them, actually. Even had wars, would you believe. I think even some Americans were involved [Pause for crowd laughter].

"Think about it, though, explain an airplane in its most fundamental terms. We have taken rocks, and we have put them in fire until they liquified, and we have taken that liquid and cooled it into shapes harder than stone. Then we have taken those shapes and stuck them together, with more magic rocks which talk to each other using lightning, and filled the whole thing with a black substance from the bowels of the Earth. And this allows us to fly. Also, while you're up there, an attractive woman in a short skirt serves you a bag of peanuts [Pause for crowd laughter]."

Fredericks: "You can hardly compare—"

Hitchens: "But I can. Absolutely, I can. Because were I to go back in time, as the good pastor suggested earlier, if I was to return, say, to eighth century France, maybe a nice little Bordeaux vineyard [Pause for crowd laughter] and present myself to an eighth-century peasant and fly—yes, my friend is absolutely right, they would condemn me as a witch; they would burn me at the stake—if they could catch me, of course [Pause for crowd laughter].

"But the exact same would have been true had I returned in an airplane. Or carrying a mobile phone. Modern medicine. Forget witchcraft, forget witchcraft. If I had arrived back in 810 AD in a Boeing 747, Charlemagne himself would have declared me Satan [Pause for crowd laughter].

"But to us, see, it's perfectly ordinary. Because we understand it. And were we to leave the Boeing 747 with the eighth-century French peasant, or the mobile phone, or the jar of antibiotics, they would eventually—hopefully, if they were clever enough, given enough time—come to understand it too. And replicate it. And it would no longer be magic. Why should our abilities be any different?"

Fredericks: "Because a phone is a machine. We are the ones who have created it. We know it. We know how it works."

Hitchens: "Do you? Can you explain to me how a mobile telephone works? Because if you can, Pastor Fredericks, I must concede you are much more technologically savvy than I am. I barely know how to turn these things on [Pause for crowd laughter]. And this is the heart of it, then [Pause to raise cell phone]. I don't know how this works. But I know there is an answer. I know it is not some antinatural creation, some product of the divine. I do not have to resort to believing it somehow exists outside of the rules of our universe simply because I do not understand it."

Fredericks: "Yes, but the obvious difference is there are people out there right now who do know how a cell phone works, and they could explain it to you. But with superhuman abilities, there is no explanation. Science has not—"

Hitchens: "Science has not found an answer yet. This does not make superpowers remarkable; it does not even make them a minority among observable phenomena. The universe is full, Mister Fredericks, absolutely teeming with things that we do not have an adequate explanation for.

"Go back a hundred years, and those unknowns multiply. Go back a thousand, and they multiply even further. And slowly, slowly, through hard work and constant effort, science has chipped away at these mysteries so that with every passing era, we know more and more. This will be no different [Pause for crowd applause].

"I have absolutely no doubt. Because there is yet to be anything that has entirely defeated our methods. There is yet to be a question to which science has provided an answer that has then been supplanted by a later, better answer provided by faith. And that's just fact. [Pause for crowd applause]."

Fredericks: "Superpowers are unnatural. They are clearly magic, and the existence of magic—"

Hitchens: "Any sufficiently advanced technology is indistinguishable from magic. Sir Arthur Conan Doyle. As applicable here as it is to any machine. Why should biological processes be any different? Why should stellar phenomenon? Ten thousand years ago, my ancestors looked up at lightning in the sky and believed it was angry gods. Now we know better. Why should we, now, seeing someone shooting lightning from their hands, automatically revert back to 'Oh, that person is clearly supernatural'? Or it is an act of God, clearly. Rubbish. Absolute rubbish."

Fredericks: "We can talk around this all we want. And we can blur our eyes, and turn our hearts from the truth, and try our hardest to make what has happened fit into our selfish worldview. But the facts remain the facts. This is not some natural phenomenon. This is not something that has existed for thousands of years that we are only just now beginning to understand. This is something that has happened quickly, which has happened spectacularly, and which defies the 'laws' that we have established for this world [Pause for crowd applause].

"For years, atheists have been saying, 'If God is real, let Him show Himself.' Now he does, he has, and as usual, they've returned to more excuses. As usual, they've attempted to explain away what we all instinctually know."

Hitchens: "Except—No, sorry, except he hasn't shown himself. Sorry, that didn't happen, actually. What has happened, what we have observed, is that a wave of stellar force, of light, impacted the Earth, caused colors to appear in the atmosphere, and following that, there was mass unconsciousness. And then we awoke with abilities previously beyond our ken.

"Nowhere in this, admittedly—and I don't deny it is—historic, unprecedented, so far unexplained but again I believe not unexplainable event— nowhere did we see the presence of the Christian God. Or the presence of any god, for that matter. Nowhere did we see any signs, any written messages, the clouds did not part and rearrange to say 'From Jesus Christ, your savior. You're welcome. See you in church.' [Pause for crowd laughter]

"God did not come down and talk to us; he did not leave a note. We simply had an experience we do not understand. Now, were my friend on the stage here arguing for the existence of aliens, I would have a much harder time. Much harder. Godlike but not godly beings, unthinkably advanced, traveling through space, finding a species at a lower stage of development and going, 'We're going to help them'—that is utterly believable. Completely baseless, of course; in terms of evidence, there's nothing to support it.

"But as a logical man, as a man who, when entertaining hypothetical ideas, looks for plausibility and reason, the idea of intervention by benevolent extraterrestrials gains a lot more ground. But gods, and the idea of gods, and this assumption of this omnipotent magical creator runs into the same problem they've always had; the same problem they've had for thousands of years, which is, quite simply, where did they come from? If God made the universe, who made God?"

Fredericks: "God is outside—"

Hitchens: "I'm sorry, Pastor Fredericks, I keep interrupting you. I feel like I'm being terribly rude, but I also feel like you were about to say something along the lines of 'God is outside creation,' 'God has always existed.' Am I wrong?"

Fredericks: "No, but—"

Hitchens: "So why. Can't. The Aurora [Pause for crowd applause]. This is the question; this is what I keep coming back to. If you are going to explain away God's existence with 'Oh well, he's outside the rules,' why can't that same explanation be applied to the universe?

"Why is God, who is presumably more powerful and complex than his cre-ations, because in theist theology, something less complex can only come from something more complex—why is God, this infinitely complex being, simply existing and then creating the universe plausible, but the universe simply existing on its own is not? [Pause for crowd applause]

"What's good enough for you, Pastor Fredericks, should be good enough for me, and I can do it with less illogical leaps [Pause for crowd applause]."

<Moderator – Mrs. Virginia Gale>

Gale: "Pastor Fredericks, your response."

Fredericks: "I . . . I . . . um . . ."

Hitchens: "Look, and again, I don't want to belabor this, but we cannot, in the face of strangeness, simply abandon scientific principles. There is no evidence—no incontestable, factual evidence—that there is a god. There is not, either, and I admit this absolutely without hesitation, perfect scientific answers for the origins of the universe, although—and I hurry to note that I am not a physicist—there is some evidence, as I understand it, some mathematics that hypothesizes that matter and antimatter may be able to spring spontaneously into being as a kind of 'equation equals zero.'

"But we do not know. We do not know. And that is okay. It is okay not to know; it is better to admit our shortcomings rather than attempt to fill the void with superstitious tripe. Because who knows? Maybe one day, we will understand the Aurora Nirvanas. But the fact that we don't, ladies and gentlemen, is not an excuse for theists, for anyone, to simply scratch their heads and go, 'Well, I don't understand, therefore God.'

"There is no evidence of a grand creator, let alone that he sent the Aurora, let alone that he knows or cares at all about our insignificant lives. And what can be asserted without evidence, can be dismissed without evidence. And an unknown should not be put forward as evidence of the impossible simply because it is, as yet, unknown [Pause for crowd applause].

"You are not so much as to breathe without my permission."

When the sun rose the next morning and Matt awoke, Jane wasted no time in bundling him out of Morningstar and teleporting home with only the most perfunctory farewells. They arrived back at the apartment with Jane's hand gripped firmly around Matt's arm, and Matt continually doing that thing where he gingerly licked his lips and stared with bleary eyes at his surroundings with the expression of someone who'd accidentally eaten sand.

The moment Will left, Matt excused himself to go lay down—but before he could move beyond the couch, Jane cornered him, seizing on Matt's hangover in the hope it might make him more pliable, and knowing she couldn't wait.

"Any time anything changes at home, you tell me. Any time you get a threatening email, you tell me. You see anyone so much as look at you weird, you tell me."

In the best detail she could muster, Jane explained to Matt what the Child had shown her, the ultimatum she'd been given, and the unimaginable threat the paradox posed. As she explained, Matt remained silent, so Jane kept powering forward, laying out one by one the new rules he had to abide by.

To Jane, the meaning of the Time Child's warning was crystal clear. Matt was in danger. Sometime, somehow, that danger was going to catch up to him, and she was going to have to choose between saving humanity and keeping Matt alive. The solution, then, was obvious. Avoid all risk at any cost.

"You do not talk to your friends. You do not talk to your family. You do not play video games with a microphone. Stay away from the windows. Stay away from the doors. Hide if you see any suspicious insects or birds. If I am not here, there is no outside world."

Initially, Jane had expected Matt to be angry, to argue, to panic or question her story or overanalyze every detail in an attempt to find a hole. But throughout Jane's entire speech, as she alternatively implored and then railed about his safety, Matt simply sat on the couch, stony faced and silent, gazing up with his hands on his knees and his face locked in a blank, inscrutable expression.

The lack of reaction, somehow, was more distressing than any pushback. It felt like hatred. It felt like Matt was shutting down.

"Do you understand?" Jane finally demanded. "Say something."

For the longest time, her boyfriend didn't respond, instead simply continuing to stare, his chestnut-brown eyes looking beyond her, focusing on nothing. Eventually, though, just as the frustration in Jane's chest had built almost to the point of screaming, Matt's lips twitched, and he spoke.

"The Time Child said this?" he asked, his voice steady and quiet. Jane's shoulders slumped in relief.

"Yes," she answered with a long and pacified sigh. It was sinking in. "He did."

There was a moment's pause.

"And . . ." Matt said slowly. He seemed to be choosing his words with great care. "Are we . . . sure?"

The rush of cool relief that had washed over Jane mere moments ago immediately flared to boiling.

"Sure?!" she cried, throwing up her hands. "Sure?! I saw it! Waiting there, this-this-this thing, this darkness, this . . . time problem!"

She launched into another tirade, her shouts ringing out around the apartment until, eventually, the sound and fury were all spent, and she stood there silent, looming over Matt, her arms hanging outstretched in an incredulous shrug. Matt's face remained expressionless. Whatever gears were turning inside his head, Jane couldn't tell, but as the seconds dragged on, it took every ounce of restraint she possessed not to grab Matt by the neck and shake him until his thoughts came flying out.

"Do you understand?" she repeated, hands on her hips as she towered over him. "This isn't a game. You. Have. To. Stay. Safe!"

Her boyfriend averted his gaze. "For how long?" he murmured, and to Jane's shock, instead of arguing, Matt's posture simply crumbled, and he slid slowly down into the couch until he was lying on his back, staring up at the ceiling, tears welling in the corners of his eyes.

Abruptly, Jane's heart dropped. The anger in her throat tightened, and she stood, dumb, frozen, and gaping at him, unable to find the words to help, unable to do anything but watch.

Matt was unhappy. Even she, who sometimes struggled to pick up on these things, could see that, this sinking gloom written over every inch of his body, which had only grown worse in recent months. The sight of it tormented Jane, because no matter how hard she tried, nothing she did seemed to stop it.

She'd bought Matt a car; she brought home ice cream—she took him flying. She listened to his complaining; she told him all these cool stories about the crazy things she did every day. And while she was doing that, yeah, Matt smiled and seemed happy, or happier, or happy-ish, but eventually, every time, after a few minutes, the smile faded. Inevitably, day after day, Jane would come home or come out to find Matt sitting silently on the couch or lying with his head on the dining room table, or sitting beside the window with his chin on his hands—just doing nothing. Saying nothing. Staring at nothing with this empty expression on his face.

Nothing was wrong, he told her. He was just bummed out, he had to see it through, he was waiting for all of this to pass. Soon, life would go back to normal. And while she understood being worried for his safety, every time Matt voiced this sentiment, Jane just felt this bubbling sense of frustration, because it was like he was saying he hated how things were now.

Because despite the ups and downs, despite the threats—and come on, that was only one aspect—the truth was, their lives were actually pretty awesome. Jane had absolutely no desire to change any of it, and she couldn't understand Matt's fixation, his obsession, on being . . . what, boring? Nameless? Some mundane college kid going out and drinking with his dumb friends?

It made no sense. They were famous. They were in the Legion of Heroes. And yeah, there was danger, and yeah, it was hard for Matt to go and see people, but he had her, didn't he? And money and clothes and a great home and video games and literally anything else he ever asked for. And yet, Matt's unhappiness persisted; this constant, recurring melancholy, this burden she kept returning home to find rebloomed despite her every attempt to purge it. And in brutal honesty, it was the only real problem she had left right now. Him, his safety, his well-being. It was the only blight on her otherwise perfect existence, her intoxicating daydream life.

Growing up, every kid at some point wanted to be a superhero. Or, if they didn't, they were brain-dead—at least that's how Jane saw it. Who wouldn't want to be able to go anywhere, do anything, fly in, save the day, soar over legions of adoring fans? And now Jane could. And she did. And it was electrifying.

Granted, the fans weren't always adoring. The mantle of Dawn had a few rough patches she hadn't really thought through back in elementary school, unpleasantness that was as much a part of the job as the glory. Critics, for one. With millions of eyes watching her every move, just by sheer numbers, there was always going to be someone being mad. You could save a puppy in a river from drowning, and some paint-drinking moron would pop up on TV or social media saying, "That's ableist; some of us can't swim," or "I don't even like dogs."

Jane viewed such critics with the contempt and derision they deserved, sparing them and their mouth-breathing brays neither effort nor thought. It was "criticism" equivalent to the shrieks of whinging children pissing themselves for attention. But it hardly mattered. Compared to the abuse Jane had endured growing up just for being an empath, the criticism she faced now as Lady Dawn was laughable.

Nowadays, people actually attempted to justify why they hated her. And the second their negative opinions got voiced, a second horde of jabbering word warriors automatically leapt to her defense, snapping back unsolicited countertirades like a stray pack of verbose guard dogs. Jane neither sought out nor paid any of it any mind. Online arguments were for idiots. Leave the petty men to their petty wars.

Then, there were the competing demands for her time and attention, which were much harder to dismiss and pretty much constant. Thinking about being a superhero growing up, Jane had only ever really imagined the big-ticket items: title fights with supervillains, terrorist threats, rescuing people trapped in landslides, that sort of thing.

In reality, though, for the most part, those clear-cut problems weren't that frequent. It was the smaller things, the constant crises on the borders of disaster, which took up most of her time; minor issue after minor issue, with pressure for the Legion to intervene being constant. Constant and blurry.

Standoffs and labor strikes, protests, threats yet to crystalize, economic or environmental problems, dubious arrests, issues with no clear-cut solution, or cultural clashes where concepts of injustice conflicted with local tradition or law. Problems, muddy and misrepresented in their thousands. Everyone was a victim. Everyone deserved immediate help.

This pressure then created this constant argument, both inside the Legion and outside it, about where they should intervene and what precedent intervention set. Okay, so they flew in to prevent violence when one factory went on strike. Were they now going to stand guard for all of them? That was impossible; the Legion simply lacked the time and manpower.

But then, if they weren't going to intervene in everything, how did they choose? Did they stick to bigger strikes, implying those workers from smaller companies didn't matter? Or did they only help a particular cause or industry, implying they didn't care about the problems faced by the other groups? It was frustrating, but unavoidable. Who they helped always said something about them, either intentionally or otherwise.

Giselle's policy, as head of the Legion, was, thankfully, not to let perfection be the enemy of good. On this, Jane wholeheartedly agreed, and although Giselle was occasionally a bit more watchful of the political aspect than she was, they were both strongly prointervention.

The point of wading in wasn't just to provide physical assistance, but in many cases, to remind those involved that the eyes of the world were watching, and that they needed to shape up and fly right. It also, on the flip side, acted as a deterrent to others considering similar misconduct. If a thousand suns of blazing fury could descend upon you every time you shot at unarmed protestors, you soon thought twice before racking your shotgun.

All this, Jane, Giselle, and Charles Farrington—the acting but in reality new head of the Ashes—discussed at length at the Legion's many formal and informal meetings. Jane hated meetings, disdaining innately the idiotic notion of a committee for heroics, and she relentlessly hammered Giselle to change the Legion's response structure to simply triage problems up to the appropriately powered person and do away with any stupid discussion.

If there was something that needed doing, just do it. The more time you gave people to wring their hands, the more concerns they found to gripe about. Giselle had thus far refused. Diverse voices, democratic institution, all that. Dumb, dumb, dumb. Jane knew what was right.

So the public feedback was idiotic, the endless debates frustrating, and the politics of it all exhausting. But the rest? The rest was exhilarating. Jane was out there helping people. Really helping people. Saving lives. She'd shoot across the sky, land on the ground, and suddenly, everything would fall silent, and the same *oh crap* expression would flash over the faces of anyone bearing guilt.

People cheered as she flew past. They gave her free things just for visiting. Kids pointed and waved and sometimes even chased after her, and adults no longer recoiled when they saw her *E*. The kids, especially, Jane loved seeing the excitement of. Jane always made time for kids.

So everything in her life was where she wanted it—except for Matt. The dangers to him just kept on coming, and Jane didn't know how to stop them or make him less miserable. Her entire life, Jane had prided herself on not caring about people. Then somehow, she'd gotten tricked into caring about someone, and suddenly, it was torment. Every day, her thoughts niggled with fear of Matt dying. Every day, she stressed over his clear, poorly hidden unhappiness. The solution, surely, was so simple. Listen to her. Let her fix it. Stay safe.

Jane let out a long sigh, staring at Matt lying on the couch.

"I don't know how long," she said, echoing his question, "until this black hole thing passes."

"The paradox."

"Yes."

"Which could be . . . ?"

"I don't know. But we can outsmart this," she said, pleading. "We can. The only way I'll have to choose between you and the world is if I'm at risk of losing you, which can never happen if you're never in danger. So please. I need you to listen. I need you to take this seriously." She paused, her jaw clenched. "Every rule you break, every tricky little bit of misbehavior, brings you one step closer to being killed. So just . . . stop, okay? Leave it be."

"Stay up here in my little gilded cage," Matt replied bitterly.

"Better a cage up here than a bullet down there," Jane retorted, perhaps harsher than she meant.

Matt sighed. "Do I even have a choice?"

"No," she said. "I'm making the choice for you. It's for your own good. The Time Child said—"

"Oh yes, what did the Time Child say?" Matt asked, sounding sour and sarcastic. Jane's eyes narrowed.

"He said"—she scowled, fixing Matt with a glare—"that he killed his own grandmother. And that I'd have to choose whether or not to lose you. The implication, I would've thought, is pretty clear."

"Oh yeah?" said Matt, his voice flat. "What's that?"

"It wants me," Jane snarled, grinding her teeth, unable to believe this sullen hostility when she was trying to save his life, "to let go of you. To let you die. But I'm not going to do that. I am never going to do that."

"I love you too," her boyfriend replied, the words droll and devoid of affection. Jane rolled her eyes, feeling the heat rising beneath her temples.

"Mope all you want," she snapped. "I'd rather you're alive and unhappy."

"Just nonstop romance."

"Shut up," Jane spat. "Idiot. Stupid, goddamn—I'm trying to save you!"

Matt let out a deep sigh. For a few moments, he didn't say anything.

"I know," he replied eventually. All the resentment had leaked from his voice, replaced, to Jane's discouragement, with more depression. "I know." Matt rubbed his eyes. "I just . . . Another day. It's a gift that keeps on giving."

Jane made a face. She reached down to shift his legs aside then dropped onto the couch beside him, leaning close to try to catch his eye. Matt didn't exactly resist, though neither did he respond to her approach with any enthusiasm. She pulled him upright by the shoulders and tried kissing him a few times on the forehead.

"We've just got to be careful," Jane insisted. "No more phone calls. No more stupid stuff. No more . . . anyone, unless we know them."

"No more life outside the twenty-third floor," Matt murmured.

"Exactly," said Jane, and she wrapped her arms around him, holding his soft body close, pleased Matt finally understood.

Three days later, forty stories above the streets of Philadelphia, a little girl swayed atop a gray tiled ledge, alone save for the wind. Her feet—black leather school shoes with clean white socks—hung out over nothingness, her frizzy brown hair not properly tied nor brushed, dried tearstains trailing down her freckled cheeks. Her eyes were red. She wore a soft blue cardigan pinned with a brooch of a bee. She couldn't have been more than twelve.

Jane descended slowly, floating down until her golden boots touched concrete. Up here, the sounds of the city faded into nothingness—a muffled, windswept hum punctuated only by distant sirens. Jane took one audible step forward, then another. The girl spun around, her expression a mixture of horror and grief.

"Please," she whimpered. "No. Stay away."

"It's okay," Jane murmured. She edged forward, holding out gold-gloved hands. "It's okay. You can't hurt me."

The girl's face crumpled, twisting from fear to incalculable sorrow—then she broke, and once more collapsed into tears.

Jane took another, cautious step toward the child. There was a slight pressure all around her, as if the air was sticky, invisibly so, like a hot, thin mist. But the sensation evaporated when it met Jane's barrier, sizzling away in an almost imperceptible hiss. Azleena had been right.

"It's okay," Jane murmured, trying to make her voice . . . calm? Kind?

The girl turned away, staring once more out over the edge of the building, over the four-hundred-foot drop. Jane moved slowly forward, keeping her steps firm and deliberate. Finally, when she reached the girl's side, she crouched on the ledge beside her and sat maybe a foot away.

They stared out across the waiting city, Jane saying nothing, the girl shaking with silent sobs.

"What's your name?" Jane asked. A few moments passed. Through short, shallow breaths, the girl finally found the words to respond.

"Melissa."

"Melissa. Nice to meet you. I'm Jane."

"I know." The girl turned to her, her jaw clenched, tears and snot intermingling beneath her nose. "Why has this happened? What's happening to me?"

Jane hesitated. "You got your powers," she finally answered.

"Oh God," Melissa gurgled.

"It wasn't your fault."

"My dad," she sobbed. "My mom."

"It was an accident."

"Why . . . Why can't I . . . I just . . . How?"

Jane stared at the girl, unsure what to say, unsure how to respond. How did anybody deal with this? How did you explain to a child they were the reason their parents were dead?

Luckily, the voice in her ear didn't hesitate.

"When you're upset," Jane repeated, word for word from the earpiece, trying to keep her voice as gentle as possible, as factual, as calm, "or angry or scared, your skin puts out this . . . mist. Like little bits of dust. Have you learned about acids and bases in school?"

The girl gave a small, miserable nod.

"This dust . . . it sticks to living things. And then it turns very acidic. It's very rare. Very unusual. It's really unlucky it happened this way."

The technical term was *idiosyncratic manifestation*. According to the genetic analysis Azleena had run on the victims, the girl's power should have been the ability to voluntarily secrete a chemical coating. It could have been protective, maybe poisonous, sometimes as mundane as glue. But it should have been voluntary; it shouldn't have been aerosolized, and it definitely shouldn't have been lethal to organic life.

Usually, these sorts of abnormalities occurred when the person had some kind of genetic disorder. Usually, they were harmless, even beautiful.

Usually.

Yesterday, Melissa McKenzie had been a normal girl with a loving family. Today, she'd killed sixteen people. Unwittingly, Jane felt her fists clench. One day earlier, and this all could have been prevented. But now, this girl's life, her entire family—all of it, forever ruined. One day, and now only pieces. Now a question of not how many could be saved but how many would end up dead.

"Why?" Melissa whimpered. "Why did this happen? What did I do wrong?"

"Nothing," Jane answered sharply, then winced as Melissa recoiled. She tried again, trying to be more gentle, tapering the edge from her voice. "This isn't your fault."

"It should've been me," the child whispered. She hugged her legs to her chest, rocking precariously on the edge of the building, eyes leaking fresh tears. "I'm sorry. I didn't mean to. I didn't mean . . ."

Her voice trailed off as her shoulders slowly sagged—too exhausted, it seemed, to endure fresh grief. The girl's movements grew still.

"Are you going to kill me?" she whispered.

"What?" said Jane, flinching. "No."

"I'm a murderer."

"It was an accident. Look." Jane reached into the bag she was carrying, pulling free a bundle of cloth. "We—the Legion—analyzed your power. We can fix it. This suit, it's got"—Jane hesitated, struggling to remember what Azleena had said—"it's got little like fans all built into it. Really little. And they can suck the dust in, and then it's like . . . bicarb soda . . . and stuff." Jane could almost hear Azleena sighing. "It neutralizes the acid," she assured her.

The girl looked up, her expression miserable. "I'll be safe?"

"Yeah. I promise. One hundred percent safe."

"Ninety-eight percent," Azleena corrected in her earpiece. *Shut up*, Jane corrected in her head.

Melissa's eyes watered. "And my mom? My dad . . . ?"

"They're gone," Jane mumbled, then: "I'm sorry."

And for the second time since she'd gotten there, the little girl well and truly broke. Jane sat beside her, helpless in the gap of distance, a horrible tightness in her chest, not knowing what she was supposed to do.

"Give her a hug," Azleena demanded. "It might be the last time anybody can."

Jane hesitated for a moment, her arms stiff, uncomfortable. Then, a memory flickered in her head. A funeral. A deep, shaking sadness—but in the middle, a tiny hand, seeking comfort in a bigger one. Twin sorrows, nesting together for warmth.

On the roof of a forty-story building, looking out over nothing, the white-gold woman leaned over to the little girl and held her close between shaking sobs.

I cannot kill a time traveler, Matt Callaghan concluded. It was all he could do not to cry.

It had been almost two weeks now; two weeks of restless nights, of distracted thoughts, of too much time on Bluin, of churning the same problem over and over. Now, at 10:00 a.m. on a Wednesday morning, as Matt sat at the dining table in his apartment pretending to read constitutional law cases while Wally Cykes sat opposite pretending to be babysitting, the slow-moving processor that was Matt's brain finally crunched the last of its computations and printed out a result.

It couldn't be done. It simply couldn't. Not by him, not with his resources, not in any way which had even the slightest chance of succeeding. It was simply an issue of causation. The Time Child could see what was coming; therefore, any trap—literally any trap—which Matt or any other temporally linear being concocted, the Child could see coming.

The best plan—the absolute best plan in the world, completely flawless, split-second precise—was still at its core dependent on the Child being too rushed, too lazy, too arrogant, or (let's face it) too negligent to look where it was going and blundering straight into the noose. Expecting that wasn't feasible. Relying on it was nuts.

Get a psychic to trap him? Well great, all we needed was a guarantee the psychic wouldn't go all Albanian Cassandra eye gouge-y from one whiff of time brain, AND the Child not already taking Psy-Block AND them luring the Child somewhere AND the Child not seeing it coming.

Make some kind of anti-time-travel field or escape-blocking Disruptance? Fantastic, so long as it's taken as a given something like that is even possible AND he could find someone way smarter than him to create it AND Matt could explain everything to them without the Child realizing AND them luring the Child somewhere AND the Child not seeing it coming.

Beyond that, what? A bear trap full of time berries? Matt was annoyed at himself for how often his brain kept popping back and brightly suggesting this "solution," but he supposed that's what he got for wasting his childhood watching cartoons.

The thing was, even if Matt hypothetically had unlimited resources—which he didn't—and even if he'd personally been some kind of Black Death-esque empath multitool—which he wasn't—the task still would've been incredibly difficult. Sure, he had Jane, who'd beaten the Black Death, and sure, she could time travel.

But as much as Matt loved his girlfriend, he'd also seen firsthand how things had gone when the war she'd been fighting had shifted into the realm of a nonphysical power. A battle between her and the Time Child wouldn't be a battle of blowing stuff up, at which Jane was a prodigy; it would be a battle of time traveling. She just wasn't proficient. It wasn't even a possibility. The Child would shred her alive.

Plus, unfortunately, their latest interaction had left Jane seemingly less sceptical of the Child and more concerned about its latest ominous warning. Matt struggled not to visibly scoff. A big, nebulous paradox at the end of space and time? One that just so happened to require him dying? Sure. Sure, you little rat bastard, there was absolutely no way that wasn't legitimate or in any way related to your numerous attempts to have someone put bullets inside his head. *Please. Give me a break.*

So he was screwed, essentially. An entire fortnight spent in furious rumination, and Matt was right back where he'd started. The Time Child was (possibly) trying to kill him. And no matter how much he strained his brain, it seemed simply impossible to return the favor.

What the heck did he do?

Leaning back in his chair, careful not to let his Wally-facing face show any signs of anxiety or disappointment, Matt shut his eyes, trying to shift his brain away from circular thoughts of murdering a time traveler and toward some other workaround. Why, he found himself thinking, why did these hypercomplex problems keep falling to him? Why did he have to be the one to solve this nonsense? He wasn't that clever, why couldn't the geniuses figure it out?

Ed, he thought into the cosmos, *if you're out there, buddy, I could really use a hand.* That, of course, only caused a twinge of sadness to blossom in Matt's stomach, but he forced himself to take a deep breath and push the feeling aside. What would Ed do? Mope? Sit on his computer a lot? Play video games?

Well, screw it, thought Matt. *Let's think about this like it's a video game.*

There is an enemy you cannot beat. You lack the power to do it harm, and any attempt to defeat it results in immediate death. What are your options?

Well, normally, Matt reasoned, anything that was unkillable had been deliberately designed that way by the programmers because the player wasn't supposed to beat it—they were supposed to sneak past or find a way around . . .

Okay then, Matt thought, straightening up slightly. Across the table, Wally glanced over; Matt paid him no heed. Another angle. Sneak around. Break things down, peel back to the most basic facts.

His existence was a threat to superhumankind.

The Time Child (possibly) wanted that threat neutralized.

So long as Matt existed, that threat remained.

He did not want to die.

Want to die . . .

Die . . .

Holy—

Suddenly, Matt sat bolt upright. This time, Wally actually leaned his head around his computer, looking concerned.

"You okay?" the psychic asked. Matt fought to keep a handle on his thoughts, struggling not to leap up out of his chair.

"Yeah, fine," he assured him. With difficultly, Matt forced his butt the inch or so back down into sitting, struggling not to rise or cackle or punch the air in manic glee. Instead, after watching for a few seconds to make sure Wally's attention had returned elsewhere, Matt reached over and shuffled through his mess of law textbooks, finally finding and extracting a notebook and pen.

He flipped the book over, his hands jittery with excitement, disregarding the notes at the front and opening to the blank pages at the back. Then, very carefully bending over the page to make sure Wally couldn't possibly see what he was doing, Matt leaned down and wrote a three-word heading:

<u>Faking My Death</u>.

"So. Reasonably sure this isn't fake."

Jane grunted, staring out the open roller door to the greater storage lot, her hands on her hips. She tried to imagine this storage lot when it wasn't daytime. A lot of gray, a lot of corners. Poor lighting. A crappy place to die.

Before her, Giselle sat crouched on the balls of her feet, gingerly using a pen to lift the victim's skull, or what remained of it, from where it hung loosely over his lapel. The man's head had been crushed like an egg, bone and brains and viscera scattered everywhere across the concrete. Disgusting, though none of the three Legion women present balked at the sight of gore.

"Did we think it was?" Jane grumbled. On the far side of the concrete storage unit, Celeste had taken the form of a bloodhound and was giving each of the corners a prodigious sniff.

"I don't know," Giselle replied, tilting her head slightly to peer inside the inner workings of the guard's pulverized skull. "A girl can dream, can't she? Someone storing Halloween props. A prank, you know. I've seen stupider."

Equally crappy place for a prank, Jane mused. A nowhere storage facility on the outskirts of some nowhere town that everyone's eyes glazed over. Real hilarious in, what, sixty years, when whoever had put something inside this one particular unit eventually died, and their kids came to clear it out.

Whoever, of course, was the government, who were not normally known for their high-level, long-term pranks. Surface-level backwoods and boring, the facility was in actuality a collection of inter-Departmental storage units used to house things classified a little under top secret, stuff that although not quite ultra deadly was still too hazardous for the public eye.

At the end of a shift a couple of weeks ago, there'd been some confusion during the guards' changeover, something to do with a snapped leash and a runaway dog. One of the grunts ending their shift, a man named Alfie Holland, had signed out and then gone missing, and for about a week, everyone had assumed he'd just headed home. His next shift hadn't been until the following Sunday, and by the time he hadn't shown up for the shift after that and it'd dawned on his boss that he might not just be slacking, Alfie's friends and family hadn't heard from him in almost a fortnight. Suspicions he might've gone camping or taken a spontaneous road trip gave way to more serious concerns. Footage was reviewed, only to find there'd been some data corruption, so in came the sniffer dogs, and finally they found Alfie's body—a decapitated corpse left lying in a pool of its own viscera in the wide, empty space where once sat a Department of Defense prototype. A little *screw you* card from the robbery. The government called the Legion in within twenty-four hours.

It did have the hallmarks of supervillainy, Jane conceded. A notch up from what might be kicked over to the police, though it wasn't quite yet destruction and doom. This machine, whatever it was, this electromagnetic wave blocker, sounded like something capable of paralyzing a city proper. It made sense for the authorities to be concerned. A theft like this screamed prelude to a bigger crisis.

Yet it wasn't the potential danger of what had been stolen that had Jane feeling disquieted, nor was it the brutal nature of the death. It was the run of coincidences. The thieves' precise timing, the failure of the recording, Alfie Holland's spaced-out roster, the perfectly balanced stack of delays in everything coming to light. It felt more than bad luck. It felt like there was something someone wasn't telling her. Something she couldn't put her finger on. Something off.

Jane shook her head, trying to refocus her thoughts as Giselle took careful photos of the body. She had no idea what the government expected them to do here other than stand around and look tough. Celeste at least could be useful. Across the empty room, the faunamorph rose up out of dog into her human form, only for her head to immediately shift into that of a giant dragonfly. The sight of that was more disturbing than the dead body.

"Nuuuzzzinnnggg weird on the color spectrum," Celeste said, the words filtering through her insect mouth on the way back to human. Once more a normal, wavy brown-haired girl, she chewed her lip. "There's a bunch of smells, but once they go outside, they've been rained on."

"How many?" Giselle asked, standing and turning away from the body.

"Six." Celeste shrugged. "Men. Mostly midtwenties; mixed backgrounds. Can't tell any powers."

"Any weird dog senses?"

"Only that that body is no longer fresh."

"On that, we can agree."

Giselle slowly stepped the length of the room, drawing a careful eye over every detail—not so much for herself, Jane knew, but for the camera glasses she wore over her eyes, which were feeding an HD stream back to the Academy and Azleena. Jane watched her go, feeling no urge to join. The unit was maybe thirty by thirty feet, bare concrete, completely empty save for the body and the scuffles where the device had been taken from. There was a bit of mold and dust. Great.

It was nice of the government to invite them here, if only as a heads-up. Maybe it was an attempt at being friendly, an olive branch in light of recent tensions and hostilities. *Let's be friends again, here's a corpse.* Personally, Jane was doubtful even Celeste was going to find anything FBI forensics hadn't. There were no fingerprints on the body; the killer had been wearing gloves.

Unconsciously, she found her gaze drawn back to the headless corpse. It was sitting, legs straight out in an *L*, as if it had sat down for a picnic before its head exploded. It stank, but surprisingly, hadn't decomposed much. Insulated from the elements a bit, Jane supposed.

She wondered why it didn't disturb her more, staring directly at brutality like that. But for some reason, it didn't. The man looked more lifelike than deathlike. It was as if he'd just sat down and dozed off, how forgetful, sorry. And then somehow, his head had popped open.

I should probably pretend to be more worried, Jane thought. Certainly, if Matt were there, that's what he'd be telling her to do. Yet by now, Jane had seen her fair share of dead bodies, many of them far more concerning than Alfie. He'd just had his head crushed by a strongman without any warning. Quick way to go.

That was odd, Jane realized. Why did she assume it was a strongman? Yet, she just sort of knew somehow. Maybe it was something about the damage to the body, a pattern she could only subconsciously recognize. Yet, even as Jane stared, she could have sworn she saw the eyes of the headless man staring back at her, as if she could see a line extending out of him, forward and backward. Like she could see the shape of his face before the incident. How he'd looked at people.

Jane shook her head like a dog trying to clear its ears of water. The images vanished as quickly as they'd come.

"I've got the scents," she heard Celeste saying. Jane forced herself to look up, to focus back in on the other two Legion members and their conversation. "Not much use unless I can cross-reference, but they're there. I'd recognize them."

"Well, it's a start," replied Giselle. "We'll have Wally go through the memories and see if he can translate the information out of dog."

"Oh my God." Celeste laughed, delighted. "Out of dog."

"What about you?" the speedster asked, turning to Jane. "Any insights?"

"Into what?" Jane scowled. "Theft? Murder?"

"The floor is open."

Jane crossed her arms across her white-gold chest and shrugged. "Hard to speak much without a head."

"Yeah." Giselle grimaced. Her gaze fell onto the body as her lips dropped in a sad frown. "I feel so sorry for the family," she said. "Can you imagine burying someone you love like this?"

Yes, thought Jane, *that's what most people would be feeling.* She tried to look at the body differently, tried to imagine it was Matt or her dad sitting there, unmoving, broken in pieces. The image came sudden, unbidden, and far clearer than Jane ever would've anticipated. She felt her heart abruptly start to race and her arms burn with nervous energy.

"Hey," said Giselle, looking worried. "Don't freak out. Take a break if you need to."

"I'm fine," Jane spat, the words coming out harsher than she would've liked. She forced herself to take a deep breath, then tried to change the subject. For some reason, the image of dead Matt wouldn't go away. "So have we actually found anything?"

"Well, I've found some dust and a dead person," Giselle remarked, leaning back on her heels, hands in her pockets. Across the room from her, Celeste guffawed. "And I've got plenty of footage for Azleena. Az? Want me to swing by anything more?"

"No, thank you," the genius's voice said over general comms. "I'm good."

Giselle shrugged. "Well, here's hoping you see something we haven't. Honestly, though?" The speedster shook her head. "I don't know how much good it does us being out here. What do they want me to do with a dead body? Run at it?"

"You could do the backward . . . man running thing," Jane suggested. "Around the Earth. From the comic book."

"It is so sad to me that I know exactly what you're referencing." Giselle sighed. "And yes, I will admit, we've all tried it, and no, it does not work."

"I was joking."

"I know," Giselle laughed. "Matt's clearly having an influence."

"Aww, Matt," Celeste sighed from the other side of the room. "How is he? He's such a sweetie."

"You saw him two weeks ago," Jane replied, fixing her with a scowl.

"Yeah, but that feels like ages. Tell him I said hi."

Jane's eyes narrowed, and suddenly, the headless person in her vision was a woman. "Tell him yourself," she said, her voice arctic.

"Come on." Giselle stepped between the two, patting Jane on the shoulder. "Let's go tell the nice army man we don't know who killed his colleague. And say thank you for notifying us." She stood with her hands on her hips, stared back through the roller door, and shook her head. "Why do I feel like this is either going to be one of those ones we never solve, or that is going to come back to bite us."

"Because there is a documented correlation between leadership and paranoia. The sword of Damocles."

"Thanks, Az. I prefer daggers."

The three of them strode from the unit and pulled the door back down. Giselle reapplied the crime scene tape.

"Do you think he's happy?" Celeste asked abruptly.

"Who?" Jane replied. She almost asked, "The dead man?" but clearly that wasn't who Celeste was talking about.

"Matt."

"What?" scowled Jane, bristling. "What are you talking about? Of course he's happy."

"He just seemed kind of sad the other night."

"He's not sad," snapped Jane, perhaps overaggressive. "He's just stressed. People are trying to kill him."

"And . . . wouldn't that make him unhappy?"

"Yes. No. Why are we even talking about this?" Jane demanded. Celeste shrugged.

"I don't know. I just feel sorry for him. Stuck at home all day."

"That's for his own good," Jane glowered.

"Don't you worry he's going stir-crazy?" Celeste nodded toward Giselle for support. "I had a cousin once, an astronaut. They made her do all this solitary confinement training. After like three weeks, she went bonkers. Filled all the instrument holes with mashed potato. They said if it had been a real mission, she would've jettisoned herself into space."

"Matt's not an astronaut!"

"And from my observations, he wouldn't waste mashed potato," Azleena piped up.

"Jesus Christ."

"I agree isolation's tough," said Giselle, ignoring Jane's visible agitation, one side of her mouth twitching into a slight frown. "But Matt's not stupid. He'd let us know if there was a problem. And he knows he's got to stay home for his safety. It's not like he's going to be up there, planning something dumb."

By lunchtime the next day, Matt was pretty sure he had narrowed down the five key ingredients of no longer being alive.

Death. How he was going to fake dying in a way that was simultaneously convincing, irreversible, and invited no further questions.

Identity. Who he was going to pretend to be after he "died," and how he was going to stay hidden.

Relocation. Tied in closely with *Identity*. Where he was going to go, what could he do without attracting attention, and what could he be.

Money. A key foundation in steps one through three. Maybe a problem, maybe not. Matt the Human, currently famous, had assets. All he needed, therefore, was a way to discreetly spend those assets, and then somehow preserve them, or at least maintain some sort of income. He needed to work out a way to put his money in a form that couldn't be traced yet could still be retrieved once the smoke cleared.

Family. Arguably the simplest; arguably the hardest. How did he shield his friends and family from the trauma of his "dying"? How did he let them know? Did he bring them along? Would they even want to come?

Matt could rule out, from the outset, going into witness relocation or some other kind of government protective services. The whole point of this was to get conclusively away from possessive overbearing authority, and blood-thieving lawsuits aside, past experience told him the government was simply too incompetent to keep a new identity free of leaks.

No, this would be a self-made, closed-circle kind of endeavour, with no one, or the very fewest number of people, involved.

He would have to involve Jane. First, because Matt loved her and—wow, this was weird to articulate, but upon reflection, he guessed it was true—he wanted them to spend the rest of their lives together. Second, because if she wasn't aware Matt wasn't actually dying, Matt knew Jane was likely to engage in—how would he put it?—extremely unproductive behavior. Screaming, rampages, destroying cities, ripping apart the fabric of time; you know, that kind of stuff.

So Jane had to be looped in. But involving Jane in his scheming—in arguably the greatest con Matt had ever pulled—carried complications. For one, she tended to become somewhat . . . *resistant* . . . whenever the idea of him and death floated too close together. But they could probably work past that with some soothing words and calm de-escalation.

The second, greater problem was that in terms of her own life, Jane was pretty much exactly where she wanted to be, and therefore pretty unlikely to want to quietly give everything up, or even concede that giving it up was necessary. Matt couldn't explain to her why he had to fake his death either, because articulating the true reason out loud would alert the Time Child—or Time Children, or whatever—that he was onto them.

Jane would also likely fixate on her own ability to protect him rather than acquiescing to the plan and being helpful. There could be no negotiation; Matt would have to deliver his death as a *fait accompli* once he was fully prepared to faux kick the fake bucket.

So Jane needed to be on board. But someone else did too.

"You know what I feel like?" he said to Giselle as they sat with books open at the dining table. Giselle had spent yesterday out with Jane admiring headless corpses in storage lockups, but today was back to babysitting. "Italian."

"Yeah?" The speedster's head poked above her laptop.

"Really, really good Italian," Matt continued. "Authentic Italian."

"From Italy." Giselle laughed. "You want me to get food from Italy?"

"Can you do it?"

"Pfft," the speedster scoffed. "Can I do it. I do it all the time. There is a little man in Chiang Mai who has been making me prawn Pad Thai every week for a year now. I've gone through thirteen pairs of shoes."

"Great, so you'll do it?"

"Italy's so *faaar*," the girl complained. "Can't I just go to New York? New York has such good Italian."

"It's original or it's nothing."

"You're nothing." She stuck out her tongue.

"Harsheel Singh would've done it," he countered.

Giselle rolled her eyes. "That is some weak, weak manipulation, and I am disappointed in myself that I respond to it."

Matt grinned. "You know you want to."

"I know I want to," she admitted. "I know my legs want to. It's just my lazy, lazy brain. Plus, this chapter is just starting to get good."

"That is a lie, and you know it. No chapter of any college textbook has ever approached *good* or anything synonymous."

"Big hater. Big, dirty, Italian-loving hater."

"You forgot *fat*."

"You're not fat. Maybe if you cut back on the Italian food . . ." Giselle rolled her eyes then grinned at him. "Fine. What do you want?"

Matt gave her his order. Giselle wrote it down.

"Twenty minutes," she said, getting to her feet. "You'll be alright?"

"First hint of danger, you're on speed dial."

"My phone will be on. Flatten the balcony once I'm out?"

"Sure." When she wasn't teleported in, Giselle used the balcony to gain access to the apartment, which otherwise had no entrance beside the subterranean lift. Once she'd hurtled herself speeding off the side of the building, Matt could press a button to retract the balcony into the apartment's framework and have the entire north side sealed by reinforced walls.

It was somewhat overkill, but Matt supposed it stopped fliers, stray pigeons, or other speedsters entering. Giselle would then phone him once she returned to have him open the wall back up.

The tall Eurasian girl stretched her arms above her head, articulating her spine with a series of satisfying cracks. Then she dipped briefly on either side to touch her toes—with casual ease, Matt noticed with envy, having never been even remotely flexible—shrugged off her jumper, blurred on a backpack, and then, with a mock salute and a laugh, disappeared in a rush of wind and vanished out the window.

Matt stuck his nose onto the balcony to make sure she was truly gone; then, feeling nervous, he sealed the terrace and turned back to the now empty apartment, steadying himself for what was to come.

Matt raised his hands, closed his eyes—and prepared to summon a god.

"Oh, omniscient Time Child," he intoned. "Oh, blue-eyed, blond-haired, all-seeing . . . note-writing . . . boy . . . person . . . hear me! I seek to know your will! Appear!" Matt paused, cracked open an eyelid, and glanced around the apartment. Absolutely nothing had changed. His chest deflated somewhat. "Um . . . please?"

The furniture looked back at him in silent judgment.

"Can . . . Can you hear me?" Matt asked, his words ringing out across the empty living room. "Oh, mighty . . . or regular . . . Child of Chronos, look upon this moment! If you are out there, if you can hear me: give me a sign!" He threw his hands back up, waited a second, then once more glanced around. Nothing moved. The apartment remained conspicuously empty.

Matt felt himself growing annoyed. "Listen here, you little albino shi—" He stopped himself, took a deep breath, then continued. "Time Child. I know—I assume you are watching. Because you see everything. Presumably. I would appreciate a minute of your time. Which I assume you have a lot of. Because you are a time traveler.

"I am planning a somewhat drastic course of action, and I want to make sure it aligns with what's on your agenda. I seek your consent." He paused, peering over on his tiptoes to see if the little boy was hiding behind the sofa. "I require a consultation." He wasn't. "Please. Fifteen-minute appointment." A pause. "Ten, max. Come on. Any time now. It's ya boy. Big Matty C. Killed the Black D. Calling in that favor, which you . . . probably don't owe me."

Matt's shoulders drooped a bit, and his mouth slid into a frustrated frown. "Alright, listen here, you little sack of crap." He scowled. "I know you're listening, so either manifest your mangy ass in my living room, or I'm going to look like an idiot yelling at the roof."

Matt stopped speaking, and the room once more fell silent. There were absolutely no signs of additional life.

"Fine!" Matt shouted. "Fine! You want to be like that, be like that! Don't appear! I don't care! We'll do it your way, fine!"

He cleared his throat and raised his arms dramatically, like a voodoo priest summoning a bog monster. "Oh, great all-seeing Time Child! If you have no objections to the path I am taking, give me no sign!" He paused and cracked open an eyelid. Nothing happened.

"If you think my idea is good, give me no sign!" Pause. Still nothing. "If this is the right thing to do, and you completely support me doing it, give me no sign!" Bubkes. "I am happy to take on any amendments, recommendations, or feedback you would like to take this opportunity to impart!" Silence. "Alright, well, if any man, woman, or godlike Child knows any reason why I should not proceed with fake killing myself, speak now or forever shut up and stay out of it."

The room stayed resoundingly silent. Matt dropped his arms, feeling phenomenally stupid. "Outstanding. Thank you, oh enigmatic godboy, for your implied blessing at this most pivotal moment."

Matt slumped back down at his laptop. Well, at least he tried.

"Prepare yourself, Lady Dawn. You face your nemesis. You face a god."

Jane stood at the gateway to the Welsh cemetery, staring out coldly at the army of rotting corpses arrayed against her. Flesh sloughing off, limbs shuffling in place, the undead stood silent and impassive, a horde of shuffling sentinels surrounding a figure at their center—a pointy-faced, pale-skinned woman in her mid-to-late twenties with dark eyes and blood-red hair. Gloves of thin, black spiderweb mesh extended up her arms and over her raised hands, and the edge of the black Victorian lace dress she was wearing dragged undaunted through the mud.

"The rising tide swallows all men," the woman called, her eyes wide and encircled with mascara. "And I will rise once more, to swallow you, to swallow—"

"You're not Ana Bloodbane," Jane interjected. "Thank you. You're not her. Don't treat me like an idiot."

Every day. Every goddamn day, it seemed, some new whack job burrowed up out of the woodwork claiming to be her archrival. Jane didn't understand. It had gotten worse since the *Tonight Show*. Didn't these people have jobs? Maybe it was her own fault, since she kept taking them out nonlethally. Maybe if she decapitated one of these so-called *supervillains*, there would be fewer candidates for the role.

She was in Wales, in the United Kingdom, standing on the green and muddy outskirts of a town whose name she couldn't pronounce, half a klick in from a police barricade, and staring down the latest contender to her nemesis throne.

This one, at least, was somewhat interesting. Myfanwy Mary Llewellyn, twenty-seven and in possession of a rare and unusual power: the ability to reanimate dead bodies. Rare, but not unique; the original Legion had actually fought someone with this power once, a woman by the name of Ana Bloodbane, who had originally actually applied to join the Legion's ranks.

She had been good, and clearly committed to mastering her abilities, but her application had been rejected by Caitlin Reid after due consideration, most likely thanks to fears of bad PR. Unfortunately, the real Bloodbane had not taken her refusal well, and in addition to nurturing a grudge, every advancement she had then made as she kept pushing the limits of her powers seemed to correspond, sadly but probably predictably, with her own sanity taking a hit.

By the time the Legion had been forced to fight her, Bloodbane's powers extended beyond just puppeteering human corpses. Capable of controlling any dead tissue, she could meld separate bodies into new monsters, and had been able to completely detach her consciousness from her original form and transfer it into any deceased flesh.

This last aspect made Ana Bloodbane a popular figure among fringe dwellers and lunatics, Jane was coming to learn, many of whom enjoyed claiming to be her, reconstituted from meat left dormant and only just now resurrecting. It was a terrifying concept, but in this case, nothing more. Jane had done her homework.

"You're not Ana Bloodbane," she repeated. Her voice rang out over the cemetery. Jane kept a watchful eye on the zombies, waiting to see if her words triggered any movement. Myfanwy's own face was too far away and heavily powdered to see any paling. "We've got a copy of your driver's license. Family photos. Necromancy is rare—you think they don't keep lists?"

The black-clad woman didn't respond. "You look the same as you did a year ago. The same as you did growing up. If you were some sort of Bloodbane flesh puppet, you wouldn't look like an existing person. You're too fresh. Sorry. Besides," said Jane, gesturing around, "zombies? Goddamn amateur hour. You might scare some locals, but I've seen the footage. I know what the real Fleshtide could do. You're not even in the same league. You're ten ranks below cheap knockoff.

"So the question is," Jane continued, stretching out her arms, gold cape billowing in the death-scented wind. "Do you genuinely believe you're an offshoot of the original, or are you just doing this for attention?"

She rolled her shoulders and cracked her neck. "Because if it's the former, you need help, and I'll do the next part softly. But if it's the latter, let me make myself clear: you have one chance, *one*, to disassemble your little undead horde, or I will break you in half."

A hundred feet away, the necromancer flinched. A second too late, she tried to cover the movement, arching her back straighter and glaring out at Jane with an attempted sneer. "F-Foolish girl," she stammered. "I traverse the deathless darkness. I command an—an army that feels neither pain nor . . . nor—"

"You have an army," Jane interrupted, "of soulless meat sacks without any sort of powers that I can pulverize with absolutely no remorse. You don't have a threat: you've got dolls made of tissue paper. This'll be the most guilt-free beating I've dispensed in weeks."

This time, Jane was sure she saw Myfanwy flinch.

"Myfanwy Mary Llewellyn," Lady Dawn declared. "You are under arrest for the murder of Sandra Milne and Christine Thomas. For sending a horde of undead to rip apart your ex-girlfriend and her new partner while they were asleep. Stand down." Jane curled her hands into fists as her eyes blazed gold. "Or the next flesh you'll hear breaking will be your own."

The following day, when Wally was in the bathroom, Matt placed a call to Azleena. The genius answered in her usual emotionless tones, which

Matt knew by now was just a symptom of her intellect, her character, or of being fifteen.

"Az," he said into the phone. "Hey. I need a favor. Is there any way you could get me a computer I can do stuff on that's utterly untraceable? I mean a hundred percent. Nobody able to check it, ever. Not the government, no one."

To his somewhat disappointment, Azleena did not seem particularly thrown by this request. Matt had prepared this whole story—a convoluted tale involving Jane, public humiliation, and a penchant for pretending to be horses—ready for deployment, only for the diminutive genius to say, "Sure," in her usual monotone and simply disconnect the call.

The next day, when Giselle arrived, she came bearing gifts: a new, sleek silver laptop complete with case and corresponding instructions.

This computer spoofs itself onto local mobile networks, the note accompanying the laptop read, *which then reroutes part packages through separate VPNs with randomized—It's secure.*

Azleena had obviously gotten bored.

Nobody can conceivably remotely trace or retrieve anything you do on this. The only way would be local, so when you're done, put it in the case, do up the zipper, and push all four green bobbles on the corners. That will dissolve it in hydrochloric acid. Six minutes, and there'll be nothing left.

Enjoy your porn.

The nerve, Matt bristled; he'd never been ashamed of his pornography. Still, he was reassured that he could now research with impunity and without having to worry about government technopaths hacking into and uncovering his plans.

With the Child summoning a nonstarter, Matt now turned to commencing his scheme in earnest, and the preliminary research required. Figuring the monkey shouldn't let go of the branch until it had a new branch to swing to, he started off with ways to assume a new life.

After only twenty-four hours of researching, Matt had become convinced he was going to have to involve Azleena. Although he'd been initially uncertain, it soon became clear that utilizing the Legion's resident genius was pretty much his only option, because holy heck were modern antifraud measures nothing to scoff at.

In the age of technopaths, psychics, and widespread shapeshifting, governments around the world took identity fraud very, very seriously, spurred on—Matt noted ruefully and with a degree of irony—in recent times by his own well-publicized clairvoyant stunt.

The American Department of Powers Regulation, in particular, had significantly tightened up their processes in light of the scandal his revelation had caused, and their mandatory-issue Ident-Cards were now pretty much essential to accessing any kind of social services or safety net. This fake would have to be elaborate. He couldn't just grow a moustache.

A regular new identity probably wouldn't be sufficient either, unfortunately. Matt Callaghan was famous—globally famous. To ditch that yoke and slip into obscurity, Matt was going to need facial reconstructive surgery, or at the very least some sort of device to make his features appear different, both options mandating Azleena's involvement. Then there was getting a power; either faking one or imitating it, if that was even possible. The clairvoyant shtick was done now, that duck never again to fly. Again, Azleena was pretty much his only choice.

But presuming he could make himself appear as someone else and appear to have powers like someone else, where would he go? It had to be somewhere remote, practically off the grid, Matt reasoned, in order to minimize the possibility of ever bumping into anyone who knew him. Hiding in plain sight was fine when nobody knew you were hiding, but when the world knew who you were, when even one tiny slipup could alert nations, any well-populated urban area was just too risky. Remote was good. The more removed the better.

"Listen to this," he told Giselle between mouthfuls of ramen, unable to resist sharing his findings (and admittedly probably going to eventually loop her in anyway). "*Pressing Paws: Life among the Dog People.*"

"What's that?"

"There's this community in California, up past Sacramento, where everybody lives as dogs."

"What?" The speedster blurred from the other side of the table and appeared beside him, peering over his shoulder at the laptop. "No way."

"Yeah," said Matt, reading down. "It's a mixture of faunamorphs and real dogs. Apparently, they live in dog form all the time, one hundred percent. There's no interaction as people. It's this big estate and"—he squinted, reading on—"I guess someone brings them dog food? Or acts as trustee?" He looked up at her. "That could be fun?"

"Too many fleas," Giselle replied, making a face. "What's this got to do with constitutional law?"

"I don't know." Matt shrugged. "Does the constitution still apply if you're a dog?"

Giselle opened her mouth to answer, then stopped. "That," she said after a moment, "is an excellent essay question. Can you renounce humanhood?"

"Can dogmen own property?"

"Enter into contracts."

"Maybe I should specialize in dog law."

"It's amazing how well that suits you," she remarked. Matt chose to take it as a compliment.

Giselle returned to her seat as Matt continued delving. Here, this might be a bit more feasible. There was a community in the Maldives—a conglomeration of depth-adjusted water breathers—who lived apart from human civilization and entirely on the ocean floor. By the sound of it, they were self-sufficient; had little cities and everything, not to mention they were isolationists, and . . . Wait, no, no. Matt clicked through some additional links. Apparently, these novus Atlanteans were periodically raided by local authorities for looting cargo ships and sinking fishing trawlers. And for some reason, a ton of them seemed bizarrely fanatical. Matt found a disconcerting number of articles about children who manifested water breathing being kidnapped in an attempt to "organically" grow the tribe.

That didn't sound good. That didn't sound like something he wanted to be a part of.

A community of pyromorphs who spent their time as fire perpetually, merged into something called the "Eternal Flame"? No. While that did sound pretty anonymous, there was a clear barrier to entry for a powerless human that was called *being burned to death*.

A Siberian floramancer commune, isolated and raising their own produce, entirely off the grid? The isolation level sounded good, but Matt would have to come up with some way to fake growing plants. Plus change his face and learn Russian.

A brothel full of shapeshifters? At least that way his face wouldn't matter, but he wasn't wild on the thought of earning his keep there, nor having to have a conversation with Jane about ethical nonmonogamy. Matt imagined she might take that as well as his actual, physical death.

He continued researching onward and onward, finding lots of possibilities but just as many problems. Nevertheless, it was a start. There were isolated pockets out there. Little communities of the like-minded, the like-powered, the closed off. Maybe, he began to think, if he had sufficient imagination, it was less a question of where he could possibly go, of what powers Azleena could pretend to give him . . . and more a question of where Matt might best fit in.

"That's them."

The police sergeant was a tall man, maybe in his midforties, who clearly took pride in keeping his uniform neat and his hair short. Standing behind the line of wooden blue barricades set up where the grassy slope of the cemetery met the street, he glared over at the protesters assembled across the road, his back straight, his jaw clenched. Jane didn't need Matt's powers of observation to understand. She'd spent enough time around soldiers.

"What are they doing?" she asked. The sergeant kept his expression neutral, but it was a close thing.

"Same as always."

"Breaking the law?"

The police officer worked his jaw. "Technically, no."

Across the street from the cemetery, maybe thirty members of the Eastborough Baptist Church had assembled, holding large bright signs bearing various repulsive slogans, colored backgrounds bearing bold black text. *Soldiers Die, God Laughs*; *God Hates Powers*; *You're Going to Hell*; *Repent or Be Doomed*. Their chants carried more of the same, interspersed with more denigration. The protesters were mostly white and middle aged, although Jane saw some children among them. Her stomach churned with disgust.

Up the small, grassy hill behind the police line, a funeral service was taking place. Though the barricades put some space between them, the protesters' signs would have still been clearly visible to those in attendance, the shouts persistent in the background to the mourners and priest.

Jane turned to the sergeant. "I'm not sure what I can do," she said, the words a pill bitter, yet truthful. "I can go scare them, flash some light. Beyond that . . ."

The police officer shook his head. "It's not right."

"You'll get no disagreement there."

"Walt Burbank was a good kid," he said, prying the words from his lips like the teeth of a steel trap. "He doesn't deserve this. His folks don't deserve this."

"I agree with you. The question's still what we do about it."

The tall man looked down at her. "Your boyfriend," he stated. "Saw what he said on Leno."

Jane sniffed. "What of it?"

"They worship him?"

"In a way."

"They listen to you, seeing as you're seeing him?"

"Doubt it. Might listen if I blast them."

The sergeant's face remained hard as he stared out over the protesters. "Going heavy's no good. They're asking for it, all of them. Angling for a lawsuit. Half the reason they're out here." His bristling head shook. "Didn't ask you out here for your powers. We can handle a few dozen lunatics. Just figured you might have an in. Be able to talk this lot into making them go away."

Talking was more Matt's thing, Jane grimaced internally. Nevertheless, she squared her shoulders.

"Happy to try. Can't make any promises."

The police officer's features remained taut as he glared off down the road. "Any attempt."

Jane gave him a curt nod before maneuvering between two blue barricades and out into the street beyond. There was little traffic along the Kansas highway, and she paid no heed to cars.

As Jane advanced, she let her powers stream out behind her in a trail of lightning gold. The crackling of her energy induced a temporary lull in the Baptists' chanting, and by the time she reached their sidewalk, two dozen pairs of eyes were boring silent hate into her skull. Jane's own eyes narrowed into slits.

She stopped about five feet away, cracking and flexing her gloved knuckles. The foremost protester, a gaunt, stubble-faced man wearing sports sunglasses and with tufts of gray hair sticking out the corners of his red baseball cap, stared at her in wide-eyed revulsion, physically recoiling in contempt.

"Devil-born," he spat.

Oh good, they had a special name for her. Jane met the contempt in his glare with her own.

"Leave," she demanded.

"Morningstar. False light. Pride of Satan's Horde."

"Walker. It's Jane Walker. Partner of Matt Callaghan. Who I know has told you to stop."

There were hisses among the assembled Baptists. Their spokesman at the center of them scowled at her, his lips pursing to bare ratlike teeth. "How dare you speak his name."

"Matt Callaghan? He's my boyfriend."

"Vile harlot. Deceiver. Babylonian whore."

What the hell did Matt see in these people? Jane scowled. She swallowed a dozen insults, forcing her temper back. *Don't say what you want to say*, her partner's words echoed in her head, through their many long debriefs and discussions. *Say what you think will get the best results.*

"Your pastor isn't with you," she observed, angling her neck slightly to take in the full extent of the crowd. "Where is he today?"

"His business is none of yours," the spokesman sneered.

"Fine," Jane responded. "But you might want to check with him what you're doing." This met momentary silence, which Jane seized on. "Matt's made it clear. I know it, your pastor knows it. No more of this funeral crap."

"We know our rights," a dumpy woman who looked as if she moisturized with butter piped up from among the crowd. "You can't make us. The First Amendment—"

"I'm not making you do anything." Jane scowled, fixing the woman with a stare, causing her to flinch. "Just like you can't make Matt take your phone calls. Everyone's free to do what they like." She swept a glare across the sullen, silent Baptists. "Maybe go check with your pastor. Ask him what's important. Access to Matt, or making this poor family's life hell."

There was a muttering as the protesters exchanged glances, and to Jane's amazement, she saw some of the signs droop. Was this how Matt felt all the time, she wondered, feeling a rush of unexpected giddiness, being able to make people do what you wanted just by talking?

The spokesman, however, was undeterred, fixing Jane with an acidic glower. "Your words are poison, golden idol. Your devil gifts consume you. You will not command us. We reject the apple; we are children of God."

"I'm not commanding anyone," replied Jane. "There are actions, and there are consequences."

"There are consequences. Oh yes, there are," the gaunt man warned, jutting out his leathery, tendon-strung neck. "A lake of fire waiting for you and all sinful souls. Repent, lest the false strength consume you. There is no true light but God's."

"I'm calling him right now," said Jane, reaching into her pocket. She held up her phone. "I'm calling Matt, and I'm putting him on camera, and you can all explain to him why you're not listening to his words."

There was further discontented muttering, but after a moment, the murmuring was accompanied by the reluctant lowering of signs.

Jane pressed on. "You've done your job. You've made your point. The world saw you." She gestured at the funeral atop the hill. "Give this family some peace. Go home. You're done here."

The Baptists grumbled but continued to shrink before the sight of Jane's still-raised cell phone like vampires before the cross. Jane spied one of the children clutching their mother's hand and whispering something worried as they leaned over. Slowly, the protesters began to turn away.

The rat-faced man was the last to go. "The day is coming," he warned. "Beware the reckoning, Lady Dawn. God sees those who fail his test, and your sins most of all. He will make an example of you, and all others like you. The Devil's Legion. The day will come when the chosen will be free of you, and we will ascend, one family at His side."

Dear Mom, Dad, Jonas, and Sarah,
I'm sorry I've had to do this.

Matt stared at the words on the screen, then sighed and hit backspace. One, he realized, these should be handwritten letters. Two, he shouldn't write them until closer to the date. Prepping too early carried the risk of the letters being discovered and the whole plan revealed. Three—the notes should be separate. One for each of them. One each to address everything they meant to him, and everything he hoped they could be.

Even looking at the blank screen, feeling himself tear up a little, Matt could see what the letters would say. That he wasn't actually dead. That he'd had no choice but to fake it. Why it didn't mean in any way that he didn't want to be with them or that he didn't love them; that he was sorry, but that this was the only way.

Then, he thought, recounting good memories, better days. The time they'd caught his dad cheating at tennis. The tale of the burnt lasagne. Sarah's phase of believing she was a fairy. Jonas's years of mispronouncing words.

From the past then to the future. What he hoped for each of them; reassurances for his parents, encouragement and advice for his siblings. A promise to get in contact, if ever possible, if ever safe. Permission to grieve. A plea to move on.

It felt selfish, he realized as he typed it down, as he made notes, as he erased them. So utterly selfish to inflict this sudden loss without any warning after he'd already turned their lives upside down. But he was doing it for them. For all of them. It was the only way they'd ever know peace.

And they would be looked after. Matt was sure of that. Whatever support they needed, whether it be emotional or financial, Jane would see to it, the Legion would. There'd be enough people to share the truth with, in his small secret circle. Enough to mitigate the trauma. Hopefully.

Mom, Dad, Jane. Jonas, Sarah. Azleena. Giselle. Wally, because he'd probably psychically find out. Maybe Will, if Wally couldn't keep his mouth shut. Already too many people. Far too many. You couldn't just extract one life without entangling them all.

Matt sighed and closed down the empty farewell letters, packing away his yearning grief and trying to return to the fun bits of his semicidal plan.

Money. Money, as always, presented an issue.

Unusually for a boy of nineteen, Matt Callaghan was very well off. This was not due to any special effort on his part, but merely his celebrity existence, which naturally, Matt had wasted no time in monetizing.

There was his and Jane's appearance on *The Tonight Show*; the use of their likenesses on a variety of licensed T-shirts, posters, costumes, stationary, action figures, and bobbleheads; sponsorships from Psy-Block, Nike, and Mountain Dew, of all companies. Jane's earnings from being paid to show up and look decorative at particular events, and royalties from a series of mental self-defense videos a corporate training company had commissioned from Matt a few months ago.

Once their income came in, minus their agent's fee, Matt was the one who managed it, Jane's approach to money being what could politely be called incautious and more accurately described as "spend it all immediately before it's stolen by some unarticulable threat."

Matt, on the other hand, had always been a very responsible saver and did not narrow his eyes suspiciously at the mere mention of bank accounts. He had therefore thus far taken charge of the couple's wealth management and (he thought) been doing a very good job.

The thing was, having money was not the issue—disappearing with it was. In his initial brainstorming, Matt had noted down a variety of potential techniques to conceal money, but all of them seemed to have drawbacks.

There was, of course, the tried and tested "withdraw a bunch of cash and stuff it into a suitcase" approach, but the problem with that was that large withdrawals prior to his purported death would raise suspicions, and it was vital no suspicions were ever raised past infancy. Similarly with offshoring large amounts of money into properties or foreign bank accounts, there was both the issue of the eyebrows the proximity to his death would elevate, and of how to access the money after him, the owner, was allegedly dead.

Matt had also done a bit of research into cryptocurrency, a relatively new field that, after an hour of research, he was one hundred percent confident he was no closer to understanding or being able to explain. Apparently, a computer solved some puzzles to make some tokens, which were uncopiable—allegedly.

Except, surely if a computer could do it, a computer could also reverse engineer a solution, or at least trace where the tokens had been transferred. Matt didn't really know. The whole thing sounded like a get-rich-quick scheme either set up by unscrupulous technopaths, or an investment that was permanently at risk of being eviscerated by them.

Then there was what some might have called the more Bond villain techniques: using cash now to buy a bunch of gold or diamonds to be sunk to the bottom of the sea or buried somewhere in a hole.

Gold no—that was entirely out. Anyone who bought gold bars was clearly up to no good. Diamonds, though? Diamonds might work.

True diamonds, Matt learned, registered at the time of mining, generally held value well and were considered difficult to fake because while there were a limited number of diamond Midas people out there who could transmute other materials to diamond just by touching, plus crystal-morphs who were able to, who knows, turn their flesh to diamond and then pull off a toenail, the former's handiwork would reverse under the right conditions, and the latter's was contaminated with organic DNA.

It wasn't inconceivable that he, a young, potentially irresponsible man finding himself burdened with a sudden influx of wealth, would *invest* in a large number of diamonds to, who knows, decorate his toilet . . . and for those diamonds to subsequently disappear from any oversight.

It all came down to how much money he had, and how much money he actually needed, Matt thought to himself. If he had heaps of money, and he only needed to keep a little bit, then it wouldn't be inconceivable for him to just buy some diamonds, maybe ostensibly to make Jane a necklace or use in some kind of gift, and then, when he died, have those diamonds get lost in the . . . explosion? House fire?

Matt was still undecided on how this whole fake death thing was going to happen. Because how he could possibly "die" so completely and convincingly that no one would ever doubt it was still a very real, very pertinent question.

What was the most foolproof, harmless method? Matt wondered. What was the safest, most convincing way to die?

INTERLUDE

I wake at 6:48 a.m., and I do not know why.

I wait for twelve minutes—one fifth of an hour—staring up at the ceiling of a house nicer than anybody my age can afford, and wishing it would burn down around me.

I am weak. I am pathetic. I am broken, fundamentally, in ways that cannot be repaired. I am suffocated by awareness of my surroundings. I need—I need to—

Vigilance. I must be vigilant, because it is my responsibility and—

Only through constant effort can I—

Vigilance is—

Vigilance—

I do not need to check the cameras, for I know that they are empty. I check them anyway, from duty and desperate hope. I am alone. There is this drowning, suffocating feeling in my chest, and I cannot—I cannot—

I make my bed because if I don't, I am a failure. I run on the treadmill until my legs burn, until sweat drips stinging into my eyes, and still, I am slower than last week. I do not get better. I am never getting better. The room hums with the notes of Beethoven's Number 14, Op. 131 on string quartet. A man who actually achieved something. A man who mattered, who will be remembered. Unlike me.

I do not shave. I do not wash myself. What is the point in papering over failure on days when no one will see it reek.

I dress, and for an instant, I want to scream because I cannot stand it. The buttons around my wrist feel like handcuffs, and the fabric around my neck chokes my life. I am a bag of broken pieces bound together and given a man's appearance. Peel apart my bandages, chip open my sarcophagus, and I will be revealed as worm-riddled sludge.

I check that my gloves are sealed beneath the sleeves and that the sleeves are correctly buttoned, once, twice, three times. I can at least manage that, this most basic task, the bare minimum required of me. I cannot escape my vigilance. Vigilance is . . .

I descend, not seeing where I am going. I do not eat. In the kitchen, I hold my head in my hands and stare at nothing, for there is nothing to stare at.

My very touch is poison, and the only thing of worth I can do is keep it contained.

It is 8:12 a.m. I have not killed anything yet. It is the only measure of success.

Eventually, I find the energy to rise. To shuffle to my study, to sit in the cold office chair and reach out to the Internet. To my world of faceless strangers.

I am alone, I tell them. *I cannot do this.*

Responses fall like rain. Persevere. Seek help. Go outside. Exercise. Have you tried this book; have you tried this medication; are you eating healthy. All useless. All correct.

You cannot understand, I write. *I can never be with her. I love her.*

Instantly, the song changes. I am a fool. I am blind. I am every man in history. I am noble. I am a coward. I just need to make a change.

Just tell her how you feel, some of the voices whisper. Things to say, things to wear, ways to test intimate boundaries with discreet movements and subtle touches. My chest aches and tears are falling, and I cannot remember when they started.

I will never touch her, I explain. *I will never hold anyone. You cannot understand.*

Yet the voices do not despair. The faceless do not retreat. *Take a chance. Take a leap,* they whisper. *Trust yourself. Believe in yourself. Take the plunge.*

What is the worst thing that can happen? Everybody gets rejected.

You can't get any more alone.

Just go for it.

Reach out.

*   *   *

I do not know when it got dark; I only know that when my phone rings and I look up, darkness has fallen and the screen in front of me sears the room with unnatural light. I glance down, the notes of the ringtone jarring, my heart hammering a startled, discordant beat. They are coming for me. They have sensed my thoughts, my weakness, my urges. They know.

No. It is just my brother. Panic gives way to resignation, though the lightheadedness remains. When did I last eat? When did I last drink? What time is it?

My fingers slide clumsily across the screen.

"Qiang, is that you?"

"Of course it's me, Liang. You called my number. Who else . . . ?" Unseen, my shoulders slump as the thought trails off.

Silence.

"I need to talk to you."

I feel a brief flash of frustration at this man, my so-called brother, who has always been an idiot, who has never worked for anything in his life. "You are talking to me."

Another pause.

"Is this line secure?"

"Is what line—Liang, grow up. Nobody is listening. This is not a spy thriller."

"Please, just say—"

"What? You want me to lie?" My insides flare with anger, and suddenly, I want to throw the phone across the room, want to reach through the screen and strangle this worthless imbecile with my bare hands. "Get over yourself. Of course this connection is private. It is every time we use it. It's encrypted; it's what we pay for." Liang does not respond. "What do you need? Money?"

Silent seconds pass.

"Brother, I did it."

"Did what?"

"I . . . I used it."

Suddenly, my heart stops. My lips move, but my mouth is dust.

"Qiang?"

"How?"

"I . . . Does it matter?"

"You fool!" I shout, and my fingers clench the phone in front of me. "You ignorant fool. How did you—What have you done?!"

"I had to, brother. I had—"

"Did anybody see?"

"No. I don't think so. Qiang, I'm sorry. I made a mistake and—"

"Who was it?"

"I cannot—"

"*Who?!*"

A pause. A sob.

"M."

"Who?"

"Melody."

"The woman?"

"My heart." He is crying now, even through the phone I can hear him, sniffing and sobbing and shaking with his soft fat hands. The room around me spins.

"Who was it?"

"Who—"

"Who was it, Liang? Who did you take?"

Silence now. Then, "Nobody."

"Nobody?"

"No . . . No one of importance. I . . . She was unwell, very unwell, and so I took her to a hospital and sat her near a dying patient, and I . . ."

Lies. All lies. I know when Liang is lying because every time he speaks, he is lying, and he is speaking now, the words tumbling forth like acid rain.

". . . some old woman, some no one. They thought she was going to die anyway, and they'll never know, Qiang. They'll never know—"

"Murderer," I hiss, and were that my words were blades to draw blood. "All your time spent lecturing me, all your patronizing, all your spite. And it is you. *You* who is irresponsible. You stupid, craven drug addict. You do not deserve your gifts; you do not deserve your life."

"Yes," my brother begs. "Yes, Qiang, I know. You are right; everything you say. But I . . . You have to help me. I—"

"Help you?" I spit. "Help you how? The damage is done, it sounds like. Liang the gluttonous. Liang the idiot. Liang who takes what he will."

"What if they find me? Brother, you have to help me. I can't go to jail. I can't—"

I force my shaking hands to stillness. "Quiet. Quiet!" I close my eyes, squeezing hard against my temples. "Did anybody see you?"

"I . . . I don't think so."

"Does the woman know?"

"Melody. No, she was . . . She won't remember."

I clench my head in my hands, and it feels as though my skull is about to break. Liang must sense my thoughts.

"Brother, you cannot tell anyone."

"Then why did you tell me?"

"You cannot. I beg of you. We can't undo this."

We can. I can. And then maybe she dies. And maybe he is taken away, the last of our family, my sole link to the truth, my sole lifeline.

"I will not do it myself," I promise. The words fill my throat like foaming bile. "If they come for you, if they ask me to do it, I will refuse."

"Please, Qiang, no. Oh God—"

There are tears in his words now, wretched misery. In my mind, I see brief glimpses of summer days. Years long past. Time spent playing together, children's adventures, conspiracies. Before that day. Before everything.

The memories are faint, but I cannot shake them.

"I will not tell," I swear, and I cannot tell if the oath feels ill or good. "It won't come from me, I promise. But Liang, you cannot do this. You cannot continue; you must make it right, be responsible—"

"I know, brother," he begs. "I know. I will change. I'll be better. It was a one-off, a mistake, I swear it, and never again will I—"

Suddenly, in the distant background, there comes a new voice. A woman's voice. Beautiful, soft, with moonlight and chimes.

"Baby, where are you? I'm alone."

"I have to go," Liang whispers urgently. And then the call drops.

Suddenly, the house is quiet. Suddenly, I am back in the darkness, in a cold chair, in silence and stillness. Unable to think. Unable to move. Alone and unloved as half a world away, my worthless, lecherous brother returns to a life devoid of consequences. To fall into the embrace of his Eurydice; to feel her compassion against his soul.

My fingernails draw blood.

BREACH

"The Most Glorious History of the Great Leader Comrade Kim Jong-il, Leader of the Democratic People's Republic of Korea, the Great Sun of Life, Father of the People, and the Only Superior Person"

[Translated into English from the original Korean]

Praise be to our Dear Leader, Supreme Commander, Great Man Who Descended from Heaven **Kim Jong-il**. His strength repels the American invaders, and his wise hands hold all powers of the world and cosmos, as he is chosen to lead the destined people of Korea and all the peoples of the Earth in glorious revolution and conquest.

The Brilliant Leader **Kim Jong-il** was born on the sacred Mount Paektu at the Paektusan Secret Camp, headquarters of the fighters for Korean freedom, on February 16, 1942, an auspicious day that is now celebrated across the globe. His father was legendary anti-Japanese hero General **Kim Il Sung**, and his mother was war heroine Kim Jong Suk. He carries forward the courageous blood of the Mangyongdae family.

At the time of his birth, an Aurora of every color filled the heavens over Paektu Mountain, and in particular, the log cabin where was born Beloved and Respected Leader **Kim Jong-il**. When the soldiers at Paektusan Secret Camp saw the sky shifting with incredible light, they fell to their knees, and tears streamed down their cheeks with joy, for they knew they had been called to witness the future savior of the Korean people.

After ten days, the Magnificent Aurora faded, and the revolutionaries saw that there remained two rainbows and a new star in the sky, and a swan flew down to herald a general who will rule the Earth. The news of the birth of Guiding Sun Ray **Kim Jong-il** spread rapidly by word of mouth throughout the country like a legendary tale, and on learning the fact, the enemy became concerned and tried to suppress the public excitement at the news of the heaven-sent boy.

The Fate of the Nation **Kim Jong-il** was the first superhuman and is the first and only Superior Human, born with the incredible natural aptitude inherited from his father, the divinely ordained Supreme Leader **Kim Il Sung**, as well as the blessing of the true Magnificent Aurora. From the moment of his birth, the Sun of the Communist Future **Kim Jong-il** wielded all powers imaginable, and all who looked upon him wept in joy and disbelief.

From three weeks of age, he learned to walk in the rustling forest amid the howling snowstorms of the mountain, and though he could fly and change the weather, he did not melt the snows nor cause the trees to bloom, for to do so would allow himself comfort while his people continued to suffer. From only eight weeks of age, he spoke articulately with outstanding intelligence and wisdom, and great scholars of Marx and Socialism traveled great distances to hear the child, the Wise Leader **Kim Jong-il,** speak unprecedented insights into the truth of the movement and their struggles for freedom.

Since the moment of his birth, his love for peace and his vision for humanity have been without precedent. Although many patriots have begged him to use his abilities, which are many times more powerful than nuclear weapons, to scour all invaders from the Korean lands, the Shining Star of Paektu Mountain **Kim Jong-il** has refrained from doing so, for as true Father to the Korean people even now, he wishes to avoid his children's bloodshed, even those taken in by the duplicitous foe.

But in 1963, in his twenty-first year, very thin waned his patience, and Fate of the Nation **Kim Jong-il** turned to the sky and proclaimed that the time had come for all people to rise up and throw off the yoke of imperialist tyranny. With a shout of "Aim High!" he called into existence a golden Aurora that blanketed the world, and all who looked upon it knew in their hearts that it was the work of the Sun of Socialism **Kim Jong-il**.

Thus did the Highest Incarnation of the Revolutionary Comradely Love **Kim Jong-il** shared his powers with the Earth and, in doing so, made his position known as the one true Superior Human.

To count the powers of the Guarantee of the Fatherland's Unification **Kim Jong-il** is to count grains of sand among the desert. He has all powers ever seen and ever known and even more he keeps hidden from even his most trusted friends, for he knows that when he unleashes them, all who witness will cower and flee in fear. These abilities are powers he was born with, not weak imitations stolen by empath thieves, and indeed, the presence of the Supreme Commander **Kim Jong-il** has prevented any empaths from ever being born among the true Koreans of the Democratic People's Republic.

When he learned of the fascist Nazi Klaus Heydrich, Iron-Willed Commander **Kim Jong-il** narrowed his eyes and spoke into the mind of the pale imitation, ordering the tyrant surrender or face justice. After seven days of Heydrich's pleading, the patience of the Ever-Victorious **Kim Jong-il** expired, and so he pointed to the sky and uttered a single devastating word. So great was the strength of Unique Leader **Kim Jong-il** that Klaus Heydrich and everything for many miles around him was immediately destroyed, a sign to the world of Bright Sun **Kim Jong-il**'s incredible power, and the true consequence of defying his will.

The Beloved Great General **Kim Jong-il** holds all records for superhuman speed and strength, and is a natural champion of all sports. His scientific innovations and transcendent writings fill more than ten thousand books, and he is recognized by every institution as the greatest artist, musician, and composer to ever live.

His films and operas are penned with such talent that they are forbidden to be shown in theaters and cinemas in Europe and wicked America, for they so completely eclipse the works of other jealous authors that they elicit tears and revolutionary fervor in audiences in the feebleminded West.

He subsists only on a single spoon of flour gruel each morning and two dewdrops from a leaf, and has never known fear or illness. He does not breathe, nor does he defecate.

Glory to Dear Leader **Kim Jong-il**! Glory to the Workers' Party of Korea! Glory to the Democratic People's Republic of Korea! Down with all false prophets of power! Down with the imperialist dogs!

* * *

"Hey."

"Hey."

The first rays of sunlight were trickling in through the window. Outside the entrance to their bedroom, Matt tugged at the edges of his pajama shirt and rubbed sleep from his eyes. Over on the couch, in front of the TV, Jane's head turned, and her tireless face greeted him with a small, tentative smile. Matt wandered over, the floorboards cool against his bare feet, and sank down beside her onto the couch, close enough for their legs to just be touching. She was already dressed in white gold.

"You want a go?" Jane asked, holding up the controller. She'd paused the game, bringing up a quietly shifting image of a serious-looking man with luscious hair and the many guns in his inventory.

"Nah." Matt shook his head. He shifted down, snuggling into her. "You keep going."

Jane unpaused, and the two of them watched for a few minutes as she ran around a derelict mining encampment shooting zombie dogs and irate Spanish peasants. For a time, the soft peace of dawn was broken only by distant gunshots and the inhuman howls emanating from the television. Eventually, a crazy lady with a chainsaw took Jane's head off.

"Dammit."

"Bad luck."

"She always gets me."

"Have you gotten the mine launcher yet?"

"No."

"Damn."

"Was I supposed to?"

"No, actually, I think it's later on."

"How long did this take you to finish?"

"A couple of days?"

"Hmm." Jane frowned. She left the game hanging on the death screen, the big bloodred words proclaiming, *You Are Dead*. "I think you're better than me."

"That may be the first time I've heard you say that about anything."

"Please," said Jane, rolling her eyes. She pushed him lightly on the shoulder. "You're better at a lot of things."

"Like what?"

"Like cooking," Jane scoffed. She indicated behind her to the large, open counter running across the kitchen. "You will notice this morning's efforts consist of milk and cereal."

"Ah. So only a fifty percent chance of fire."

"Ha-ha. You think you're so funny."

"Woman, I'm hilarious."

"Well, there you go. You're better at telling jokes."

"Only because I tell so many bad ones." Matt leaned up and kissed her on the cheek. "Numbers game."

They lapsed into a few moments of peaceful silence.

"You're better at mental defense," Jane added eventually, seemingly wanting to keep making a list. "You're better at talking, just generally."

"Worse at shutting up, though." He glanced at her with a small grin, but Jane kept gazing ahead at the TV. A slight sadness swam around the edges of her eyes.

"You're better at being nice to people," she murmured. She gave a dry sniff.

"Hey." Matt put his hand in her lap, laying it atop hers. "What's going on? You okay?"

Jane rubbed one eye with the heel of her palm and let out a sigh. "Yeah. I'm fine. I . . ." She hesitated. "I just feel like we haven't been talking much lately."

"You hate talking," Matt pointed out.

"You know what I mean." She shook her head and turned to him, making a face. "I know there's . . . a lot going on, and you don't like being stuck inside, but it's—"

"It's fine," Matt sighed. "We don't have to talk about it." He tried to smile, and to make the words conciliatory rather than confrontational. "I know you care about me."

"I do."

"And you know I care about you."

"Sometimes," Jane mumbled. Matt lay his head on her shoulder.

"Always."

"Why do we keep arguing, then?" she murmured.

Matt shrugged. "People can disagree and still love each other. We just . . . believe different. True souls can disagree on the color of a garden."

"That's nice. Who said that?"

"A crazy person."

"Oh good." Jane sniffed again. Then she sighed and set the controller down on the couch. "If you're up, I should . . ."

Matt flicked a glance over her uniform. "Big day?"

Jane's lips twitched, somewhere between a smile and a frown. "Gonna make some enemies."

"Well, at least there's a queue." He reached over and squeezed their shoulders together. For a moment, they just sat there, heads resting against one another. "Do good," Matt said eventually, pulling away. "Get the bad guys."

"I always do," Jane chuckled weakly. She turned to him with a small, sad smile. "Don't eat just Cocoa-Puffs."

"Excuse me, I . . . Fine."

"And cardio?"

Matt sighed. "Yes, dear."

"Good." Jane's smile grew a bit brighter. She kissed him on the forehead, then pulling back from their sideways embrace, she rose from the couch, leaving Matt alone with the controller. Matt watched over his shoulder as she walked away, cape shimmering in the sunlight.

"Beautiful day for it," he called after her. He turned back to the blood-stained words still lingering on the TV as Jane's shining figure stepped out onto the balcony. "Give my regards to the outside."

Eight miles above the Earth, Jane Walker drifted among the clouds.

Alone, wind rippling through her hair, she floated like a swimmer on her back, carried forward by simple momentum across a clear and open sky. Ahead, sunlight crept over the horizon, shining up from beyond the Earth's curve, drenching the world in gold. Her cape fluttered, flowing beneath her, licking at clouds like cotton wool. On and on she glided, crisp and breathless, gazing up into the heavens, watching the flawless expanse around her spread from blue to indigo and all the way back down.

Jane smiled, breathing in the bracing cold and the glorious, whispering silence.

Then she closed her eyes, drew a long, deep breath . . .

And dropped.

Her body limp, Jane hurtled in a calm backward dive, plummeting down into the clouds, rushing through layer after layer of wet and cold, a world of swirling gray, blinding, down, down, and down, until abruptly the clouds parted, and she emerged into open air—

Into a hail of gunfire.

Jane's eyes opened. Her smile spread into a wicked grin. She spun to face the dark ground rushing up to meet her, and in an instant, her body erupted in golden flames.

BOOM.

Chaos. Pure, electrifying chaos. Chattering machine-gun nests spewed streams of white-hot bullets while antiaircraft missiles spiraled from mobile emplacements, exploding in midair all around her, as across the base, North Korean soldiers in archaic olive military fatigues screamed at each other, scrambling over concrete walls and staircases like ants doused in fresh piss. Jane rocketed through all of it, the maelstrom, unstoppable, a gleeful comet of burning gold.

She dropped through strings of artillery fire, plunging headfirst toward the earth and pivoting sharp right a half second before impact, shooting off horizontally two feet above the ground as the helpless turret emplacements struggled to follow, spewing bullets into the walls. Everywhere, North Korean soldiers screamed words she couldn't understand but didn't have to.

Fire streamed from their hands, and lightning arced from their fingertips, hitting empty air or hitting her, it made no difference. Faster. A boulder erupted in her path—Jane grinned and blasted straight through it. Faster. She angled her body, turning in a tight blazing circle around the compound's interior, racing round and round and round in a slipstream of burning energy, destroying everything in her way.

Artillery piece. *Boom.* Troop truck. Straight through. A North Korean soldier screamed obscenities and turned into a tiger midleap, lunging at her with razor claws. Jane twisted, caught the big kitty with her boot, and kicked it into the cement.

She burned harder, flying faster, golden flames billowing like a storm, sending men and military equipment flying, cleaving fissures in the defensive redoubt. Soldiers scattered. Concrete crumbled.

Then, Jane pirouetted out of her spiral and flew straight for the hangar doors.

BOOM.

* * *

"Don't stop me now, I'm having such a good time, I'm having a ball."

The song danced out from the kitchen speakers, and Matt found himself quietly humming along. He crouched in front of the oven, pulled open the door with his white-floral oven mitt, and slid in a tray of unbaked cookie dough. Chocolate chip. Something of a speciality.

It was midafternoon, and Matt was alone in the apartment. Jane was out doing something superheroic, the details of which he couldn't remember beyond that it was something she'd been looking forward to. He was taking a midstudy cookie break because it had been a while since he'd baked anything, and because it made the day feel marginally less fruitless.

With the dough set and the speakers slinging tunes, Matt slid around the kitchen in bare feet, enjoying the magic of creation and the freedom to sing free of judgement. (Giselle was out getting Chinese food.)

"Don't stop me—'Cause I'm having a good time. Don't stop me—Yes, I'm having a good time—"

"Don't wanna stop at all," Matt hummed as he placed the second tray on the lower rack and closed the oven door.

Three hundred and fifty degrees, fan-forced. Did he set a timer? No, Matt decided after a moment's consideration. There was no need for that. He'd live dangerously.

Jane exploded through the hangar doors, sending the fat slabs of steel tumbling back like windblown cardboard.

"*Aiiiiieeee!*"

"*Sagyeok! Sagyeok!*"

Beyond the doors, there ran a large concrete tunnel, dual security stations built into both walls. The left door plate, some thirty feet wide and twenty feet high, spun off in a pirouette and flattened the left-most station in a crash of steel and glass. The right door went higher, crashing into the concrete wall above the right-side guardhouse. There was screaming and scrabbling as those inside scrambled to get clear as the metal began to creak and groan, threatening in mere moments to fall.

Before her, beyond the debris field, an army of soldiers was scrambling into formation, arrayed eight rows deep, aiming guns, hands, rocket launchers. Some man, a commander with a quarter-chest full of medals, stood at the front, screeching and gesticulating wildly.

In the half second it took for Jane's eyes to adjust, the platoon opened fire, and suddenly, the air around her screamed with bullets, flames, lightning, missiles, lasers, acid, sound. The assault slammed into her in a deluge as impotent psychic intrusions simultaneously scratched fruitlessly at her mind, scrabbling in vain against the Psy-Block. Jane cackled and rocketed forward.

Boom. She slammed through the rows of soldiers, blasting them aside like tenpins, being sure to direct a quick energy burst at that cheeky little neutralizer who was standing in the back holding his hands up and hoping she wouldn't notice.

"*Janggun-nimeul wihayeo!*" Through the scattered bodies and debris, a large, muscular man ran at her. He leapt as she passed, managing to grab hold of her ankle. Instantly, he was not one man but twenty, fifty, dozens of identical bodies that swarmed over her, holding on even as she kicked and twisted, shaking some loose, the rest dividing like camouflage-colored bubbles trying to slow or weigh her down.

Jane grinned and clenched her teeth. The light around her began to burn brighter, white hot. The replications cried out in distress.

Boom. The air around Jane exploded in blinding brilliance, sending the clones flying off into the walls, popping into nothingness. Jane rocketed on, unstoppable, out the main entrance chamber and down the narrow bunker hall.

Boom. Through a checkpoint. *Boom,* people scattered to the side. Jane hurtled at breakneck speed through twisting tunnels, curved concrete walls a foot away in every direction.

She skidded to a halt, her feet touching down for the first time since she'd entered North Korean airspace, recognizing a sign from her brief.

BAM! Her golden boot kicked open the steel door.

"*Geuman! Salyeojuseyo!*"

Behind the locked door, which had probably previously been guarded, lay a bunkhouse of a kind. Cramped metal cots in endless rows stacked floor to ceiling filled every scrap of available space, and around them scurried a horde of thin, terrified Korean people, all of whom now looked at her.

The smell of rotting flesh and rancid sewage hit Jane in a wave as she struggled not to gag. She glanced up, noting the cameras lining the roof and the remote-controlled gun turrets hanging in the corners. Jane raised a steady hand and blasted the guns out of existence, causing every person in the unwashed, starving crowd to flinch. A few turned their heads on instinct, allowing Jane a glimpse at the wounds festering on the back of their necks. Bombs implanted to detonate should there be any escape attempts.

Good thing she'd just blasted the mother-loving crap out of the monitoring stations and communications array.

Jane let out a sharp, wordless shout. The North Korean prisoners all turned to look at her. She pointed her chin, motioned overlarge slapping the back of her neck, then gave everyone a thumbs-up before she gestured those in the middle out of the way.

A rush of huddled whispers, fear, and uncertainty spread over the prisoners' faces. Only a few people moved. Jane rolled her eyes, squared her stance, and cupped her hands together, causing a ball of searing energy to begin growing between her fingertips. Suddenly, the Korean prisoners were moving very, very fast.

CRACK-OOM!

Jane twisted and fired, unleashing a devastating blast of golden energy that rocketed through the center of the room, annihilating the middlemost bunkbeds and tearing through the steel plating on the far side. As the smoke cleared, the damage was evident: an enormous hole punched floor to ceiling in the wall, which continued on through the outer concrete and barbed-wire fences until all that was left was a singed tunnel to the distant smoldering countryside.

Jane relaxed her stance, smiling at her handiwork. The pale, emaciated inmates gaped between her and the smoking, house-size crater.

"*Bbali bbali*," she told them, pointedly directing a finger at the very large hole in the compound leading to freedom and outside. Azleena had assured her that meant *hurry up*. Jane turned on her heels, leaving the North Korean prisoners to their freedom, and shot off once more in a blaze of golden fire, rocketing down the hallway.

2:39 p.m. Ooh. Matt looked up from the newspaper where he'd been doing the crossword. Time for cookie check. He put his pen down and waddled over to crouch on the balls of his feet in front of the oven. Oh. Yep. Still pale, but the centers had made the dough-to-cooked transition. Perfect.

Matt pulled on his mitts and opened the oven door, still humming.

* * *

There. Down the far end of the halls of the concrete bunker, Jane's golden eyes spied a door unlike the others. Walnut brown and inlaid with beautifully polished panels, jade, and gold, and carved into intricate patterns of mountains, rivers, and cherry blossoms, it was guarded by six of the biggest, toughest-looking North Korean soldiers she'd seen so far.

The six spotted her as she shot round the corner, raising cries of alarm, one turning to liquid steel, one raising an antipathic hand to their forehead, and one throwing up hard-light force fields before her like panes of glass. Two more snapped up high-caliber rifles, and the last one leveled what looked like a trash can–size flak cannon at her, the contents of which he held his hand to, imbuing a pulsating violet glow to the shrapnel inside.

The elite guard took aim. Jane grinned.

Twelve seconds later, the door they were guarding exploded open, and the white-gold figure of Lady Dawn shot through.

Jane's boots skidded to a halt, burning black tracks in the ornate Persian rug. The room she'd breached into was palatial, completely discordant with the military sparseness beyond: high-roofed faux-wooden ceilings, plush carpet interior, luxurious French-patterned lounges, and a vanity chest lined with whisky bottles and crystalline decanters.

Huge, gold-framed oil paintings twice her height hung from the walls, depicting the face of a plump, glasses-clad dictator and smiling Korean citizens, soldiers, and workers united gloriously under arms. To her right, the room sloped down into a private twelve-seat cinema, complete with personal side tables and recliners. To her left, long steps ran upward into a fifteen-foot-high, sweeping office, the walls leading up to the far corners lined with antique tomes and mahogany bookshelves.

On the far end of the office, the wall farthest away from her was comprised almost entirely of an enormous fish tank, spotlessly clean and bursting with coral and exotic fish of every shape and color. Running parallel in front of the fish tank was an enormous oak desk. Behind the desk was a short Korean man in gray whose portrait hung on the wall.

Jane's face split into a wolfish grin.

"*J-J-Jeongji!*" the little man demanded, his voice cracking as he raised a trembling hand and pointed. Jane strode up the stairs toward him, undeterred. The short, plump-faced man in the gray, high-buttoned military jumpsuit and square clear-frame glasses shrieked and waved his fat hand frantically as the empath marched toward him, his froggy eyes bulging beneath high, frizzy black hair.

"*Non jugutda, yi gan-na saekkiya!*" he screamed, but absolutely nothing happened, and Jane did not pause. The dictator's eyes raced frantically around the room, looking for his guards, his soldiers, anything, finding nothing but Jane stalking toward him, smiling like she'd won the lottery.

Finally, when the empath was maybe seven feet away, something broke in the short man's psyche, and he slammed his face desperately up against the fish tank, mouthing silent, hysterical pleas into the glass. Instantly, the fish in the tank grew agitated. One of the larger ones, a salmon, wriggled furiously out from the air gap at the top and hurtled itself out into the office, coming to land with a splat at Jane's feet. It remained there, flopping as aggressively as a fish could flop on carpet.

The sight of it caused Jane to actually pause for a moment, stopping dead in her tracks as she stared at the flailing, pointless creature, momentarily stunned.

Then she looked back up and locked eyes with the North Korean dictator, stepped around the fish, ripped the two-hundred-pound desk between them aside with one hand, and grabbed the fat man by the collar.

"Ow," muttered Matt, shaking his hand where he'd accidentally touched the hot baking tray. "Ow. Hot. Ow." He sucked furiously on the offending finger. This stuff was dangerous.

Matt pivoted, gingerly juggling the half-eaten chocolate chip cookie into his other hand so he could alternate between taking bites and running cold water over his boo-boo.

His finger cooled, Matt redonned the oven mitt, moved the trays over onto the stovetop next to the waiting wire rack, and began spatulaing cookies over to cool down. When both trays were empty and the racks full, Matt gazed upon his crop of baked goods with a deep sense of personal satisfaction.

See? He'd accomplished something.

"*AIIIEEEEEE!*" the North Korean leader screamed, and Jane cackled. One hand held firm around the scruff of the dictator's neck, the other punching forward, Jane flew unrestrained through the concrete corridors, a freight train of golden force, unstoppable. Everywhere, people screamed and scattered. Korean men in lab coats hurled themselves out of the way while soldiers scrambled to aim but then froze when they saw Kim Jong-Il's flailing.

The little man squirmed helplessly in Jane's grasp, his pudgy cheeks flapping as they rocketed forward, snot and tears streaming intermingled down his face, begging—she thought—for someone to save him while simultaneously screaming at the soldiers not to shoot, his words lost beneath explosions and the rush of air.

The hesitation of the army arrayed against her was fleeting, but by the time they'd processed what they were seeing, Jane had already flown past, powering effortlessly through the disorganized North Korean ranks as she dragged their leader one-handed behind her like a sack of wet cats.

Bam! Back through the crumpled gates and out into open air. Shouts went up around her, but again, men hesitated as they saw whom she was carrying, many of them—in her brief glimpses—seeming to be undergoing some kind of existential shock. Jane didn't wait to let them process. She skidded to a halt, looked up at the sky, and with the fat little Korean dictator in one hand, shot straight upward, a comet of shining gold.

The wind whipped through her hair as she let out a triumphant laugh, looping through the air with her infamous prisoner dangling helplessly in one hand behind her. She pulled out of a turn, and the little tyrant threw up, a rain of brown-green chunks that quickly dissipated down onto the fortress below. Jane cackled and angled sideways.

Alone once more save for her cargo, Jane soared above the clouds, out over the Yellow Sea, and to a waiting US Army cargo plane chugging patiently through the sky. As she approached, the rear loading ramp opened. Without hesitation, Jane flew up and flung the terrified Kim Jong-Il inside, his round body bouncing with a thud off the metal cargo hold floor like a porpoise tossed on the beach.

The dictator curled into the fetal position, his formerly gray jumpsuit now a patchwork of bodily fluids, cowering his head between his hands and alternating between trembling whispers and the occasional hysterical shriek.

Jane turned away without a backward glance, leaving the small man to the circle of large US marines advancing to surround him, blocking his quailing body from view. She closed her eyes and tumbled back behind the plane, reveling in the bluebird cold, and spinning in golden spirals through the sky.

Ping.

Matt raised his head as the ding of the elevator chimed from underneath his music. His brow furrowed. That was odd. Will was off with Wally on some private retreat, Giselle hadn't called for him to reopen the balcony, and Jane was on another continent. Was she home early? Had she teed up with Will? That other teleporter, what was his name, Enrique? Was he imagining things? Had the Legion sent someone else?

Matt set his cookies aside and strode frowning over to the security panel next to the front door. He pushed the touch screen buttons controlling the external cameras, and sure enough, the elevator light was on—the lift was moving. Matt leaned close, peering at the screen.

His heart stopped as the elevator doors opened, and from their depths emerged two, then four, then a dozen heavily armed soldiers.

Giselle Pixus whistled as she strode through the streets of Guangzhou marketplace, idly throwing and catching a small Hello Kitty purse full of freshly exchanged yuan. The morning sun was bright and the sky blue and clear, the air around her suffused with the scent of fresh herbs and the cries of stallholders calling to suppliers or shouting instructions at family members and staff across the cobblestone streets.

Giselle meandered with a discerning customer's gaze, thoroughly out of place in her sleek dolphin-gray activewear, yet unwavering in her confidence as she strolled from storefront to storefront, peering curiously at the produce arrayed inside. Matt had requested pork buns and broccoli stir-fried in garlic, but that still gave her, oh, about twelve thousand calories to work with.

A thin, hexagon-pattern navy backpack sat flat against her shoulders, currently crinkled and deflated but able to be smoothed rigid and aerodynamic with a button press to keep shape and stability on the run home. As was always the case whenever she stepped out from Matt duty, Giselle felt a small twinge of guilt, as if her foray into the outside world was shirking some responsibility. But she was being ridiculous. She'd been gone, what, a few minutes? And at Matt's insistence, too.

She pulled her phone—a Kinetic™ Tempest K10—from her pocket and glanced briefly at the screen, which showed no new messages. See? He was fine. The apartment was secure.

There was nothing to worry about.

"Giselle," Matt whispered frantically into the phone. "Giselle!"

He quick-dialed the number again, and again, the call failed to go through. Matt's eyes flicked to the reception in the upper right corner. No signal. No signal? How was there no signal?! This place had signal out the wazoo; it should never—

As if on cue, the music coming from the wireless speaker in the kitchen fizzled and died.

Crap, Matt thought.

They had a scrambler. Whether superhuman or man-made, some sort of device or ability to block electromagnetic—

Crap.

Matt turned back to the security screen and the secure camera feed. Outside, black-clad soldiers continued assembling. One woman had gone back down in the lift, causing another ding, another light to go on above the doorway inside the apartment. The elevator doors reopened, and a second group of armed assailants stepped out.

Crap, crap, crap.

The attacking force was both men and women, some wearing black helmets, some just balaclavas. They weren't armored in any kind of uniform but a motley array of tactical vests and cargo pants, though predominantly black in color. Every one of them Matt could see either carried a gun or had one holstered. Even through the fishbowl lens of the camera, that was impossible to miss.

His chest tight, his breathing shallow, Matt's shaking fingers quietly pressed the button to relay sound.

"—breaching charges—"

"—is that every—"

"—why can't we just cut—?"

"—don't know if it's—"

They army of attackers amassed before his door, and Matt's heart hammered in his chest.

Stall. He needed to stall.

Panic flared across his brain, but before the fear could go anywhere, Matt furiously corralled it, instead forcing his fingers to flick rapidly through the audio files on his phone, looking for—

There.

Matt raised his phone to the intercom panel, pushed the microphone button, and pressed play.

"Attention, dead men," Jane's voice rang out from the prerecorded message. "You are trespassing on private property. You have exactly one chance—*one*—to turn your sorry asses around and go the hell away before I come out there and annihilate you. This is not a courtesy to you; this is a courtesy to me. We just repainted these walls."

Outside, the gathering army froze. Frantic heads turned to each other, exchanging glances, wide eyed. Matt saw a few take off their helmets or pull up their balaclavas to better look at one another, revealing generally white, worried faces. A few powers flickered and faded.

"Is that—?"

"I thought you said she was—"

"—supposed to be—"

"—we can't—"

"Quiet." A harsh bark, a woman's voice. "Faces down." There was a muttering, a shuffling, as those who had removed their balaclavas struggled to pull them back into position. One of the soldiers, the closest to the door, removed her own helmet to reveal a freckled, midforties woman with a shock of short hair bleached blonde. She peered around cautiously, eyes tracking over every inch of the cramped landing, the reinforced door, until her gaze found the camera. Her eyes narrowed.

Matt scrolled furiously to the second recording.

"You think this is a game?" Jane's voice snarled from the phone. "You think I'm gonna go easy on you? This is my home. You take one more step forward, and your families will be burying you in doggy bags."

Again, the soldiers on the outside flinched. Several in the center exchanged glances, and a few at the back shook their heads.

"Screw this, dude—"

"I was promised—"

"Suici—"

"Shut up," the lead woman hissed. She had wild, sunken eyes, and a scar cleft into her left upper lip. The woman inched closer to the door, getting as close as she could without touching it—then she leaned her head back and drew a long, deep sniff.

"I don't smell her," she muttered. Suddenly, she spun back to face her comrades.

"It's him. It's only him. Our info's good. Go, quickly, get the door."

Inside, Matt's face paled, and he frantically flipped through his phone until he reached one of Azleena's custom programs.

Load, damn you. LOAD!

Outside, there was more murmuring. The woman in front continued to glare, and slowly, the faces and postures of those behind her began to harden, the eyes of his attackers turning once more toward the door.

Come on, come on, come—Yes! The program opened. Matt's trembling fingers pressed onto the big red button to record.

"Your info is not good," he snapped—but it was not his voice that came out of the phone's speakers but Jane's. A custom voice modulator. "Your info is dog crap. You want to sniff something, Marine-wife Barbie doll? How about you take a real deep breath when I rip off that peroxide-soaked head of yours and shove it four feet up your salon-bleached ass?"

Crap. Not so intricate. Jane mainly just threatened and swore at people. Matt leaned back to the phone voice modulator and added in a bunch of curse words for good measure.

"I am a hundred percent serious," he continued. "You idiots think you're the first group to find this apartment? You're actually the third. You know where the first two are? Some vacant-ass patch of the Pacific Ocean, their spines about a hundred miles from their assholes, probably wishing they listened, and with none of you other morons ever knowing their names."

Come on, Giselle, he urged mentally. *Come on.*

On the camera screen in front of him, Matt saw his words take effect. The blonde lady flinched, her eyes wild like someone had spat in her Frappuccino. Behind her, he saw several other attackers shake their heads, retreating a few steps back from the door.

"Screw this, man," said one, a shorter (what sounded like a) man clutching some sort of hunting rifle to his chest. "She's here. We gotta run; we gotta—"

"Nobody's running!" someone else snapped, but a second later, the first guy's sentiment was echoed by another.

"I'm out. I'm not killing myself; I've got kids—"

"Don't! Move!" hissed the blonde woman, but it was too late: someone pressed the button to the elevator, and when a second later the lift opened, three people crammed themselves and their weapons inside. Ignoring their comrades' howls of protests, they frantically hit *door close*, and a few moments later had disappeared. The elevator dinged going down.

Back in the apartment, Matt's heart skipped a beat.

"Wow," he continued, drawling in Jane's dulcet tones. "Guess there goes half your collective brain cells. Well, I spy with my little eye three less dead men out there than I did two seconds ago. Should we have one last go at getting out of here without your children becoming orphans, or do I really have to get intestines on my favorite top?"

The hall outside fell into frozen silence. Matt's eyes burned into the screen so hard it felt like they were going to explode. A bead of sweat dripped down his forehead.

"Did somebody check DawnWatch?" a tall, lanky figure in a balaclava and black skateboard helmet murmured.

Someone shuffled beside him. "My phone's not working."

"Idiot, we're jamming the—"

"I thought it was just him!"

"How could it be just him?"

The hall descended into argument, a few of the attackers holstering their guns to access phones or gesture at their companions. A few pushed at those with whom they were arguing, and to Matt's excitement, for a moment, it almost looked like a full-on fistfight was about to break out right in front of his door.

Yet, at the forefront of the assault, the scar-lipped blonde woman remained silent. As the noise behind her rose, her eyes narrowed.

"Too much talk," she whispered. And then, to Matt's horror, she looked up directly into the camera—directly into his soul.

"Shut up," she commanded, and despite the rabble, her words seemed to carry. The bickering died down. The black-clad woman took a single step, tilting her head, before turning back to her companions.

"There's been too much talk," she said. "She's not here; otherwise, she'd have come out by now. It's a trick; he's trying to stall us. Get the charges, now. Get us inside."

The muttering faded, the mob exchanging glances, but a moment later, there was a flurry of nodding, and suddenly, the attackers were moving with renewed purpose, shuffling some of their numbers closer to the door. Matt felt bile building in his throat. That had bought him less time than he'd hoped.

Second hurdle.

"Stop." He returned the phone to his pocket and faced the intercom screen square on, his finger on the microphone. His own voice rang out, unadulterated. On the screen in front of him, the attacking army paused. Two dozen pairs of eyes turned to stare up at the camera. "Stop."

There was a brief, breathless silence. Then:

"Matt Callaghan."

"One and the same."

"You should open this door."

"I'm not going to do that." He paused. "Jane's on her way."

Even through the screen, the blonde woman's eyes glinted like shards of obsidian in firelight. "I doubt it. You're a liar."

"This time, I'm not."

"I'm sorry, kid. This isn't personal."

"Feels pretty personal." He paused again. "You should turn around and leave."

The woman sneered. "We're not going to do that."

"Well," Matt said, "then you should know there's an antipersonnel mine embedded above the doorframe, ready to go off the second someone touches it."

The conversation slid to a shuddering halt. Outside, despite them wearing masks, Matt thought he saw several faces pale.

The blonde woman flinched, but after a few seconds, managed to recover.

"Lies."

"You sure about that?"

"Yes. You're a liar, Matt Callaghan. No good will come of you."

"I don't always lie," Matt replied conversationally, leaning one arm over the intercom. "I didn't lie to Klaus Heydrich."

"Yes, you did."

"What did I tell him?"

A pause.

"What did I tell Klaus Heydrich? Come on, don't play games with me; you all saw the interview."

"'If you take my blood, you'll lose.'"

"Wasn't lying to him then. Wasn't lying to you now. There is a high-yield, outward-facing claymore pointing directly at each and every one of you, and the second anything happens to that door, it'll blow apart every one of you racist hicks."

The blonde lady scowled. "We're not racist."

"Oh, so what, I personally wronged you?"

"Human isn't a race."

"Human's literally the original race, you idiot. What were you, home-schooled by a cat?"

"We don't have time for this," a stocky man behind the blonde leader interjected. "He's bluffing. Break down the goddamn door!"

"I'm not bluffing."

"Does anyone have X-ray—?"

"Is Lady Dawn actually—?"

"I'm warning you."

"Just breach it, go!"

Suddenly, one of the masked attackers pushed forward. He shoved the blonde lady aside, raised an arm that turned to bright, jagged stone, and with a roar, slammed his bare fist into the door.

There was an immediate crack, an electric howl, as the man's body hurtled back into his companions. Most managed to yelp and dive out of the way, but a few were not so lucky. The terramorph's body slammed into the far wall, pulverizing two other black-clad figures. The crushed men lay gurgling, twitching in a pile of blood and broken limbs beneath four hundred pounds of flesh turned rock.

Matt pressed the intercom.

"Oh yeah," he said mildly. "It's also electrified."

A moment of horror passed as the attackers processed. Then:

"EMP—"

"It won't open—"

"That's it!" cried another man, turning back to face the door, ecstatic. "That's all of his defenses. Go now, go now!"

"Don't," Matt warned, voice raising in alarm. "I'm serious, don't touch it." He took a step back, the microphone staying on. "I'm serious; I'm not joking about the claymore."

Outside, the attackers swarmed, oblivious to his warnings. Matt took another step back from the screen, looking on in horror as hands moved to satchels, as blocks of plastiline-like explosive telekinetically floated out and onto the edges of the door.

"You're killing yourselves!" he cried.

"Don't listen to him!"

"This is suicide!"

"Blow it! Blow it!"

Matt turned and ran. He vaulted over the marble island to the other side of the kitchen and huddled down in a ball, back pressed against the countertop, clutching his ears with his hands.

Outside, someone pressed the detonator.

BOOM!

"*Xiexie ni,*" Giselle attempted, bowing low as the Chinese vendor handed her a wrapped parcel of food. The little bald man in an apron bowed and said some words she didn't understand yet. Regardless, she could make out the gist of it.

Giselle turned and walked away a few steps, shuffling the backpack around and off her shoulders, hands juggling the dumpling containers in their plastic bag. She placed the food on the ground, sped her hands as she undid all the zippers, then expanded the backpack to its full reinforced size.

A tinkling jingled from her pocket. Giselle pulled out the phone, glanced at it, and put it to her ear.

"Dude, relax, I'm coming. I had to translate pork buns—"

"Giselle!" Matt's voice, terror, the sound of screaming. "Come home, I'm under—"

Before the next word could hit the air, the girl was gone, vanished into a blur, the stack of food left abandoned, leaving only a trail of blinding dust.

* * *

"ARGH!"

"OH GOD."

The phone fell silent, and Matt's shaking hands fumbled as he moved it back into his pocket. Beyond the counter, screams drifted in from the ruined hole where the door to their apartment once stood. Sounds of movement. Sounds of pain.

"HELP."

The secret to good deception was knowing how to intersperse lies with truth. Matt had not been lying about the claymore. He had, however, been lying about there only being one.

All throughout the apartment, the air hung thick with smoke, dust, and the sound of agonized wailing. Matt didn't dare look up, didn't dare think of the dying people, how many lives had just been ended. Instead, he dropped to all fours and began crawling desperately to the other end of the kitchen counter.

"I told you," Matt muttered furiously to no one, teeth gritted, fists clenched. "I"—he swore—"told you."

He shuffled around the corner, smoke stinging his eyes, trying to block out the moral and existential terror of the carnage which lay beyond. He didn't know how many had died. He didn't want to see.

"ARGH!"

"PLEASE!"

A ringing in his ears, the smell of smoke and blood in his nose, Matt clambered into a low, ungainly run, loping step by step, keeping as low as he could go. Fourth hurdle, fourth hurdle.

"Disco, disco, disco!" he shouted. Matt jammed his fingers as hard as he could into his ears, kept running, and scrunched his eyes shut.

Suddenly, the whole house plunged into darkness. Blackout blinds shot down over the windows, blocking the last of the afternoon sun, and every light switched off.

"I CAN'T SEE—"

"Night-vision goggles!"

"OH GOD, MY LEGS—"

Please, let this work, Matt pleaded. *Be mostly dead; be mostly dumb.* He scurried around the corner, seizing the sudden darkness to make a break for the south-side corridor, moving off memory in the dark as he ran toward the gym, the laundry, the spare room. The panic room.

"Wait, I can almost—"

"Get some fire—"

"Can you hear—?"

Matt kept his eyes and ears shut tight.

Suddenly, the house exploded in blinding light. Not golden light, not "Jane finally turned on her effing cell phone and came to save him," but multicolored, strobing light of blazing intensity, as every lightbulb in the apartment suddenly surged with electricity dialed to two hundred, three hundred percent.

In the living room, Matt heard his attackers shriek, and then a moment later, heard their cries swallowed as a cacophony of the worst sounds known to humankind screeched from the apartment's surround sound system. Howler monkeys, psychotic geese, fingernails down a chalkboard, high-pitched fire alarms, children playing recorder—all blasted out from a dozen speakers, some visible, some hidden, the sounds crashing, overlapping, leaping from every direction in a delirious, deafening mess.

The prerecorded sound of Matt's own voice interspersed among the chaos, flittering off into the ceiling, out over the balcony, and into the bedroom beyond—a flock of screaming, delirious mockingbirds skittering off in every direction but one. Outside the apartment and in the living room, Matt imagined the attackers desperately clutching their eyes and ears against the sudden assault of blinding techno light and a hundred-and-fifty-decibel hell. He had never been much of a musician, but he had been an amateur DJ, and this was his seminal work.

There was a bang behind him, the unmistakable sound of gunfire, breaking glass, and crackling speakers, then suddenly, the house dropped back into pitch black and silence.

"We got it!" someone shouted, which was very premature. A second later, the surviving lightbulbs flared back on, and the cacophony of discord screamed pounding back to life, this time interspersed with crying babies and moans of furious sex.

Gunfire. More gunfire. The shattering and spluttering of speakers. Matt sprinted into the far bedroom and yanked closed the door.

* * *

Across the Pacific Ocean, Giselle Pixus raced.

Faster than a bullet, faster than a jet. Her feet barely touching water, a slipstream of waves fanning metres high in her wake, shooting out behind her.

Giselle Pixus ran as fast as she could, as fast as her legs could carry her, a one-woman missile, racing back toward the continental United States.

The door slammed shut behind him, and Matt ran his fingers over the touch pad three times. There was a click, a thud, as internal dead bolts locked into place.

Okay, he did it. He just had to hide. He just had to stay safe. Giselle would be back any minute, any second. Just had to—He whirled around the room, scanning desperately. The door was reinforced steel, the lock technopathically coded. There were sprinklers in the ceilings, and a gas mask under the bed . . .

Matt's heart pounded. Wait. Just wait. Stay quiet. They didn't know he was here.

The room was long and rectangular, about three lengths of the single bed nestled in the far corner, the bed foot facing the door, the right wall the color of burnt orange, the left a line of windows medium size and dull. Empty, save for the bed and a small chest of drawers.

Matt felt himself unconsciously moving backward until his back was against the far wall, facing the sealed door. To the left of that, the door to the bathroom, the panic room proper. Where he should go, where he should seal himself . . . Except, in the face of actual danger, the idea suddenly seemed ludicrous. If they could get through this many defenses, what was that going to matter? What was going to be accomplished by trapping himself in a steel box?

Shouts from the main room. The ear-shattering chaos, muffled and far less deafening in here, sealed off from it. Matt's breathing came hard. Time. He wasn't playing for safety; he was playing for time—

Suddenly, a hot, sweeping presence. Telepathic fingers raking through every corner of the building, reaching for Matt's presence, searching.

"I've found him!" he heard the telepath shout, and in his excitement, Matt felt the man leap, claws outstretched, into his mind.

Big mistake.

Matt Callaghan did not take Psy-Block. Matt Callaghan did not *need* Psy-Block. Matt Callaghan had fought off the best telepaths in the world, and for a few brief, brutal seconds, been telepathic himself. There was only one place on Earth he was powerful, and this amateur idiot had just thrown himself enthusiastically inside.

The psychic barreled into Matt's consciousness, charging in haphazard with the whole of his being. Matt let him advance, not putting up any resistance, allowing the telepath to advance until his mind had completely come over. The man invaded with reckless abandon, lunging furiously at Matt's gray-mist thoughts—only to abruptly hit a wall.

An unbending iron wall.

I AM HUMAN.

The attacker turned, but the wall was behind him, around him, above. He was no longer a marauder cavorting free; he was trapped inside a box, surrounded, a solid cube of unbreakable steel suddenly rushing inward with unnatural speed, without hesitation or remorse. The psychic screamed, trapped, crushed in every direction, his consciousness scrabbling desperately to return to his body, his fingers clawing against the walls—

But there would be no escape. There would be no mercy.

The iron-willed cube compressed to a pixel-size dot, and out in the real world, Matt felt the psychic's eyes roll back into his head. Wordlessly, the man collapsed.

"Wrong neighborhood," Matt snarled, dropping his fingers from his temple.

BANG! BANG!

Heavy impacts, pounding on the door. Matt shook his head, trying to draw himself free from the purely mental sensations. He strode over to the bathroom, and without going in, swiped his fingers three times over the keypad lock.

Schloom! A solid steel door slid shut as from outside, Matt could hear whirring and clicks.

"Break it! Break it! Something's going on!"

Without hesitation Matt ran back to the bed tucked up against the room's right corner, grabbed the bedposts with both hands, and pulled with all his might. The bed slid forward a few inches, staying flush with the wall. Matt pulled forward until there was maybe a half-foot gap between the wall and the tall wooden headboard, a gap visually undetectable from the view of anyone coming inside.

He slid down between the bed and the wall, crouching low, breathing hard.

BANG! A more solid sound this time, a rending metal crunch, and suddenly, the air was once more full of unmuted noise. There were footsteps on the carpet. People entering, people turning around.

"Another one?! Goddammit, how many—"

"Just get it open!"

Two men's voices. Could they really be down to two? Matt smelled the scent of charcoal and heard a crunch, which made him think one of them might be the rock man, the one who had previously been electrocuted . . . The other . . .

"We're out of C4."

"Reach in, see if you can loosen the hinges."

BAM. BAM. BAM. Jarring impacts, like a battering ram. Behind the bed, Matt's jaw clenched, his teeth rattling with every thud.

"Are you moving the—?"

"I'm trying!"

Reach in, they'd said. *Reach in.* What did that mean? Intangible phaser? No, every room in this place had Disruptances on separate backups. Telekinetic. He was trying to reach into the locking mechanism.

"There."

"There?"

"Hit it!"

BAM. BAM!

"I got it. I got the corner!"

"Go again, keep going!"

"We're coming, human! We're coming!"

Matt's heart was deafening in his throat. He closed his eyes, clutching his hands to stop them from trembling, while men intent on his destruction broke down solid steel mere feet away. *Think I'm cleverer than I am,* he pleaded. *Think I've pulled off the impossible.*

BAM!

"Wait. Wait, it's empty!"

"How is it empty?!"

"What?!"

"Check the ceiling!"

"There's—It doesn't open!"

"Check the—Check the sink!"

"How the hell would he go down the sink?!"

"I don't know!"

Keep going, Matt pleaded. *Look for secret passageways. Hidden escape pods. Rip it apart, tear everything to pieces, just please keep trying to find me there.*

"Where'd he go?"

"He couldn't have come out."

"He's not in here!"

"Did you see him come in?"

"No, but Jake, I—He pointed this way, then he screamed—"

"This is bullcrap. This is bullcrap!"

"Do we check the other rooms?"

Yes, Matt pleaded, *check the other rooms.*

Silence.

"No." A hard voice, Southwestern, with a growl. "Something's wrong. Why were the doors closed if there weren't nothing in here worth protecting?"

"Maybe they lock automatically." Younger, higher, more unsure.

Crunch, crunch. Heavy footsteps on the carpet. "Then he'd get locked in. What's the point? No. Search."

Matt silently swore. Okay. Okay. The sound of two sets of footsteps now, drawing close. Seconds. He had seconds. Got to . . . Got to . . . More time.

Final hurdle.

Matt sprang out from behind the bed, facing the men, hands held high.

"Stop!" he cried. "Please. I'm here; you've found me. Just stop."

The two attackers he faced both flinched, and for a second, there was no sound save for the labored breathing coming from Matt's chest. In the apartment beyond, the wailing noise fell silent, the mix ended, the speakers all fried or shot. Matt stared at the two men in front of him, both covered in dust and blood, both who had torn their masks off sometime during the assault.

The foremost one was taller, his face grizzled and pockmarked, with brown hair only a shade darker than his skin, and a jaw lined with sandpapery stubble. His forearms were bare and made of thick, jagged, tan-colored stones, which, as Matt watched, faded back into his flesh as the man swung a semiautomatic pistol out of his leg holster.

The other man was shorter, paler, less muscular, with thin fluffy hair a soft coffee color, and a trembling in his eyes, lips, and body. He, too, slung a gun from his back—a single shot, bolt-action rifle—but only raised it halfway, staring at Matt with disbelieving eyes.

"We got him," he whispered.

"Yeah," snarled the tall man. "Now, let's finish it." He straightened the gun.

"Wait!" Matt pleaded. He clasped his hands above his head, not daring to take a step. "Wait, please. Just . . . I forgive you."

The man in front recoiled, his features pulling back like he'd swallowed something sour. "You forgive us?"

"Yes," babbled Matt. "I understand what you're trying to do, and I . . ." At that moment, he allowed all the terror and the fear to wash over him, and he doubled over in wretched, defeated sobs. "Just promise me," Matt begged. "Promise me you'll destroy it. Promise me you'll take it back."

"Wait," said the smaller man, taking a step forward. "Destroy what? What are you talking about?"

"Lionel, shut up!" snarled the terramorph. Gritting his teeth, he aimed the gun at Matt's head. "It's a trick!"

"No, hold on," the man named Lionel protested. He reached forward, pushing aside his companion's gun. "What if he's—What are you saying? What do we have to destroy?"

Matt shook his head, tears streaming from his eyes, the words stumbling between his teeth through wet hiccups. "I didn't want this," he pleaded with them. "I didn't want any of this. They forced me; I had no choice. They—They took it . . ."

"We don't care what you want!" the terramorph roared. He tried to shoulder Lionel out of the way, but the telekinetic refused to budge.

"Took? Took what?" he demanded, breathless. Out of the corner of his eyes, Matt saw him crouch slightly, trying to look up into Matt's hunched-over face. "What did they take?"

"My blood," Matt confessed, recoiling from the word as if stung. He heard sharp, twin intakes of breath. "They've had it for months; there was nothing I could do. They were trying to keep you distracted while they worked on . . ." He hiccupped. "I've been trapped here. Jane, she wouldn't let me leave. She—They made me say, and I—I never wanted—You have to—You have to—" Matt's shoulders heaved with a gigantic sob, and he hunched down on himself, almost into a ball, openly weeping. From his periphery there came only stunned silence.

"I knew it," Lionel whispered.

"Where?" the terramorph demanded, suddenly grabbing Matt by the front of his shirt, pulling the limp boy upright, glaring at him, a wild intensity raging in his slate-gray eyes. "Where have they taken it?"

Matt panted, drawing several fast, hysterical breaths, then forced himself to breathe deeper, to stare up at both of them through tearstained eyes. "There's a place," he blabbered. "Somewhere in the US. Area . . . Area 60. I don't . . . They had me blindfolded every time I went there, but I still . . . It's cold. And I heard the sound of waves and seagulls and someone talking; something about Kodiak bears, or a lion—"

"Kodiak Island," the tall man whispered. "Port Lions." He rounded on his younger companion. "I know that place! Alaska! I had a friend who used to go there hunting."

Matt forced himself to nod.

"Please," he begged. "You have to destroy it. Kill me, burn my body, burn this entire place to the ground, but then find it—you have to find it. It's our only hope. The next round of flu vaccines, they're not going to be . . . You have to stop it. Please. Please! You're the only ones who can!"

For a moment, nobody breathed. The two assassins stood perfectly still before finally exchanging glances drenched in understanding and horror.

"It's worse than we thought," the terramorph murmured.

"We've got to tell people," Lionel whispered.

"We will, kid," his companion promised. "We will." He turned back to Matt, the gun now hanging loosely in his grasp. "Thank you. I can't believe I'm saying this, but . . . thank you." Almost reluctantly, he once more raised the semiautomatic pistol. "I know you didn't choose this. And I'm sorry. But it's—"

Matt shook his head, resolute and defiant. "It's the only way. I know. I've made peace with it. I just . . . get them for me, okay?"

The two nodded. The terramorph placed a hand upon Matt's shoulder.

"Turn around," he told him. "It'll be quick. I promise. You won't feel anything."

Matt nodded, giving another sob. He turned around halfway but stopped, laughing out a weak, hiccuping cough.

"I don't suppose either of you fellas have a smoke?" he asked. He looked back over his shoulder, contorting his face into a pathetic smile, wretched and miserable. His would-be killers exchanged glances. The sides of the terramorph's lips twitched.

"Sure, kid," he said sadly. He reholstered his gun, reached into his left breast pocket, and drew out a box of cigarettes and a lighter. He motioned the tip of the box to Matt. Matt took it.

"Careful," Lionel joked. "Those things'll kill you." He recoiled back down into himself as his companion shot him a glare. Matt lit the cigarette, sighed, tried desperately not to cough, and trudged a few steps over to the window.

"I never wanted this," he murmured. He reached over, undoing the latch and sliding open the pane of glass.

"What are you doing?" the terramorph warned, his voice suddenly wary. He looked between Matt and the window, his eyes narrowed as his hand went back to his holster.

"What?" Matt shrugged, looking perfectly innocent. He exhaled smoke out through the open window, then looked back as if only now realizing what he was doing. "Oh. Sorry. Habit."

The terramorph scowled. Slowly, he raised the pistol. "Well, hurry up. No offense, kid, but the longer we wait here, the longer we risk Lady Dawn showing up."

"She's not coming," Lionel told him. He reached into his back pocket and pulled out his phone. A gold and orange website—DawnWatch. "See? She's in North Korea, going after Kim Jong-Il. Right now."

"The Legion, then. The cops."

"Can I finish the smoke?" asked Matt. The tall thug glared.

"Quickly," he snapped. "Quickly." Matt drew in another breath then exhaled out the open window, not being obviously slow. A second passed.

"Oh, screw this," the terramorph snarled. Matt let out a yelp of surprise as the man grabbed his wrist and yanked him away from the window. The cigarette fell, smoldering and forgotten on the carpet.

Don't revive me, he begged Jane silently. *Don't fall into the Time Child's trap.*

"Sorry, kid," the tall man muttered. He raised the pistol, aiming it directly at Matt's forehead. Behind him, Lionel closed his eyes. "This is just the way."

He took a step back. Matt braced himself, staring down the barrel of the gun. The world seemed to slow. His breathing filled every facet of his consciousness, smothering all other sensations. The slight breeze on his left cheek; the tightness in his chest. The blurred tears in his eyes; the gross, acrid taste of cigarette. The smell of smoke and dust and blood.

Inside his chest, Matt's heartbeats spread in an endless distance, the blood in his ears hushing like distant waves. The vain straining of life. He saw the sweat beading on Lionel's forehead; saw the tendons clench in the terramorph's jaw. Saw his finger squeeze the trigger.

Matt tried not to close his eyes.

Giselle Pixus ran.

Faster than sound. Faster than thought. Through outskirts and city streets, between cars and people caught almost frozen in hyperperception. Closer, closer. Three suburbs away, two, then she could see it, the building, twenty-three stories, but as she raced forward, she saw the seal still down over the balcony, smoke and dust and debris—

Around the base of the tower she flew, panting, desperate, looking for an opening. There, a glimmer, a glimmer and a void—an open window. Too small for her to stop on, too narrow for her to climb—No time to think. Giselle ran, legs burning, racing up the side of a nearby building, flying across the rooftops, five stories, ten, hurtling across, hurtling up—

Until she was on the small roof directly opposite.

Ten stories below the chest-size opening, Giselle Pixus roared and poured on every ounce of speed.

Then leapt, arcing like a javelin toward the window, her arms outstretched.

BANG!

A sudden rush of air. A deafening noise. Matt flinched, recoiled, cowering from his death—then he blinked.

There was no darkness.

There was no pain.

There was only the gun barrel, staring three feet away from him, the tip wisping gray with smoke.

And to his right, Giselle Pixus, a bullet clenched between her fingers.

The assassins' faces blanched.

"Oh no," whispered Lionel.

"Oh yes," hissed Giselle. Having run halfway across the Earth, leapt a hundred and fifty feet off a neighboring building, and hurtled head-first through Matt's open window, the leader of the Legion of Heroes now stood between Matt and his attackers, outnumbered, red faced, covered in sweat. But none of that mattered. Because as Giselle slowly straightened, her shoulders slid back, and she rose to her full command-ing glory. Her eyes shone with something close to madness. A smile twitched at the corners of her lips.

"Run," the terramorph whispered.

"I will," the speedster promised.

"Nonlethal," Matt requested, standing back. He leaned casually against the windowsill, any trace of terror forgotten.

"Less lethal," Giselle compromised.

Then she bared a vicious grin and disappeared into a blur.

INTERLUDE

Every time you look at her, you see a corpse.

She does not know, and she does not notice. There is nothing dead about her now, no pallor on her lips or empty grayness in her eyes. Her touch is warm, and her movements fluid, and when she rises on top of you, she sways with the same frenetic energy that stopped your heart and stole your breath. Yet, in every moment now, you watch for it. No matter how alive she seems, how vibrant, all it takes is a single moment of stillness, and you know for certain she is dead.

She whispers in your ear, and you hear hissing rainfall in the alley.

She kisses, and you taste vomit on her lips.

You close your eyes and shut it out. You close your mind, but inevitably—

Moonlit shadows twist upon her face as you writhe together. Suddenly, the body beneath you is decayed and rotten, the red scratches drawn across your back gouged by the broken fingernails of a corpse.

The truth is an infection you cannot cure.

But you have ways of making yourself forget.

Every night, every bar in Hong Kong welcomes you with chemical anonymity. You dance until your feet bleed, until sweat drips through your silk shirts, until you are febrile with mirth and intoxication. Drink gurgles down your throat, powder fizzes up your nose, tablets dissolve beneath your tongue. A dead man and a rainswept alley hound your thoughts, and the only way to make them flee is to destroy your capacity for thinking.

Every morning you awake in a cold sweat and wretched nausea. You start pouring hair of the dog on your waking nightmares, and Melody laughs and calls you a fiend. You cannot stand to turn on the news for word of the murder being discovered. You recoil at every knock on the door, be it for pizza, medicine, or work. You do your job in silence, eyes averted, aggressively sober and deliriously certain that the government knows, that everyone knows, that the truth stalks you, waiting to come out.

You give life almost as an afterthought, counting down the moments until you can behold Melody again; until you can know, relieved and certain, that she is still warm and beautiful, that she still rests above the ground.

THE DAEDALUS DRIVE

"Study of Idiosyncratic Manifestations in Monozygotic Twins"
Harvard University Faculty of Science and Medicine, 1998

Figure 4.1

Subject Names [birth order]	Ability: Elder (observations/notes)	Ability: Junior (observations/notes)
T. Tong I. Tong	Enhanced hearing (subject congenitally blind)	Enhanced sight (subject congenitally deaf)
S. Clark A. Clark	Absorb electricity (no detriment)	Create/release electricity (severe lethargy)
S. McDonald G. McDonald	Intercept and interpret electrical signals (rapid comprehension)	Create and send electrical signals (high impact; multiple devices)
J. McKinley A. McKinley	Telekinesis (high precision)	Spatial awareness, proximate object sense (high precision)
P. Holmes M. Holmes	Vary skin colouration, patterning, camouflage	Vary body shape, physical composition, elasticity

J. Roberts D. Roberts	Comprehend animals*	Command animals (high volume; simultaneous)
J. Benedict V. Benedict	Size expansion (very large), contract to original	Size diminution (very small), expand to original
T. Barber R. Barber	High physical force output#	Specific durability; resist heavy loading.
O. Phelps J. Phelps	Create fire (high volume; low lethargy)	Control fire (high precision; high control)
M. Kelly S. Kelly	Specific durability; resist change to temperature, pressure	Close system sufficiency; input oxygen, nutrients, sustenance not required
M. Hermano L. Hermano	Control, merge self with plant mass	Create, enhance, expand, propagate plant mass
Y. Lee X. Lee	Superspeed$	Thermal and acoustic absorption and release$

*Subject exhibits high agitation once removed from beta blockers. Observation ceased due to ethical concerns.

#Subject reports feedback pain when exerting superhuman force. Observation ceased due to ethical concerns.

$Subjects' abilities appear linked. Use of ability by elder subject causes contemporaneous energy build-up in junior subject. Continued failure to release energy by junior subject results in injury to elder subject. Observation ceased due to ethical concerns.

Jane Walker landed in the street outside her home to find sirens, dust, and death.

She'd been accompanying the cargo plane back to American airspace, oblivious to what waited for her until they landed, until she turned on her cell phone to hundreds of missed messages, dozens of missed calls. She'd left her prisoner behind, racing up through the clouds in a slipstream of thundering air and golden panic.

She descended on the city, windows shattering in her wake, and when she landed in the center of the street, her feet drove a crater into the asphalt. But none of that mattered, for all Jane could see was the smoke billowing from the remains of their apartment, and the bodies of the dead being laid out in front.

"Matt!" she cried, sprinting toward them as the crowds parted. "Matt!"

To her relief—to her eternal, desperate relief—a familiar figure raised his hand above the commotion. Pushing policemen, paramedics, and gawking civilians aside, Jane stepped through the crowd to see Matt resting in a small pocket of space beside an ambulance, Giselle carefully wrapping bandages around his legs and arms as she argued with a paramedic.

"I can heal it," the short-haired African American ambulance officer was saying. "This is ridiculous; I understand if you don't trust cops, but I'm not—"

"Touch him and I'll break your filthy neck," Jane swore, storming over. The paramedic turned, saw her coming, blanched, and abruptly stepped back. Matt watched Jane's approach with tired eyes.

"Hi."

"What happened?" Jane demanded. Then, before anyone could even answer, she launched forward, snatching Matt up into a bone-breaking hug.

"Ow," Matt winced. Jane pulled back abruptly, although her hands still held a trembling vise grip on his shoulders.

"What happened?" she repeated. Giselle shook her head and—the paramedic now retreated—continued to silently minister to Matt's superficial wounds.

"I left the gas on," replied Matt. Jane's eyes widened in disbelief, only to narrow half a second later.

"Come on, man," Giselle sighed beside him.

"You—"

"Don't freak out," Matt told her. "Everything's cool." He kept his gaze fixed on her, clearly trying very hard to ignore the street scattered with bits of mortar or the black-clad bodies either moaning or lying silent. "I was maybe a little bit attacked."

"Absolute circus," Giselle said.

Jane's heart skipped a beat. Her breathing began drawing in fits and starts, and the air around her started to tinge.

"How . . . You . . ."

"I'm fine," Matt assured, making a grab for her hand. She stiffly pulled away. "I'm fine. This is . . . We'll get through this, okay? It's going to be alright."

Jane could barely hear. Her ears rang and her head pounded, and her fists were clenched so hard she thought her fingers were going to tear through her gloves.

"Where are they?" she hissed, and her eyes began to seethe with gold. "Where are they? I'll kill them. I'll burn every last one of them. I'll rip their heads off. I—"

"Most of them are already dead," Giselle interrupted. She indicated over at the bodies. All around, the growing crowd was staring at the three of them, craning their necks despite being pushed back by the disorganized police officers. Jane neither noticed nor cared. "The mines worked," the speedster continued prattling. "And then Matt's strobes kept them down long enough for me to get back—"

It took every ounce of Jane's restraint not to grab Giselle by her throat. "Get back?!" she demanded, turning to tower over the crouching woman, eyes ablaze with fury. "Get back?! Where the hell were you?! How could you let this happen?! You were supposed to be watching him; you were supposed to—!"

"Jane!" Matt barked. For a moment, Jane barely heard him, could do nothing but glare at the silent, stone-faced speedster, who had slowly risen to her feet, staring back. But eventually, the feeling of Matt's eyes boring into her forehead made Jane swear and turn away. She met Matt's furious gaze, his face caked in a thin layer of dust. "Enough." He glanced at Giselle. "Give us a minute."

"I'll see to the Legion stuff," Giselle said, not reluctant at all to leave. "Thanks."

The speedster flicked Matt a brief, almost sad smile before risking one last look at Jane and walking—not running—briskly off toward the police line. Jane watched her go, teeth clenched.

"She saved my life," said Matt.

"Where was she?" Jane growled, the words black and guttural.

"It's fine."

"Where was she?"

"She was getting lunch. She—"

Jane let out a deep, savage growl. "I'll kill her," she snarled. "I'll kill her; I'll kill every last one of those useless—"

"Jane!" Matt grabbed her by the wrist, hard, and pulled her to face him. The shock of the contact caused the death threats to slip momentarily from Jane's lips.

"Calm. Down," he ordered.

"Calm down? Calm down?!" Jane wrenched her arm free from Matt's grasp and reeled away from him, hands clenching and unclenching within her gloves. Without realizing it, she began to pace back and forth beside the ambulance, boots kicking cracks into the ground. "Are you kidding me? Are you freaking kidding me?!"

"Take a breath."

"This was our home!"

"I know. I know."

"How are you not upset?!"

"I *am* upset," Matt said, his voice deliberately even. "But don't make a scene."

"Scene?" Jane snapped, lunging her face an inch from his. "You want a scene?! I'll give you a scene." She spun back to the crowd and the corpses. "Where are they? Where are those miserable scum? I'll kill them; I'll burn—"

"Do you want me to be safe?" Matt demanded, and suddenly, all balance vanished from his voice. Jane turned back toward him, incredulous, only to find Matt's glare resolutely matching her own. "Or do you want to throw a tantrum? Get a hold of yourself." Jane flinched as though he'd slapped her. "You're better than this."

"I—"

"I don't need anger," Matt snapped. "Anger is worthless. I need you to shut up, take a breath, recognize what you're doing, and do something else."

"How—?" Jane spluttered, incredulous. "Like—" She forced herself to stop midsentence, and through curling lips and gritted teeth, drew in a long, angry breath. "Like what?" she finally managed.

"Like, geez, Jane, I don't know. Talk to the survivors. Look at the bodies. Do something other than rage and punch things." Jane felt heat rising inside her chest, but before she could snarl out a response, Matt held up his hands, his eyes squeezed shut, waving down at her. "I'm sorry. I'm sorry," he said. "That wasn't fair. This isn't your fault. I'm just stressed." He opened his eyes and looked up at her, his expression sickened and sour. "Turns out, this isn't just fringe lunatics anymore. It's coordinated."

"Matt—"

"Just . . ." He held up his hands again, as though even talking right now was too painful. "Go. Find out what you can. Do . . . Legion stuff. The training. I don't know. I don't know anything. Just . . . give me some time."

A hot, tight pain crept through Jane's chest and up her throat, constricting her voice. She took a step forward, hands reaching toward Matt, but Matt shied away, averting his gaze as he pressed farther back into the side of the ambulance.

"Please," he murmured. "Just . . . please. Find something." He looked back at her with miserable, defeated eyes, which a moment later caught on something off in the middle distance. Jane glanced over her shoulder, following his gaze over into the waiting crowd to a familiar blonde head. "Plus," said Matt, folding his arms, "seems like our lawyer's here, so I'm pretty sure she'll have fires that need putting out."

"I'm not leaving." Jane scowled, turning back to him.

"And I'm not going anywhere," sighed Matt, dropping his arms to his side. "Clearly. So just . . . go figure out who all these people who want to kill me are."

Jane grumbled something inaudible and frustrated, but in the face of Matt's dejected stare, she finally relented, storming over toward where Giselle was on the phone calling in more of the Legion to help.

Alone against the ambulance, Matt sighed as he watched her go—then groaned as another painful conversation appeared over by the barricades with a distinctive *pop*. Their two FBI handlers, Fiona Cree and Tom Richardson, stepped out of the sulfur and surveyed the devastation, their own teleporter and posse in tow.

Great, thought Matt. *Just perfect.*

"Please leave me alone," he whispered to the wind.

"Mr. Callaghan!" Matt looked over to see the senior FBI man mouthing instructions to his fellow agents and pointing rapidly at their surroundings. The group he'd jumped in with began to disperse, each heading toward their respective targets: a few agents moved to talk to the cops, while the plain-faced Fiona bustled across the road to sidle up to Jane and Giselle.

Halfway across police lines, Matt saw Rana take quick stock of the situation and correctly assess which of her clients needed the most pressing legal counsel. Matt watched his lawyer hurry over and arrive just as the air between Jane and the FBI woman started to spark.

"Mr. Callaghan." Matt turned and looked up to see the male FBI agent standing beside him, his graying hair clashing with his tan suit, face plastered with faux concern. "Thank goodness. We came as soon as we heard."

"Outstanding," said Matt, dry enough to be a fire hazard. Richardson took a step closer, leaning in to rest one big fist on the ambulance, his expression pained.

"Let's get you out of here. There's a safe house barely—"

"Mr. Richardson," said Matt, cutting him off. "Come on. Do we have to?"

"Have to do—?"

"For Christ's sake. Enough!" Matt interrupted, his temper flared. His voice ran roughshod over Richardson before the big man could get a chance to speak. "Let me save fifteen minutes of our goddamn lives from your agonizing, ham-fisted bullcrap! I do not care what you have to say. I am never going to go with you!"

Matt paused to let the last sentence sink in, glaring at the FBI agent, his tongue loose and venomous. "I know you think I'm a child," he continued before Richardson could get a word in edgeways. "Clearly, that's how I must look to you or, you know, to everyone. But let me make one thing abundantly clear." He pointed his fingers like he was finally snatching from the air some maddening fly.

"This false friend thing? This 'caring paternal figure,' 'arm around my shoulder, baseball and bald eagles' shtick that works maybe on dumbass kids from broken homes with twelve IQ? It is never"—and

Matt reemphasized that last word—"*never*, going to work on me. I am never going to fall for it.

"So GIVE UP! Give up, go away, leave me alone, and stop trying to . . . what, capitalize on a near-death experience?" Matt paused, and an edge of resignation crept into his voice as he gazed away from Richardson and out over the destruction and the bodies accumulated outside his home. "Save your breath. Death's been stalking me for a while now. It's beginning to lose its impact."

For a moment, the man said nothing, merely stared at Matt with his lips barely open, his rugged face curled into an inscrutable expression. He followed Matt's eyes out onto the open field, up to the half-ruined, hollow shell of the apartment, then back down and over Matt himself, scratched and bruised, yet safe.

"Alright," the FBI agent said finally. "Serious, then."

"Oh, for crying out—" Matt began, but this time, it was Richardson who cut him off.

"These people are trying to kill you," he stated. The words came factually, like he was doing nothing more serious than giving a presentation on the price of grain. Richardson's back straightened, his arms moving to clasp behind him so he stood almost to attention.

"The fabled Bureau observation," replied Matt, rolling his eyes.

"They're not going to stop trying to kill you," the agent continued, ignoring the jab.

"Doesn't seem like it," Matt sighed.

"We want your blood." A small jolt of surprise ran through Matt's body, and he actually turned and looked up at the large FBI agent standing beside him.

Richardson unclasped his hands from behind his back and crossed his arms, gazing down at Matt, his eyes devoid of emotion. "We being the American government and affiliated associations." He waved a dismissive hand. "People whose names you don't know, whose orders I can't question, whose decisions have unknowingly shaped fundamental aspects of our lives.

"It's irrelevant. They want your genetics. They want to study it. They want the strategic advantages it will confer. May confer." Another contemptuous wave. "It doesn't matter. These are the facts. You know it, I know it, everyone knows it, even if no one will say it with your lawyer around."

"Well, I appreciate the honesty," Matt said, a little taken aback. "Not, you know, a lot, but—"

But the man in the tan suit wasn't finished.

"Sooner or later, Mr. Callaghan," Richardson told him, holding up and examining the nails on one thick, muscled hand, "one of two things is going to happen. One: someone is going to get your blood. Maybe it's us. Maybe it's another player. Doesn't matter. Sooner or later, there'll be an opening. Sooner or later, you'll slip up."

"We'll see," Matt murmured.

"Scenario two," Agent Richardson continued, undeterred, "is that one of these people"—he gestured broadly around at the debris, at the bodies lying on the pavement—"is going to get you. Put a bullet through your skull. Burn your corpse. That's not even a threat. It's inevitable."

The tall man shook his head, staring down at Matt with cold, emotionless eyes. "You are special, Mr. Callaghan, but not unique. I don't mean your powers; I mean how you're viewed by marginal society. You are the subject of conspiracy." He said it like a self-sure doctor presenting an unusual diagnosis. "You have stirred into agitation a small yet pervasive crust of America for whom reason does not enter into their worldview. They have fixated on you, in the way in which they periodically fixate, and they will remain fixated on you until you die, and then possibly after. And you will die."

He paused and let out a short, humorless bark of laughter. "This is not some organization, some cohesive group trying to kill you. This is a plague. An incurable infestation of vermin spawning from fringe stupidity, a lingering madness at the bottom of the bell-curve. And they will keep coming, and coming, and coming until they see you dead."

The FBI agent shrugged, nonchalant. "I've seen it before. You're a fixture for them now, the idea of you, and it will keep spreading indefinitely. All it takes is one mistake from your fledgling Legion—from your girlfriend—now, a week from now, ten years. One slipup, and they'll pounce."

Matt said nothing, merely continued looking out at the crowd, at Jane and the Legion members now rapidly appearing in the street. Striding, barking orders, sweeping and setting the perimeter, doing their duty, their rounds.

"These people are hunting you," Richardson said, quiet yet unrelenting, "because they think you're with us. No amount of evidence, nothing you can say, will convince them otherwise. That's the nature of conspiracy." He paused. "And if that's the case, then what's the point? Why suffer the detriment of their beliefs while refusing the benefits we offer? You're a rational man." The agent gazed down at him with dark, indifferent eyes. "Don't make an irrational trade. Make it better. Take the protection. Live out your days free from this endless danger and let what's going to inevitably happen come."

"Inevitable," Matt snorted. But the word rang hollow and solitary.

"We can hide you," the FBI agent promised. He leaned in. "Really hide you. A new face, new name, fake powers. There are things we can do that aren't known to the public. Technologies."

"I'm fine where I am," Matt lied.

"You could be useful to us, Matt Callaghan," Richardson pressed on. "Not just for your blood. Really, actually useful. I'm not making this offer to her"—his eyes flicked over at Jane—"I'm making it to you. Because you're realistic." He leaned in closer, just a fraction of an inch. "You're a voice in her ear. A calming voice. Perhaps the only one. How long before she makes too many enemies? How long before it isn't just the fringe you're fighting but entire countries, special forces?"

His dark eyes gleamed. "You can steer her away from that. You can guide her into diplomacy, even caution. We can show you how. And in return, we'll give you anonymity. A proper career. The life you always wanted. You, your family. Anyone."

There washed between the two of them a few moments of silence before Matt finally managed to find his voice. "I'm going to start saying very rude things now," he told the FBI agent. He kept his face blank and stared straight ahead, refusing to meet the gray man's eyes. "About you and all the people you work for. It probably would be better if you moved on before that happens."

Richardson's only response was an empty smile. "The offer's open, Mr. Callaghan," he said. "Until it isn't. Until it's too late to play that card." The man stood back up to his full height. "Make the rational call."

"Kill yourself," answered Matt, borrowing one of Jane's. The agent didn't reply, but instead, with an uncharacteristically compassionless smirk, stepped over to one of the nearby assailants, lying handcuffed on the ground.

"So you don't get lonely," Richardson said, and with a single strong movement, jerked the man to his knees. The assassin yelped, his shoulder clearly broken, or some other part of his arms, and stayed kneeling, swaying as his pained gaze flickered from the FBI agent to Matt. There were cuts and bruising to his torso and forehead, and his hands and feet were bound. Matt recognized the soft face and fluffy coffee-colored hair. The younger man who'd come close to killing him in the spare room. Lionel.

Richardson looked on in amusement as Matt and his assailant stared at each other, then without another word strode off, strolling with only a brief backward glance toward his companions, who were engaged in an animated three-way discussion between themselves, the police, and the Legion of Heroes. Matt watched him go in silence, then indulged in the aforementioned barrage of swearing anyway.

"Well said," Lionel mumbled.

Matt turned to his attacker, kneeling hog-tied like Christmas ham not three feet away.

"Oh, so now you feel like talking?"

The black-clad man sucked in air between his teeth. "Doesn't feel like I'm going anywhere."

"Yeah, well, that'll be the sedatives or whatever they've injected you with. Plus the broken bones."

"I can't feel my legs," Lionel murmured.

"Yep, well, that's Giselle Pixus. 50ccs." Matt folded his arms, scrutinizing the assassin with an imperious eye and making no move to approach. "I suppose this is the part where you say, 'Come closer,' so you can telekinetically slit my throat."

"My head hurts. Hard to see." A bead of blood was trickling down his forehead. "Was never good at body parts."

"Well, isn't that nice."

Lionel's voice faded. His eyes wandered over to where the FBI, the police, and the Legion were clustered, then back toward Matt. His tongue moved gingerly over cracked lips. "I didn't . . . You were lying," he said, as though that was some hard-fought revelation.

"Yeah, well, sort of the only thing I've got left," Matt replied with a scowl. He sighed, resigned. The assassin shook his head.

"All that stuff about them already having it. A secret facility. All lies."

"Absolute nonsense."

His assailant lapsed back into silence for a moment. "Could've fooled me," he said.

"I did fool you," replied Matt. "And before you ask, no, I don't feel bad about it. You were trying to kill me. All morality is off."

Even with his hands bound behind his back, Lionel's shoulders slumped. "I didn't want to kill you."

Matt shook his head, staring off at Jane and Rana arguing in the distance. "Even if I believed you, Lionel, which I don't, I don't care about your internal dilemmas. All that matters are your actions. You feeling bad doesn't change the fact that you tried to put a bullet through my skull, and it sure as heck doesn't change the fact that you just blew up my house."

The wind whipped between them, blowing silence and dust. Lionel once more dragged his tongue across chapped lips.

"I heard you guys talking."

"Good for you."

"They don't have your blood." It was a statement, not a question.

"No, Lionel." Matt sighed, still not turning to look at him. "They don't. They never have." He shook his head, gazing out over the carnage. "Not that you or anyone with your level of inbreeding even remotely cares."

The two fell silent, their words giving way to the whispering air, the hum of voices, the wail of distant sirens. There came the sound of someone far off moaning, an injured person, their screams piercing up against the sunset. Matt closed his eyes, trying to let the sound slide off him. He would've given anything just to curl up into a ball and sleep.

"Wrong," Lionel murmured beside him. "I was wrong."

"Hooray for you," replied Matt, who genuinely didn't care.

"I think I was set up."

Suddenly, the hair on Matt's neck stood on end. He opened his eyes, and for the first time, turned to look directly at his assailant. The man stared at him, unwavering, his words a bare whisper beneath the wind.

"What did you say?"

The attacker gave the barest shake of his head. "All along, I wondered," he whispered. "Something didn't feel right. Something felt off. It was all too good to be true. And then it wasn't."

"What wasn't?"

"The intel. You. The drop." His head turned, and his gaze moved blankly out over the bodies of his companions. "They knew exactly where you were. What Lady Dawn was doing. The gap in the basement. All perfect, on a platter. But nothing about the land mines? Your defenses? And no mention of the speedster. No word that she could get in."

"What're you saying?" said Matt.

Lionel looked back at him, and despite the pain swimming in his eyes, beneath it lay focus. "False flag," he whispered. "I think this was a false flag."

"By who?" But then, Matt followed the assassin's eyes over to where the FBI agents were standing—over to Richardson and Fiona.

"They used us," the man who'd tried to kill him murmured.

Matt didn't respond.

"You can't say yes to them." A plea.

"I'm not going to." Matt turned back to face his bound attacker. "I know I'm pissing into the wind here, but listen to me, genuinely: I'm not with them. I'm never going to be with them. I will be dead in my cold, unmarked grave before I voluntarily give them my blood. I've lived my life as a useless human, and I don't intend to inflict that on the world. The government can eat me."

He fixed his eyes on the back of Richardson's tan jacket with a cold, bitter stare. "The Chinese can eat me. All those private corporations can eat me. Everyone I love has superpowers. And if they think I'm going to help make that a privilege, they can suck my pale white balls."

"I believe you," Lionel murmured. He bent his head, glancing slowly around, then suddenly, with a grunt of pain, he twisted his shoulder toward Matt.

"Here," he urged him. "Quick. Before they realize. I've still got a little juice."

"What, you gonna hurl a rock at me?" Matt said with a frown. But the jab fell short and hollow, because as he watched, the attacker's face clenched. Lionel's teeth gritted, and the tendons in his neck strained, droplets of sweat beading across his forehead. His skin reddened; his whole body began to tremble. And then, slowly, slowly, with the smallest, most infinitesimal movement, the top pocket of his vest peeled open.

And slowly, like a splinter being extracted, there crawled out from the pocket a thumb drive.

"I don't . . . like . . . being . . . lied to," Lionel panted, and as his shoulders shook and his chest heaved, the drive inched up and outward before suddenly tugging free and tumbling down into the dirt. Slowly, the bound man's eyes boring into it, the USB scraped along the ground between them, a pebble tugged along by the wind, almost unnoticeable, until the edge brushed against Matt's shoe. Abruptly, Lionel's shoulders sagged. His head drooped, and he let out a low groan, his forehead slick with sweat. Silently, as though in a dream, Matt bent and wrapped his cold fingers around the USB.

"Figure . . . it . . ." the man who had tried to kill him whispered, and a moment later, he passed out.

A trio of Acolytes—one telekinetic, one speedster, and one who could change the size of objects by touching them—boxed up what remained of Matt and Jane's things while a contractor trusted by the Legion (who could excrete quick-setting concrete foam) made sure the roof wasn't going to collapse. Jane did not speak to them. Matt was ninety percent sure they were the same group who had helped his family move last time.

"Thanks, guys," he said as they unloaded and rescaled the last of the miniaturized boxes into Morningstar's top-floor guest room. The youngest, a tan kid with tricolor hair who couldn't have been more than sixteen, flicked him a salute, and Matt resisted the impulsive urge to tip.

A part of him wondered if these Acolytes resented being repeatedly used as movers, though none of the tireless three seemed irritated. More likely, the young recruits were simply pleased to show off their skills in front of the big boss. Not that Jane was in the mood to notice up-and-comers at present. Not that she was in the mood to do anything besides veer between self-loathing and rage.

So long, brief flash of independence, Matt sighed. *'Twas rash to think we could ever be.*

"You are never leaving my sight," Jane ordered, storming back into the bedroom as soon as the movers were gone. She had yet to take off her uniform, though the tips of her cape were caked in what he hoped was dust and mud. "You are staying here, under round-the-clock guard, unless you are under guard by me on mission."

"At least I'll see the world," Matt said mildly, which was the wrong response because it set aflame the oily rags of fury Jane had been stock-piling all afternoon.

"How could you be so stupid?!" she erupted, throwing up her hands, waves of golden light radiating from her shoulders. "Sending Giselle away?! What were you thinking?!"

"I was thinking it was twenty minutes and I wanted dumplings," Matt replied, trying hard not to let frustration get the better of him. "I'm sorry. I genuinely didn't think there would be an assault team waiting to literally beat down our door."

Jane didn't seem to be listening. Instead, she paced with increasing rapidity to the point where Matt was worried her empowered boots might burn holes in the floorboards. "I should've been there. I should've been back quicker. It's all my fault." Abruptly, she stopped, gripping her head in her hands, borderline manic. "How did they know?" she demanded, and then louder, "How did they know?!"

Matt didn't have an answer, so Jane resumed pacing.

"We were so careful," she almost shouted. "So goddamn careful. I don't understand; I don't . . . Urgh!" Again, she threw up her hands, and had anybody stepped through the door at that moment, Matt would have given even odds of Jane simply vaporizing them right then and there merely as an outlet for stress.

Jane spun around to face him. "I'm going back," she growled. Her eyes kept skipping over where he stood, and thin wisps of gold were rising from her *E*. "I'm going to go back. I'm going to wait for them; I'm going to stop them."

"No," said Matt, his voice suddenly rising, suddenly firm. "Absolutely not."

"You can't stop me."

"No, but I can— We are not time— *playing Pokémon* over this!"

"I want them alive," Jane snarled. "The dead ones. I want to track them down. I want to be waiting. I want to see where they come from, and go back through their miserable little jump scars and beat them all within an inch of their lives until they tell me how they knew."

"And then what?" Matt snapped back. "What if they aren't the end of it? What if there are no good answers?"

"I AM TRYING TO KEEP YOU ALIVE!" Jane roared. Suddenly, she was turning on him, lunging right up close to his face, causing Matt to recoil, heart racing, head pressing back into the wooden wall as Lady Dawn's golden fury bore down upon him.

"Don't yell at me," he murmured, recoiling.

Jane's palms splayed on the wall either side of him, trapping Matt in place. Her face moved so close he could see the individual sparks of light dancing across her irises, the thin spindles of saliva dripping from her teeth. "You are an idiot," she hissed. "An ungrateful, petulant child who values . . . Chinese food! Over his own life!"

Abruptly, she reeled back, leaving Matt standing there against the wall stock-still while she stormed, raking her fingers through her hair. "Why can't you just listen?" she moaned. "Why can't you do what I tell you, just once? Why can't you follow the rules?"

"It was a mistake!"

"Everything you do is a mistake!" she shouted, throwing up her hands. "No matter how hard I try, no matter what I do, you just keep— ARGH!" She clutched her face with both hands, her palms aglow.

"Right," replied Matt. His arms trembled, but his words were frozen stone. "My apologies. Screw me for getting lunch. Screw me wanting twenty minutes to myself without somebody watching. Sorry for not wanting to give you *absolute control* over EVERY ASPECT OF MY LIFE!"

Jane spun and marched toward him, thrusting her finger into his face, her features twisted in pure contempt.

"You," she whispered, the words low and dark and bloody, and for a single, wild moment, Matt thought she might actually hit him, "are the only thing I *constantly* have to worry about. Day in; day out. You don't care if you live or die? Fine. But I do. And I am *not* going to let you die," she snarled, her voice rising. "Even if it takes me every moment of every day *for the rest OF MY GODDAMN LIFE!*"

Matt's eyes narrowed an inch from Jane's. "I'm sorry I'm such a burden," he sneered. Suddenly no longer afraid, he pushed her hand out of his face and shoved free, stomping toward the door.

"Where do you think you're going?" Jane demanded, her voice rising to a roar. "Get back here!"

"Or else what?" Matt snarled, spinning on his heel. "You going to physically restrain me?"

Jane's nostrils flared. "I will if I have to!"

"You going to stop me walking around the Legion of Heroes? You going to stop me using the restroom? You going to stop me seeing my family?"

"I . . ." Jane's voice suddenly faltered, and her thin brows arched suddenly inward, anger replaced by anxiety. "You can't . . . without . . . It's not safe!"

"I don't care," Matt spat. "Seems like that's more your problem than mine."

And with that, he turned, stepped into the hallway, and slammed the door, leaving Jane standing in the center of the guest room, shining and alone.

For the longest time, the room lay silent save for the retreating patter of Matt's footsteps and the ragged sounds of Jane's breath. Alone, still wearing the uniform of a so-called hero, surrounded by an empty bed, a stranger's antique furniture, and the last of their worldly possessions, Jane stood, feet rooted to the floor, her teeth clenched, her fists balled, her shoulders heaving.

No, her thoughts muttered. *No, no, NO, NO, NO!*

"AAAARGGGGGHHHHH!"

The pulsating fury exploded in Jane's chest, and without thinking, she turned, grabbed the side of the four-post bed and hurled it into the farthest wall. *CRASH.*

The old wood shattered, mattress bouncing back and knocking over some of their boxes, the room's paneling buckling where the frame impacted. And for some reason, the fact the bed had broken rather than the wall she'd flung it into, filled Jane with such unimaginable rage that with a wordless roar, she threw out her hands and fired, blowing a hole clean through the side of Morningstar and out into the night beyond. The warm air scurried out, carrying with it a wave of dust and splinters. For a while, Jane just stood there, panting, staring into the starlit hole.

A moment passed. Then two.

"Urgh," Jane eventually groaned. She mashed her face into her gloves, then clenched shut her eyes before opening them again. The broken wall lay silent in front of her, cold night air continuing to creep and circle round the heels of her boots. Jane's shoulders drooped.

"Goddammit," she muttered. Jane pinched the bridge of her nose, suddenly feeling like the biggest idiot in the entire freaking world. *yOu'Re NoT a GoLdeN hAmMer.* Well, tell that to the enormous effing hole in the wall. Jane let out an exhausted sigh. What was wrong with her?

Her rage suddenly reduced to cinders, Jane trudged over toward the jagged opening, grabbing the upturned mattress with one hand and dragging it behind her. She drifted out into the open air, pulling the bulk of the mattress into place so that it clogged up the opening, and then just sort of hung there, four stories above the Academy grounds, gazing in resigned defeat back at the white patch on the manor's upper floor. Someone was going to have to fix that, she lamented internally, closing her eyes and rubbing her temples. She'd caused a literal security breach.

Already outside and unwilling to go take the stairs like a regular person in case she ran into anybody—or God forbid, Matt—and had to explain what the hell had just happened, Jane instead floated down toward the maintenance hut that lay on the Academy's outskirts, a small cottage next to a larger shed where she knew the Legion kept repair equipment and supplies.

Her feet touched down outside the cottage door—white planks with a single window—and she rapped her knuckles on the wood, letting out a deep sigh as she stared down at the nondescript brown doormat. Jane was so caught up with thoughts of what she was going to say, the attack on Matt, and her own stupidity, that she didn't put two and two together until the door opened, and she found herself face-to-face with someone familiar.

"Jane?"

Jane opened her mouth for a few seconds before shutting it, abruptly thrown. Standing in the doorway, her father's weathered brow furrowed, his face creased with concern.

"Dad."

"This . . . This is an unexpected surprise."

"I . . . Yes."

"Is everything okay?" he asked, sounding worried. Though it was late, Peter Walker still had on denim jeans and a thick flannelette shirt, and as he stood gawking at her in concern, his oil-stained hands wiped themselves unconsciously on a dirty rag hanging from his left back pocket. His hair was its usual tangled brown bird's nest, and his cheeks bore a few days of scratchy stubble, but his movements were alert, his eyes weren't bloodshot, and there were no bags underneath them.

"I, ah . . ." Jane forced a swallow, shook her head a little, and focused on why she'd come. "I, um . . . Sorry. I needed some repairs."

"Oh." In the dim porch light, she saw her father's face fall slightly, but he picked himself back up before it could be down for more than an instant. "Seemed a bit late for a visit."

"No, it's not . . . I just . . . There's a hole in the manor."

"Ah," he said, nodding sagely. "Right."

"It's my fault," admitted Jane with a sinking sigh. "I know it's late, and I'm an idiot; it's just—"

Her father held up a hand. "Say no more," he replied, level and calm. "Not the first and won't be the last. Happens more often than you'd think. We've got some good kids here who can fix it."

"Thank you."

"No problem. Most pressing question, though," the old man asked, "is anything on fire?" As far as Jane could tell, he was being completely serious.

"No."

"Well." Her father flashed her a small, dusty smile. "I've learned that's what they call around here a 'lower grade emergency.'" He extended his hand and held the door open. "Come in. Sit."

Jane hesitated, but after a moment, she sighed and stepped across the threshold, doing what she was told, if only to be polite, with a minimum of grumbling. Her father's cottage was small and basic but cluttered with so many tools and plates and knickknacks it made it seem cozy, if not quite comfortable.

A small TV sat in the corner next to the sink and a landline telephone, and the edge of an ironing board poked out from a thin built-in wardrobe. Jane saw lots of bits and pieces from their old home stacked up around the place—favored mugs and a few old keepsakes, plus lots of photographs. Kid pictures of her. Photos of Mom.

"It's, ah, not the Ritz-Carlton," her father noted, standing on the doorway, hands shuffling to his hips, "but I don't know. Does the job."

Jane sat down on the single bed, on the russet-colored blanket knitted by her grandma, smoothing her cape out between her legs. "It's nice," she said, genuine.

Her dad gave her a wry smile. "Ms. Pixus offered to build me something bigger, but I figured . . . Ah, I don't know, don't fix what ain't broken. Besides"—he gazed around at the warm, cluttered home with a sense of contentment—"I just rattle around, give me too much space."

Jane nodded, not feeling the need to say anything further. After a moment, her father clapped his hands together.

"Tea?"

"Tea?" Jane scoffed. "Since when do you drink tea?"

"Since seven months sober," he replied, shuffling past her with a little glance back, half proud, half cheeky. He filled a clear, metal-rimmed kettle from the sink and returned it to its base, flicking a switch that sent blue lights glowing up through the water. A thin whistle began to rise.

"Congratulations."

"Thank you." He opened his mouth as if to say more, but then closed it again a moment later. They lapsed into silence while the kettle boiled, her sitting, him standing, a small distance apart. Once the high whine subsided, Peter Walker pulled open a wooden drawer and set out two mugs, dropped a tea bag in each, and poured in a stream of steaming water.

"Milk?"

"Who are you?" Jane asked. Her father's mouth twisted in a wry grin.

"That British girl who's always in black's been teaching me a thing or two. We got to chatting a bit, you know, since she's also psychic."

"Natalia. And you mean she saw your thoughts while you were making tea one day and told you you were doing it wrong."

"'An insult to civilized society,' I think were the exact words," he replied with a laugh. "Now I'm under strict instructions. It's called milk, not cream, and so help me God if I ever put it in first, I'll be right out on the street."

Despite herself, Jane chuckled. "She's not cuddly."

"All prickles," her father agreed. "But it's nice in a way. Reminds me of someone a bit taller." He handed her the tea, and the two of them sipped at it, drifting back to peace and quiet.

"So," her father said eventually, leaning on the sink across from her. He crossed his heels. "How come there's a hole in your wall?"

"Got blown up."

"Who blew it?"

"Me."

"Well," said her father, raising the mug to his lips and taking a long draw. "Guess that's not ideal. But better than the alternative: people blasting your house in."

"Might be simpler."

"Suppose. Give you someone to blast back."

"Exactly."

"Your mom was a fighter," he murmured. Jane gave an exasperated sigh and roll of her eyes. Peter immediately put up his hands.

"Sorry, sorry," he said, chastised, apologetic. "That's on me."

"Come on. We almost had a record."

"Yeah, I know. Sorry. Sorry." He let out a deep sigh and took another long sip from his mug. "So," he continued, deliberately changing the subject, "hole in the wall. All the way through?"

"Yes."

"You meant to put it there, or you missed something?"

"I . . . When do I ever miss anything?" Jane replied, bristling. Her father laughed.

"Sorry, forgot who I'm talking to."

"Goddamn right."

He grinned at her. "I remember when—" But midway through the sentence, the old man abruptly stopped and shook his head. "Scratch that. I don't remember anything. Here and now. Hole in the wall. You put it there. Go."

"I . . ." Jane shifted uncomfortably atop the bedspread. "Does it need explaining?" she asked, frustrated. "Do I really need to tell you?"

"No," her father replied with what might've been intended to come across as an indifferent shrug. "Just thought you might want to, that's all."

They fell into another long silence. Jane avoided her dad's gaze, turning her eyes instead up into the corners of the cottage and forcing herself to take another sip of tea. The taste was warm and bittersweet.

"I . . . Matt and I were arguing," she finally relented, a sigh accompanying the admission.

"You blasted Matt?" her father responded, his eyes suddenly widening with panic.

"No," Jane grumbled, waving away his concerns. "He wasn't in the room."

"Ah." The old man's shoulders relaxed.

"I just . . . I was angry."

"Okay." Her dad paused. "Happens to the best of us."

"Pfft," replied Jane, puffing out her cheeks. "Don't think the real Captain Dawn blasted many holes in his building."

"No," her father conceded. Then he raised a finger. "Though there was that one time that French diplomat guy said something rude about his wife, and he dropped a train on his Citroën."

Jane laughed. "How do you know about that?"

"I've been reading books," Peter said, sounding a little proud.

"Yeah?" she grinned. "Plundering the Legion's library?"

"Well, when in Rome . . ." He smiled as he let the sentence fade. "So you were fighting. Okay. What about?"

"He . . ." Jane's voice trailed off, and she rubbed the bridge of her nose. "There was an attack. On the apartment."

"I heard. You okay?"

"I'm fine," she replied, dismissing the notion with another wave.

"Was Matt hurt?"

"No."

"So just a normal day for the two of you then, huh?" He forced a smile, which Jane thought trembled a bit, though he tried to keep the words light. "Par for the course."

Jane shook her head. Without knowing why, she brought her knees up to her chest and tucked them beneath her chin. "It was close. Closer than people are saying. And Matt . . ." She sighed, running her hands through her hair. "I don't know. It's like he doesn't want me to protect him."

For the longest time, her father said nothing. Jane stared off into the kitchen counter, watching the wisps of steam rise from her teacup, stomach churning too badly to take another sip. Eventually, her dad set his mug down on the counter and motioned toward her to shift aside. She did, and he sat down next to her on the bed.

"I . . ." he began. Then he stopped. The corners of his mouth twitched, and he turned to her, hesitating. "Can . . . Can I talk about your mother?" he asked, the words tentative, almost worried. Jane rolled her eyes, but after a few seconds, she nodded.

"Sure."

"Thanks." He drew in a deep breath. "Back in the day, when we . . . when she . . . when your mom was working, I used to get worried a lot about the places she was going. You know, this jungle here. The Arctic.

I'd worry she'd be going somewhere and get sick, or maybe get kidnapped . . . Half of these places were war zones, and I didn't know the people she was going with and . . ." He paused. "Maybe part of it was jealousy. I was worried she was gonna find some other man, someone more her speed, more intelligent. More exciting. I don't know.

"But the point is"—he turned back to Jane—"the point is, every time she went to go somewhere, we'd argue. About whether she should go or not, whether it was safe. And I'd get so frustrated with her, and she'd get so frustrated with me, and it wasn't hatred, really, or selfishness. I cared about her. I was just scared for her. I didn't want her to leave."

He sighed, and his shoulders slumped. "But she had to, you know? She had to; that's what she kept coming back to. 'It's a great big world out there,' she'd say. 'And if you're not out in it, what's the point in even living?'"

He blew out his cheeks. "Which seemed crazy to me. But now, I think I get it. Some people are just like that. They don't see danger. They only see a cage."

Jane hung her head, gazing at the dusty floorboards. "So that's your advice?" she mumbled. "If you love something, set it free?" But to her surprise her father shook his head.

"That was where I finally got to," he told her, "'cause that's what everyone said. And I eventually thought that they knew better, so I listened. I reasoned. And I gave in, time and time again, because I knew it'd make her happy. Even if it'd make me worry. And it worked. She kept coming back." He choked up a laugh, little more than a dry, joyless cough. "Every time, she came back full of stories, full of life." And in the warm cottage light, his eyes faded, and his limbs grew limp. "Until she didn't."

There came a long, awful silence. Then Jane's father turned to her.

"I learned then—or maybe it took me ten years to learn," he said, and his black eyes burned like coal, "once I pulled my head outta my ass. But I learned, finally, that pretty sayings are just that: sayings. Dead is dead. Gone is gone. The world was no less empty because your mom had been smiling when she died. You didn't grow up any less alone."

"Dad . . ."

"No." He shook his head with sudden violence, tears leaking through his wrinkles. He wiped his eyes with the back of his hand. "It is the greatest regret of my life, not protecting your mother. I should never have let her go. I should've locked the door. I should've held her down. I should've . . . anything. Everything. Even if she hated me. Forever."

He stared at Jane, his face a mask of raw determination. "I would give a thousand years of anger," her father whispered, "to stop her from getting on that plane. Because it would mean she'd still be living." The old man shook his head. "When it comes to the people you love, the first question can't be if they're happy. It has to be if they're safe. Unhappy people can get happier. Dead people only stay dead."

In the quiet glow of the cottage, Peter Walker took his daughter's hand, and beneath his skin, Jane felt once more his telepathy—that piercing diamond opening in her mind.

"You do," he urged, "whatever you have to do to protect the people you love. Lie about it. Apologize for it. Then do it anyway." He paused. "You don't love someone to be thanked. You don't even do it so they'll love you in return. You do it for better or worse."

Within Jane's chest, clad in white and gold, a yearning, aching warmth opened, and the girl felt her closed throat shake. She drew back a hearty sniff and wrapped her arms around her father.

"Thanks, Dad," she whispered.

And a moment later, he embraced her in return.

They stayed like that, the pair of them, for neither knew how long. Eventually, Jane's father pulled back.

"Now," he laughed, wiping the tears away, "enough whinging. Let's go fix that hole."

"Mom. Knock-knock."

"Matty? Hey . . ."

His mother was standing out the front of their house when he approached it—their Legion house, not their actual home, which of course was many miles away, sitting empty where they had left it. This was Ironbound's house, Matt supposed, the founding Legion member, a one-and-a-half-story family home with a suburban triangular roof, wooden front porch with white trimmings, and walls painted light gray.

From a distance, coming across the grassy grounds around the side of the Academy, the house seemed still and silent, the dark shingles of the roof merging into the night sky beyond, the white porch light the single point of illumination, staining the walls with shadows. Yet, as he approached, Matt saw a figure moving, standing just beyond the front porch, their back to the door. For a moment, Matt was worried, but then he remembered: she would've been waiting for him.

"Mom." They embraced in the mottled glow of the porch light. Kathryn Callaghan's long brown hair was loose, sitting in its natural curls; she wore a light blue shirt, black track pants, and slippers, with a maroon knitted shawl wrapped round her shoulders. She squeezed Matt tight, then after a moment released him, cupping his chin with both hands.

Matt's brow furrowed and he sniffed, smelling something acrid and unpleasant. His eyes fell on the lit cigarette held between her fingers.

"Mom," Matt repeated, a complaint this time. He fixed her with a disapproving gaze.

"Oh, shush," Mrs. Callaghan hushed, swatting at him with the hand not holding the cigarette. "It's only one."

"I thought you told Dad you quit."

"What your father doesn't know won't hurt him," Matt's mother replied. She took another long draw and blew the smoke away from him before throwing the cigarette on the damp grass and squashing it underfoot.

"So many years of lectures . . ."

"Yes, well, when my children can scrub their own lungs . . ." She let the sentence trail as she took in the expression on Matt's face. "Oh, Matty. Are you okay? What happened?"

"Is Dad . . . ?"

"He's asleep. Kids are out. There was a commotion . . . somebody mentioned . . . but I didn't want to scare them." She paused, peering at him. "Is everything okay? Are you alright?"

Matt sighed. Together, they walked around to the side of the darkened house, to where a two-person white wooden seat swung from the branches of an old oak tree. They sat, and Matt ran his mother through a blow-by-blow of the day's events: the attack, his escape, the FBI's coercion. He left out Lionel and the USB drive tucked quietly away in his pocket, but little else. Not Jane's anger. Not the violence of the attack.

"God."

By the time the tale was told, Matt's mother was leaning forward in the gently swaying chair, her face pained. "Oh, Matty. You poor thing."

Matt forced himself just to sniff. "It's fine," he told her. "I'm okay."

"Of course you're not. Don't be ridiculous." She shook her head, gripping his hand tight as they looked out across the night at the manor. "And you're here now?" she asked him. "The Academy, I mean. At least for the time being."

"I guess," Matt mumbled. "Yes. No. Maybe?" He sighed, sat up, and shook his head. "I don't know. I don't . . . I've been talking all about me. How're you?"

"I'm fine. Worried about my son." She shook him by the shoulders, and Matt gave a weak chuckle.

"Dad?"

"Still thrilled at being off work."

"Jonas? Sarah?"

"Your brother has been taken under the wing of that Charles Farrington person," Matt's mother mused, "though I'm not entirely sure how it happened. He's normally quite reserved, Charles, the few times I've seen him. Anyway, he was walking by as Jonas was throwing a few fire moves around outside one afternoon, you know, which he's started doing lately in hopes of catching the attention of one of those active-wear-clad girls, and he stopped and watched for a bit before offering to give Jonas some pointers."

"And Jonas accepted?"

"Heavens, no. Ungrateful little brat laughed in Mr. Farrington's face and said, 'I don't need help, old man.'"

Matt rolled his eyes. "He's such a little—"

"For which I was ready to ground him," his mother continued, firm. "Or at the very least power wash his cell phone. Anyway, turns out I didn't need to because Mr. Farrington was not in the least bit offended. Instead, he simply shrugged and said, 'It's your choice if you want to be useless.' Then he erupted into this fifty-foot phoenix of flames and flew directly over the castle." Matt laughed, and his mother raised a meaningful eyebrow at him. "I have never seen Jonas so quiet."

Kathryn Callaghan scoffed. "Of course, your brother spends the next two days running through every room in Morningstar until he at last finds the poor man reading somewhere and begs-begs-begs him to teach him how to do that. I'm told there was even groveling involved. And now, my son is being privately tutored by the greatest pyromancer in America while every single other branch of his education atrophies, and I don't know whether to be proud or annoyed."

"A little of both," said Matt. "With Jonas, it's always a little of both."

"And then Sarah, God." Matt's mother sighed. "I'm going to lose Sarah to the same thing. Ever since she manifested, it's been like the Tasmanian Devil hurtling through our living room, and, 'Please-please-please, Mom, can you go running with me, please-please-please.'"

"And are you?"

"Matt, honey, one day you are going to wake up middle aged and understand what I truly mean when I say unfitness runs in our family."

"Nobody runs in our family."

"Well, someone does now." She shook her head. "Giselle Pixus comes by and races with her sometimes. You should see the look on Sarah's face; you would think she was back being five again, staring up at a real-life Disney princess. Nothing in the world—nobody—can compare. Definitely not her slow old mother." Kathryn Callaghan shook her head, though she smiled as she did. "She's a wonder, that woman. I can't believe she makes time."

"She saved my life today."

"Did she? Well, she's invited to Thanksgiving."

They lapsed into silence, gently swaying on the swing in the cold night air. Matt's mother turned to him.

"Matty," she told him, "I am so, *so* sorry you've had to go through all this. I am so, so sorry about your home." And in the darkness, Matt's reserve crumpled, and he folded into his mother's arms, and she held his head and stroked his hair as he sobbed, quiet tears running down his face.

Eventually, Matt hiccupped, wiped his cheeks on his sleeve, and sat up.

"You're not secretly"—hic—"secretly pleased?" he asked her, drying his eyes between sniffs. "Not happy I'm moving back in with you?"

"Pssh," said Kathryn Callaghan, dismissing the idea with one hand. "My son's nineteen; he's saved the world and started college. I'd have to be crazy to want him home. No." She shook her head. "You'll always have a place here, Matty, as long as you need. But you and I both know your wings are a bit too big."

"Yeah," Matt chuckled, half a laugh, half a sniff.

"Besides," his mother continued, "any child of mine who can consistently lie to me for five years deserves their own apartment."

"Oh, come on. You said you weren't still mad about that."

"I was never mad," she countered, sounding only a touch resentful. "I was impressed. Shows you're my son, at the very least. Your father couldn't lie about what tie he was wearing."

Again, Matt laughed. And again, before too long, the laughter faded, and silence took over, and both parent and child found themselves sitting quietly side by side, gazing out at the starlit world.

"Mom?" Matt finally asked.

"Yes, Matt?"

"Are you going to be okay if I die?"

In a way, he'd expected wrath or hysterics, for his mother to angrily demand how he could even suggest such a foolish notion or descend into tears at the very thought. But deep down, he knew her better than that. He knew his family.

"Oh, Matty," his mom whispered, and she turned to him, her weak smile brimming through silver tears. "When you die, a piece of my soul will die with you, and nothing will ever be the same."

Her gaze wandered back toward the manor, and in the glow of the porch and the moonlight, sorrow wrapped and swayed around her voice. "When the Legion first picked you," she said, "God, it feels like a lifetime. But when these people at this place first picked you, God, I was so scared. I was certain I was going to lose you. That you'd be killed, swept up. My baby boy."

She tilted her head back and stared up at the stars. "I didn't know what to do. I couldn't stop you; I dared not. What kind of mother . . . Yet the world was so big, and you were so small, and every day I was certain, 'This is it. This is the day they bring home a coffin.'" She sniffed. "So I did the only thing I could. I spent the first three months while you were away finding every piece of you I had with me—every photo, every school report, every finger painting, all those pointless awards and participation ribbons and scraps of homework we'd kept lying around. And I brought them all together. And I put them all in order. Bit by bit."

His mother let out a quavering sigh. "It took me months," she admitted. "Months and months and months, but now I have a scrapbook—this big, blue scrapbook of every moment, every memory, every piece of you I ever had. It made me feel like such an old lady, but I did it. I did it anyway. And I keep adding to it. Oh yes," she told him, "every day. Anytime there's anything in the newspaper. Some of my friends keep their eyes open for me, plus your grandma; she always had an eye for scrapbooking.

"Every piece of that book," his mother continued, "is a sign that you were here. Is your life made real; is memories I can look at and bring surging back like they were never forgotten. And I want it to keep going. I want you to live for a hundred years, to do everything conceivable, so by the time you die, that book could fill a library. But if your time ends tomorrow, then it'll still be there, and I can look back at it when I miss you and remember how you were and the joy it was to be in your life."

She turned and cupped his head in her hands. "Don't be afraid of death. Not for you, not for what it'll do to me. The worst thing you could do, the absolute worst thing, is to let the pages of that book grow empty. Because right now, they're bursting, and that fills me with so much love."

In the moonlit night, Matt's mother faced him. "What am I going to do if you die? I'm going to keep living. I'm going to cry a lot, and I'm going to eat, and I'm going to wish every moment you were there. And I'm going to read this book, every day you're not with me, and you will live again in my memories, because no amount of silence ever stole a second of song.

"When that day comes," she told him, taking both of his hands, tears flowing in rivers down her cheeks to a warm, defiant smile, "should it ever come, and may it never, but if it does. When that day comes, we'll stand over you, and we'll paint your coffin in a hundred colors, and we'll sing and we'll cry and we'll tell stupid, stupid stories. And we will adorn you in light and flowers, and wave to Death when he takes you, and say to him, 'That's our boy—you be gentle now.'

"And then," Kathryn Callaghan said finally, and though her voice broke, she held her chin up high, "then your father and I will leave, and we will search, and we will keep searching if it takes us to the Earth's end, 'til we are old and gray and broken—and with your ashes on our hands, we will find the one who killed you, and we will boil them alive."

The night was still dark when Matt returned to the guest room, his heart equal parts full, weary, and relieved. He found Jane there, and to his surprise, also her father, and to his even greater surprise, a car-size hole in the wall which Jane's dad was filling with expanding foam.

"What happened?" Matt asked, feeling the strain of his body shifting to a state of alarm *again* at yet another emergency. "Were we attacked?"

He glanced around the room, taking in Jane, who was sitting on a packing box resting her elbows on her knees, seeming neither concerned nor riled up, as well as the king-size mattress propped up against the adjoining wall, and the carefully laid out pieces of a destroyed four-poster bed. His panic subsided somewhat.

"Just an accident," Jane replied. Her eyes flicked over to meet his for a few moments then shuffled awkwardly away, which Matt took to mean her agitation levels had fallen back down somewhere between *annoyed* and *resigned*. Her dad flicked a quick glance back at Matt, reholstered the spray can of expanding sealant in his tool belt, then turned to the both of them and clapped his hands.

"That should hold until morning," he said. "Come sunup, I'll have the boys swing round to do repairs proper."

"Thanks, Dad," replied Jane. She gave him a small, sad smile. Peter Walker opened his mouth as if to say something but hesitated, glancing between Matt and his daughter, and after a second or two, seemed to think better of it. He closed his mouth and stepped away from the foam barrier, walking back out the room with only a brief pause to rest his hand on Jane's shoulder and to flick Matt, who was standing beside the doorway, a short, nervous smile.

"Accident, huh?" said Matt, once Jane's father had left.

"Don't start," Jane sighed.

"I'm not," he replied, placating, holding up his hands.

There was a pause. After a moment, Jane blew out her lips. "Look, I'm sorry I was mad."

"I'm sorry I yelled."

"Guess we were both a bit keyed up."

"Yeah." Matt paused. "Is your dad okay?"

"Yeah," said Jane, waving a hand. "He's fine. We're fine. No, we, ah . . . I don't know. Don't worry about it." She shook her head and glanced over at him, still seated on a box. "Where'd you go?"

"Talk to Mom."

". . . And?"

"She's going to be very sad when I die."

Jane's face twisted in pain. "Don't joke."

"I wasn't."

Jane shuffled over on the box she was sitting on, and Matt crossed the room to sit next to her. She was still dressed in the uniform of Dawn, and still scowling slightly, though the intensity of her gaze seemed to be directed at the world at large now rather than just him.

"So," he said finally, gently poking her leg, "you want the good news or the bad news?"

Jane sighed and rolled her eyes. "Any. Either. Both."

"Well, the bad news," Matt started, "is that it's 2:00 a.m., I'm exhausted, and something has destroyed our bed." A grunt was Jane's only response. "Luckily, by my estimation, the mattress is the part of the bed you actually sleep on, and that seems to be intact."

"Hngh."

"Use your words. The good news is that I may have a lead."

"Yeah, that's—What?" Jane suddenly sat bolt upright, her eyes widening and her face recoiling back like she'd just strode headfirst into a plank of wood. "Lead? What lead? What're you talking about?" She leapt to her feet. "On the attackers?!"

"First things first," said Matt, holding up a finger. "Can you please change? It's 2:00 a.m. I feel like we've just come back from a costume party and any second now I'm going to be hovering over you in the bathroom, holding your hair as you throw up."

"There's no time for—"

"There's time," Matt sighed, exasperated. "Please go, dress like a normal person, have a shower and—I mean you're—the other way around. Have a shower then put on clothes."

"But—"

"And then, *please*," he continued, putting as much emphasis on the word as he could, "I would be forever grateful if you could, while I wait here in the designated safe room, go downstairs and find me some chocolate chip cookies."

Jane stared at him, flabbergasted. "I'm not your errand girl," she said. "And it's the middle of the night, what do you need cookies for?"

"Because mine got destroyed," Matt replied, doing his very best to keep his voice level. "And I am tired and hungry, and I have had a very long day, and I just want this one thing, just this little something nice."

The hard lines around Jane's face softened. Her pulled-back chest deflated, her shoulders slumped, and she ran her hands through her hair. And then, before Matt could do anything, she leaned forward and pulled him into a hug, pulling him up to standing, holding him tight and warm and close.

"I'm sorry," she murmured, and in the soft words, there crept the beginning of cracks. Matt held her in return.

"It's okay," he sighed. He slid underneath her cape with one hand and rubbed gentle circles atop the small of her back. "I'm okay. We're okay."

Jane let out a big sniff and pulled away, eyes wavering but still dry.

"Go." Matt gestured with his chin toward the room's ensuite. "Change. And then please, I wasn't joking about the cookies. Jesus Christ, I'm so hungry; I haven't eaten all day."

Jane rubbed her forehead, clearly torn between wanting to be caring and needing the lead right away right now give it. "What if it's time sensitive . . . ?" she asked, peering at him, though at least having the courtesy to do it bracing through half-squeezed eyes.

"What if it was time sensitive half an hour ago?" Matt replied, rolling his eyes so hard he rolled his head. "Lord have mercy; at some point, you've gotta just take the risk. I promise, Jane, I promise, I will look at this with you right away, but if I do not eat something soon, my stomach is literally going to consume me."

"But—"

"I am dead serious," he repeated. "No shower, no cookies, no lead."

Jane took in Matt's immovable expression and hung her head in defeat. "You're an idiot," she sighed.

"And you're amazing. Now go be amazing in the shower, then get me food while I . . . I don't know. Sit here with the door closed pretending I don't exist."

"What if they don't have chocolate chip?" Jane asked.

"You're a big girl; think of something," Matt replied, a tad impatient. "Use your phone, look up a recipe. Make some."

"I don't know," his girlfriend retorted, sounding dubious. She paused and flashed a shy glance. "Morningstar's already burnt down once."

Matt's next words died on his lips, and he was forced to stand there for a few moments, staring at Jane in shock. "That," he said finally, "was actually really good."

By the time Jane returned to their room some twenty minutes later, exactly as Matt had anticipated, a lot of her residual tension had subsided. Basic behavioral psychology: a shower and fresh clothes subconsciously marked to the brain a new chapter, and a simple selfless goal provided an easy sense of self-worth and accomplishment. It was all about directing energy. So much, Matt knew, of what Jane was used to feeling was in terms of fear and anger, he had to occasionally give her permission to express herself in different ways.

"There weren't chocolate chip," she announced, walking back into their bedroom in gray track pants and a hoodie, her arms laden with blue boxes, "but there were Oreos. Are they all right?"

"At this stage," Matt replied, happily relieving her of her burden and tearing open a packet, "I would eat Pop-Tarts slathered in dog poo."

"Ew." Jane frowned as she watched him devour a handful of the chocolate cream cookies, making no move to sit. Matt raised a guilty eyebrow, his mouth full.

"You said you had a lead."

"Yesh."

"I got you your dumb cookies."

"Shure." Matt swallowed a mouthful of Oreo and cleared his throat. "One of the attackers gave me a USB."

"What? Why?"

Matt explained what had seemed to be Lionel's thought process. Jane looked stunned.

"So what's on it?" she asked.

"How would I know?" Matt shrugged. "Haven't exactly had time to sit down in front of the PC with a cup full of hot cocoa."

"Okay, well, we need to look at this. Immediately."

"It's like two thirty," Matt complained.

"You can go to sleep."

"Yeah right, like I'm going to trust you with detective work, Miss *Captain Dawn is so great and most definitely alive.*"

Jane's face fell, and Matt immediately regretted his words.

"Sorry," he apologized, slapping his own cheek. "Sorry. That was uncalled for. My brain has lost its capacity for good jokes."

"Ass," Jane muttered, though a quick squeeze of her shoulder seemed to wipe away most of the hurt.

"Let's go look at this USB."

There was no objection. "Did they manage to save your laptop?"

"Doesn't matter," said Matt. "I don't trust my eyes on this either. We need an expert."

They set out from the ambassadorial suite, boxes of Oreos and thumb drive in hand, down Morningstar's refurbished high-ceilinged hallways with their soft, powder-blue carpets and variety of old pictures and awards on the walls. Replicas or reissues, most of them, Matt knew— he'd heard about Giselle assigning the task to a particular Acolyte who'd been struggling socially so as to the give the poor kid something to talk about and some purpose—though you'd never have known by looking at them.

In the muted light of nighttime, it was hard to tell the Academy had even been destroyed in the first place. The biggest change, Matt felt, was the people they encountered in the hallways; most were young and unfamiliar, and the way they whispered reverential greetings or stepped aside as Matt and Jane passed, maybe even bowed their heads, was definitely new. Neither of them had gotten that treatment before, and Matt wasn't sure he liked it.

Though the part where even at two o'clock in the morning there was an abnormal number of fit, attractive people awake training, tinkering, and studying—well, that part at least hadn't changed.

They alighted upon a familiar third-floor computer room to find the door closed and a light glowing out from underneath it. Matt stared down at the glow and shook his head, struggling not to roll his eyes.

"It's not even a stereotype at this point," he told Jane. "It's just the truth."

"Is it weird she's using Ed's old computer room?"

"No. I thought I'd be offended, but being here, seeing it, it's actually less offensive because I just know it never once crossed her mind."

He knocked on the thick wooden doorframe.

"Enter," answered a flat, familiar voice.

They walked in.

"Azleena Hossein," Matt announced, swinging the door open and stepping through into the computer lab. "How did I know you'd be awake at this hour?"

"Sleep is for the weak," said the small genius, not looking up from behind her multiple computer screens.

"I'm having déjà vu," said Matt. He didn't know if it was the lack of sleep, the near-death experience, or just emotional exhaustion, but he suddenly found the young girl's mannerisms strangely endearing. She'd been trying her best, and though she'd taken on Ed's role, she wasn't trying to actively replace him. She was just her own person who happened to be filling his gap, and her weird deadpan approach was just her way of dealing with people.

Who knows, thought Matt, semidelirious from exhaustion, maybe he just had a soft spot for psychotic, emotionally stunted women.

He swung around a chair opposite Azleena's desk, and without needing a word of encouragement, Jane did the same. "We've got a thumb drive," Matt said.

"I'm presuming there's more to that statement," the genius replied, monotone.

"I got it off one of the attackers this afternoon."

"How?"

"He gave it to me."

"Interesting." Azleena stopped typing and peered out from behind her computer for the first time since they'd entered. "Step into the scanner."

"What?" asked Matt, somewhat taken aback.

"I'm going to scan you for adherents or toxins," explained the genius. She pointed with some impatience toward a new mechanical addition in the corner of the room, a ceiling-height open white double donut–looking thing that Matt had just assumed was some kind of temporarily stored upside down MRI machine. "Which hand did you pick up the drive with?"

"Right, but—Oh." Matt stared down at his thumb, feeling stupid. "You think it's poisoned?"

"I think we should rule out someone who has tried to kill you continuing that endeavor."

"Right," said Matt, his sensation of stupidity intensifying.

He got up and walked over to the big circular machine, sliding carefully between a pair of smooth white metal rings at head and feet height. Azleena tapped a few buttons on her keyboard, and the machine whirred, the two donuts sweeping twice up and down Matt's body. Matt saw Azleena's screens flash with a series of images and readouts.

"Negative for nanomachines. Negative for toxins. No symptoms of concern." She paused and spun back on her chair to fix him with a flat gaze. "You're low on dopamine."

"Nobel Prize." Matt scowled, narrowing his eyes slightly, unable to tell if the small genius was taking the piss.

"He's fine?" Jane asked from the other side of the desk.

"He's fine," Azleena confirmed. She beckoned Matt forward from the machine. "Out. And hand me the USB."

Matt grumbled something inarticulate about his life being a series of commands from demanding women, but nevertheless obediently stepped out of the scanner and handed Azleena the thumb drive. The genius took it, peered at it, and, without so much as a shrug, stuck it firmly into her computer.

"Are you worried it might have viruses?" asked Jane.

"Are you worried about getting shot?" the girl replied.

"No."

"Same reasoning."

"I'm worried about getting shot," said Matt, but neither paid him any attention. Jane carried both his and her chair around the table and set them down behind Azleena so they could see the full run of the computer screens.

"No viruses," confirmed the genius. New windows flew up as she rapidly opened everything. "Looks like a regular store-bought storage device, and your attacker just saved everything he was sent. No, had access to. He got a link to a private server. Let's go—No, there's an authenticator." Without warning, her cursor left the files and white server login screen, clicking quickly through to a program for making voice calls. There was barely a ring before whoever was on the other end picked up.

"Helen," Azleena said without any preamble, "third floor."

"Coming."

Azleena terminated the call, turning back to the open files. "In the interim . . ." she murmured. She flicked rapidly through, engrossed. Behind her, Jane leaned over to Matt.

"Which one's Helen?" she whispered. Matt kept his gaze level.

"Helen. The robot."

"Oh, the robot. Yup."

"Cyborg," Azleena corrected, not looking up. "I think I've figured out the chronology. He's gone back and saved chat logs. Diligent." She glanced back at Matt. "You said the attacker was carrying this on his person?"

"Yes," Matt confirmed.

"Phenomenally stupid," Azleena replied, turning back around. "This is what those in law enforcement call an orgy of evidence."

Matt blinked slightly at the incongruence of the word *orgy* coming from the mouth of someone who appeared about twelve. "He said he had suspicions beforehand that maybe they were being set up."

"Who's 'they'?" Jane demanded. "Who is this person? How did any of them—?"

"I'm getting to that," the genius replied, cutting her off. Jane fell silent. Azleena leaned in closer as she opened screenshots of Bluin message boards. "I'm not familiar with these phrases or acronyms."

"I am," Matt piped up. He quickly ran his eyes over the chat logs and explained all the slang he was familiar with while Jane looked on, her eyebrows furrowed in increasing confusion.

"How do you know—?"

"Shh-shh," shushed Azleena, poking a tiny brown finger aggressively back toward Jane's face. She nodded at Matt. "Much clearer, thank you." The genius paused, reading quickly over the images of comment chains spread out on the screen.

"Here we go. So he gets contacted, our guy, Arquebusier127. Private message through the site. 'I see you've been active on,' etcetera. Invitation to private subgroup. Joins—modded. Yes, obviously. Rule 1: after twenty-four hours, all content will be deleted. That would've made them feel secure. Here we go, screenshots. Blah, blah, blah, take action, blah, blah, blah, go in force . . ."

Azleena suddenly leaned back and scoffed. "Look, one of them has half a brain. 'How do we know this isn't a setup?' Except the rest then just back pat each other into complicity; they know each other already from the site. Familiar usernames."

She leaned forward infinitesimally. "Alright. Here they're talking about DawnWatch. Speculating on its usefulness, its accuracy." A pause. "Summating it's reasonably correct. Dependable."

"I knew we should've had it taken down," Jane snarled.

Azleena didn't spare her a second glance. "Cut one head, and another . . . Here we go. New thread. 'I've had something come to me.' Says the sender was anonymous, a 'concerned citizen'—Ah."

"Ah?" asked Matt. "What's *ah*?" He tried to look at whatever Azleena was staring at on the screen, but all he could make out at a glance were columns full of numbers.

"Money." Azleena swore. She sounded both frustrated and resigned. "It's always the goddamn money. They've got our financial records. The Legion's." She shook her head. "That's how they got in."

"Wait," said Jane, looking aghast, "we've been hacked?"

"No, not us." The genius scowled. "Our accountants, maybe. The IRS." She shook her head. "It doesn't matter how strong our security is; we can't control the integrity of other groups. Or account for every one of their staff." She turned back to the computer, her face blank. "Maybe one of them has a leak."

"But I don't get it." Jane scowled. "So they know what our expenses are; what does that matter? How would that . . . ?"

But Matt thought he understood, and as Azleena maximized the financial records to make them more prominent, he felt like he could almost have predicted what the genius was about to say.

"See this?" Azleena explained, highlighting a particular line of numbers in the expense table for Jane to clearly see. "This is electricity costs for your apartment. It doesn't specify an address, but still. Here, water. Internet. Insurance. Repeating costs. Take the date and dollar value and you can reverse engineer a locality and an approximate-size residence."

She pulled open another spreadsheet. "They had older figures, too. Costs still unaccounted for. Now, our income—prior to you two moving in. You take time to go through and cross-reference everything the Legion manages, and you're left with these outliers." She clicked her tongue. "Logical to assume off-the-books residence. Logical to assume safe house. From there, it's just detective work."

"Who slipped up?" asked Matt, already feeling like he could see where this was going.

"Let's see . . ." Azleena murmured. She flicked quickly to another screen, then scowled. "Insurance company. Of course. They put the street address on the certificate and thought they were being safe by just leaving off the apartment. Idiots. See, there's a second info dump. Courtesy of whoever this is, Connect_Conclusion24."

"Different to the first person?"

"That was throwaway_user4876. She's prominent throughout these chats. Connect Conclusion is quieter."

"So the insurance company got hacked?"

"Or it was someone working there. Or someone just called up the main line and got through by human error." Azleena shrugged. "Minimum-wage call centers; what do you expect?"

"I'm confused," said Jane. Azleena ignored her.

"Second dump has a wider array of documents," she told Matt, pointing to the screen. "Building plans, title searches. Nothing incriminating on there, but you put it all together, and you begin seeing—"

"Holes."

"Exactly." She looked at Matt. "There was a terramancer among them?"

"Terramorph."

"Near enough if he'd mastered form flowing. This is him. TheOldLandAndTheSee. Another thread; he claims he's gone by the building. Sensed around underneath." A further pause. "Says he's found a bunker. He wants a teleporter to try jumping inside."

"A blind jump into solid rock. That's a bold ask." Matt suddenly felt ill at the thought of these people who had been trying to kill him having been so close for so long. All this time, he'd been blissfully unaware, safe up in his little tree house, as all the while, people who had been trying to kill him scurried away only a few stories underneath.

"Yep," Azleena continued. "But someone does it. There's a confirmation thread. They have access."

"Pity that wasn't one of the times Will and Jane were coming home," Matt said with a weak laugh.

"Yes," the genius said flatly. "Pity." She paused, reading more. "From there, it's logistics. Arranging to meet. Make sure everyone's armed, buying breaching ordinance. As soon as Dawn's spotted in North Korea, they're ready to go." Azleena tilted her head. "This is nice. JOEY3X is offering to mail pcthrow13 cash so he can afford a bigger gun. Real community spirit."

"How many are there?" Jane demanded. "Who's controlling them?"

"There doesn't seem to be anyone controlling them," Azleena replied in a mild tone. "There're about a hundred, but the information seems to be coming from different sources. Connect Conclusion is a member of the group, but throwaway user's account records' source isn't. I mean, maybe . . ."

At that moment, the door to the computer lab opened, and a woman stepped inside. Although *woman* was not Matt's first impression as he glanced up over the monitors; the more accurate term was *machine*, because that was the first thing anyone who saw the person now stepping through the doorway would notice: that her right arm, left leg, and significant portions of her torso had been replaced with silver metal cybernetics.

Matt knew Helen by sight from having seen her around the Academy a few times, in particular with Giselle at the dinner party, but he still always found himself doing a double take whenever he saw her. She was a big woman, probably taller than Jane by an inch, and a few inches wider, with light-brown hair shaved down to a boot camp buzz cut, a septum piercing, and round, pimpled bodybuilder shoulders. Her right robotic arm ended in a rotating three-claw pincer, and her artificial leg was marginally thicker than her natural one and looked like someone had cannibalized the hydraulic press from a construction crane. She wore a dirty white tank top and black gym shorts.

The technopath blinked when she saw Matt and Jane were present. "Sorry," she said, seeming to struggle with the words somewhat. Her human hand and leg moved slightly to cover up her cybernetic body parts. "I didn't know that . . . um . . ."

"They don't care," interjected Azleena, leaning up and peering all five feet of herself over the monitors. "Come on. I need to spoof an authenticator."

"Okay," Helen echoed quietly, and with deliberate steps, she shuffled around the desk toward the computers, still flushed slightly at being in her nightclothes. Matt stood and pulled Jane back with him to give the two some space.

"Were you asleep?" he asked jokingly, trying to catch Helen's eye and smile. The cyborg flicked a nervous glance at him, looking like a big shy bulldog.

"I . . . Okay, I—"

"Enough small talk," Azleena snapped, clicking her fingers. "Let's go."

She leaned down near the screen, and a moment later, the technopath joined her. Their two heads beside each other gave Matt the impression of a coconut leaning against a passion fruit.

"I want to get into this server."

"Yup."

"Is it TP encrypted?"

A pause while Helen closed her eyes. The screen flickered.

"Yup."

"What level?"

"Store-bought."

"Not military?"

"Nope."

"Great. Where's the weak spot?"

"If you input a code and get rejected, it retains data on how you were wrong. It'll return it to counter if you make a straight challenge."

"And then you've got the one-and-done as a data point."

"Yup."

Beside him, Matt could see Jane squinting in confusion, words beginning to form on her lips. Matt reached out and wrapped a discreet hand around her wrist, causing her to glance at him, to which he silently shook his head to indicate no, he didn't understand what they were saying either, but nevertheless just shut up. Jane closed her mouth.

"Excellent. No limiter?"

"There is, but it's stupid," the machine woman grunted.

"Excellent. Start spooling."

Helen's eyes closed, and with her hand on the computer tower, a surge of numbers suddenly began flashing all over the screen. A second later, Azleena's entire rightmost monitor turned white, and a dense list of six-digit codes began cascading down column after column, line after line.

A few seconds passed. The numbers continued to race, filling up the screen as Azleena stared at them without blinking.

"Is . . . Is this good?" Matt tentatively asked. Beside him, Jane tilted her head and leveled him with an incredulous stare, eyebrows furrowed at his blatant hypocrisy. "Lots of . . . random . . . numbers. Is that good?"

"There's no such thing as random," Azleena murmured, her eyes fixated on the screen as the columns continued to grow, pushing the list further and further down, "only machines . . . taught to pretend . . . Eventually . . ." Helen's eyes stayed closed, and the lines of six-digit numbers continued to race. ". . . you find . . . the pattern . . ."

"Close?" asked the technopath.

"Almost . . ." Azleena breathed. Her eyes shone wide as satellites, and her face was so close to the screen, the tip of her button nose was almost touching it. "You . . ." she muttered, staring transfixed, twitches of madness darting across her features, and her words uncharacteristically guttural, "are not . . . as smart . . ."—her thin lips curled—"as you think . . . you are."

Suddenly, the genius snapped back in her seat.

"Got it," Azleena announced, blinking rapidly while quickly shaking her head like she'd just been mildly electrocuted. "Now. Login screen plus bring up source code. Show me their timer."

"Yup."

"727, 867."

"Got it." Helen entered the authenticator code. Suddenly, they had access to the server screen. Matt let out an involuntary gasp.

"Well done," he told them.

"Rudimentary," Azleena replied, although the way she flicked her hair as she said it and shuffled slightly in her seat made Matt think it probably wasn't.

"Does that mean it's not the military?" he asked her.

"It means it's got the highest level of protection there can be before you start getting suspicious why it's so well guarded," Azleena replied with a shrug. Matt wasn't sure if that counted as an answer.

Helen stood up and stepped back from the screen, allowing Matt and Jane to peer in. Disappointingly, the private server that Lionel had been given access to only seemed to contain stuff they'd already seen—folders containing some of the Legion's financial records, which the attacker seemed to have just saved directly.

"Are they all the same?" Matt asked Azleena, feeling his heart drop somewhat. The genius quickly opened the documents one after the other, scrolling rapidly through.

"Yes."

"Darn." Matt put his elbows on his knees and leaned forward, resting his chin on his hands.

"So there's nothing more?" asked Jane, sounding extremely disappointed.

"Looks that way," the genius responded. But as Matt stared at the screen of predominantly white and empty folders, a sudden thought bugged him.

"Azleena," he asked, "how big are these files? All up."

The genius blinked, doing quick math. "Thirty-eight meg."

"And what's the Bluin upload limit?"

"Twenty."

"And how much would the security package on this have cost?"

Azleena glanced up at Helen, who shrugged. "I don't know," the technopath answered. "Several thousand bucks?"

Matt turned back to Azleena. "And setting up private cloud storage?"

Azleena met his eye, realization suddenly dawning across her face.

"Inconsistent, if that's the only use."

"Exactly," Matt agreed. "Why not just upload twice?"

"Sorry," interrupted Jane, looking between the two of them with a mixture of frustration and confusion, plus the occasional glance at Helen's looming robotic form. "I don't get it. What does the cost mean? What's being uploaded twice?"

Matt turned to her. "It's overkill," he explained. "Way too much effort for simply transferring forty megabytes of files. If that's all you're doing, why not just put a password on the files and send them in two batches? Why spend a whole bunch of money setting up this secret server? Unless you already have the server ready. Unless that's not all you're going to do with it."

Helen glanced down at Azleena, perched small and eager in her chair. "False face?"

"Could be." The genius nodded. She pointed back to the open, empty folders. "Go digging."

Helen reached down to put her natural hand back on the computer tower and, once more, closed her eyes. Her lips twitched.

"There's more," she murmured. "We're not seeing it. We're getting . . . Hngh. It's very clever. It doesn't want to talk."

"Make it," Azleena ordered. Beneath their lids, Helen's eyes continued to slide back and forth.

"Shh, shh, shh, shh, shh," she whispered, and the words began flowing from her mouth, uncharacteristically open and tender. "Shh, shh, shh. I know you're there. No hiding. I've got you. Yup. Yup. There. There!" Her eyes flashed open. "I've got admin view."

Suddenly, the white on the screen blinked, and the contents of the server they were looking into were no longer blank but overflowing. Folders and folders and folders—terabytes of material, all alphabetized and labeled. All with different names.

"Bloody hell," Azleena muttered. She leaned forward. "Look at it all. What the hell."

"Jackpot," mumbled Helen. "Told you."

"What is it?" Jane demanded, also leaning forward. "What's there?"

"What isn't?" Azleena murmured. She was clicking through files and folders at lightning speed, opening and closing documents so quickly nobody else could keep up. "This is—These are Bluin profiles. Spoof VPNs. Connect_Conclusion24, the one who sent the building info, that's all from here, same with JOEY3X. At least a dozen of them. Usernames and passwords." She flew out of one folder and into another. "Holy crap. These guys are DawnWatch."

"What?" Jane yelped.

"Yup," Azleena stated, files racing across the screen like leaves in a tornado. "Wow, I mean, they didn't just—They created the whole site. This is all the keys, the back code. They've even—Wow, there is complex data feeding into this. Satellites. How are they piggybacking off satellites?"

Matt and Jane exchanged horrified looks.

"Mary mother of—Half the world is compromised," Azleena continued, her words flying as thick and fast as the images on the screen. "Company records, government departments; this is—There is so much confidential stuff. So much. How are they getting this? How are they— Wait, here we go. Big . . . psychological profile? On this guy. This man, who is . . . I don't know. But this reads like military. Lots redacted. But that's historical . . . No, here, they're keeping watch."

She clicked over before any of them could get a word in. "Screw me sideways, there's another one. Except he's . . . identical? And they—Goddamn, they've got everything. They've got taps on this guy's phone, his computer logs. Every search. And again, all these Bluin accounts. They're—" Azleena abruptly stopped. "They've got his porn."

"Pardon?" said Matt, still struggling to take everything in.

"Yeah!" The genius laughed, although the mirth died out quite rapidly. "There's an algorithm tracking the features of every woman he looks at, and then it amalgamates and . . ."

Her voice trailed off as she clicked an image file open, the screen filling up with a picture of a woman, heart faced, red haired. Full lipped.

"What the hell . . . ?" Jane whispered.

"This is incredible," Azleena continued. "It's an averaging of features whoever they're profiling is attracted to. I mean, the level of depth, of focus, they—Oh look, there's Captain Dawn's DNA."

"What?!" Matt and Jane both yelled at the same time. The genius didn't even look back at them, simply gave a weak-wristed wave.

"Oh, that's not that big a deal; that's been out for a while now. It got shared with a few labs in the seventies. I mean, it's supposed to be kept confidential, but compared to the rest of this . . ."

Azleena's voice trailed off, becoming lost in the sound of her clicking as she sped folder to folder. "What's this, then; this one's huge. I've got . . . message logs to an escort. They wanted her focused on one man . . . Thousands of dollars. Tens of thousands. Weeks of her time. For . . . talking? Reports back. 'Today I talked to him.' 'Today we flirted.' 'He's interested.' 'He said he's left his girlfriend.' I don't—" Azleena clicked over to something else.

"Okay, and now we've got complaint forms to the Board of Veterinary Medicine. Complaints . . . about a student? I mean, why bother . . . Well, she's expelled. Okay, that's nonsensical. Next folder. Social media ads. Targeted. Ultra targeted? They've practically hacked this girl's phone. To put job ads?"

"Slow down," Matt said. "I can't follow." But Azleena just kept powering onward.

"All for some delivery place?" she murmured. "But they're in there too; they own it, subcontracted from a bigger company for one very specific route . . . Wow, that's a lot of money. Why would you pay that—Anyway, I don't . . . Hey, it's the same girl. Same girl, same—Why are they so focused on . . . I don't—Wait, no, I've got it backward. Image searches."

She opened a folder, and the screen filled with tiny thumbnails of photographs, thousands of them. "Social media image searches. Driver's licenses. They—And then profiles of them. A lesser number. They're narrowing it down. Down and down and down. Until it's only her. Her and her and her. This one girl. She's no one, but they've got her bank statements, her credit cards, her registration, her lease agreement. Family history, psychological profile. Everything about her, everywhere she goes. Every facet. Why?"

In the neon-lit night of the computer room, as the bulk of the Academy lay sleeping, Matt, Jane, and Helen watched the files flying across the screen and stayed silent, stunned, as Azleena spun in her chair to look at them, her tiny face scrunched in confusion, and asked what they were all slowly thinking, the question that rapidly dawned:

"Who the hell is Emily?"

A thousand miles away, in a house of unwitting sleepers, a man lay in a room with no doors or windows and waited alone in the dark.

He lay atop a single bed, an intricate wooden bedframe carved from a dark, almost fire-tinged wood, his head resting upon a feather-filled pillow, a thin woollen blanket drawn across his chest, the colors of autumn soft. The room was no prison, not unless he wished it; the floor was smooth-polished cedar, the walls stone and mahogany, and beyond the foot of the bed rose a modest desk and bookshelf.

The air did not move, save for the shallow rise and fall of the man's breathing. There was no light, no noise. The man lay with closed eyes and restless twitches, his world naught but darkness and the smell of faint sweat and cold wood.

Try as he might, he could not sleep. He yearned for sleep, but sleep eluded him. It was a stranger now, no longer treading comfortably across his threshold, repulsed by his vile deeds and the inkling horrors swimming beneath his mind.

Suddenly, from across the other side of the sealed room, there came a creak—a muffled footstep atop the floorboards. The sleepless man's eyes shot open.

"Leviathan," he whispered. He rose from his bed, staring out into the pitch-black darkness, and swung his legs out over the wooden floor. "Leviathan."

No answer came. The man stumbled to his feet, taking one cautious step and then another, fumbling blindly out with his mind. He sensed no change, no shape or presence, but that was the way of it, the abyss of His true nature. The man made a small motion with his hand, and a seat of liquid timber rose to waist height beside him from the floorboards. He collapsed, sitting, staring into nothingness, his face mere inches away from what he knew was empty wall.

The man leaned forward, holding out a trembling hand, trailing the barest trace of his fingertips over a section of solid stone, causing an opening to unfold, a square cavity atop the floor, four feet by four feet. A pinch, and a slab of stone nearest the center crumbled, shivering like liquid until it reformed into unnatural wood. The man clicked his fingers, and the wood caught ablaze.

Fire flickered up and danced before him, stinging his eyes, throwing tongues of light and shadow dancing across the room. The man glanced up to where smoke rose from his fresh-forged fireplace, and motioned disinterestedly with a downturned palm. The fumes ceased, billowing no longer into smog that would inevitably choke the sealed room but instead changing, after they rose past some certain invisible point, to droplets of snow, floating down through the firelight and settling harmlessly upon the ground.

The man shuffled in his chair, glancing over his shoulder behind him to see a shadow which had not been there before.

"Is it time?" he whispered to the interloper, the cupbearer, the only friend to his cause.

Guide them when I am gone, he pleaded. *See that it is done.*

The figure in the firelight remained silent, unmoving.

"I am done," the man murmured. "Everything is ready. The third pillar. They will clash. There'll be necessity. And then . . ." He breathed out, his chest shaking, staring up at the snow-specked glow, not daring to look behind. "And then I'm ready."

He turned, spun around suddenly, and the entire world rippled in tune with the fever in his mind.

"Say the word, and I will send them. Speak, and I will know it's time."

From a place no one could perceive, the blue-eyed boy stood silent, watching the insane man breathe unnatural air in his cold, impossible sanctum; watched him cling to hope too terrible to speak. Watched the final piece of the puzzle, who knew everything and nothing, whisper flickering pleas for reprieve from his abyssal, excruciating terror. A salve for his broken soul. A lie for the inescapable truth.

"*Soon*," the boy whispered. "*Soon*."

The man's heart raced.

ABOUT THE AUTHOR

Benjamin Keyworth is an Australian author born and raised in Newcastle, New South Wales, and currently living in Sydney with his wife, dog, and many plants. A lawyer by day, Ben has wanted to be a writer since he was five years old (before which he wanted to be a dinosaur). He holds a master's degree in creative writing at the University of Technology Sydney, and in his spare time he enjoys baking, playing basketball badly, and playing video games pretty well.

Podium

DISCOVER MORE

STORIES UNBOUND

PodiumEntertainment.com